The Three-Faced Women

Her Challenge

by

M a r i a   B á r k á n y i

Never think there's no way further,
for it is worth the fight.

PART 1

For everyone who has ever been cheated on,
or strangled upon, for a better life;
Be strong. Find ways.

This is for you.

CHAPTER 1

There was hardly any traffic on the road. Vicky drove her car at a leisurely pace. She wasn't in any hurry. Her baseball cap was pulled down low on her forehead. The sun was starting to slant down the sky, so she flipped down the sunscreen and glanced out at the sea, which was shimmering in the heat. The horizon practically merged with the blueness of the sky.

She slowed down as she reached a village and looked for a parking spot before strolling over to a nearby bar, which was deserted in the late afternoon hours.

"*Hola,*" she greeted the bartender. "*Un café, por favor. Solo.*" The truth was, she was feeling hungry. She glanced at the three sandwiches lined up in the display case. A few minutes later, the dark-faced man handed her a cup of fragrant coffee.

"*Gracias,*" she said passively.

The Spanish man nodded appreciatively before turning away and getting back to work. He didn't seem particularly busy and was lining up glasses on a shelf.

She slowly sipped the dark, sugar-free, aromatic liquid. She loved spending time in bars like this one, where there was always something to be found at the right price. This time, however, it seemed she was out of luck. She glanced back at the sandwiches but they weren't right where she wanted. She noticed some fruit displayed on a table. She took two apples and a banana from the basket.

"*Cuanto?*" she asked the man.

"*Dos.*"

She put two Euros down on the counter before walking out to the washroom, which had seen some better days.

Meanwhile, a Jaguar pulled up at the parking lot. Two men climbed out of the dark green vehicle and approached the café. The bartender looked up attentively, quietly clicking with his tongue as he continued wiping the bar.

Vicky left the bar and walked towards the parking lot. Glancing at the Jaguar, she hummed something in appreciation. It was lovely. She would never own such an expensive car, she thought. Still, she wasn't overly ambitious. She knew where her place was in the world. As she reached her little car, she noticed a young girl with a backpack sitting awkwardly on the side of the road, eyeing her. Vicky raised her right hand to shield her face from the blaring sunshine.

"Could you give me a lift?" asked the teenager.
Vicky was about to turn away, but then she changed her mind and motioned for the girl to hop in.
"What's your name?" she asked indifferently.
"Lucy," answered the girl a bit reluctantly, cautiously swivelling her head around with a thin smile on her face.
"My name's Vicky," she said openly, starting the car. She glanced at her watch and thought she might make it home by eight.
"Where are you headed?" asked, to break the silence.

"Marbella."
"Home?"

The girl hesitated for a moment before nodding. Vicky didn't want to force the conversation and didn't bother to tell the girl she was headed in the same direction.

"Want a banana?" she asked instead.
"Oh, thanks."
"It's there on the back seat. Give me one too."

When they finished their bananas, Vicky pulled out a plastic bag from the door compartment and dumped her peel in it before handing it to the girl. "You can put yours in there too. We could toss it out the window, but I'm not that type. There's plenty of garbage as it is, right?"

The girl didn't answer. Later on, she fell asleep. Her head leaned against the window as her hand slowly slipped down into her lap. She looks too young to be running around on her own, Vicky thought to herself. Later on, she noticed that the Jaguar she'd seen before was catching up to her. She slowed down, but the car wouldn't pass her by. Instead, the car started tailing her. They're probably just fooling around, she thought.

A guy driving a Jaguar won't mug you, she assured herself. She smiled because all she had with her was sixty Euros. She'd left her credit card at home, and her car wasn't worth much either. The kilometres flew by. The gasoline meter was getting close to zero. She'd have to stop at the next gas station.

Warm air flew into the car through the open window. It was getting dark outside, and the young girl was still fast asleep. Vicky finally reached a gas station and saw in the rear-view mirror that the Jaguar had stopped nearby. She hesitated for a moment but had no choice but to get out. After filling up the car, she quickly went inside to pay.

On her way, she hurried back to the car and got in, noticing too late that someone was sitting behind her. She tried to get out, but a hand pressed down on her shoulder.

"You better not cause any trouble. Please, get going and follow the Jaguar," said the stranger in subdued tones.

Vicky glanced at the girl, who averted her gaze. She tried to make out her new passenger in the mirror, but the man was wearing a straw hat pulled down low and a pair of sunglasses. She saw his dark beard, but the stranger quickly slipped back down behind.

I would never recognise him; she thought and reluctantly started the car. She glanced back at the girl, who paid no attention to her. They probably knew each other.

Why did I bother to give her a ride? Vicky chided herself. I'm far too gullible. I'm just not crafty enough for today's world, she thought. She pushed down too hard on the accelerator, and the car came to life with a roar.

"Take it easy," warned the man in the hat.
"What do you want from me? I don't have any money," Vicky shouted anxiously. The man said nothing just cleared his throat. The girl seemed to stifle a giggle. At the end of the road leading to the highway, Vicky spotted the car she was being forced to follow, gritting her teeth. The Jaguar turned on its indicators before Marbella.

"Follow the car," warned the man. She obeyed him with annoyance. They passed through narrow roads, first down and then up, before reaching a neighbourhood of mansions.

The Jaguar pulled up in front of a wrought-iron gate which automatically opened. The car was parked in the unlit lot next to the building. The driver hurried inside at once.

"Get going," urged the man impatiently. Vicky parked next to the other car with growing anxiety as the gate slowly closed behind them. The man sent the girl inside in a subdued tone, and she reluctantly obeyed him.

"You're coming too," added the man.

Vicky reluctantly got out but didn't move. The stranger walked up to her and took her by the arm.

"Come," said the man, leading her inside a faintly illuminated living room before turning around and heading out of the room.

"What do you want from me?" she shouted after the man. He stopped, yet didn't turn around. "Nothing. Please wait a minute," he said before disappearing behind the door.

"How rude," she muttered in exhaustion.

A simple lamp in the place, barely illuminating the spacious living room he spotted a sofa, two broad armchairs, and a low coffee table. Under the lamp, an old chest was set next to the wall.

The furnishings were rounded out by a few stools, a huge vase on the floor, and a dark-screened television next to the fireplace. A flight of steps led upstairs from the back of the room. The curtains in front of the window were drawn shut. She pulled the heavy fabric to the side to peek out. She saw the outlines of a few dark bushes lining the edges of the unlit patio, and she seemed to hear the ebb and flow of the sea in the distance.

"I've brought you a refreshment," said a friendly voice behind her. Vicky spun around.

The woman approaching her cautiously set the tray down on the table before introducing herself with ease.

"I am Patricia Gomez. Please, make yourself at home," she said, showing towards the sofa. "I'm sure you're exhausted after that long drive," the Spanish woman continued in a neutral tone.

"Of course, but first I want an explanation, and I want to leave as soon as possible," replied Vicky, firmly looking the stranger in the eye, somewhat comforted by the woman's warm gaze.

"Oh, yes. My daughter eloped with her girlfriend in Barcelona. Fortunately, my brother managed to find her. I guess she asked you for a lift."

"Yeah, right. Then why did the man in the hat make me come here?"

The woman flashed a barely perceptible smile. "Because we didn't want to cause a scene. We expected my daughter to come up with something and make a big fuss about it. This isn't the first time she's done something like this. She's barely more than fifteen, yet she's fiercely independent. She always did whatever she wanted to. I know, it's my fault," she complained with a heavy sigh.

Vicky muttered something in response. She doubts the woman's story, but actually, she isn't particularly intrigued. She was too tired to listen to this stranger and wanted to leave this uncomfortable situation as soon as possible.

"Okay then, I'll get going now."

"It's late. Why don't you stay for the night?" asked the woman kindly.

"No, thanks," Vicky curtly replied.

The woman's face hardened. "I'm sorry. In that case, I won't keep you waiting any longer. How much do I owe you?"

Vicky glanced at her in surprise. "Nothing, of course."

"Thank you for your efforts. Have a safe trip, and sorry for the inconvenience," the woman said dismissively. She nodded and walked out of the room, closing the door on her way out.

The lights were on in the corridor. The front door was open as well. When Vicky left the house, she noticed the gate was slowly opening. She didn't hesitate and quickly got in her car – where she was surprised to find the girl.

"No way, I'm not taking you anywhere, do you hear me?" Vicky demanded impatiently.

"I … I just wanted to thank you."

Vicky was starting to feel awkward, so she asked in a softer voice, "Is everything alright? Will everything be okay with you?"

"Yes, I think so," said the girl with a stubborn look in her eyes. "Listen, if you have some problems, call me and I'll see if I can help," Vicky said uncertainly, fishing out her business card. "Put it away, you might need it."
The teenager nodded and left.

Vicky drove off, and the gate slowly closed behind her. She kept looking back and was relieved that she wasn't being followed. As she reached the highway she looked back, noticing nobody following her. She smiled. Perhaps what the lady told her was true, but she wondered. She had no idea whether she and the woman would ever see each other again.

The weeks and months went by, and the events became fuzzy to her. She was fully caught up in her work, and her life went on day after day without any difficulties or surprises.

CHAPTER 2

One morning, Vicky was showing a few houses to a Scandinavian couple. She felt they were probably just killing some time. In the summer months, she often had to deal with clients like them who weren't intent on actually buying real estate.

She lazily leaned back in her chair and slowly sipped her chilled orange juice. The heat was oppressive and drying her out like a piece of parchment. Most people stayed in the water or on beaches in times like this, she thought as she glanced out the window. Only a handful of people strolled down the piers of Puerto Banus at the end of the siesta. A host of yachts were lined up next to each other, listlessly moored in the water. All of this would change around eight in the evening when the neighbourhood suddenly came to life.

Her thoughts were interrupted by a stranger who headed straight over to her after seeking her out in the office.
"Can I help you?" she asked with a polite smile.
"I sincerely hope so."
"Have a seat.
"David Stone," said the man in the introduction, getting right to the point and explaining what he was looking for. She showed

him a few houses on her laptop but quickly noticed that her client wasn't too interested in her offers. "Would you show the previous one?" asked the man suddenly.

"This one?"

"Yes. Where is it located?"

"Las Chapas. It's a great neighbourhood, with sandy beaches – it's a popular place," she added in a business-like tone.

"That might be what I'm looking for, or something of the like," he noted, glancing at his watch. "If it's okay with you, I'll be coming back around eleven o'clock tomorrow. I'm sorry, but I have to go now."

He handed Vicky his business card, stood up and disappeared from the office with a curt nod. She jotted down the appointment in her notebook and read the name on the card.

She was surprised to see that he was one of the heads of a five-star hotel built years ago, "Hmmm," she uttered, wondering absently about how young the man seemed to be. Vicky recalled an image of the building's smoke-coloured, impressive glass façade, shown mirrored the hill of La Concha, the symbol of Marbella.

She read through her notes again on Monday. Except for Tuesday, seem it was going to be another uneventful week, although she could never know for sure. Things usually slowed down in Andalusia due to the great heat.

Everyone tried spending their free time close to the shore. Since there were a lot of tourists. The estate agents stayed open until late at night. She was just about to head home when Lucy appeared.

"I never thought I would see you again," Vicky noted with surprise. "What is the purpose of your visit on this occasion?" she asked, leaning forward, suspecting the worst. "Something happened again, right?"

The young girl hopped down on the chair in front of the desk, looking glum and sullen. Vicky gave in and held up her hands.

"Okay, I'm done for today." She quickly gathered her belongings.

"Let's go," she said, and they soon disappeared into the crowd on the street.

"I almost forgot about you at all," said Vicky. "If I remember correctly, we met a year ago, right?"

"That sounds about right," the girl said without particular interest.

"You grew a lot – you're almost as tall as I am. Lucy walked on without a reply, pursing her lips. "Come on, I'll get you a drink," offered Vicky. They found a table on the pleasant-looking terrace of a bar. Vicky ordered some drinks and took a good long look at the girl squirming in her seat. The young waiter brought their freshly squeezed orange juice while cautiously sizing them. He was busy, so he soon gave up and hurried off. Beads of water trickled down the sides of their glasses in the heat.

Vicky sensed Lucy's hesitation.

"Come on, just get to it," she urged, getting fed up with the waiting game. The girl fidgeted with the hem of her skirt without looking up. Suddenly, she raised both her hands and ran them through her auburn hair, with a few unruly locks falling across her face.

"My mother's boyfriend has disappeared," she began suddenly.

"Are you sure about that, or is that just a theory?

"I know that's what happened since I saw it myself."

"What did you see?" she asked cautiously, but the girl fell silent. Vicky waited for a moment before patiently continuing.

"Listen, I guess you're here to share your problem with someone, but if you're not sincere or you've changed your mind, maybe you should leave now."

Lucy bit her lip as her eyes flashed with annoyance.

Vicky noticed the reaction and gently smiled as she moved closer and put her arm around the girl. "Don't worry, I'll help if I can – but please don't make it hard for us, okay? I only want to hear the truth."

Lucy reached out for her glass, took a sip, and then started her tale, faltering and pausing from time to time.

"The first time we met, I did run away to my girlfriend in Barcelona, but Nick and Pedro quickly found me, and I hated them for that. I didn't want to go home – or maybe I did because of my mother, but I hated Nick."

"He was the one sitting behind me in the car?"

"No, that was Pedro, Mom's younger brother."

"Well, who's Nick, then?"

"He's my mom's lover," she explained with suppressed hatred.

"And what about your father?"

"My parents divorced a long time ago. My father remarried and is currently living in Seville, so I rarely get to see him."

"Tell me about Nick," she urged, to get back to the story.

"I don't know what he does for a living. I know he travels a lot to London and stays there for months, but when he's here, he mainly stays on our yacht. He practically has it all to himself," she exclaimed hatefully.

"How old is Nick?" asked Vicky. Lucy shrugged. "I don't know. Around 30? Maybe older."

"What about you?"

"Me?" exclaimed Lucy in surprise, before instantly replying: "I'm 18."

"Come on!" exclaimed Vicky, raising her finger in protest.

"OK, 16."

"That sounds more like it."

"Fine, but what has my age got to do with it?" protested Lucy angrily. Vicky recalled how hard it was for a girl to be a teenager, suppressing a smile as the memories came flooding back to her.

"So why do you hate Nick? Are you in love with him?" asked Vicky provocatively. Lucy blushed. "Oh, come on, he's a lot older than me and sleeps with my mother," answered Lucy. It was clear that her anger was seething beneath the surface.

"He was my father's friend, and later she hooked up with my mom." She quipped excitedly. She was confused by the question, which had never occurred to her. She reached out for her glass and took a sip. For a while, she silently stared at the sea and then carried on in a softer tone: "I love the sea."

"Have you known him for a long time?" asked Vicky, shaking the girl up from her reverie.

"You mean Nick?"

"Precisely."

"Oh, sure. Whenever we took the yacht out for a spin, Nick always was tagging along. I was close to him when I was younger. I always sat in his lap and played a lot with him," she recalled as her face brightened.

"I remember I was barely 8 years old when I went swimming with him in the sea, looking at the fish under the water. Whenever I got tired, I held on to him. He even caught a little octopus and put it in my palm. I was terrified and started crying, but he taught me not to be afraid. Then …"

Lucy's face darkened, she nervously tousled her hair again before sighing heavily as if shouldering a heavy burden before carrying on.

"Two weeks ago, Mom, Nick, Pedro, and I were on our way to the yacht. The very last moment, Mom turned back, saying she was feeling sick. I had a feeling it was because of Nick. I didn't like going with them, but I was just bored and I didn't want to stay at home." Her voice faltered, and fear shone in her eyes before she carried on in a quieter tone.

"A bank of fog rolled in from the distance, slowly blanketing us in vapour. Visibility was getting increasingly worse. Pedro stopped the motor and yelled out to me that he was going down to the cabin. Nick suddenly stumbled over to me and sat down next to me on the edge of the yacht with a drink in his hand. He grinned as he leaned in closer, lifting the drink to my lips. "Have some," he urged me in a lurid tone. I heatedly pushed him away, and he lost his balance and fell into the water."

"And?"

"I looked over the edge but couldn't see a thing through the dense fog. For a moment, I thought it was just a joke, but I quickly realised it wasn't. I stirred from my reverie and shouting his name, even threw out a life vest into the water. I rushed down into the cabin to get Pedro and then back up on deck, and we started calling his name, but all we could see was the fog quietly billowing over the waters. We still couldn't find Nick when the visibility improved," she continued.

"Unfortunately, we never found him. As we reached the port, we reported an accident to the coast guard. As expected, I completely freaked out," she concluded her odd story.

"It was all because of me," she sobbed, rubbing her tears away. Vicky opened her purse, looking for some tissues, which she held out to Lucy. She tried her best to hide her shock.

"When did this happen?" She asked, looking pale.

"I told you, two weeks ago. I can't get any sleep since then, and I keep on replaying the same scene over and over in my mind."

She blew her nose and carried on, starting and stopping.

"Yesterday, someone called me – a man called Ali who wanted to talk to me about Nick," she said, glancing at her watch.

"I have to get going. I'm meeting him at a Sangria bar nearby."

"Do you want me to go with you?"

"No, it's alright, I can take care of it alone," she said naively.

"You better be careful, and call me if you need anything."

Lucy nodded, jumped up and stormed off. Vicky kept going over what she'd heard, over and over again. There was no doubt that some dark dealings were afoot. Perhaps it would be better for her to get going and stay out of this.

CHAPTER 3

On Monday, the good-looking client showed up at the office again, right on time. Vicky sized him critically. His winning looks, sporty shape, and confident attitude made her feel a bit awkward.

"Act professionally," she muttered to herself.
"Did you say something?" asked the stranger.
"Oh, not at all, I was just coughing," she replied evasively.

A few minutes later, she was calmly driving the car down the lanes. The traffic was stiff on the roads as always. In the inner lane, a truck blew right past them.

"I hate trucks. They always drive around like madmen. They're responsible for most the accidents on the roads," she said. The man glanced at her.

"Have you been doing it for a long time?"
"What, driving?"
"No, your job."
"Only about a year, but I keep dreaming about having an office of mine own," she explained, suddenly leaving the main ac-

cessway and continuing in a calmer tempo down the side roads. For a moment, she glanced at her client.

"But it's okay to dream, right?"

"You never know. Things can change in a fraction of a moment," said the man in a thoughtful, ironic tone. Vicky nodded and slowed down as she peered out the window and finally parked in front of a stone wall. She rummaged through her bag before fishing out the keys.

The garden had seen better days. Yes, its neglected state still radiated beauty and tranquillity. An old carob tree sprawled in the left half of the terrace with branches dangling to the ground, its small, crescent-shaped fruit scattered across the lawn.

"There's so much carob here, you could raise a donkey," noted the man with a chuckle. "It burns well in the fireplace once it's dried out," added Vicky, go back to a stop in front of the entrance.

"Look, you can turn it into a top-notch real estate with a minimum investment," she added in a business-like tone before slipping the key into the lock. However, the heavy oak door wouldn't budge.

"Let me help," suggested the man.
Vicky stepped back, and the client tugged on the handle, turning the key and opening the door.

"Go ahead," he suggested with a hint of sarcasm in his voice. In his experience, women usually had problems with locks, not to mention technical matters. He recalled his wife often bickering with him over the lock of their house in London, which they had to replace in the end.

"Thank you," said Vicky, with some annoyance. She began to open the windows. "The place could use a paint job, but all things considered, the price is still very reasonable," she explained.

"Do you live nearby?" asked David Stone suddenly.

"You could say that," said Vicky evasively.

"On your own?"

"Oh, well, um …" she stuttered but changed her mind. She nodded after a pause and awkwardly moved on to the next room. The client followed her. He often gazed at her and noticed she wasn't flirtatious or encouraging as most women tended to be with him. Instead, she seemed distant and coldly reserved.

They visited two more houses that morning, so time flew by quickly. "Come, let's get a drink," David suggested once they had finished. Vicky hesitated.

"Oh, come on, I won't bite," he urged with a laugh, trying to ease up her official attitude. "OK, but I don't have much time. I have to be back in the office."

They were soon sitting on the shady terrace of a nearby bar. It was hot, so, they both enjoyed sipping their cold drinks.

"Well, what do you think about Andalusia?" she asked.

"I don't know much about it yet, but it's promising." He scrutinized her expression, yet she was doing her best to avoid his gaze.

"The weather is still good in the winter, right?"

"Hmm, well it gets a bit damp."

"Well, it doesn't rain as much as it does in England."

"No, of course not," she said kindly, shaking her head. They both glanced out at the sea. The beach was full of people, even though it was around noon. The coloured multitude of parasols, the familiar din of voices, and the carefree murmur of the sea reminded them of the pleasures of slow days.

"Do you like the sea?" he asked.

"What a question!" She glanced at him before suddenly averting her gaze, annoyed by the way her inexplicable nervousness wouldn't go away. Get a hold of yourself, she warned herself inwardly.

Changing the subject, she asked, "Are you looking for an investment or is your family …?" She left the sentence unfinished, speaking once again in a confident, official tone.

A shadow crossed the features of the man. "I'm not sure yet. Nevertheless, I'm planning on staying here for a few years. My wife got a good job in London, which she doesn't want to give up." He didn't add that his wife was seeing someone, or that this was why he was here.

A lengthy silence set in. The man gazed at Vicky again, wondering what to ask her to keep the conversation going.

"What are you doing here?" he asked.
She shrugged. "What all the others are doing," she said tersely.
"Oh, come on, don't be like that."
Vicky raised a hand to her mouth while a smile played in her eyes. I grew up next to the Atlantic Ocean at Algarve. That is all. As I said, I've only been here for a year," she concluded her story.

"So, what are your plans for the weekend?"
"Oh, that's still a long way off," she replied evasively, practically in a rough tone.

"Please, I don't wish to impose, but I have an old friend who I've been trying to hunt down for some time now." He gestured with his hand. "He's renting a house somewhere around Tarifa. I don't remember exactly where, but I have it written down. Would you like to come with me at the weekend? The truth is that I would like to see the Atlantic coast, and I might manage to find my friend," he explained and then fell silent. He quizzically eyed Vicky, before raising his hands in the air.

"No obligations," he added, firmly with a smile in the corner of his mouth. She certainly felt lonely sometimes. After all, why not? At least she could put his trustworthiness to the test.

"So?"

"OK, that sounds acceptable," she noted, glancing at her watch. "Unfortunately, I've got to go now."

"Sure, no problem," he said, motioning for the waiter. They parted company when they reached the office and agreed he would call her on Thursday. Vicky watched her client walk off with firm strides, disappearing down the street.

This isn't good at all, she thought with a shake of her head. She was annoyed that she had said yes since he was married. That's okay, she would cancel the invitation on Thursday, she decided firmly. Yet she still wondered if they could be friends. She spent most of her time selling real estate, and in the rest of her free time, she hung out at the beach. She always noticed when guys were looking at her, and it made her feel awkward. Still, she'd always toyed with the thought of having a Latin lover.

Thursday the phone rang around six.

"David Stone," said a pleasant male voice.

"Hi," replied Vicky in a reserved tone.

"So, can I get a yes from you?

Vicky paused for a moment.

"No, or rather yes," she agreed uncertainly. "I'm pleased by your decision," he told her. "So, as I mentioned, we're leaving on Saturday. Is it okay if I pick you up around nine?"

"Yes."

"Great, then see you on Saturday," said David, hanging up. Vicky held the receiver in her hand for a while before slowly putting it down. She cursed herself for being such a weakling, but she was still glad she'd said yes.

CHAPTER 4

On Saturday, they met as agreed. David got out of the car, took Vicky's bag, put it in the trunk, opened the door for her, and hopped back down on the front seat.

"Aren't you sleepy?" he asked, starting the car. He was glad to have the redhead sitting next to him.

"Not anymore. Road 340 was lined on both sides by apartment houses, bars, and restaurants.

"Do you know this road?" asked David, trying hard to strike up a conversation.

"Yeah. Like the back of my hand."

"I wouldn't like living here. It's too noisy."

"True, and the traffic keeps picking up. I would set a speed limit of fifty kilometres or less from Malaga to Gibraltar." The man bit his lip to suppress his grin. *So, the redhead is a smart one,* he thought to himself.

Vicky caught his smile. "What is it? What's so funny? You can see for yourself how many buildings are here. I don't think the people living here appreciate the noise. If, someone who is in a hurry can use the highway. It's not far from here."

"You could be right."

In less than an hour, the outlines of the Rock of Gibraltar appeared in the distance.

"What a sight!" David exclaimed. "If you don't mind, I'd like to take a closer look, since this is the first time I've been here. I take it you've seen it before?"

"Yeah, more than once. Let's go, it's worth a peek."

As they crossed through the city, Vicky guided her new friend upwards before stopping at a bypass road with a magnificent view of the bay, which glittered in the morning sunshine. She spotted a few monkeys sitting on the narrow stone fringe of the road.

David kept taking pictures, busily clicking away. "Do you mind?" he asked. Vicky smiled into the camera, ruffling her boyishly short hair. They got back in the car and visited the southern part of Gibraltar. The view was spectacular. Africa was just a stone's throw away. To the right, a ferry approached the mouth of the bay, most likely approaching from Tangier.

"One of these days, I want to visit Morocco," noted David suddenly. "Unfortunately, I don't have much time. Have you been over there?"
"Yes, twice."
"Can you take a car over there?"
Vicky nodded.
"But trips like that can be pretty dangerous," David mentioned. "Why?" asked the other, raising an eyebrow.
"Because of drug smugglers."
"Then I've got nothing to worry about."
"That's just it. That's what they're looking for on the other side."
"What do you mean?"

"I heard a messed-up story a long time ago," she started. "A couple went over to Ceuta in their car. They were arrested on their way back. A big packet of hash was glued to the bottom of their car. The man tried proving that they had nothing to do with the drugs and had no idea how they got there. They released the wife, but the man was arrested."

"That can't be true."

"It seems to show that you can't be careful enough."

Once they reached the city, they were lucky enough to find a parking place. They had some coffee before walking through the throng flowing down Main Street. David stopped in front of a jeweller's shop.

"Wait a minute. I'll be right back," he said, entering the shop. Vicky kept on staring at the window display.

The man returned within a few minutes. He took Vicky by the hand and slipped a small parcel into her palm.

"What's this?" she asked.
"Just a memento from Gibraltar."

Vicky curiously opened the lid of the tiny box and saw that it contained a tiny heart-shaped coral. She felt a sense of warmth spreading through her body.

"It's beautiful and kind of you," she said, gently smiling up at the man, "but unfortunately I can't accept it since I hardly know you."

David turned grim. "Please, accept it. I insist."

Vicky sensed that it was a sincere gesture and she shouldn't turn him down. "Thank you," she whispered awkwardly, blushing through her freckles.

"Let me slip it on your bracelet." Vicky silently removed the souvenir she had received from her mother a few months ago, for her twentieth birthday. David slipped the heart-shaped charm onto the bracelet, which he clasped back onto her slim wrist.

"Think of it as a lucky charm and let it take good care of you," he said. Later, as they drove out of Tarifa, the ocean water began churning.

Near the shore, they spotted an array of colourful kite surfers bobbing in the air. An hour later, they reached Caños de Meca. It was sweltering hot, yet they still walked up to the Trafalgar light tower. The Atlantic Ocean glowed in a deep blue hue in the sparkling sunshine.

"Isn't it just lovely?" asked David.
Vicky replied with a nod. "Indeed, it is."
They walked back to the car to continue their journey. As they reached El Palmar, David drove up and down the shore, unable to find the house they looking for. Finally, they decided to visit a restaurant. Both of them relished the cold beer. David spoke up.

"So how about dropping the official tone now?" he asked Vicky, who gladly nodded. "You forgot something," he added, leaning to Vicky over the table.

He sat back down in his chair with satisfaction after she kissed his cheek and his gaze lingered on her. Her boyishly short hair and freckled face made her look like a teenager.

"What is it?" she asked, noticing a change in his expression. "It's nothing. I'm just glad I met you." Vicky blinked and fell silent, feeling a bit uncomfortable. She turned her bristly head towards the ocean. She was silently wondering whether or not it had been a good idea to go on this trip.

The waitress brought them their lunch, which they hungrily devoured. Naturally, David picked up the tab.

"Could you help me?" he asked the waitress, who spoke a few words of English. "I'm looking for an old, antique-looking stone building on the shore."

"Sure. It's on the other end of this road, about two kilometres away. Are you still hungry?

"Oh, no, no. The lunch was delicious, I'm stuffed."
The waitress cleaned up the table with satisfaction.
"See you next time," she remarked in a friendly tone as they walked out of the restaurant.

"Well, let's see if we can find it this time," suggested David as they got back in the car. "Then let's hit the beach. I hope you brought a swimsuit!"

"Sure – don't leave the house without it!"
They locked eyes for a moment, but Vicky quickly broke off, feeling awkward. Driving down the shore, they finally managed to find an old stonewalled inn. David stopped the car in front of the building.

"Come on, I think we're in the right place," he said cheerfully. They found a small street directly behind the antique structure. He furtively looked around. "This might be the house I was looking for," he noted hopefully, motioning her to follow.

The shutters on the second-floor windows were all closed shut. However, the front door was open. They spotted a figure lounging in a hammock on the shaded front patio. He held a newspaper in his hands and was engrossed in his reading.

"Hello!" cried David over the low fence.

The stranger dropped the newspaper and looked up at them. He suddenly stood up.

"David?" he gasped in surprise and rushed over to the gate.

"Hey, dude, I can't believe my eyes – you came to Andalusia after all! Come on, get inside," he cried enthusiastically, eyeing the girl at David's side.

"Let me introduce you to my friend," began David. The young, charming man held his hand out to the little redhead, who awkwardly stayed in the background.

"Nick," said the man, gently squeezing the girl's fingers.

"Vicky," she muttered quietly. She felt oddly attracted and revolted by the man's handshake. He was undeniably good-looking, she realized at once.

Nick offered his unexpected guests a seat at the old cracked wooden table on the patio. "It's great to see you, pal," said Nick, patting David on the shoulder. He walked inside and shortly returned with three cans of beer. He sat down on the other side of the table, exactly opposite Vicky.

It was an old habit of his to sit opposite the girls he was interested in to inconspicuously take a good look at his next possible target. He opened one of the cans and pushed it over to the girl.

"Cheers!" he cried, lifting his beer to his mouth while eying the freckled face.

"So, when did you arrive?" he asked, glancing at David.

"Oh, about a month ago."

Nick realized without asking that David had come alone, otherwise, his wife would have been there. He glanced back at the girl, who suddenly stood up.

"I'll go look around if you don't mind," she said awkwardly, disappearing behind the house. She didn't notice Nick's searching, voracious gaze.

"What's going on?" asked Nick once Vicky was gone. "I'm sure you're in a mess, if you came along."

"Not, since we'll soon get divorced anyway," said David quietly.

"Your new girlfriend is really cute."

"She's not my girlfriend, but I wouldn't mind if she was," he replied with a grin.

"Okay, okay, I hope you're staying for a few days!"

"I was hoping you would ask us to stay," he replied with a laugh. Nick stood up since Vicky had returned.

"Come on, I'll show you around the house," Nick offered politely. They entered a spacious living room. On the left side was a grand open kitchen, and on the right was a sizeable fireplace, its outer wall covered in soot. A massive flight of wooden stairs ascended opposite the entrance, where there were three bedrooms and a bathroom.

Nick opened the door to the bedroom in the back. "Will this be good for the two of you?"

David glanced at Vicky and quickly spoke up. "If you don't mind, I'll stay in the other room," he said awkwardly.

"You know, pal, I didn't have the chance to tell you that we only met recently, and we're just friends," he added, stressing the last word in the sentence. Nick shrugged. "Whatever you say, but just so you know, there's a bedroom and a bathroom downstairs, so you can choose whichever one you want." He gave Vicky an ambiguous glance.

Vicky instantly chose the room on the ground floor and quickly disappeared behind the door. "How could I put myself on the spot like this?" She muttered to herself. She was annoyed by this awkward situation. I should've stayed at home, she pondered tensely.

There was a knock on the door.

"Yes, I'm here!"

"I just wanted to say that we're heading down to the beach," cried David through the door. "I'll be right with you," she replied at once. She slipped into her swimsuit and slipped a T-shirt over it. A few minutes later, all three of them were strolling down to the shore.

The water was crystal clear. The waves ceaselessly approached and splashed ashore before the mass of seawater retreated, only to let the next wave crash in with renewed force. They basked in the sun and had a lively chat before Vicky stood up and waded into the water. David followed her in at once. Nick went in with them for a while but then walked back to the shore where he could shamelessly eye Vicky as she came out of the water.

She had an immaculate figure, and the water was glistening in her red hair. She surely hadn't gotten much sun this year, as her skin was still pearly white. Vicky noticed the man sizing her up. His predator-like eyes furtively feasted on her, but she coldly ignored him. She sat down on the reed mattress, turning towards David.

Nick's phone rang. He stood up and went for a walk before finishing the call and returning in a hurry.

"I'm sorry, but I've got to go at once, and I have no idea when I'll be back. Stay as long as you want to. Come on, I'll give you a set of keys," he said, turning to David, before saying goodbye to Vicky.

"Oh, I almost forgot," he added. "There's some cold drinks and some food in the fridge. I recommend the restaurant next door, they have a good chef, but there's a store nearby as well. Make yourselves at home!" He showed David the place where he hid the keys.

"Ask him to put them back before leaving."

"Thanks, but I have to return to Marbella tomorrow," said Vicky.

"That's up to you. I'm sorry, but I've got to go now. We'll make up for it, next time," he said in a hurry. He quickly drove off in his Land Rover, leaving a cloud of dust and sand in his wake.

David was glad to be left alone with Vicky, but he wasn't pushy, and Vicky wasn't giving him any encouraging signs. They chatted at length and went swimming, and thus the weekend quickly come end. They parted as friends when they returned to Marbella.

CHAPTER 5

A week went by with no sign of David Stone. That was understandable since they hadn't gotten any closer over the weekend. He finally got in touch with her after two weeks.

"Hi, it's David," she heard him say on the other end of the line. "Can I see you sometime?"

Vicky didn't know what to say.
"I was off travelling, and I just returned," he explained.
"Fine," she agreed after some hesitation.
"When exactly?"
"I'll get off work in an hour if that's OK for you …"
"I hope I can make it. Please don't leave if I'm a bit late," he said before hanging up.

David showed up in front of the office at the previously agreed time, and they stopped by a local bar for a drink. He ordered some drink and furtively eyed the peevish-looking girl. "It's been quite some time since I've seen you," he began, "and I must admit that I've been thinking a lot about you."

Vicky was reticent and didn't admit that she had been thinking about him too. She couldn't explain her feelings for him. Whenever they met during their brief friendship, she simply couldn't overcome her nervousness. It was good to be with him and talk to him, but she didn't feel anything else.

"I had to urgently travel to London," explained David, "which is why I didn't call." He changed the subject and asked her a question. "I would like you to come to the hotel on Saturday. We're hosting a charity ball." Vicky thoughtfully gazed at him and finally nodded, pretending to be at ease. "I would love to go, but no strings attached."

David tried suppressing his grin. "I've heard that before," he muttered half-seriously. The waitress brought some *tapas* for them. David didn't fail to notice that the short-haired young man at the next table couldn't take his eyes off the little redhead. *She's a truly lovely girl, but fairly stubborn,* he thought to himself. During the conversation, he noticed Vicky's nervousness but decided not to ask her about it. He felt there was some kind of invisible wall between the two of them which prevented them from getting closer.

Suddenly he realized that perhaps it was the big age difference between them and the fact that he wasn't free. He had recently visited London to get divorced and wanted to tell all of this to Vicky, but the place and time weren't suitable. He glanced at his watch.

"I'm sorry, but I can't stay any further," he explained, picking up the change that the waiter had left on the table. "Unfortunately, I have an important meeting to attend. I'll call you on Wednesday. Again, I'm sorry. I just wanted to see you," he added before leaving in a hurry and disappearing into the crowd.

After David deserted her, Vicky slowly walked along the road next to the harbour. The bars and inns were filled with tourists and locals.

When she got home, she leaned up against the counter and thoughtfully started munching on the sandwich she'd just prepared. She didn't understand why she said yes. She was certainly very lonely – and convinced by now that Luis wasn't going to get in touch with her. They'd broken up for good. But what did she want from David? He was married, for God's sake! He was good-looking, but she was fairly certain there was no sense in getting into a relationship with him.

She showed up at the hotel's reception on Saturday evening. Several people were in the lounge. She looked around and spotted the elegantly dressed shape of David in a tuxedo, directing a group of people into the ballroom. Vicky didn't move and stood around hesitantly, waiting for a while before glancing at herself in the mirror on the wall. She failed to notice David approaching, sizing her up appreciatively. He snuck up behind her, grinning to himself.

"It's a beautiful evening." He smiled as she spun around. Vicky was wearing a deep green dress which enhanced her red hair and freckled face. The dress left her nicely shaped neck uncovered. She wore tiny earrings in her ears with a golden bracelet on her arm – with the coral heart she got from David.

There was a light layer of makeup on her face, which accentuated the natural beauty she wasn't entirely aware of. However, her green eyes revealed nothing of her feelings.

"Well, someone is looking fabulous," complimented David. "Come on," he urged, putting his hand on her shoulder. She had a fresh, pleasant fragrance to her. He didn't like women who doused themselves with racy perfumes. He crossed through the masses, leading her into a grand hall.

"Let me introduce you to a few of my colleagues," he suggested. They stopped in front of a table where people were happily chatting with each other.

"David you, lucky bastard," noted one of the men.
"Well, what can I say?" asked David sheepishly.

The waiter balanced a tray full of cocktails over their heads. "Cheers," David cried happily, lifting his glass into the air. He suddenly leaned close to Vicky and planted a kiss on her face. They quickly emptied the contents of their glasses, and Vicky's excitement eased.

At one end of the room, a huge selection of dishes wa arrayed for the guests and they all took part in the reception. At the end of the dinner, David whispered to Vicky, "I'll be back soon" and hurried off into the crowd. Suddenly, the lights came on upon the
stage, and David appeared to deliver a brief charity speech.
Vicky took a good long look at him. She was sorry that he was taken. She had to admit that she fancied her new friend.

Still … Suddenly, a woman from the other side of the table sat down next to her. "You know, David is a great boss," she began. "He sure knows a lot about hotels. I knew his wife, who left him recently. I still don't understand why she did it since everyone loves the guy. However, they finally put it down in writing. He's a free man now," she added, meaningfully glancing at her. "Did you know that?"
"No, I've only known him for a few weeks."
"You can trust him."
"Thanks, that's very kind of you," added Vicky thoughtfully.
"I'll go back to my boyfriend," added the woman with a wink of an eye, since David had finished his speech.

Now that Vicky knew his secret, she thought of him differently. She started wondering whether she could love him. Her thoughts were distracted once the curtain opened. A group of people dressed in black were sitting on typical rustic chairs in a rigid posture. The man at the edge of the group started playing the guitar while the others accompanied him by clapping. The woman sitting in the middle of the group starts singing while rhythmically tapping on the floor with her foot. She accompanied her singing with her head, expression, and unusual mimicry and motions.

Suddenly, a woman fluttered onto the stage, captivating the audience with her amazing flamenco dance moves. Her hair was tied up in a bun. She proudly raised her head, rhythmically tapping a beat with her black shoes, going through the steps and moves that had been handed down generation after generation. The dance became increasingly hard and wild.

Her frilled skirt twirled and dipped in the air, flashing her leg and knees on the stage. The arms twisted and twirled up and down, bending at the wrist. The woman's head bobbed up and down rigidly while her face displayed a proud, practically stubborn expression and her black shoes beat against
the stage, faster and faster.

At the end of the dance, they all stood up and rewarded the deeply a bowing artist with a round of relentless applause. The woman in her forties next to Vicky whispered to her, "She's a very famous dancer called Patricia Gomez."

Vicky suddenly recognised Lucy's mother, whom she had met over a year ago. A short intermission followed the performance.

"Did you like it?" David asked Vicky.
"I loved it! The stirring melody, the dance – I think they express just how fiery the Spanish emotions are."
"You might be right, that's about how I felt," he said, nodding his head uncertainly. "To be honest, the melody was a bit too hard for me."

"It does sound a bit forced if you're not used to it," she agreed. "Either you love it and feel it or you don't. Once you've got to know Spain, you'll think of it like this fiery flamenco and bouncing beat," she added, glancing at him with a mischievous grin.

"Of course, you might think of bullfights or the fiesta, the Holy Week or even the siesta." This made them laugh. They had a few drinks. Vicky felt flushed, and she became more talkative. After a brief pause, she carried on,

"I guess you know that for centuries, Andalusia had a mixture of influences – the Moors, the Arabs, the gipsies, all of which can be noticed in their traditional outfits and the spirit of the people. But what captures this the best is the flamenco."

David attentively listened to Vicky. "If you think about it," she continued the cultural heritage shows all the influences in the architecture and the arts. Think of Alhambra, for example."

"I guess you like the Spanish people?" he asked.

"Yes. Modern art is stunning. Just think of Picasso, Gaudi, and Dali. Right?

"Yeah, you have a point."

"Also, we mustn't forget the painters of the previous ages, like Velázquez, El Greco, and Goya. They have a rich culture, and their history has brought together a grand nation. You know the Spaniards and Portuguese went on adventurous sea trips centuries ago. Their campaigns of discovery brought them great plunder, which made the adventures rather tempting for all the participants. Yet we mustn't forget that these people also gained a lot of external experience which also greatly enriched Spain. To get back to our original subject, their dance and music perfectly mirror the sentimental side of Spanish people. I feel this is what makes the land so mysterious and beautiful."

"Those were some lovely thoughts," noted David appreciatively. "And what do you think about the Spanish people living around you?" he asked, jolting Vicky back to the present.

"Well, you know, if you've been living here for years, you can notice that most people are friendly and helpful, but of course, there are exceptions to that. The most interesting is how sensitive they are. They cry easily, even the men."

Vicky suddenly realized she's been talking too much and quizzically eyed David, who attentively listened to her reasoning. They drank a few more toasts and later went dancing before Vicky finally said goodbye at the end of the night.

"I'm sorry," she said, "but I have to go away tomorrow." While waiting for the taxi to arrive, David sighed deeply and squeezed her hand.

"Can I call you again?" he asked.

Vicky awkwardly nodded and reached up to plant a light kiss on his cheek. David wanted to hug her, but the night was fast receding, whisking away this peculiar girl with it.

CHAPTER 6

After Gibraltar, the serpentine road provided the same spectacular view she'd experienced the last time she came this way with David. For a few minutes, she stopped at a rest stop on the other side of the road, admiring the unparalleled view. She just couldn't get enough of the natural beauty.

Where the Mediterranean Sea met the Atlantic Ocean, just a stone's throw from her was the deep blue spire of the Riff Mountain on the African side.

Maybe she would make it over to Morocco in the fall, she thought. Due to the extreme curves in the road, she could only drive at low speeds. The right side of the road was lined with tall, slim wind turbines which rotated silently in the brisk wind. She slowed down to take in the junction ahead of her before heading down a barely noticeable dirt road which led into the mountains through the forest of turbines.

Soon she reached an enchanting cork tree forest. The crowns of the trees linked over the road, and the sun's rays filtered through the branches. In a bend of the road, two beautiful foals galloped across, but as soon as they noticed the car, they pranced and disappeared down the gently sloping rocky terrain.

Vicky regretfully watched them race off. In the next bend of the road, she found a few white-washed buildings, so, she decided to park the car.

She pulled out her girlfriend's letter from her bag and pored over the instructions again. She got out of the car, hoping she was in the right place, and uncertainly rang the bell at the gate. A few minutes later, she heard the click of the lock.

Sarah appeared at the gate with a broad smile on her face and her several-month-old baby in her arms. The two women warmly hugged each other.

"I thought you weren't coming. Did you change your mind?"
"I was running a bit late, but thanks to your perfect instructions, it wasn't hard to find my way," Vicky explained, leaning closer to the baby.

"And what is the name of this little angel?" She caressed a tiny little hand.
"Angela," replied the mother proudly.
"You live in beautiful surroundings. This cork-tree wood is amazing."
"Isn't it? I remember it was love at first sight when we came here with Juan."
"Quite a hiding place."
"Yeah, if hiding is what you're looking for. What counts is that it's close to Tarifa. As you know, my husband works there at a health clinic. We have phone lines, and it's only a few kilometres away. Come on, let me show you the house. Are you hungry?"

"A little bit."

"Me too, so let's go the kitchen. Oh, wait for a second. Let me put this little darling down to bed first," Sarah added cheerfully, planting a little kiss on the baby's rose-coloured cheek.

"I just finished feeding her," she added. "I'll be back in a few minutes. Look around and get washed up. There's the bathroom, and your room is just next to it." Sarah pointed towards the corridor.

Vicky looked around the rustic living room with a hammock of colourful canvas dangling from a girder, a sofa, and a dinner table that was huge but somehow cozy. The walls were covered by a few old timbers hanging from chains and used as bookshelves. They were loaded with well-used books.

"I'm back already," said Sarah, returning to the room without the baby. "I was waiting for you, so I wasn't able to have lunch either." She headed over to the kitchen, taking up two dishes and serving some steaming hot stew for the two of them. "Come on, let's go out on the porch, it's nice and cool."

"Is Juan at work?"
"Not at the moment. He went down to the *playa* with some of his friends. Do you like it?" Sarah asked, motioning to the soup.
"Yes, it's very tasty."
"You seem tired, so I suggest we get some rest while the baby is sleeping because there's going to be a party later on."
"Good idea. I didn't get much sleep, so I could use some rest," Vicky explained, recalling the previous night's events.

Vicky woke in the late afternoon to the sound of laughter. She quickly had a shower and got herself together before walking down to the porch. Juan noticed her at once and stood up, warmly welcoming her.

"Oh, there she is! I haven't seen you in ages," he said, planting a kiss on her face.
"She's my wife's best friend," he explained to the others.

Sarah motioned for Vicky to sit next to her as she attentively eyed the others. The young man sitting opposite from her holding his hand out to her.

"Pedro," he introduced himself, while handing her a glass. "Would you like some?" He poured some beer in the glass, with the foam spilling over the side. "Oops, too fast," he said, apologizing for his clumsiness.

Vicky smiled at him.

"Thank you," she said awkwardly, feeling something like a shock of electricity as they looked at each other. She quickly reached out for the glass to hide her embarrassment, since the man's proximity seemed to upset her entire existence. Even his voice sounded familiar.

They started chatting after a few minutes, and it felt like she was meeting an old friend. The man couldn't take his eyes off her, which Vicky didn't mind at all. The sun slowly slipped down behind the treetops. Sarah was busying herself with the baby. They were having a great time, and one of them suggested they should go for a walk in the woods before it got dark. A little exercise after the hearty meal would be good for everyone.

"Care to join me?" asked Pedro, approaching Vicky.
"Sure," she replied at once. The man undeniably had a great effect on her. She'd never felt this odd sensation before – a kind of inner tension which made her tremble all over her body.

The air in Spain is always charged with a kind of peculiar romance, especially when the orange trees are in bloom. Although she couldn't sense the blossoms' overwhelming odour at the moment, she still blushed when she gazed into the man's dark eyes. They lagged a bit behind the others. Pedro directed her towards a group of rocks. They were talking about several different subjects and hadn't noticed that they had lost sight of the others entirely. Nevertheless, Vicky continued to follow the man. The cork wood rustled in a light breeze, and the trees created a romantic kind of half-light. They suddenly came to a stop.

"We'd better go back. It'll get dark soon," suggested Vicky, almost.

Pedro glanced at her. "Are you cold?"

"No," she told him, whilst shivering in the draft. She turned around but suddenly slipped on a rock. Pedro reached out for her, but he also lost his balance, and they both fell to the ground. Vicky felt the embrace of his strong arms, which wouldn't let go of her.

"Are you hurt?" he whispered, hovering over her. She shook her head, and they magnetically locked glances. The man sensed Vicky's smell and the heat of their bodies, and their lips irresistibly touched.

By the time, they made their way back to the house, it was dark, and the others had left. They silently parted company. Vicky quietly slipped into her room. She took a shower in a daze and fell onto her bed. Her face was still burning, and she still felt Pedro's embrace and passionate kiss. She was puzzled by herself, yet she couldn't stop thinking about those brief moments of bliss.

It was a starry night when she woke with tears in her eyes. The pale light of the moon streamed through her window. She'd had a nightmare but couldn't recall the details. All she knew for certain was that she had gazed into a faded mirror and couldn't see herself. She felt an unspeakable sense of sorrow from the dream and from the fact that Pedro might never want to see her again. They hadn't said a word in parting as he solemnly left her.

The dawn was still far off, but she stared at the stars with her eyes wide open. She tossed and turned as her thoughts strayed back to last night's encounter, and she just couldn't forget the embrace of her Latin lover. She wanted to see him again and felt she could love this warm-hearted man forever. She banished the thought of her bad dreams and longingly buried her head in her pillow.

CHAPTER 7

She didn't dare ask any questions from Juan over breakfast so he wouldn't get suspicious. She silently sat next to the table. She was sure Pedro wouldn't get in touch, which was no surprise. What would he think of a girl who lost herself suddenly in the embrace of an unknown man?

"Pedro just called and invited us to his seaside house," Juan told her. "You're coming too, right?"

"Oh, I don't want to impose," she replied quietly.

"But he invited you too," insisted Juan, eyeing her quizzically. Suddenly, she perked up. A smile appeared on the corner of her mouth.

"I'd love to go with you – and if you and Sarah don't mind, I'd like to stay here a few more days."

"Don't be foolish. You know we're glad to have you. If you have the time, you could come more often," interrupted Sarah, sitting down next to them. Vicky stood up with a smile on her face.

"Well then, I'd like to take this opportunity to thank you both for the invitation," she said, rushing into the house. A few minutes later, she reappeared with a flushed complexion, holding a bottle of booze in her hand as well as a lovely photo album from Andalusia and a little rattle for the baby. "Thank you again for your kindness," she gushed, setting the gifts down on the table.

"That's very kind of you," said Sarah with pleasure. Juan also nodded and thanked Vicky for the gift.

"I'd like to look around the neighbourhood for some business before heading over to Algarve."

"You're going to have your work cut out for you," warned Juan. "I'm sure you've heard that constructions aren't allowed in the area. Still, there are a lot of people who break the law." He stirred his coffee before continuing. "One of my patients told me that the local council in Tarifa recently tore down an illegally built structure with bulldozers, right in front of the owners."

"No way! That sounds a bit harsh. What's the point of that?"
"It's simply because this area is a nature preserve."
"OK, that's important, but it's hard to stop developments close to the shore."
"Sure, especially when so many people want to spend their vacations here and settle down. I'm sure you heard that kite surf and windsurf people love coming here, but because of the limited accommodation options, the prices have been high for years. Still, the tourists keep coming, especially young people. The transportation is far from decent, but the sandy beaches are undeniably beautiful, unlike the stretches, east of Gibraltar. Although Marbella and its surroundings are the Florida of Europe. I still swear that the beaches west of Tarifa are the best in Europe, of course, excluding Algarve."
"I love Algarve."
"Yeah, me too, but if you see this stretch of beach, I'm sure you'll fall in love with it," Juan concluded. "I've got to go now. I'll be back soon." She closed the gate after Juan's car and walked off towards the cork wood again, which looked stunning in the morning sunshine. The leaves were motionless on the branches, and the enamoured girl thought longingly of Pedro.

After her stroll, she spent some time with Sarah and the baby. Sarah didn't mention their plans for the afternoon since her every moment was occupied with the child. Vicky didn't speak much either. Later on, she listened to Sarah's stories about the baby and their day-to-day life before helping her friend out with lunch.

In the meantime, Juan returned and then went out tinkering with his car after lunch.

"I'm ready to go," he yelled to his wife.
"You better bring a toothbrush," warned Sarah, mysteriously planting a kiss on Vicky's face.

Vicky blushed and rushed back to her room. She quickly pulled out her bag, throwing a few things into it. Her heart was pumping in joy, and she could hardly wait for the embrace of her Latin lover.

They headed out along the serpentine road, which ended after Tarifa. They spotted countless colourful chutes in the air over the Atlantic.

"The best kite surfers come here," explained Sarah, pointing out towards the ocean, where the yellow sands encroached on the hillsides. Juan turned left onto a narrow road. Enclosed farms and cows were grazing in fields as far as the eye could see. As they passed through Barbate, they entered a shady pine forest. When they moved down the slopes, the crowns of the trees seemed to open up, offering a view of the blue Atlantic.
"A few weeks ago, I drove down this particular road with David," Vicky recalled with an odd sense of premonition. Juan slowly and leisurely drove the car down the road.

"These flatlands aren't particularly beautiful, but the shores are," he explained. The road led straight down to the edge of the ocean. Vicky paid close attention once Juan turned to the left. Oh, this can't be true. What an odd twist of fate. She knitted her hands together, looking ahead with pent-up excitement. "Don't worry," she whispers as she tried steadying herself. "Coincidences like this never happen in real life."

After they passed by the stone inn, they turned onto a dusty road, and Juan parked in front of a house.

"We're here," he exclaimed cheerfully, taking the baby in his arms and walking through the gate. Vicky's face grew pale, and her heart raced. A few weeks ago, she spent a weekend in this very same house with David. The unexpected situation made her feel awkward and deeply upset. It seems there are coincidences, after all, she sadly thought to herself. The same table awaited them on the covered patio, but instead of Nick, she saw Pedro standing in front of it with a broad smile on his face.

"Finally, you're here! I'm glad you brought Vicky with you," he added nonchalantly, giving her a meaningful glance. Vicky felt so awkward she forgot to smile. She clenched her trembling hand into a fist and peeked into the house over the man's shoulder, expecting Nick to show up as well. Pedro noticed her tension, but he attributed it to the pleasant memories of the events that took place the previous night.

"Come," he invited her, taking her cold little hand in his palm and leading her upstairs. The ceiling of the sizeable bedroom was supported by wooden girders. The window provided a fantastic view of the shore, where the waves softly lapped on the sand.

"Beautiful," she noted appreciatively.

Pedro approached her from behind and tightly hugged her around the waist, whispering in her ear, "Yes, it's beautiful. I hope you'll stay here with me."

Vicky's worries were suddenly washed away. At that moment, she forgot everything, experiencing only joy in the arms of her Latin lover.

CHAPTER 8

They didn't live in the house for two days. Their love brought them together again, and again. Their eyes hungrily searched each other out. The spacious bedroom upstairs was home to tempestuous embraces, sighs, and whispers.

In the quieter hours, Vicky looked for a chance to tell him about her friendship with David and that she had visited this house before, but she never found the right opportunity to do it. She simply felt happy in Pedro's arms – profoundly happy. She didn't feel like explaining herself, since nothing had happened with David, after all.

The waves pounded harder on the beach. The gleaming body of saltwater covered them for a moment. They fretted and fumed, clinging to each other as they waited for the next wave to hit them before finally lying down on the beach, feeling refreshed. The sun was smiling over them in the clear sky, and the lovers gazed deeply into each other eyes. Later, they went for a lengthy stroll on the sandy beach. Vicky pulled her baseball cap down low. Pedro scrutinized her face and suddenly recognized her. He remembered the time Lucy asked for a ride in Vicky's car, causing quite a stir. Yes, there was no doubt about it, it was her. Sometimes odd coincidences like this happen, he thought.

"What is it?" Vicky asked, eying him quizzically. "Is there something on my face?"

Pedro scratched his chin and suppressed a smile. "You should have put on your cap sooner."
"Why?"
"Because the sun has burnt your nose," he grinned, pulling her close. Vicky shimmied up to the man and rubbed her nose on his chest.

"This is such a wonderful place," she said, looking up at him lovingly. She thought how great it would be to stay here with him forever. "That's why I love being here," he said. "The shallow beach is fantastic, no doubt about it." He hugged the girl to him as they slowly headed west.

"Is there any property here for sale?"
"I don't know. It's possible, but you can't do any construction work. It sounds hard to believe, but most houses in the village were built illegally. Including mine."

Vicky perked up.

"The local council fines the owners," he continued. "We can't know for sure, what will happen later on, but they could demolish the whole village."
"This isn't the only place with a problem like this," she added hopefully. "Perhaps it would be better for them to be tougher on new buildings and leave the completed ones intact. It would be cruel to ruin someone's house after they spent all their money building it. But things would be different if they would intervene at the beginning of the construction. You know, it's hard to make sense of the Spanish regulations. And of course, there's always corruption to deal with."

"That's right," Pedro agreed. "The other problem is that more and more people are coming here. See how many of them are here already? It seems they proved my point. From Tarifa to Cadiz, this stretch of the Atlantic is simply fabulous. All this could provide businesses, investors, and local citizens give a huge opportunity. Visitors and tourists need accommodation, food,medical care – the list goes on."

"However," he continued, "the government treats all of these areas as nature preserves, thus artificially holding back development and tourism which could provide the locals with a range of employment opportunities. It's no secret that unemployment is at record high. The unresolved problems will burden the weakened elements of the chain with growing crime and drug smuggling."

"At the same time, however, Costa de Sol is overdeveloped," interrupted Vicky, clearly enjoying the subject. "Perhaps neither is a good solution."

"I don't know. Still, if they would allow a certain degree of construction near the shores, they would have enough nature preserves further away from the coast," explained Pedro.

"Sounds good to me," she agreed, burying her foot in the fine sand before turning serious and facing Pedro.

"Tell me something about the African refugees. I remember over the winter I saw on TV that once the waves kept washing bodies ashore, and another time they captured a ship or fishing boat filled with frozen, miserable Africans."

"Unfortunately, that's all true. A lot of them come when there's a new moon, the night is dark, and the waves on the ocean are the mildest. I've seen a few incidents myself," he noted grimly.

"I once saw a bunch of people desperately clinging onto a boat tossed around by the waves. They huddled together soaking wet and trembling, barely alive at all. The water was almost up to the edge of the boat, it was so overburdened. A smaller wave was enough to send them to the bottom of the sea for good. Unfortunately, the winter period often brings nasty scenes."

Vicky shuddered.

"What happens to the ones who survive?" she asked. "Are they dangerous?"

Pedro firmly shook his head. "No. These unfortunate people disappear as soon as they arrive so they won't be sent back home. The people they catch usually won't admit where they came from, so it's rather hard to send them back home."

"You mean, they don't know which African country they should send them back to?" she asked in surprise, laughing.

"That's right."

"Well, you have to hand it to them, that's a pretty smart move."

A police car slowly drove down the road behind the dunes. The officers in the car were carefully checking the beach. "See, they're patrolling the area day and night," Pedro pointed out. Vicky was disheartened by the lengthy account but soon asked another question.

"And what do you know about drug smuggling?" she asked naïvely. Pedro eyed her quizzically. "Well, not much, but I heard a lot of people make a nice living out of it."

On their way back, they had lunch at the local restaurant before go back to the villa for the customary siesta. They quickly fell asleep in each other's arms in the cool room.

Vicky suddenly woke up. With her eyes closed, she happily thought of the man she loved. She reached out for him, but the other side of the bed was empty. He must be out on the terrace, she reasoned. She lazily got out of bed and gazed out the window. The area was quiet, with the distant murmur of the people on the beach as the only sound.

"Pedro, where are you?" she called out down the steps. Since there was no answer, she headed down to the living room. Much to her surprise, the door was locked. She noticed the key on the dining table with a piece of paper telling her that he would be back soon.

She waited at length and finally walked down to the sea. She went for a swim and then lay out on the beach. The huge mass of water was glittering in the setting sun. The ocean and the beach seemed just as beautiful as before, but she wasn't so certain without the man. She slowly headed back to the villa as her stomach nervously quivered.

Where was Pedro, and when would he come back? What should she do, now? The street was deserted, yet she heard a rustle and suddenly spun around. An unknown, possibly Arab man ran past her and scampered over the gate of the neighbouring building. Vicky saw him getting a bicycle from the bushes, riding off through the backyards, doubling over the cycle.

She entered the house feeling increasingly anxious, quickly locking the door behind her. She went upstairs to the bedroom and sat down in the armchair next to the window, gazing out over the street, but the man she was waiting for just wouldn't show up. After a while, she spotted a police car at the end of the street. Pedro was right, she thought. Twilight slowly descended over the area, and she sadly turned away from the window. There was still some food in the fridge, but she wasn't hungry. After taking a bath, she quickly fell asleep.

She slept restlessly and stirred around midnight. She heard the distant murmur of the ocean and some far-off noise, so she crept over to the window. Distressed from all the waiting, she stared out into the darkness. The new moon cast a barely perceptible glow over the dunes, and she could see a car pull up in front of the house.

Finally, he was back. She sighed in relief. She could faintly see a figure entering the garden, but suddenly, she was certain it wasn't Pedro. She would not sim easily. Her heart was beating heavily in her chest. "Pedro?" she called out uncertainly from the window.

"*Buenas noches*. I have a letter from Pedro," said the man from the dark. Vicky rushed down the stairs at once and opened the front door. She tensely took the folded-up letter from the man before heading back to the illuminated living room where she excitedly read the message:

Please go back to Juan's house at once.
This man will take you there.
I will get in touch.

This was the last thing she'd expected. She packed up her belongings and searched the drawers for a piece of paper to write a reply. She found a photograph of a bearded man in a hat with Lucy at his side, smiling. She was shocked to recognise Pedro. So, he fooled me, she thought sadly. She blew her nose and walked through the house, quickly packing her belongings and closing windows before placing the key in its hiding place with trembling hands. She stumbled onto the street where the stranger was waiting for her in the car.

When she arrived back at Sarah's, her friend was still awake, watching TV. When she saw the expression on Vicky's face, she asked her at once, "What happened?"

"Nothing. Pedro disappeared and told me to come back to your place," she said in a rattled tone, suppressing a bitter sigh Sarah noticed the tears glimmering in her eyes.

"You should get some sleep. If you want to, we'll talk things over in the morning with a clear head."

Vicky gratefully nodded and disappeared into her room with an awkward smile on her face. The events and the long period of waiting deeply disturbed her, and she cried out in bed over the way Pedro had fooled and deserted her.

CHAPTER 9

She woke up early because the baby was crying. Her head was reeling from the lack of sleep, but she couldn't go back to sleep either. She suppressed a yawn and trudged out to the bathroom.

Sarah was busy, so they didn't have a chance to talk – but then, Vicky didn't feel like talking. This was her business alone. She had been a fool, no doubt about it. Pedro used her and then got rid of her. The whole thing had ended just as fast as it began, she concluded to herself, trying her best to forget about it. Yet her heart ached, and she still felt the embrace of the Latin lover who left her without a word.

"I'm heading down to Tarifa. I want to look around," she said after breakfast to Sarah, who was busy cooking in the kitchen.

"Do you need anything?"
"Yeah. Two loaves of bread and at least three cartons of milk."
"No problem." Sarah eyed her friend anxiously but didn't ask a thing since Vicky's red, tear-stained eyes said it all. It seems

the promising love affair hadn't worked out, after all, Sarah thought forlornly. She had hoped they would have a decent relationship since Pedro wasn't the cheating type. She thought of Juan and how she never had any problems like this with him. Their lives had been relatively hassle-free, which was a rare thing nowadays.

As soon as Vicky arrived in Tarifa, she stopped by a few real estate agencies, since she wanted to gather some information about the local conditions. She quickly realized that the real estate on the market was rather overpriced, to say the least.

"Tarifa is a popular place, especially among young people," explained a girl at the office smugly. "And the selection isn't too big."

"I see," Vicky replied patiently. Yet there knew that there was a huge difference in quality between Marbella and Tarifa. Still, the Atlantic Ocean is unbeatable, she thought to herself.

After finishing her rounds, she stopped by a few shops. She picked up the milk and bread for Sarah as well. A teddy bear in a store window caught her eye, and she bought it at once for baby Angela. She recalled the time a few years ago when her parents invited an English couple to their villa. The couple bought some cheap crackers and a lousy bracelet for her mother. During their stay, they had used her father as a taxi driver.

She's seen money-grubbing behaviour like this before. It was hard to understand people sometimes. She hated dealing with spineless characters who made friends just to benefit from them, only to turn their backs when those friends are in need.

While driving, Vicky kept thinking about Pedro. Finally, she shook her head. "Enough of this. I'm heading over to Algarve, the first thing tomorrow morning. That's where I wanted to go in the first place. I want to forget everything!" she cried in annoyance, loading a CD into the player in her car. The music just made things worse, and she started sniffling. She wiped away her tears with the back of her hand and bit her lower lip, feeling angry at everyone. How could she bump into him like this?

And how good he was at hiding the fact that he recognised her! She had felt from the get-go that his voice sounded familiar, but his hat had covered his face the first time they met in the car.

Her eyes were getting blurry from the tears. Why was it that he used and dumped me when he no longer needed me?

What was wrong with me?
Why are you so surprised? She wondered mockingly.
You quickly fell for him in a matter of hours, you are a gullible fool! You were such an easy mark for him. You foolishlly thought you'd found love.

Well, maybe you did, but the guy just dumped you.

Vicky's agonising never seems to end. Slowly drive through the cork wood. Everything was motionless in the shade of the trees. She hopefully looked around to see the foal, she spotted the first time, but the forest was silent and still. By the way, she reached the house the sun was setting.

Juan was bathing the baby in the tub, lifting her and dropping her back down into the water. The baby submerged and then quickly kicked herself back to the surface, only for her father to lift her delicate little body for a moment, as it glistened in the sunshine. The baby cried out in delight. Sarah sat on the patio, happily watching them. Vicky felt a twinge in her heart at the peaceful scene in front of her.

"I envy, you know that?" noted Vicky sadly, sitting down next to her girlfriend.
"Come on, I hope you'll be doing the same things soon," Sarah reassured her. "You're beautiful, kind, and smart to boot. You

have everything it takes for someone to fall for you – or maybe you already found the right guy, eh?" she asked, meaningfully eyeing her girlfriend.

"I wish you were right," Vicky sighed.

"Come on, I'll whip up a cocktail for you. So, you fell for him, right?" Vicky bowed her head without answering.

"I'm sure he'll get in touch," said Sarah. "I know Pedro well since he's a friend of Juan. Still, they hardly see each other lately, since the baby is taking up all of his daddy's time. Plus, Pedro lives in Marbella. He rarely comes here."

Vicky still didn't say a word. She was crushed by the way she had been abandoned.

"I'm off to see my parents, tomorrow," she explained with some effort. "They're expecting me." Sarah glanced at her.

"I would like you to stay, but I perfectly understand if you have to go," she said, feeling for her friend and caressing Vicky's arm. "Come on, let's lure them out of the water," she went on with a mischievous smile, lifting the tray and cautiously approaching the table. Juan laughed.

"You'd make a lousy waitress," he noted, winking at Vicky, who finally shared a laugh with them.

CHAPTER 10

The following day, Vicky drove through Seville to the Portuguese border, arriving in Gale by the afternoon. It was good to be back home, yet her tension and restlessness just wouldn't subside.

Her mother quickly noticed that something was amiss. Vicky, however, remained calm and silent. She often walked down to the shore, wanting to be left alone. *They're indeed only our children until they grow up,* her mother reflected.

Once they start on their own lives, their parents are pushed into the background, and the family relations change for good. Adult children focus on the future, their career and livelihood, and finding love. Once they find a partner, settle down, and have children, they form a new community, and the parents are slowly far away. That's just the way things are.

Love is the strongest tie in one's life

You're lucky if you find it, yet still, a lot of people feel it's like a game you can't win. Once you're disillusioned in someone, you're left alone, licking your wounds. You mourn the closeness you lost, yet the wounds heal and fade in time. She felt that's probably why her daughter was feeling blue.

Vicky slowly walked alone down the shores of the Atlantic through the charming *playa* in Gale, which ran for several kilometres, all the way to Armacao de Pera.

The comfort of being at home gave her a sense of ease, but unfortunately, it wasn't enough to truly shake her up. She simply couldn't stop thinking about Pedro. She wanted to run and hide like a fox hunted by hounds, so after a few days, she decided to get back in her car and drive off. In parting, she turned back towards her parents and blew them one last kiss.

"Take care of yourself, honey!" cried her mother in concern, wiping the tears from her eyes.

Vicky kept on waving until the turn in the road. As she looked back, she could see they were still waving at her. This image would haunt her for years. She felt anxious, and a grim expression appeared on her face. She couldn't explain why, but her heart felt unspeakably heavy.

CHAPTER 11

When she arrived in La Perla, Vicky was welcomed by the cool interior of the townhouse she was renting. She tossed her bag on the sofa, quickly donned her swimsuit, and walked up to the pool. She relished the water after her long drive; it loosened her up, and she comfortably stretched out on a deckchair. Her eyes wandered up to the summer village on the mountain. The colourful houses looked lovely spread over the terrain.

The zigzagging streets had a romantic atmosphere to them. The balconies, patios and stairs were covered with pots and plants. She loved living where people welcomed each other in the street even if they were strangers. Most of the houses were owned by foreigners, most of whom only came here temporarily. The inhabitants of the sleepy little village didn't disturb each other. Not a sound of loud radios and televisions, nor dogs barking, can be heard.Everyone loved living a quiet life.

After sunset, the shadows grew, and the heat was trapped amongst the houses. Vicky smelled spicy barbecue as she strolled back to her house. She took a shower, washed her hair, and went down to the living room. She had some fruit for dinner while channel-surfing on the TV.

As she flipped over to the local TV channel, she spotted an image of Lucy on the screen. The speaker briefly explained that the daughter of a flamenco dancer Patricia Gomez went missing eight days ago. Vicky was so stunned that she dropped the fork in her hand. She thought of Pedro at once and was practically convinced that this was the reason he left her that night at the house on the beach.

What could she do now? How could she help?

The last time she spoke with Lucy, the girl mentioned that she was meeting an Arab man named Ali in some Moroccan bar. Vicky recalled seeing an advertisement for the bar in the recent edition of the local paper, so she quickly flipped through again, searching for it. She found what she was looking for and eagerly pored over the highlighted article.

She had been looking forward to a good night's sleep after her long drive, yet she suddenly made up her mind and hopped into her car. Although she found the bar she was looking for, the man at the bar wore a mask of hostile silence, so she decided to leave, disheartened.

"Wait, I might be able to help," cried the man as she was about to walk out. He quickly turned away and made a phone call. After finishing the call, he gazed at her with his black eyes, spread his arms apart, and shrugged.

"Unfortunately, I know nothing," he told her, "but if you can come back around eleven, I might have some information for you. If you give me your phone number, I can call you back," he noted indifferently. Vicky gave him her home number without hesitation, deciding to return if he didn't call.

The doorbell rang shortly after she arrived home. She looked through the peephole, and her heart raced. She opened the door at once and silently hugged the man she thought she might never see again. The heavy wooden door slammed shut behind her with a quiet thud.

Pedro explained everything to her at once, including the way Lucy had disappeared without a trace. That was why he'd had to leave the house on the beach so quickly. Vicky had been fast asleep, and he didn't want to wake her up.

"You know, they've invented the phone," she noted reproachfully.

"I know, but my mobile died and I couldn't remember your number by heart. However, I didn't forget your address. Pilatos Street. I know La Perla well, so it wasn't hard for me to find the place. I came here several times, but you weren't here."

"Why didn't you tell me who you are and that you recognized me?"

"You're right – I did recognize you when you put your cap on at the beach. I wanted to tell you, but I was afraid you'd walk out on me, and I didn't want that to happen," he admitted while holding her tightly.

"It seems you recognized me too.
When did you catch on?" he asked teasingly.

"After you disappeared. I was looking for some paper and found a picture of a bearded man in a hat with Lucy. It wasn't hard to figure out it was you in the picture. That's all." Pedro let go of Vicky and dropped the previous subject. He paced up and down the room in concern.

"I found a business card in Lucy's room," he began, "but there was no one at the address listed on the card. The mobile number was out of service as well. However, I met a man at the bar next door who gave me some hazy information on the owner of the card – a certain Ali. In exchange for a little money, he told me that Ali was currently residing in Marrakech. He said I would find him at a hotel named Sahara in the medina. I knew the owner for a long time ago. His name is Sarhan, and he might be able to give me a lead," he explained excitedly.

Vicky interrupted.
"I just came back from a Moroccan bar. I was also looking for a man named Ali, but I couldn't find him." He eyed her in surprise.
"How do you know about this?"
"I met Lucy a few weeks ago before I met you, and she gave me some background information." Something occurred to Pedro.
"I'm heading off to Morocco as soon as I can," he told her.
"I just wanted to see you first. I have to get going now. I'll get in touch when I get back."

She made up her mind at once.

"Wait. I want to go with you."
Pedro was surprised; "But I don't know how long I'll be staying there."
"That's okay. Take me with you, please!"
He gave in to her at once. "Fine," he agreed, "but I have to go home first." He glanced at his watch. "Look, I'll be back for you about an hour from now," he promised and left in a hurry.

Vicky danced in joy. After a moment of hesitation, she quickly packed a few belongings in a duffel bag put her papers in her pockets and called up her boss to urgently ask for leave.

The doorbell rang.
Has Pedro come back so soon? she wondered. Without a thought, she opened the heavy door. Much to her surprise, instead of Pedro, two dark-faced men burst into the house. One of them kicked the door in, and it slammed into the wall. The other suddenly flashed a knife in front of her face with a sneaky look on his face.
"If you speak a word, you will taste the chill of my blade," he hissed. She slumped down into the armchair behind her in fright. She was speechless with surprise and could only nod in terror.

She lifted her arms to shield her face.

The dark-faced man yanked her arms down, looking her in the eye. "How do you know about Ali?" he asked in a subdued tone. Vicky told him Lucy's story at once, adding that the girl had mentioned him to her.

"And why are you looking for Ali?" asked the other with a growl.

"Because Lucy disappeared – I saw her picture on TV an hour ago." The men exchanged glances and started bickering in the Arabic language. The shorter of the two pulled out his mobile. After a lengthy conversation, he said something to the other man before hostilely speaking up.

"Come," he said to Vicky, pushing her towards the door. He didn't treat her nicely as he pushed her towards the jeep parked in front of the entrance. She desperately gazed out of the window of the car as the vehicle silently crept down the deserted street and slowly approached the exit. The man sitting in front of her turned, around flashing his knife. At the very same moment, she saw Pedro's car turn in from the road.

"You're late," she muttered in agony, her throat constricting in pain.

"If you say a word, you know what will happen to you," threatened the Arabas he climbed out of the car.

The knife flashed in the hand of the other man, swishing in the air just inches from her face. Vicky was so petrified that she could barely get out of the car. She had a bad feeling about what would happen to her. Her eyes darted around on her pale face as she looked for a way out, but she had no chance to escape since the men flanked her on both sides.

After a brief walk, they led her onto a yacht and locked her inside the cabin. Her stomach quivered from the unexpected events as she stared out the round window. A great crowd of people passed down the illuminated promenade. It was odd to see her freedom just an arm's reach away. She could even see her own office. She grimaced, unable to come up with an acceptable explanation for why she had ended up in this impossible situation.

That morning, she was still saying goodbye to her parents. Pedro had finally returned, and now here she was, dragged against her will into some dark dealings because of Lucy. She felt she was going to be sick because of her heightened anxiety. The door to the cabin slammed open, and the Arabs rushed into the room. Vicky stared at them, growing pale. She lifted her arms in front of her face again and backed away in fear. The shorter one suddenly held her down while the other one jabbed her with a needle which drugged Vicky before the door silently closed behind them.

As their car had passed, Pedro had accidentally spotted Vicky as she stared out of the vehicle in fright. He knew she was in trouble. He quickly turned around in the parking lot and tried trailing the jeep, which quickly headed towards the Puerto Banus yacht harbour and finally came to a stop at the back end of the marina.

He rushed over to the promenade after parking, but no one was in the jeep by the time he found it. Feverishly trying to come up with a solution, he rushed back to his car, picked up his belongings, and rushed towards his yacht, which was moored nearby. As he reached his ship, he scanned the illuminated yacht with his spyglass, including the jeep and the sailboats moored in front of it, but he didn't see any suspicious movement. Suddenly, he spotted a man moving from a small yacht not too far away from him, hopping into the jeep, and driving off. At the same time, the yacht left the harbour.

Pedro quickly started the motor, but by the time he reached the open waters, the other boat was far away from him. He was certain it was heading towards Africa. He followed the distant light as far as he could but soon lost track of it within the dark mass of waters bobbing in front of him. When he reached Ceuta, he went through the formalities and exhaustedly slept for a few hours. In the morning, he checked all the ships in the area but couldn't find the yacht he was looking for.

Vicky was still lying in the cabin in a drug-induced sleep. She had no idea that her fate was sealed and that perhaps her life was about to plunge into darkness.

CHAPTER 12

She felt herself being jolted around in the backseat of a car. She raised her throbbing head to look through the window of the rundown vehicle she was in, which was driving across an unknown, desolate landscape. She couldn't think clearly, so she slumped back on the seat and fell asleep again.

A few hours later, she woke to someone slapping her face.

"Hey, get up, hey, we're here," urged the Arab man.

She sat up with some difficulty. Her head was buzzing, and she had no idea where she was. She uncertainly clambered out of the car. At this point, she noticed she was wearing a long, ungainly dress. One of the men glanced at her in passing and adjusted the veil on her head before taking her by the wrist.

"Come."

They slowly fumbled along before reaching an alley. Vicky occasionally stumbled, and her brain felt numb. The Arab thought it was better to take her by the arm. The deserted alley seemed to run on forever. She was hot since she was still wearing her clothes under the flowing shift. She cautiously prodded at her jeans pocket, which contained her papers, and she was reassured to find them intact. If she was strong enough, she could run off now, but she knew she wasn't fit to do so in her current condition.

They turned left and disappeared behind a bright blue door. Crossing through a square-shaped patio, they reached a narrow corridor. Her companion pulled a bolt to the side on a door and pushed her into a room.

"You better lie down," he suggested before locking the worn-out dark brown door.

Vicky heard the door slamming behind her and hesitantly looked around. The shutters of the smallish window were closed, and thus she couldn't see much. When her eyes grew accustomed to the half-light, she spotted someone motionlessly lying on a mattress, turned towards the wall. Since she was too exhausted to investigate at the moment, she decided to sit and then lie down on the other mattress, where she soon fell asleep.

In the morning, she woke to a rustling sound. She saw a middle-aged woman in a long, featureless grey shift leaving two glasses of water on top of a dark nightstand before leaving the room. She shortly returned with a conical topped earthenware dish and a plate of fresh flatbreads, the smell of which reminded Vicky at once of how hungry she was.

Vicky lay motionless, watching, but the servant woman didn't look at her. *I'm probably in Morocco,* she thought to herself, puzzled. She tried recalling the events that had led her here. She faintly remembered the two dark-faced Arabs holding her down on the yacht and one of them jabbing her with a needle, which explained why she still felt so dizzy. Nevertheless, she got up and peered at a low door at the end of the room. The door led to a tiny bathroom, but the shower wasn't working.

She tried composing herself before returning to the room. She had a drink before lifting the lid of the dish and peeking inside it. The contents smelled good, and she decided to sit down. She couldn't find any utensils so she tore off a piece of the flatbread and dipped it into the saucy food. While eating, she glanced at the person lying motionless on the cot on the other side of the room. She hesitantly approached the sleeping figure and tenderly shook the person's shoulder.

"Come, eat."

"Leave me alone," said an unfriendly voice.
Vicky prodded the shoulder again.
"Please."
The person slowly turned around, and Vicky recoiled in terror. "No, this can't be true! I can't believe it's you. What happened to you?" she asked in shock, shivering in fright.
The young girl's face was swollen, and there was a dark smudge under her left eye. Lucy broke down and silently started crying, sobbing partly in relief that she was no longer alone. She opened her mouth to say something but then changed her mind. She turned away again.

Vicky stopped bothering her since she was growing sleepy too now that her stomach was full. She fell back on the bed and shortly fell asleep.

CHAPTER 13

The door suddenly slammed open, and an unknown man entered the room. He spread his legs apart and squinted, motioning towards Vicky. Vicky glanced at Lucy in fright before anxiously following the lanky man, who walked at a leisurely pace in front of her.

The patio, illuminated with dim light, was lined with old painted tiles. The wall under the arcade was lined with wrought-iron seats filled with pillows, providing comfortable seating for the people living here. She looked up at the two-story-high building which encircled the patio. She was undoubtedly in some Arabian country, but this old, quaint riad reminded her of Morocco. She touched the man's arm.

"What do you want?" he growled, whirling around.

Vicky didn't understand a word he said. "Morocco?" she asked. The man nodded, approaching a barely noticeable, narrow, and steep flight of steps under the arcade. The lanky man wore a long, striped, hooded caftan with worn-out white leather slippers on his feet.

She followed him while her heart raced, yet she still paused to admire the staircase and walls decorated with beautiful, coloured tiles. As they reached the upper floor, she found herself in a spacious living room. Her companion disappeared, carefully closing the door behind himself.

A servant appeared from somewhere, leading her to a spacious bathroom, opening the faucets above the tub and sprinkling bath salts into the water. The woman said something in the Arabic language, pointing at the tub before disappearing from the room. Vicky hadn't bathed for days now, so she quickly removed her clothes and enjoyed the pleasures of the bathroom.

In the meantime, the servant gathered her clothes and left a robe on the sofa in the living room. She scanned the room with her dark eyes one last time to make sure everything was in order before leaving. Vicky couldn't find her clothes after her bath, so she donned the robe waiting for her, which was made from very thin fabric. She suddenly remembered her papers she had kept in her back pocket, which made her nervous. She cautiously peeked into a neighbouring room, but the suite seemed deserted. She opened another door and found a bedroom, illuminated with a faint light. A man was lying on a broad bed, perhaps sleeping. His arm was draped over his face. She silently started backing out of the room, but the stranger leaned up in bed and addressed her.

"Come," he said with an English accent.

His voice made it seem more like an authoritative order than a request. Vicky didn't move. For a moment, she stared wide-eyed at the man, whose face was covered in shadows by the lampshade. A wave of panic washed over her since it wasn't hard to figure out what the man wanted from her.

He lost his patience and jumped up. The features of his unclothed athletic body shone even in the half-light.

"I was waiting for you," he said hoarsely, suddenly wrapping his arm around Vicky's waist as if she was an old lover. Vicky did her best to break free from his embrace, but his muscled arms lifted her with ease and tossed her onto the bed. She quickly flipped over on her stomach to protect herself. The man chuckled, reaching out, and ripped the robe off of her while pushing his heavy body down on her.

He slowly slipped his hand under her stomach.

"Don't worry, honey, I won't hurt you," he purred into her ear while his mouth clamped down on the back of her neck like a vampire. He tightly wrapped his arm under her chin and turned over to the side with her. He wrapped his strong leg around her knee, thus holding down her fragile body.

"It's better if you don't put up a fight," he said with bated breath, skilfully reaching her most sensitive point. "Be a good girl," he panted excitedly.

The scared girl desperately tried to break free of the embrace of the stranger, but she simply wasn't strong enough. Her anger slowly mingled with more potent senses which she simply couldn't fight. Her body trembled as the man penetrated her. This method always yielded him a fast and successful result. He loved the sense of female bodily fluids, which gave him a boundless sense of pleasure. She felt like a demon was grinning at her from the corner of the room. She silently sobbed and thought of Pedro.

The stranger got up without looking at her. "If you behave, you won't end up like the other one," he said, heading over to the bathroom. The light illuminated his face, and she suddenly recognized Nick, whom she saw once at the house on the beach where David took her. She almost cried out in surprise and instinctively turned away.

Later on, she heard the man's voice.

"Talk some sense into her and tell her there's no sense in putting up a fight. If you do as I say, no one will harm you."

He raised his hand to press a bell next to the nightstand and left the room satisfied, without even bothering to look at her. Vicky lay on the bed motionlessly for a while, blankly staring at the floor even when the servant knocked and entered. She stirred and rushed over to the bathroom. She opened the faucet and started rubbing and scrubbing at her body as if washing off some invisible stain.

She felt disgusted with herself.

She found her clothes in the living room next to a long black robe. She got dressed, but her papers were missing. She desperately peeked out the Moorish window which opened out onto a gangway, but a moment later the lanky Arab appeared, motioning for her to come with him back to her room on the ground floor.

CHAPTER 14

Lucy eyed her, puzzled. "What happened? Did they tell you anything?" she asked impatiently. Vicky, however, sullenly turned away.

"So, you're hiding something from me, huh?"

"Leave me alone. Nothing happened, they just gave me some clothes,"

Vicky lied with constraint.

"That's what took so long?"

"They were too big."

Lucy looked at her with doubt since her nightgown-like robe needed no adjustment and the size weren't of much importance either.

"Where are they?"

"I left them there."

"But why, when you have to wash the clothes on you sooner or later?"

Instead of answering, Vicky turned around and asked the girl, "How did you end up here?"

"Simple – I was incredibly foolish. Remember the Moroccan I was going to meet in Marbella?"

Vicky nodded. "Ali?"

"Yes. He told me that Nick was alive and wanted to see me. So, I unassumingly went to see him a few days later on his yacht, but the boat took off while we were talking."

"You've been here ever since then?"

"Yes. If I'm correct, I've been in this bloody riad for the last two weeks," Lucy snapped angrily.

"Who did that to you?"

"Nick," she explained in a faltering tone.

She lifted her left hand to wipe the tears from her eye.

"What did he do to you?"

"Nothing."

"Then why did he hit you?"

"We argued over something two days ago, and I suddenly slapped him. As you can see, he punished me for that."

Vicky sighed in relief.

"Listen," she explained quietly, "If you want us to get out of here somehow, I suggest you pretend to agree to everything. Don't protest, OK? Can you promise me that?"

Lucy hesitated for a moment. "I still don't know why he brought me here or what he wants from me."

"I don't know either, but I hope we'll find out soon," Vicky said, although she didn't sound too convincing.

"I don't want to sit here locked up like this either," agreed Lucy.

"Neither do I. Don't forget, the door is locked, so I think we better not cause a scene."

Their situation changed over the next few days. They were free to come and go in the house. They often sat under the arcades of the patio or upon the terrace. During this time, they observed everything, including the way the blue gate was always carefully locked.

No windows looking out onto the narrow alley. From the terrace upstairs, they had a view of the city over the flat-roofed houses, and from there on to the slopes of the Atlas Mountain. It wasn't hard for them to figure out that they were in Marrakech. They reluctantly agreed that it seemed impossible for them to escape without any help.

An older servant tended to the girls, whilst another one did the cleaning. Nick didn't show up at all. The tall, lanky man and his nasty looking gorilla-like partner, were almost always located in the room next to the entrance, usually killing time with some game played with balls.

The door to their room was always open. Everything seemed peaceful and quiet in the riad.

Vicky restlessly tossed and turned in her sleep at night. She heard footsteps outside and peeked through the window. The corridor was dimly lit. She could see them bring three girls to the room opposite from theirs, and the guard carefully locked the door to their room. Could it be that Nick and his henchmen were trading in girls? she wondered excitedly.

Later on, she heard more footsteps. She cautiously slipped out of her room and silently paused in the darkened corridor, waiting. The moon and the stars in the sky illuminated the square-shaped patio. The girls were just being escorted out of the gate. Once she had seen enough, she slipped back into her room and lay down. She pulled the coarse blanket over herself, feeling cold. She was horrified at the thought that perhaps one day they might suffer the same fate. *We have to escape somehow*, she thought.

"Are you asleep?" Lucy asked.

She was surprised when Vicky answered her. "No."

"Do you think we'll ever make it out of here? It would be good to be back in my bed at home."

"Good question," muttered Vicky, barely able to keep her eyes open.

CHAPTER 15

The next night, she woke to the sound of a quiet knock. She leaned and listened, her heart beating in her throat. Someone rattled the window again. She sat up and pushed the curtain aside.

"Who is it?" she whispered.

"Vicky, is that you?"

She recognized Pedro's voice and excitedly answered him.

"Yes!" she gasped, jumping up and rushing to the door at once. "What are you doing here?" she asked in amazement.

"I'll explain later on. Get dressed quickly, it looks like we can get out of here."

"We're coming. Lucy is here too."

"Great. Hurry up," replied Pedro, waiting for them in the dark, thrilled and surprised.

Vicky stumbled over to Lucy's cot. "Wake up," she said, shaking the girl by the shoulder.

"Huh?" asked Lucy sleepily.

"Get up, Pedro is here."

She jumped up as if stung by a bee. "Where is he?"

"Wait. Get dressed first," Vicky warned her quietly. Two minutes later, they moved out of the room. Pedro quickly kissed them on the forehead.

"Follow me in silence," he whispered, scurrying over to the stairs which led up to the second floor and from there onto the roof. Lucy stumbled on the stairs with some noise.

"Ouch!"

"Hiss!" hissed Vicky.

As they made their way onto the roof, Pedro ascended at once before landing with a thud on the neighbouring roof and lifting his arms to help the girls down. Vicky landed without any trouble, but Lucy made a thumping noise as she descended next to her uncle.

Pedro shook his head and helped her get up.

"Are you hurt?"

"A little bit, but I'm OK."

"Then hurry up," he whispered and headed off at once.

They clambered onto another roof from where a steep set of stairs led down. They soon found themselves face to a face with a steel door. Pedro turned back and looked around in the silvery moonlight to get his bearings.

A bit further, off he saw some light beyond the rooftops.

"We're headed that way," he quipped, noticing two figures moving on the distant rooftop.

As they made their way onto the next terrace, they crept under a line of drying clothes. Pedro slipped down into the narrow alley. Vicky followed him, nimbly climbing over a low wall.

"Come on," Pedro urged Lucy.

"I'm right here," she said quietly, slipping downwards as her feet dangled in the air.

"Let go!"

"Oh, God," Lucy whispered silently.

"Don't worry," Pedro urged, helping her down. "Hurry up, or we'll get in trouble," he warned, thinking of the dark figures.

The lights in the sky cast a bluish glow on the flat roofs of the buildings as their pursuers rapidly approached them as shadows.

Lucy noticed them. She started shivering in fear and let go of the edge of the building.

"Good girl," praised Pedro, "but now we've got to hurry up to get rid of the goons."

"I saw them. They're trailing us," warned Lucy.

The three of them raced down the depths of the shadowy alley. They panted, out of breath, running as hunted prey, and spotted a narrow flight of steps leading up to a flat roof. They heard some bustling noise nearby and spotted the illuminated square on the other side of the house.

"Muster your strength," urged Pedro.

"We have to make our way down there and disappear in the crowd." However, he couldn't find any way down.

On the far end of the flat roof, he spotted two hooded figures with their shadows trailing behind them. At the very last moment, Pedro spotted a narrow arcade.

"This way!" he cried, and they finally reached the Djemaa el-Fna square, where they melted into the crowd in joy.

The square was blanketed in the spicy fragrances of cooking meat, and it was filled with people despite the late hour. They found themselves, in right in a bustling city scene. Their bodies were soaking wet with perspiration after the exhausting run, and their matted hair clung to their, foreheads, yet they still shared a joyful burst of laughter.

"We made it, but stay close to me," urged Pedro, hurrying on in relief. Lucy stopped for a moment since she felt a cramp in her side from the long run. She still panted as she pressed her hand down on her crotch. She wanted to cry out to Vicky and Pedro to wait for her, but suddenly a stab in her back silenced her as two heavy hands clamped down on her arm.

"Silence," said the Arab threateningly, wrapping a shawl around her head and jerking her back.

Pedro's tension faded away since he knew he could lead the girls to a safe spot from here. He turned around and saw Vicky right behind him, but Lucy was nowhere to be seen. He gripped Vicky by the hand.

"Where is she?" he cried, eyes wide open, desperately scanning the crowd.

"She was just behind me," gasped Vicky.

"I'm sure they caught her," he noted angrily, standing up on a bench to scrutinize the smoky square. There was no sight of Lucy. He slipped down from the bench, disheartened.

"Unfortunately, there's nothing we can do for her at the moment. Come on, let's get out of here. I'll figure out something later on," he said with a crestfallen expression.

He took Vicky by the hand, and they blended into the crowd. It seemed they could never know for certain what would happen to them in a moment, despite his relief over freeing them with ease. His plan was only half-successful, but he was comforted by the thought that his niece was still alive.

Once they reached the hotel, Vicky related her ordeal.

"But how did you find us?" she curiously asked.

"I visited that riad a few years ago, with Nick, whom I thought was my friend. On the other hand, I spoke with Sarhan and thought over the events and realized that all the leads led to the riad.

"It's late," he added, caressing Vicky's face. "I suggest you go lie down. You need some rest."

"What are you going to do?"

"I'll go back. I have to try freeing her again. I have to do something. I can't just leave her there." She opened her mouth in concern, wanting to tell him not to go, but she knew she couldn't ask that from him.

"Be careful," she said instead. Pedro nodded and quietly closed the door on his way out.

Vicky was left alone. After taking a bath, she soon fell asleep, breathing evenly. Pedro was exhausted, yet he still set out on his uncertain journey. He silently rushed down deserted alleys, quietly treading on the cobblestones in his tennis shoes. He uncertainly stopped at a corner. Only the locals truly knew their way down the zigzagging alleys of the medina. He instinctively headed left. Once he reached the riad, he climbed up the ivy-infested fence and silently slipped down the narrow stairs. For a moment, he glanced up at the sky; the stars seemed to flash close to him, palely illuminating the patio.

At the end of the dark corridor, he quietly rattled the open window, but there was no answer.

"Lucy," he whispered as he knocked again, moving up to the door and pressing down on the handle. The room was deserted. The next-door opened at his touch.

"Lucy," he called out again before rushing back upstairs like a shadow. The riad was engulfed in a mysterious silence. He cautiously pushed down on the handle of the door opposite to him, but it was locked. He quizzically stopped for a moment. He quietly rattled the window one more time, but the lights suddenly came on in the corridor, so, he was forced to run away.

After his fruitless attempt, he sullenly backtracked to the hotel. He was annoyed at having lost track of his niece at the very last moment. However, he was glad that at least Vicky was safe. He was so exhausted that he couldn't fall asleep. He kept tossing and turning, wondering how to get Vicky back to Spain without any papers.

He'd talk to Sarhan in the morning and hopefully, get some help. Things were more complicated now that had Nick resurfaced. Pedro had always suspected Nick was involved in some shady dealings, so he had been avoiding the man for some time. He simply couldn't understand why Nick had brought Vicky and Lucy to Morocco.

CHAPTER 16

In the morning, Pedro quietly got out of bed. He wanted to go see Sarhan. He planned to get Vicky on the yacht and then return at once to somehow save Lucy. He would have to ask for the help of the police if there was no other solution. However, things don't always play out as planned.

Vicky restlessly sat up in bed.

"I was afraid you would leave me again," she said, blinking and trying to shake off her cobwebs of sleep. Her short red hair stood up on the back on her head. Her freckled face made her look like a hedgehog. She rubbed her right eye with her fist and suppressed a yawn.

Pedro couldn't take his eyes off her. He sat down on the edge of the bed and hugged his sweetheart, who fell more deeply in love with him.

"You know I adore you," he whispered into her ear, heating the air in the room. Vicky hugged him tighter and tighter. She never wanted to let go of him again. *You are my man, forever*, she recalled from a song as the joy washed over her.

Later, they were standing under the shower in the bathroom, soaping each other's back, but Pedro restrained himself.

"We'll go down and have breakfast once you're ready. Good, strong coffee will do the trick."

Vicky regretfully gazed at Pedro.

"Come on," he called, throwing the towel on her and forcing himself to avert his gaze.

Sarhan came to see them during breakfast. Pedro introduced him to Vicky and turned to the Arab man.

"We have to head to Casablanca at once; that's where my yacht is."

"Fine." Vicky excitedly intervened. "But we surely won't leave Lucy at the riad. Let's go get her now, right away. Trust me, this is the best time. There are only two guards and the servants there during the day. Nick hasn't been around for days," she added.

"So, you met him?"

"No, no," she replied quickly. "I just saw him from the corridor." Pedro acknowledged her answer. "Look, I'm planning on doing the same thing, but first I want to get you on the boat. I want to make sure you're safe first."

"But we'll lose time that way," she insisted, shaking her head. "I want to go with you. Please," she insisted.

"You know it can be dangerous," he protested. "This isn't a trip for girls."

"Don't worry about me. I can take care of myself."

Pedro eyed her, pondering. "Okay then. If you want to, then come with me. If something happens, you can find your way back here, right?"

"Yes. At least I hope so."

"If you get lost, ask around for the Sahara Hotel. Sarhan can help you." He started rummaging around in his side pocket and handed her a few hundred Euros.

"You might need this," he explained.

"Thank you. You know I don't want Lucy to suffer any harm." It occurred to her that they might be getting into something dangerous.

It also occurred to her that if she didn't show up in the office tomorrow morning, she'd probably lost her job, yet she was certain she couldn't get back by then. Still, she didn't mind. She worried about nothing when Pedro was at her side. At the same time, she had a faint sense that they didn't have much hope of saving Lucy from the henchmen. Nick might be there by now as well. Nevertheless, she decided to stay with Pedro, imagining the frightened look on Lucy's face. In the end, this started a landslide of events.

They moved from alley to alley as they approached the riad. Suddenly, they backed off, pressing themselves up against the fence as the blue gate opened. A servant appeared, heading in the opposite direction with a shopping basket.

They exchanged relieved glances.
"One less person to worry about," whispered Vicky hopefully. They could hear the faint din of the city in the distance, yet the alley was deserted.

Pedro didn't hesitate and climbed up the same way he did last night when he brought the girls out, motioning for Vicky to follow. She stepped upon a stone outcropping and grasped Pedro's outstretched hand, managing to reach the parapet from where they could move to the rooftop. They silently slipped up the narrow stairs and stopped when they reached the patio to listen, but they didn't hear any movement.

Pedro had just started to move when suddenly they heard a muffled gunshot, and events escalated. Pedro faltered and fell over with a reddish stain on his shirt. Vicky rushed over to him in terror. She wanted to lean down to him, but then another shot was fired. She felt a searing pain and a rush of heat on her face. She lifted her hand, but suddenly the world around her was plunged into darkness.

Pedro stood up. He spotted Vicky at once, lying motionlessly next to him with blood on her face. He winced in pain and leaned over her, shaking her. She's dead, he realized suddenly. He sought her pulse with trembling hands but couldn't feel a thing. He heard footsteps now from the arcade and only had enough time to drag himself over to the stairs.

He glanced back at the girl in parting before struggling up to the rooftop. He knew he was in trouble. He mustered all of his strength, clenched his teeth, and somehow managed to descend to the alley. He took off down the alley, pressing down on his side with his hands.

Don't give up!
Hurry up!
He urged himself.

Much to his surprise, he found Sarhan rushing towards him, coming to his aid.

"It's good to see you. I don't think I could make it without you."

"I heard the shots, so I stayed behind. Where did you leave the girl?"

"She was shot and died," he croaked.

Sarhan uttered an Arabian curse and wrapped his arm around Pedro as they disappeared down the labyrinthine alley.

CHAPTER 17

One of the doors upstairs opened shortly after the shot was fired. Lucy peeked out onto the patio and spotted Vicky's motionless body. The blood ran out of her face in terror as she rushed down the stairs at once. She knelt on the ground and tenderly shook Vicky, but the woman didn't move. Vicky's face was unrecognizable from the gunshot and the blood.

"What happened? Who did this to you?" she shrieked hysterically, clinging onto Vicky's arm.
"Please don't leave me here," she sobbed out loud.

At that moment, Nick walked through the gate. He had been out of the house all night long, and thus he didn't know that the girls eloped. He exchanged a few words with the guards, who related the story with anxious gestures.
He approached the site of the tragedy with an ashen expression on his face. He leaned over and picked Lucy up from the ground.
"Don't cry," he said in a muffled tone.
"Come on, you've seen enough of this"

He took the sobbing girl back upstairs.

"Listen to me. Stay here, and I'll come back as soon as I can," he ordered.

"Don't worry, I'll take care of everything and take her to the hospital at once. I hope she's not dead," he added hurriedly.

He was deeply annoyed by the unpleasant incident. It's a good thing we got rid of one of them, he thought. One less problem to worry about.

But who was the other person?

Hardly anyone knew about his hiding place. Who helped, the girls escape? Perhaps Pedro? he wondered. Yes. It must be him. Nick stopped in front of the motionless body. He crouched down and gripped her wrist. He felt uncomfortable as he looked at the blood-soaked face, unwilling to touch her artery.

He motioned for his henchmen to come over.

"Take her to the hospital at once."

It was hard to believe that this poor thing had been his one-night stand a few days ago. He couldn't even remember her face; the room had been in the half-light. Nick never suspected that the girl was the same one who visited him with David at the house in El Palmar.

"Why did you have to shoot?" he demanded of his guards with flashing eyes.

"Because we thought the same person returned with this," explained the guard, pointing at the unfortunate girl. Nick didn't feel like bickering since that wouldn't help things at all.

"Hurry up now. Take her in without attracting any attention, got it?" he asked, glancing upstairs and calming down before carrying on. "Tell them of the hospital that you found her in some alley. I don't want any trouble. Oh, and quickly get rid of this mess," he added, pointing at the bloody pavement.

The taller, lankier Arab removed a tablecloth from a nearby table and wrapped it around the girl's injured face to somewhat stop the bleeding. The other wiped up the pool of blood, and together they carried out the unconscious girl to the end of the deserted alley, panting and putting her down on the ground.

"Go and get the car; I'll stay here with her," said the lanky man. "Do you think she is still alive?"

"I don't think so. Go on, what are you waiting for?!"

In the meantime, Nick hurried back to Lucy, who was still huddled on the bed.

"She's dead, right?" asked Lucy, raising her head.

"I don't know yet."

"Poor girl," Lucy said in a faltering voice. "It's all my fault." She sobbed out loud.

"Okay, get your act together. What's done is done – we can't help her anymore, she's on her way to the hospital."

"Thank you. You might've saved her life," she sniffled.

"There's nothing to thank me for. I'm just doing my duty," quipped Nick.

"But … what do you think? Who did it and why?"

"I don't know. Trust me, I don't know. I wasn't home last night. I just came back and found the gate was ajar. Someone might have broken in."

"Can I visit her tomorrow?" asked Lucy naively.

"Unfortunately, you can't, since that could get us into trouble. Don't forget, they took her to the hospital with a gunshot wound. If the police get involved, they might harass us, and that's not good for anyone, right? They might even suspect you," he noted suggestively.

"Me? I wasn't even there. I've never held a gun in my hand my whole life."

"Luckily, honey," he noted, making a face. "The cops don't care about that at all."

"Then who shot her?" She repeated her question stubbornly.

"I told you already, I don't know. Look, I know you're mad at me for hitting you, but trust me, I brought you here because you weren't safe in Marbella. I was afraid they might kidnap you or try to murder you," he lied smoothly, looking her in the eye.

"Do you think I'm in danger?" she asked in surprise.

"Yes, but not just you – me too."

"But why?"

"It's better if you don't know about this. After what happened, I have a good reason for both of us to get out of here. Trust me," he added calmly.

"I have a feeling the person who got you out of here is part of the gang."

"No, Pedro isn't one of them."

Nick suppressed a smile since he had managed to find out what he wanted to know. He had to leave with Lucy at once since he didn't want to confront Pedro.

Lucy pondered their situation in confusion.

"You might be right, but promise me you won't abandon her," she noted unsuspectingly.

"Of course, that goes without saying," he assured Lucy, leaning in close to plant a kiss on her teary face. "Again, I'm sorry for being so hard on you recently." He pulled Lucy close, and the girl leaned her head on his shoulder. Still, he had a lot of things to do, so he gently pushed her away after a few minutes. "I've got to go," he noted, leaving Lucy on her own.

After two days of intentional stalling, he entered Lucy's room and found her lying on her bed. He sat down next to her and told her in a faltering tone that Vicky had died. Lucy sat up, looking deathly pale, and began sobbing, huddling close to him. Nick cautiously lifted her up and tenderly lay her back down on the bed.

"It's okay, honey, don't cry," he consoled her, finding the scene too theatrical for his taste. "You know I've loved you for a long time," he added cleverly.

His arm slowly slipped around her waist while the girl looked up at him with teary eyes. Nick's mouth suddenly pressed down on her moist lips.

This was the first time Lucy had been kissed by a man, so it's no wonder she shuddered from his embrace. She faintly felt that perhaps this was the moment she had been always waiting for. She was already attracted to him when she was a little girl when they went swimming together. She jealously watched him make love with her mother. She subconsciously idolized him for years. However, her thoughts were now distracted. Her body was whipped up by an unusual, urgent sensation. The man reciprocated her passionate yearning with a heated embrace until a thin scream emitted from her swollen lips.

CHAPTER 18

The sailboat barely moved in the wind. Pedro sadly gazed out on the choppy sea. Although the bullet had gone through his side, he hoped it hadn't injured any organs. The pain was tolerable, yet he felt increasingly exhausted. He lifted his T-shirt, and with a little mirror, he could see that his bandages were soaked through.

He recalled the way they finally reached the hotel after limping through the city. There, they had disinfected his wound. Sarhan applied a bandage and brought him back to his yacht. The trip seemed rather lengthy and it was hard for him to tolerate the car's shaking and rattling. They would make it back soon, he hoped, lifting his head and staring at the approaching harbour.

His thoughts strayed back to Vicky. Poor girl, he thought as the tears welled up in his eyes. He simply couldn't believe that he'd lost her for good. He could still see her face rendered unrecognizable by the gunshot. He knew he couldn't have helped her even if he had stayed behind. The only reason he managed to get away was by using this last moment to escape.

He should have never taken her with him – then she would still be alive; he accused himself as the tears slowly flowed from his eyes.

The yacht slowly entered the harbour of Puerto Banus. His side throbbed in pain. He knew he had to urgently find a doctor. By the time, he made it to the hospital, his body was seething hot, and his chest was panting. He was taken to the operating room at once.

Pedro soon recovered and was discharged from the hospital. It was hard for him to move, and he could only walk by doubling over and supporting himself with a walking cane. He usually rested at the shady patio while thinking over the loss of the poor girl again and again.

His only companion was his sister, Patricia, with whom he talked a lot. One day, she sat down next to him.

"Lucy finally called from London," she began.
"How did she end up there?" he asked in surprise.
"I don't know. All that counts, is that everything is okay with her. Nick told me not to worry, he would take good care of her. He also asked me to tell you that Vicky died. Please tell me what happened!

How did my, daughter get close to Nick, and who was Vicky?" she asked, training her lovely green-eyed on Pedro. He pondered in silence for a few moments.

"I don't know a thing about Nick and Lucy's relationship," he said haltingly.
"And what about the girl who died?"
"She was an unfortunate girl who was at the wrong place at the wrong time," he concluded. It was obvious he didn't want to discuss the subject.
The woman stopped questioning him. She stood up and left her morose brother, who leaned on the table, cradling his head in his

hands. The news didn't surprise him at all since, he already knew that Vicky was dead, and he continued to blame himself for it. At the same time, he felt increasingly angry at Nick.

He'd known the man for a long time, and Nick had been well-known as a womanizer ever since they'd first met, but Pedro never thought he would get his hands on Lucy. Nick was a low-down scumbag who always takes the upper hand. This diabolically planned-out love story was simply ridiculous. The notion of revenge kept revolving in Pedro's mind, but he didn't want to get involved in the girl's life without his sister's permission.

Six months later, Pedro received a postcard from London. It was from Lucy, tells him that she was married to Nick.

Her mother wasn't pleased by the news that Lucy had married at such a young age, especially to a far older man. Athough Patricia had broken up with Nick a long time ago, it was still hard for her to believe that after all his victims, he would get his hands on such a young girl.

"That bastard!" she cursed semi-audibly. Her hatred for him was rekindled. She somehow wanted to get her daughter back, but she was entirely sure that she couldn't accomplish this with force. Perhaps time would resolve the matter, she reflected wisely.

CHAPTER 19

Nick treated his new wife with confidence. He knew how to seduce the fairer sex, especially a teenager. However, it wasn't so easy to deal with Lucy, since she was a smart and rather distrustful wildling of a girl. Of course, she didn't have much experience with men, which Nick regularly made good use of. After a while, his little wife learned everything he needed to know in bed.

The man's shady business dealings were flourishing, and thus they travelled a lot. After a brief stay in Hong Kong, they flew to Tokyo, surrounded by impenetrable clouds.

The "fasten your seatbelts" sign turned on. The plane descended and suddenly turned into a dip. The stewardess who was handing Lucy her coffee suddenly lost her balance and fell backwards. Fortunately, the drink cart in front of her got caught in one of the seats, and she didn't suffer any injuries. She looked pale as she tried her best to stand up – and then the plane tilted again.

Lucy looked around in fright, and since she saw no one coming to the aid of the helplessly fumbling stewardess, she unfastened her seatbelt and grabbed the woman by the wrist. In the meantime, the passengers sitting nearby clung to their chairs in terror. Lucy looked around for someone to help until finally, an older man sitting nearby was willing to come over.

Lucy sat back down and gazed at her husband reproachfully. Nick averted his gaze and looked out the window.

"I hope we'll land in one piece," sobbed a woman behind them. The plane dipped again. Lucy grabbed onto the seat in front of her in terror. A moment later, she started to throw up and reached out for the sick bag with trembling hands, yet Nick completely ignored her. It wasn't hard to figure out that she could only count on herself in difficult situations – if they reach the airport at all, she wondered anxiously.

The plane trembled as if hopping down an uneven road. The captain's a voice came on over the loudspeaker.
"We're going through some turbulence and preparing to land." Lucy reclined in relief, but the minutes seemed to draw out for an eternity until they finally landed with a jolt.

"Well, it seems like we walked away from another tight spot," said Nick, thoroughly shaken despite his cool demeanour. His brow was wet with perspiration.
Lucy acknowledged the incident with a wry smile. An hour later, their taxi parked in front of the hotel. After dealing with the formalities, they were racing up an elevator within a few minutes. Once they reached the tenth floor, they entered a spacious hall with a glass wall that offered a spectacular view of the city.

Nick headed straight over to the minibar and produced two tiny bottles. He held out one of them to his wife, who rejected his offer. He shrugged and drank both of them before dumping the bottles in the waste basket.
"I'll be back soon," he hurriedly promised. "In the meantime, you can unpack."

"Where are you going so late?" she demanded.

"Business," he snapped, slamming the door on his way out. Lucy angrily opened one of the suitcases and hung some of the clothes in the closet. She quickly got fed up and decided to rest instead. Nick returned surprisingly soon, so Lucy felt at ease. They went for a lengthy tour of the city before ending up at a nightclub after dinner.

Two days later, they moved to Bangkok. The city's teeming mass of people verged on the unbearable. Women sat in sweat-soaked clothes on the street and the sidewalks, whipping up a range of dishes with moisture beading on their foreheads. The taxi changed direction and took them towards an elegant neighbourhood, and their surroundings changed at once.

Modern buildings, skyscrapers, and flashy shops glared at them from all sides. As usual, Nick left once they reached the hotel. In the meantime, Lucy went shopping. In the evenings, they went to boring dinners, yet Lucy noticed that Nick seemed to have friends wherever they went who kindly welcomed them and eyed her through their slanted eyes.

On the last day of their Oriental travels, they visited the royal quarter and even attended a party at night.

Once they returned to London, Lucy quickly grew accustomed to their new lifestyle and her freedom without control. She enjoyed her life, spending money; she even enjoyed Nick, who let her do anything. She attended school and even went to singing classes in the evening. With Nick's backing, she was signed in a year. With her lovely voice inherited from her mother and her fluid motions, she quickly reached the pop charts, and her career took off like a shooting star.

One day, Nick announced that they were moving to Barcelona. "But why?" she cried hysterically. "What am I going to do there?" she bawled in desperation. "What about my career?"

"It's business. Don't worry, you can sing there too. I might even be able to put together a tour for you," he encouraged her, while downing a hit of whiskey. Nick couldn't care less about the fact that his wife was now an in-demand pop star. It allowed him to travel alone and tend to his business in peace.

His wife flounced like a fish at the end of a line. She often flew to London for performances. If Nick left on business, she shrugged it off, since she was occupied with her tours and band, whilst her nightlife unintentionally led to an increasing number of affairs. Her flings were dealt with promptly and disappeared without a trace. She even smoked pot from time to time.

Whenever she met Nick, she embraced him tightly and slept with him as soon as possible to cover up her sinful liaisons. Nick didn't ask any questions, and they silently developed an understanding, since they both knew fidelity wasn't their strongest trait.

"How about a baby?" asked Lucy one day, jokingly.
"What did you say?" he asked heatedly.
"I asked, how about having a baby?" she repeated a bit impatiently. Nick's face turned grim. He faced the window to compose himself.
"That wouldn't be a smart move," he replied, wrapping his arm around his wife's waist. "It would ruin your career."
"OK, I was just thinking," she noted, while wondering how successful she would be if she would show her tummy off onstage. Nick could barely sleep at all at night since he had too many problems to deal with lately, and he was upset by this sudden notion of having a baby. He decided when he was half asleep to take Lucy to their beach house in El Palmar, where they would probably stay for an extended period.

The house belonged to Pedro, who had been living in Rio de Janeiro for some time now and didn't look like he was coming back any time soon. Nick didn't give the matter much thought, since after all, Pedro was his wife's uncle.

CHAPTER 20

It was December, and the waves were crashing against the coastal breakers. Lucy stared at the churning Atlantic through the window while humming a tune to the baby in her arms. The little one sleepily winked and slowly fell asleep. She cautiously put the child down in the crib and tiptoed out of the room. She descended the stairs to the living room before heading out to the garden with a magazine in hand since the sun was shining warmly in the sky.

"*Hola,*" a young woman called to her from over the low fence. Lucy nodded reservedly.

"Can I have a word?" asked the stranger. "I'm Vicky's girl-friend." Lucy perked up and attentively hurried to the gate.

"Come in," she said readily, and they introduced themselves. "Sorry for coming to you as a stranger," the woman said, "but you might be able to give me some information on Pedro and Vicky. My husband and I haven't heard anything about them for quite some time," she explained.

"The last time we saw them was a few years ago, in this house, and since then they both disappeared without a trace. Vicky spent a few more days at our house, but we haven't seen her either since then. We live nearby and we often came over here, hoping to see them or someone else, but the house was always closed."

Lucy bowed her head. Sarah had a bad feeling and ominously asked her.

"Somthing happened to them, right?"

"Yes. Vicky died. She was shot."

"Excuse me?" Sarah cried in disbelief as her eyes welled up with tears.

"This happened about three years ago."

"Oh God, no, I can't believe it," Sarah gasped, pale as a ghost. Yet still, she knew the words Lucy spoke were true.

"Who shot her and why? Vicky had no enemies!"

"I don't know," said Lucy nervously.

"The police in Morocco couldn't find out more about the matter."

"So, it happened in Morocco."

"Yes, in Marrakech," Lucy explained with sympathy.

"Would you like a glass of water?"

"No thank you," she replied quietly. "And what about Pedro?"

"My uncle went to Rio de Janeiro after the incident. He's been working at a hospital there ever since."

"They loved each other," whispered Sarah, her thoughts wandering off. The terrible news deeply upset her. "I don't want to get in your way. Thank you for sharing the news, but I've got to go now," Sarah explained, swallowing her tears.

Lucy sadly walked her to the gate before returning to the patio, yet she no longer felt like flipping through the magazine. In her mind, she saw Vicky's motionless body and bloody face in front of her again. Hearing the phone ring, she hurried back inside.

"Hello," she answered the phone quietly.

"Is that you?" asked a pleasant male voice.

"Yes, it's me," she replied, and the line went dead. She didn't recognize the voice. Lucy thoughtfully put down the receiver before running upstairs to check on the baby, who was still fast asleep. She quietly opened the door and went back outside into the garden.

Fate can be unpredictable at times, she reflected, still surprised by what the woman told her about the affair between Vicky and her uncle. It was hard to believe that Pedro would have met her after the incident in Barcelona. He probably didn't even know where the real estate office was, she thought.

Sarah ran back to the beach, where Juan was chasing their daughter up and down the dunes.

"What happened?" he asked with a start.

"Someone's in the house, right?"

"Yes." Her pent up, emotions burst out, and she sank to the ground, sobbing. Once her daughter saw her mother crying, she also started sobbing.

Juan took the little girl in his lap and sat down next to his wife, comforting both of them.

"Come on, tell me what happened!"

"Vicky died, and Pedro is in Rio," she explained, sniffling.

"What?" asked Juan in shock.

"So, that's why they didn't get in touch."

"I tried calling Vicky so many times, but I could never get through to her," Sarah sobbed. "Do you remember how happy they were together? Their love ended so fast."

"Still, he could've dropped a line," noted Juan disapprovingly.

"Look, I perfectly understand Pedro. I'm sure he didn't want to see or talk to anyone after that horrific event. He probably felt it was better to go somewhere far away. He simply wanted to forget about everything. If you would have experienced a tragedy, you won't feel like meeting or seeing friends, relatives, or anyone else, for that matter. He wanted to run away from his memories by leaving."

"I don't know, you might be right. Poor Vicky. It's so hard to believe that she died so young," sighed Juan with a heavy expression on his face. "She was a kind girl."

CHAPTER 21

Nick finally arrived when it was getting dark. He planted a kiss on his wife's forehead.

"Honey, I have to leave again today. You know business is business. I will probably have to stay away for a longer time."

He noticed that Lucy didn't react to what he just said.

"Did something happen?" he asked, raising her chin.

"You could put it that way."

"Well, tell me, what was it?"

"A woman showed up this afternoon, asking me about Vicky and Pedro"

"What did you tell her?" he asked, looking at her sharply.

"What could I say?" she responded daringly. "I told her the truth. Vicky died."

Nick had to be careful. He didn't ask any more questions and just turned his back on her. He wasn't thrilled that Vicky's friend had appeared out of nowhere.

An hour later, they silently sat down to have dinner, yet the tension was still tangible in the air.

"I'll go upstairs and take a shower, then I'm leaving," said Nick, breaking the icy silence.

"Whatever. If you have to go, then go," she shrugged, "but the baby isn't well. I'll take her to see the doctor tomorrow."

"What's wrong?"

"It might be nothing, but she didn't sleep much last night and cried a lot."

"Call me if it's something serious," he noted, hurrying up the stairs. Lucy stayed at the table. It had occurred to her for some time now that whenever she tried talking about Vicky, Nick became dismissive and reticent. She had a gut feeling that something wasn't right about the murky events.

She still loved him, though. She could say they had an ideal marriage which was working just fine. It looked perfect, but maybe it was too perfect, she wondered. He'd been kind and caring since the baby was born. Still, they weren't emotionally close to each other. The sex was different, she thought.

Nick appeared, all dressed up and ready to go.

"I'll come as soon as I can. I'll call you," he added, planting a kiss on her forehead and leaving. Lucy wasn't exactly bored with the baby. She had everything she needed, and they financially could spare no cost. A young girl called Rose came every three days to clean up and covered as a babysitter if needed. Lucy absently removed the leftovers of dinner from the table. Her thoughts strayed back to that day in Morocco when she last saw Vicky.

It was true that Nick tried saving her, but unfortunately, he wasn't successful. He helped Lucy a lot too, but she still wasn't sure whether she was ever in any danger. He'd explained at the time that he bought all sorts of antiques and rugs, which was why he travelled so much. That's how the charming man won the trust of an inexperienced girl, she thought sarcastically.

At the same time, Nick was driving down the road, lost in his thoughts. When he was on the yacht and Lucy pushed him into the water all those years ago, he easily climbed back aboard and hid in the cabin, since he wanted to teach the unruly girl a lesson. Later on, this was why he took her to Marrakech. Then things turned out differently, and he ended up marrying her. That way, he fended off any possible revenge attempts on Pedro's behalf.

However, the marriage didn't change his life, since he was still mostly occupied with making an easy buck and getting with beautiful women. He was well aware of his nature, yet he still decided to go through with the wedding. It wasn't his style to end up in a situation like this. Still, he was glad that he could deliver an impeccable performance.

There was a lot at stake, after all. Lucy would inherit a fortune – plus this way, he could take revenge on her mother, who was his lover for years. He had to admit that ever since he got married, his business dealings were running smoothly. His bank account in Switzerland was getting heftier every day. Had he known things would turn out like this, he would have never married Lucy.

The baby just wouldn't fall asleep and kept crying. Her tiny little hands seemed hot. Lucy took her temperature and suppressed a shriek. She called the ambulance at once, but it took them an hour to arrive. The baby was barely breathing by then and died by the time they reached the hospital. Lucy couldn't get through to Nick.

She held on to the baby's tiny hand as it grew lifeless and cold. The devastated Lucy clung on to her dead baby.

"She left just as easily as she came," she cried in anguish. The nurse gave her a tranquillizer injection and finally removed the lifeless body from the mother's tight embrace. This was the second time she'd experienced the pain of loss in her life.

First was Vicky's death and now the death of a tiny soul. She simply couldn't believe that her baby's life had ended so suddenly. Only hours ago, she had cradled the baby in her lap, singing lullabies. Lucy and Nick's relationship suffered after the baby's death. She carried on with her whirlwind lifestyle in London. She often toured with her band, yet her popularity faded, as with many other pop stars. Nick went to Marseilles to continue his dealings.

The house in El Palmar was left locked and deserted. There was no one to open its wide, worn-out doors. Lucy never wanted to go back there because of the memory of the baby. Nick quietly maintained the place, considering it a good strategic hiding place. He thought he would surely make use of it sooner or later. He also kept his hiding place in Marrakech. After the unfortunate incident, he replaced the staff, just to stay on the safe side of things. He washed his hand like Pontius Pilate and kept on living his busy life.

CHAPTER 22

The sound of a baby crying resounded from the back room of the riad. The man shouted from the corridor upstairs, "You better silence that little runt or I swear to God, I'll go down there and smash its head into the wall!"

The woman wearing a black *djellaba* desperately crouched down and quietly hushed her son.

"Please don't cry. You know if you keep on crying, we'll get in trouble," she said anxiously, gathering the toys on the floor with trembling hands.

"Look, here are your little clay soldiers, waiting to be sent into the desert with the camels," she whispered.

The tears glowed in the boy's eyes. The mother kissed him on the top of his head, wiping his tears away with the fringe of her robe. "Captain, prepare your legions," she ordered, winking at him. The little boy started giggling.

She stood up and got back to the work she had just finished. She dumped the dirty water from the bucket on the corridor and filled it with clean water to continue her washing up. When she was done, she hurried back to her room and her child in exhaustion, lovingly cradling him and telling him a story. In times like this, they both entered a world of dreams. The boy always listened carefully to his mother's stories. She usually told him about a seaside house which was the home of good, loving people.

"Please take me there," he demanded suddenly, pouting in sorrow. Her heart ached. *What could she say to that?* She wondered in grief.

"Why don't you say something? Will you promise to take me there?" urged the little boy.

"Yes, one day I will," she uttered involuntarily. She sadly turned away, since she knew she could never fulfill her promise.

Nevertheless, she had a decent life in Marrakech. She did her job around the house while raising her son, who sometimes could be rather unruly. He had an unpredictable nature. She often spanked him because of his tantrums before regretfully cradling him in her arms.

The boy's black hair and even his gestures were reminiscent of someone she'd lost forever five years ago. She was all alone with only this daredevil of a boy as a company. She squeezed him tightly and often planted a kiss on the top of his head, relating her dreams to him.

Every night the mother recalled the sad events that took place years ago. She still couldn't accept the fact that her life had changed so drastically. These last five years, she could hardly leave the riad, where she was employed as a maid. Her previous life had come to an end since her face was irrevocably damaged. She had given up all hope of ever returning to Europe a long time ago. She would be forced to live out the rest of her life here, tolerating Nick's tyranny and coarse behaviour. She had no other choice.

When Nick appeared from time to time, she always noticed movement in the house. Girls came and went, and two Arabs were posted in the room next to the gate at all times. This is the third time they'd been replaced since she'd been here.

Nick came here more often lately, even though he'd disappeared for long periods in the past few years. She wasn't interested in his dirty dealings. All that counted was that they had a place to stay, and she tried her best not to think of her former life.

They usually rested during their siesta after lunch, but her son started crying for some reason. The fly cover hanging in front of the door suddenly rustled, and Nick unexpectedly burst into the room. He approached her threateningly, and she jumped up in front of her child. Nick approached her and suddenly slapped her face. She uttered a soft scream and lost her balance, tumbling to the floor. Antonio cried out and crawled under the table.

"I told you to keep your child in order. I won't tolerate him making any noise. Plus, why aren't you working?" he yelled, as he points at the terrified child. "I didn't take you in with this runt for you to sit around and do nothing!"

The miserable woman sat up. She painfully groped at her face with one hand, suddenly adjusting her shawl. Her eyes filled with tears. The man eyed her in disgust. "Get out of my house!" he yelled again.

"You can't throw us out. This runt is your child too … or have you forgot that?" she warned him, losing her cool, leaning over the crying boy.

Nick kicked her rump with helpless rage. The woman sprawled on her face and the boy hollered as he crawled back under the table. Nick leaned over her with a reddish face and yanked the boy out of his hiding place by his leg. The man lifted the boy with ease and shook him.
"Shut up," he hissed nervously, yet still he didn't hurt the boy, instead of dropping him down to his mother and storming out

of the room. The mother remained on the floor as tears coursed down her face. She pulled her son close and hushed him until she slowly lulled him to sleep, laying her sleeping child down on the bed and continuing her work.

She entered the tiny bathroom late at night and removed the shawl from her head. She could barely move her jaw. She painfully groped at her face, which ached and was slightly swollen from the blow. She soaked the tip of a towel in water and cautiously applied it on her skin. She unconsciously gazed into the mirror above the sink and saw a twisted complexion looking back at her. She felt a surge of deep, unspeakable pain bursting forth from her heart, as it always happens when she sees her face and leads to tears streaking down it in silent sobbing.

With her nearly bald reddish hair, she looked like some kind of African albino, which made her bruised face, look even worse. After a while, she went to bed, yet sleep eluded her peturbed mind. She lay on the bed with her eyes open, staring into the darkness for hours. She knew she couldn't change her life, and she cried herself to sleep, as she had for the last couple of years.

She imagined herself again lying on her hospital bed, agonized by seemingly never-ending pain. However, her helplessness was just as torturing as the pain, especially after they removed the bandage from her face and she was sent out into the street. In parting, the nurse gave her a black shawl to cover her face.

"It's better if you put it on," she said in pity.
She only saw the reddish scars later on. Her face was unrecognizable and plunged her life into the shadows for good. She felt like a gazelle locked in a cage. How could she carry on living? She wondered in terror. She couldn't get a job without any documents or money and with her disgusting face. She cried, wandering along the streets.

She found the riad after a lengthy wandering, but Nick wasn't around. She lurked in front of the gate for weeks until he finally arrived. After she begged him at length, he finally took her in.

"You can stay here for a while. Try busying yourself around the house," he told her dryly. "The new staff will arrive tomorrow. The guards will arrive in the evening. You can't leave the house for the time being, but I guess you don't want to," he added coldly.

"I'm entrusting the new cook and servant to you," he added, turning his back on her and leaving.

He hadn't decided what he wanted to do with her, but he was sure that it would no harm to keep her at the riad for a while. Still, Nick decided to kick her out after a month. She begged him in terror to let her stay since everyone would spurn her because of her face. She was mentally broken and promised to do everything he asked her to.

Nick finally changed his mind.

"Fine, you can stay. That is if you're not lazy – otherwise, I'll get rid of you," he threatened her. "You have to take care of everything. Keep the house clean with the staff."

From that point on, she worked as a shadow in the riad. Her face was repulsing because of her reddish scars, so the typical Moroccan garb suited her perfectly. She slowly grew accustomed to the black djellaba that hung to her ankles with a shawl around her head, carefully masking her face. She didn't want to see the pity in the eyes of the others since she suffered enough as it is.

It often occurred to her that it would have been better for her to die that day. She longed for death, but there was something that stopped her from this a few months later. Yet this secret tortured her body and her soul. The djellaba hid her secret for a while. She took care to avoid Nick whenever he appeared.

CHAPTER 23

She couldn't sleep at night again. She thought about her pregnancy. The second half of her ninth months were going by slowly. Her round tummy showed clearly through her robes. It was getting harder for her to move, and she often had to sit down due to the heat.

Then one day, Nick arrived with a woman she remembered. She heard the sound of quiet music and laughter coming from their room. She was puttering around in the kitchen when Nick stumbled down from upstairs with an empty whisky bottle in his hands. She could tell from the look of him that he'd had a lot to drink. He stopped on the doorstep and looked at her in shock. "Come here," he said with pent-up rage.

She slowly approached him with her bulging tummy. Nick looked her over one more time with a deranged look in his eyes before his hands came to life. He suddenly gripped her clothes and dragged her across the patio. He opened the gate and pushed her out into the street. "Get out of here, you whore!" he croaked hoarsely, slamming the gate behind her.

"Don't let her back inside!" he yelled to the stunned staff. She was left miserably crying in front of the gate all night long until she finally fell asleep huddled next to the wall.

The following morning, she was sitting in the deserted alley feeling clueless until she finally dusted off her clothes and started to hammer on the gate determinedly. Her first started hurting, so she listlessly sunk to the ground. What should she do now, where should she go? She wondered hopelessly. She was hungry and thirsty. The gate opened. Nick saw that she was still sitting next to the wall.

He approached her with his eyes throwing sparks.

"I already told you to get out of here," he snarled. "I don't want to see you around here anymore, do you understand? I took you in, but you misused my trust. I can see that you got pregnant, even with that face of yours," he added, angrily tugging her shawl to the side, raising his other hand to strike her.

Although she was mentally broken, Vicky suddenly stood up and furiously raised her voice.

"Don't you dare lay hands on me again," she shouted, "since I'm carrying your baby," she uttered hatefully. In truth, she wasn't able to determine whose child she was carrying, but it made no difference in her current situation. The baby would soon be born, so he had to provide a place for themselves to stay.

The man's hand first came to a stop in mid-air. He stared at her in shock for a few moments before silently turning around and storming back inside – leaving the blue gate open. She followed him in quickly with a triumphant smile playing on her lips.

That afternoon, Nick lay on his bed without a cover. The ventilator stirred the air above his head with a quiet buzz. He tried to remember the day he slept with the girl, even though it only happened once. However, try as he may, he just couldn't recall her face. It occurred to him that it was no wonder since the room was often dimly lit. Plus he'd been with countless women since then.

The faces got mixed up. He shrugged. One more or less, who cares. Still, he never thought in his wildest dreams that he would be a father again. His wife was probably in London at the moment. However, he had nothing to worry about, since he would never bring her here again anyway.

After thinking about the matter at length, he walked down the stairs and approached the girl's room. In the dim light, he spotted the huddled figure of the girl motionlessly sitting on the ground, looking him in the eye without fear.

"You're in your final month, right?"

She nodded. Nick paused for a moment.

Finally, he broke the awkward silence.

"I decided you can stay, but on one condition," he eyed her coldly. "You are never to tell anyone that it's my child," he said, pointing at her tummy. "Do you hear me?"

She nodded again.

"If you tell anyone about this, you'll be sorry you brought your little runt into this world." He contined in a threatening tone. "And oh-," he added, turning back suddenly, "you won't say a word about the things that happen in this house. You hear nothing, you see nothing, you speak nothing. Stick to these rules, do your job well, I'll leave you alone." She averted her gaze so the man wouldn't see the hatred in her eyes. "Do you understand?" he cried sharply.

She shuddered and nodded again, quickly adjusting the shawl to cover her face. Nick left the very same evening.

On that morning when Nick kicked her out of the house and then decided to take her back, she decided to take good care of herself. Two weeks later, she became a mother. She recalled how one morning her water broke and the pains got more intense. The servant saw she was going into labour, so she called for the midwife. The baby was born by the afternoon without any complication. When Vicky saw the little boy for the first time, her motherly instincts stirred, and she lovingly caressed him.

"You're so cute," she kept saying over and over, and the joyful months after the birth flew by quickly. One day, the boy gripped onto the bars of her crib and managed to pull himself up from a sitting position, screeching to his mother to show that he managed to stand up.

After Antonio was nine months old, she often took him out of the crib and started taking steps with him by reaching under his arms and then cautiously letting go of him. She stepped back a few steps and called him closer. The baby shyly teetered and took a few steps before falling to his bum, quickly frowning and bursting into tears. The tears rolled down his plump little face. She picked him up, kissed him, spun him around in the air, and made him giggle through his tears.

Antonio soon started toddling around the room. While she was working, he played in the enclosed patio. The servant often planted a kiss on his head, and he even won over the guards, so the months flew by without a care in the world.

CHAPTER 24

After a lengthy period of absence, Nick finally returned. He halted when he walked through the gate. He squinted at the boy playing on the patio. He thought he was a cute little kid, but then he moved on without a word. The mother watched the scene from the darkened corridor. She never saw Nick approaching the boy in the future either. He simply looked through Antonio as if the child didn't exist at all.

The young mother took great care to avoid any conflict while he was at home. She always kept an eye on Antonio while she was working, and if possible, sent him to play in their room. She was terrified that Nick would shout or harm them some way, so she stayed out of the way and avoided meeting him. Still, if Nick was there, her young body rebelled, and she unintentionally dreamed of him.

The macho-looking Nick was undeniably attractive to women, so it was no wonder that she secretly admired him from a distance from time to time. She suffered, trapped in a young body with an ugly face since she had no ties with the opposite sex. She knew she had to forget all about love and a man's embrace. She was free to come and go from the house, but she could never take her son with her. She carefully masked herself and usually averted her gaze while walking down the streets.

As the years went by, she noticed some odd things at the house, yet she kept reminding herself of the Oriental saying Nick had told her to stick to:

"See no evil, hear no evil."

She learned a few words of Arabic and could hold her own in French. She slowly grew accustomed to this life. She had decided a long time ago that is better to stay in the shadows with a face like this. Still, whenever Nick appeared, she started rebelling and longed to find some way to get rid of this unpredictable, cruel man.

However, these thoughts quickly dispersed if she looked into the mirror, and thus she gave up on her hopes of escaping. After a few years, the boy's features increasingly reminded her of Pedro. She was terrified that Nick would notice this since he might kill the child or both of them.

One day, she was walking alone through the deserted alleys of the medina. She didn't like these abandoned pathways, but they were still a shortcut. The sun wouldn't shine through the old walls of the quarter. She looked up at the buildings and noticed a window covered with a grate. There was probably one or more women living there, she thought. As she moved on, the neglected-looking win-dowless buildings, locked gates, and musty smell in the air made her quicken her steps.

As she passed the tiny butcher shops of the souk, she turned the corner. Fragrant spices were heaped in the palm-sized stores, which stubbed out the heavy fumes of the previous alley. She stopped to purchase some spices for their kitchen. The vendor searchingly eyed her, since her clothes made her look like a local.

The "Arab woman" paid two dirhams without a word before disappearing into the teeming crowd. Ever since she had been forced to live here, she had been wearing a black djellaba with her shawl. This typical Moroccan outfit masked her face without attracting any attention. Although the times were changing and more and more women were wearing European clothes in the city, the senior generations still insisted on the old traditions.

She found her way to the Djemaa el-Fna square, which was thronged with tourists, yet it was also regularly visited by Berbers and nomads from the Atlas mountain and the Sahara – and in fact, from all over the country as well. This was no wonder since this famous square was always a busy place, perhaps even since the beginning of time itself.

The colourful, picturesque site led her to stare at the multitude of people. As always, the place was full of people. She spotted the well-known street water carrier, who smiled at her. He was wearing a red tunic and a worn-out old wide-brimmed hat. On his shoulder, he carried water in a stained leather sack, stopping here and there as he passed through the crowd. He occasionally rang a copper bell, attracting the attention of the tourists, who loved taking pictures of him.

Since it was early in the afternoon, the square was full of snake charmers, musicians, dancers, acrobats, fire-eaters, monkey trainers, magicians, storytellers, and similar sorts. The various spectacles were surrounded by a ring of people. This colourful multitude livened up and heightened the square's atmosphere reminiscent of the old ages.

Behind the mass of people, the square was lined with a row of small shops which slipped into the labyrinthine alleys, including several vendors selling the wares typical of the craftsmen of Morocco. After sunset, the square changed. The various performers disappeared, replaced by a mass of steaming, smoking cookeries and long tables and benches. The cooks dressed in white garb busied themselves, with their, food, cooking, and baking, producing endless varieties of tempting dishes and offering their services to the mass of people passing through the square. A bit further away, mounds of fruits, vegetables, and salad were heaped. At night, the Babel-like confusion was heightened by a smokescreen billowing over the masses.

The benches were crowded by tourists of various nationalities, local or rural guests who sampled the various Moroccan dishes with delight. The atmosphere of the Djemaa el-Fna square and its throbbing, vibrant nature tempted visitors from all corners of the world. She was swept away by the mass, ending up next to a ring of people. She tiptoed over to watch the Berber musicians – women dressed in dazzling outfits and dancing with expressive movements and gestures.

She forgot all about her duties as she gazed at the dancers. She failed to notice that the Arab man standing next to her was eyeing her and suddenly whipped the shawl from her face. The man recoiled, surprise and horror gleaming in his eyes. The people standing around her also recoiled, openly displaying their disgust. A few children made faces and started giggling.

The poor woman felt like dying right on the spot from the shame and humiliation. Her hands trembled as she covered her face with the shawl while backing out of the crowd in confusion. She stumbled through the masses and stopped next to a stall on the other side of the square to compose herself. She looked around in alarm, but luckily no one was paying any attention to her.

She made a few purchases from a vendor before heading down a deserted alley in despair. Her hands were full of baskets and bags as she carried home her spoils like a lonesome dog. She was lost forever; she winced as if they'd split hot water on her. This is worse than death, she thought. Then a voice inside her warned, *get yourself together, you have a son waiting for you!*

`This won't happen again if you take care of yourself. Don't worry, no harm will come to you since the shawl covers everything. She felt momentary consolation in these thoughts, sent perhaps by her angel.

Oh God, help me, she begged again, to no avail.

By the time, she reached home, she had composed herself somewhat, yet mentally she was still deeply shaken. It was better if she didn't leave the house at all, only if she had to, she decided finally as she silently crept through the blue gate.

CHAPTER 25

In the morning, she started her work as usual. She prepared breakfast in the kitchen since Nick had returned the night before. Later on, she went upstairs to the guest room to change the sheets. She walked over to the window to the pull the curtain aside, but her hand stopped mid-air.

On the opposite side of the corridor, the door to Nick's room was wide open. She wanted to walk away, yet she couldn't since Nick was sitting on the bed, cradling his new partner in his arms. Her heart leapt at the sight of them swaying in bed. Her young body starting aching; sweat trickled down her forehead, and her lips went dry as she motionlessly watched the entwined bodies in bed. After a while, she moved away from the window. She wandered over to the bathroom and removed her shawl with trembling hands. She opened the faucet to cool her face since the previous scene had rocked her entire being and whipped up her long-suppressed, healthy desires.

"God, help me," she prayed in a whisper. "Please rid me of this sensation, since I know full well that I will never feel the embrace of a the man again," she cried silently.

From that day on, her body suffered and ached. Whenever she spotted Nick, she retreated to the furthest corner of the house to crush her feelings, yet every night, she saw the bodies entwined in bed in front of her.

On the week, Nick and the woman both left.

"Did they leave for good?" she asked the servant.

"I don't know, they didn't say," the servant replied in a jaded tone.

In the morning, Vicky wrote down the things she had to purchase and picked up her basket.

"Keep an eye on my son, I must go down to the souk," she said to Fatima before she hurried across the patio where her son was chasing a little kitten. She approached him and planted a kiss on his mischievous face. "I have to go. Be a good boy. I'll be back soon."

"Take me with you," begged the boy, forgetting all about the kitten.

"I can't. I have to go alone."

"But I want to go!" pouted the boy.

"You know you can't come, I told you already," replied the mother impatiently, hurrying off to the gate.

Antonio ran after her sobbing. "I want to go with you!" he shrieked, and the patio echoed with the sound of his crying. One of the guards curiously peeked out of the room.

"What's the matter?" he asked.

"You know, the same old thing. He wants to come with me." The other man appeared, and they exchanged regretful looks. They both knew they mustn't let the boy leave the riad.

Suddenly, the gate opened. Nick appeared, looking groggy, with the blond woman at his side.

"What's this noise?" he demanded with bated rage.

"He wants to go with his mother," explained the shorter of the two guards. The blond woman kindly approached Antonio.

"Why are you crying?"

"I want to go with Mommy," he muttered shyly.

"And why can't you go with her?" she asked, looking around, before glancing at Nick.

Nick didn't feel like explaining himself, so he motioned to the mother that she could take the boy with her. The unknown woman winked at the boy, who gladly ran over to his mother.

"Cute little kid," she noted to her boyfriend. Nick didn't reply and instead coughed and walked on inside the house. Ever since he first saw the boy, he kept eyeing him at length.

He sometimes looked down from the corridor upstairs if he heard him playing under the arcades. He noticed how cute, smart, and level-headed the boy was. He's my son, he thought proudly – but whenever he got to this point, he brushed off his thoughts and the absurd feeling accompanying them.

Years ago, when his daughter had died so suddenly, his fatherly feelings died with her. His relationship with his wife ended, and they got divorced. He was free again, and Lucy had disappeared from his life for good. However, lately, for some odd reason, he often thought about the curly-haired little rascal.

The mother gladly took her son by the hand and led him down the narrow alley. She suddenly thought she could seek out Sarhan, who could help her escape. *Crazy woman, just looks into the mirror*, she chided herself.

"Look, Mommy, how big I am!" said Antonio, interrupting his mother's train of thought, holding his arm out to the wall next to him. "If you hold your arm out, we can close the street and no one can come this way."

"But this isn't our street. Anyone can use it, honey."

"But …" He opened his mouth to continue the sentence, yet faltered since they had reached a busy street which ran into the distance in both directions. The narrow street was lined with shops on both sides. The boy stared at the strange sight in awe. They stopped in front of the shop selling sweets.

"Give me some of these" said the faceless woman to the vendor on the other side of the rickety table.

The young man measured out the goods, nimbly walking around the table and handing the bag to the young boy.

"Here you go."

The boy shyly accepted the bag.

"Shukran," he said quietly, hiding behind his mother's robe. He started rummaging through the bag with his thin little hand at once. He dug out a sweet and gladly popped it into his mouth.

A scrawny little cat was meowing in front of the next stop. Antonio took out the sweet from his mouth at once and held it out to the kitty.

"Come on, honey, cats don't eat sweets."

"But why? They're delicious!"

"Animals don't like it, only people," she explained patiently. Suddenly, she spotted a tiny bookshop. They entered the store at once. Much to her surprise, she found quite a few Spanish and English books on the shelves. She purchased two books from her meagre allowance. One of them was a storybook.

"This is yours," she said, holding the book out to the little one.

"Mine? It's mine?" gasped Antonio in awe.

"Of course, it's yours!" exclaimed the vendor.

"You have a lovely son," she added, turning to the mother.

"Stop by again, some time."

"I would love to, but I don't have much money," she explained sadly. "Look, if you take care of the books, you can swap them for another one once you're finished with them. You don't have to pay."

"I will come back," she promised cheerfully. "Shukran,"she said, thanking the man for his kindness. Antonio silently gaped in awe at the sights of the Djemaa el Fna square and forgot all about the bag of sweets in his hand. Everything was new for him which was no wonder since this was the first time, he'd seen the colourful multitude surrounding him.

The sun was climbing high in the sky, warning them to return to their, home. Vicky adjusted the pack on her back, and they headed back.

"We have to go. It's getting late," she said to her son. She could tell that the boy was exhausted even though he still had a long way to walk home. She couldn't carry him since her pack was heavy.

At the far end of the square, she suddenly came to a halt, staring at the two approaching people. She thought she was going to faint since it was Sarah and Juan standing right in front of her, wondering which way to go.

"Do you speak English or Spanish?" asked Juan suddenly of the Arabian woman standing next to him, holding the hand of a cute little boy.

The woman was so petrified that she couldn't say a word.

"Forget it. She doesn't understand a word you're saying," noted Sarah, turning around and moving on. Vicky suddenly snapped out of it and yanked her son's hand. "Come quickly," she said, pulling him excitedly along with her, rushing after the tourists.

As they caught up to them, she held her hand out, wanting to embrace her long-lost girlfriend and whisper to her that she was Vicky, but she came to her senses at the very last moment. Suddenly she pulled her hand back and quickly adjusted her shawl and spoke up right behind them. "Can I help you?"

Sarah turned around. She eyed the woman they had just approached, explaining herself a bit timidly.

"Um, we're lost. We're looking for Hotel Atlas."

"Oh, it's not fair, you can reach it on foot," replied the *Arabian woman* holding back her pent-up emotions, pointing towards the other side of the square.

"Thank you for your help," said Juan politely, caressing the boy's head. Vicky was left standing alone, quizzically eyeing them. She stared at the tourists walking off with unspeakable longing until they had disappeared into the crowd. She wanted to run after them and tell them everything, yet she sadly wiped at the tears welling in her eyes. She knew well why she had passed upon this once-in-a-lifetime opportunity.

"Mom, let's go, I'm thirsty," urged the boy.

The young mother came to her senses. She adjusted the pack on her back again, which she felt was growing ever heavier – or perhaps it was the burden of her heart. She sighed heavily before they hurriedly disappeared down the alley.

CHAPTER 26

That night, she awoke from a noise. She quietly got up and cautiously peeked out the window. In the dim half-light, she saw them bringing in two women. She quietly opened the door and heard some movement and the sound of approaching footsteps from the patio, so she quickly turned back.

Eh, it's better not to get involved, she convinced herself.

There's no sense in getting curious. This has happened many times before, she concluded, laying back down in bed.

For some reason, she changed her mind later on and left the room, quietly rattling the door on the opposite side of the corridor.

"Who is it?" asked someone anxiously.

"That's not important. Where are you from?" she asked in English.

"Paris. We're at the medina, right?"

"Yes."

"Look, I don't know who you are, but I ask you to help us," sniffled the unknown voice.

“Hush. Quiet.”

“Can you help?”

“I don’t think so.”

“Please, please help. I have enough money. I’ll pay you handsomely if you help us,” begged the stranger on the other side of the door.

“I have to go,” she said quietly before quickly retiring to her room, where she was consumed by her thoughts. I could give it a try, she pondered, but her fear overcame her. She didn’t want to mess with Nick.

The dawn was fast approaching, yet she was still tossing and turning in her bed. She recalled all the things that had happened to her, including the gunshot that had ruined her face. It would have been better to die like poor Pedro, she thought, rebelling against her fate. Hers was no way to live a life. Her accidental encounter with Sarah and Nick brought back memories of her past which she had buried for years. She thought of her previous carefree existence when she was working at the real estate agency. Now look at me, I’m just a servant, she thought. She was doomed to live her life out like this, even though she was only 25 years old.

No one would ever find out who she really was. It had been five miserable years. The love-crazed girl she was had died forever, yet not in her heart. She sighed and pulled the covers over her head to rid herself of her painful memories. The following morning, she prepared breakfast with tear-stricken eyes and took it into the strangers.

“It was you last night, right?” asked one of the girls sleepily. She hesitantly nodded and quickly turned around to leave the room. The French girl suddenly reached out for her to stop, accidentally tugging at her shawl, which slipped aside, revealing her ravaged face. The stranger recoiled and covered her mouth in surprise.

“I just wanted to know who you are, since your eyes and accent show you’re not Arabian,” she stammered in confusion, suddenly averting her gaze in shock.

Vicky quickly replaced the shawl covering her face.

"Yes, I'm not an Arab," she said with hostility.

That's great, though the French girl suddenly. She didn't hesitate and quickly sized up the situation and made a decision.

"I'm Yvonne," she said, holding her hand out in a friendly way. "And she's Zoe," she added, pointing at the blond girl sitting on the bed, staring at the blank wall.

"Listen, I'll help you if you help us. I'm talking about your face."

"Please, you can't help me."

"I think I can, and I'm willing to do so," she quipped.

"Look, a good plastic- surgeon can do wonders, and my father just happens to be one," she added firmly.

Tears welled up in Vicky's eyes.

"You can't help me," she repeated.

Unless … she thought. No.

She didn't dare think of running away.

"Yes, I can. Trust me, I can help."

"That's impossible."

"Look, if you help us escape, you can come with us, and your life will change."

Vicky shook her head. "No. My son is here with me, and I won't leave him, and I don't have any money."

"Don't worry, I'll cover the costs," exclaimed the girl excitedly. "You know very well that we're in trouble. I don't want to end up in a harem or a brothel, sleeping with smelly, unkempt men," she explained with tears in her eyes.

"We only arrived in Marrakech yesterday. We got wasted at the hotel bar last night. That's why we got in trouble. Please help us so we can help you," she begged.

"OK, I'll try to help, but I'm not going with you."

"No. Don't say that. Think of your son, his studies, and your future. You have a chance now, and this might be your last one, so don't miss it."

Vicky left the room in a hurry without replying before tensely doing her day's work. Her perturbed thoughts kept wandering back to the girls. She knew they might be taken away at any time. She had to help them.

She's right, I have to do this for my son, she decided suddenly. She knew she had to do her work quickly since the girls brought here were usually taken away in a few days. She went back to the kitchen with her emotions churned up.

"Listen, take care of my son," she said to Fatima, picking up her basket.

"I forgot to buy fresh fruit yesterday. You know how Nick likes fruit."

CHAPTER 27

As she crossed the patio, she carefully adjusted her shawl as usual. "I'm going shopping. I might come back late," she said, peeking inside the small room where the Arabs were having breakfast. One of the guards wiped his mouth with the back of his hand, passing her the key.

"You could buy a few guavas," he noted, letting her out the gate. She quickened her steps. She knew she had very little time to carry out her plan without getting caught, but the hope of escaping had captivated her heart.

She faintly recalled the hotel where she spent a few blissful hours with Pedro many years ago. She finally managed to find the archaic building by asking for directions multiple times.   S h e entered the smallish lobby, which was entirely vacant. She quietly tapped on top of the counter. She impatiently waited for a while before knocking again on the desk. She heard some motion in the distance before an elderly man shuffled into sight.

"What do you want?" he growled at the poorly dressed woman.

"I want to talk to Sarhan," she replied timidly, nervously running her hands over the surface of her shawl.

"Sarhan? Who's Sarhan? I don't know anyone by that name," replied the Arab man.

"You must know him, he was Pedro's friend," she begged with growing anxiety.

The man eyed her searchingly, yet didn't say a word.

Vicky was crestfallen. It seemed like her plan had failed. But why wouldn't it fail? She had been nothing but unlucky in the past five years, she thought with teary eyes. The old man changed his mind once he noticed he wasn't dealing with an Arab woman.

"Wait," he noted.

The young mother's eyes glimmered in hope.

"Sit down over there on the sofa," he said, standing up with some difficulty. He adjusted his ankle-length djellaba before walking down the corridor to the right, shuffling along in his worn-out, pointy leather slippers. She waited at length, barely able to contain her excitement. She saw Pedro's body and his bloody T-shirt in front of her.

Oh, she sighed quietly, this is where they had decided to go back and get Lucy from the riad. Had they made a different decision.

"Assalam Alaykum," welcomed the familiar man.

The woman excitedly jumped up from the sofa. She searchingly stared at the stranger, whose hair turned grey over the last five years.

"What do you want from me?" he asked with a good deal of reservation.

"I would like to ask for your help."

"Who sent you here?" he pressed on, ignoring her request.

"No one."

"How do you know Pedro?"

"From a girl called Vicky who stayed with him at this hotel five years ago. You might remember her. You might know Nick and the riad as well. I've been living there with my son for some time," she pressed on firmly.

Naturally, the man didn't fail to notice that she was non-Arabian, even though she was wearing a djellaba, yet still, he decided to remain wisely silent. He motioned for her to follow him and offered her a seat in his office.

She hesitated for a moment before carrying on.

"Recently, they brought two French girls to the riad. One of them offered to take me and my son with them if I help them escape. We have to somehow make it back to Europe. The problem is, we have no papers. Look, if you agree to help us escape, they will pay you handsomely," she added, without taking her eyes off the man who wisely still didn't say a word.

"If you want to help, we must hurry up, since we have very little time left. We have to somehow leave tonight, otherwise, it will be too late. Nick might take the girls away at any moment now."

Once she concluded her story, she waited for a reply with pent-up excitement, yet Sarhan's face remained expressionless. Vicky, on the other hand, was simply unable to hide her excitement. Her eyes fluttered nervously while she dug her nails into her palm.

"Please help us."

Sarhan still didn't say a word. His expressionless face revealed nothing; only his eyebrows were furrowed as his gaze bore into her. Although the shawl covered her face, when he looked into her eyes, he had a faint suspicion. He suddenly spun around and started pacing up and down with concern before coming to a stop in front of her.

"Fine, I'll help you, but I warn you – this is a very dangerous gambit. Even if you manage to escape from the house, Nick has a long grasp. This isn't the right time for the crossing. Life is cheap on the top of the churning The Atlantic Ocean."

She forgot all about the dangers at the moment, and his words took a load off her mind. She sighed in ease, full of hope. Subconsciously, the spark of escaping, which she thought had gone out forever, suddenly rekindled inside of her.

"We'll do anything," she cried, and her eyes sparkled in joy. Her voice clearly showed her determination and pent-up excitement.

"Can you get out of the house?"
"I don't think we can without some help," she explained, excitedly relating the same plan that Pedro had used to get them out in the past. The man thoughtfully stroked his chin for a moment.
"Fine. I will wait for you under the roof garden at midnight. Don't forget, you must stay as quiet as you can. Do you have more clothing like that?" he asked, pointing at her *djellaba*.

Vicky nodded.
"Then make the girls put them on. It's safer that way, understand?"
"Yes."
"Go now and have luck."
So, he knows the house, she thought with satisfaction.
"Yes, I have to run now. Time is running fast," she noted.
"Thank you for everything," she added gratefully, before turning around and leaving in a hurry.

Her heart was thrilled by the prospect of escaping. She carried her sack with ease after she did the shopping. Sarhan's warning lingered in her mind for a while, but she didn't understand why the crossing was so dangerous.

Her tension increased during all her chores. She knew she didn't have a moment to waste. She was afraid she would forget or ruin something, but the worse thing would be for them to come and take the girls away. Her plan was ready, yet her stomach was still quivering from excitement. It all depended on luck. She kept herself from remembering again that her luck had departed her a long time ago.

CHAPTER 28

When she returned to the riad, she found her son sitting on a rug under the arcades, drawing a picture. The sun weakly shone down on his head.

"Look, Mom, I drew you a picture!" he cried, lifting the sheet of paper.

She crouched down next to him, and her eyes got blurry as she looked at the drawing.

"It's the house on the seashore you told me about!"

"Yes, honey, that's right. All you need now is some trees and flowers next to it," she added, pulling her son close for a minute. "I have a lot of things to do, so please draw your picture in quiet."

"I'll draw it again," muttered Antonio, turning the paper over. It was getting dark outside by the time she returned to her room, exhausted. She nervously rummaged through the bottom of the rickety dark closet, where she spotted her only sweater. She packed an old coat with some warm clothes for her son in a bag made of a hand-woven rug and pushed it under the bed.

Her meagre wardrobe consisted of three hooded djellabas,

which she kept wearing, one after the other. She wore one while the other two were hanging from the coat hangers on the door.

She heard the blue gate slam shut. She had a bad feeling in her stomach. Nick had probably come back, she thought in terror. She peaked out the door and indeed, she heard his deep, erotic voice from the direction of the patio. She waited a while before heading over to the kitchen. The cook was just putting the steaming couscous on a tray.

"He's back," she noted indifferently.
"I heard his voice. Is it for him?"
"Yes, I'll take it up for him, so it won't go cold."
"Did you give the girls anything for dinner?"
"Not yet. I will when I get back. It's over there," she said, pointing at the brown glazed jars which kept the food warm under the conical lids.
"I'll give it to them," offered Vicky indifferently.
Fatima shrugged. "Sure, if you want to," she replied, picking up the tray and disappearing from the kitchen.
Vicky picked up the keys and headed out with the food at once. On her way, she picked up the two djellabas. The girls were sitting on the bed. Vicky put the food down on the table.
"Eat, it's still warm," she noted with a mysterious smile.
"Could you arrange something?" asked Yvonne without looking at the food.
"Yes. If we're lucky, I'll come to fetch you at midnight," she whispered. "Do you have a watch?"
"Yes," replied the French girl, covering her mouth to hold back her joy.
"Fine. Before we leave, you must put these on, but only right before midnight," she explained, handing them the djellabas.
"Cover your mouths with the shawls as I do. I have to go now. Eat," she added, pointing at the food.
"You're an angel, our guardian angel," said Yvonne in joy. Vicky raised her finger in caution.

"Shh. Don't get too happy yet, but let's hope for the best," she added. She walked out the door and hurried back to the kitchen. She carefully replaced the key in the drawer before heading off to her room with a tray of food, where she quietly had dinner with her son.

"Want some more?" she asked briefly, her thoughts still focusing on the escape plans.

"No thank you, I'm just thirsty."

"Come here. Bring me those two empty bottles," she said, pointing towards the windowsill.

"We'll fill them with water in case you get thirsty during the night," she said, thinking about the difficulties ahead of them. She slowly filled the bottles through the filtering system in the kitchen and handed one of them to Antonio. The house was quiet, as usual. She bathed her son and put him down to sleep.

"Try to fall asleep, I still have things to do."

"Tell me a story."

"There's no story tonight, but I'll make up for it tomorrow," she promised, leaning down and planting a kiss on his little face.

"Go to sleep, darling. Sweet dreams."

She hurried back to the kitchen. She slipped two flatbreads and some meatballs into a bag which she hid under her clothes before stepping out into the corridor.

Fatima was just coming down the narrow stairs. "The boss wants to see you," she noted indifferently.

"You're still here?" she cried in surprise.

"I thought you left long time ago."

"I'll clean up the dishes in the kitchen and then I'm leaving," she replied in exhaustion.

Vicky was startled as she hurried back to her room. She took a peek at her son, who was already fast asleep. She put the food down on the table and quickly hurried up to Nick's luxurious suite. The man was in a good mood.

"I have to leave tonight," he started.

Vicky was devastated.

I'm late, I'm late, she thought bitterly.

"You just came back," she noted timidly. She averted her gaze so Nick wouldn't notice her anxiety.

"Well-well, did you miss me?" he asked sarcastically, glancing at her for a moment and absently lifting his glass to take a few sips.

"Don't worry, I'll be back in a few days."

Vicky shifted from one foot to the other.

"Well, what is it?" asked Nick.

"I need some money. Antonio needs some warm clothes. It's November, and it's raining a lot. I'm afraid he'll get sick."

"OK, why not?" agreed Nick. He walked over to his dresser, pulled out the top drawer, and took some money.

"I've only got Euros, but you can change it anywhere," he noted, handing her a few bills.

"Thank you," muttered Vicky awkwardly, heading towards the door.

"Wait."

She turned around in alarm.

"I didn't tell you why I wanted to see you."

"I'm sorry," she noted quietly. She cursed herself for forgetting that he was the one who asked to see her.

Nick glanced towards the slightly open door to the bathroom, from where she heard the sound of running water and the humming of his new girlfriend. She suppressed a grin and turned back to face him.

"Get the girls ready. Buy them some lovely, thin dresses. You know what I have in mind?" he added, handing her a few more hundred Euros.

"Now, get lost," he motioned with his head, taking off his T-shirt. Vicky took one more glance at his upper body before blushing and backing off, nimbly rushing down the steps.

She was thrilled that they could carry out their escape plan tonight. She smiled since she never dreamed that things would be so easy with Nick. The unexpected money also came in handy. It would solve her problems for a while. Fatima was still busying herself in the kitchen.

"Go home, I'll finish it," she offered in a pent-up good mood. The girl glanced at her gratefully. She thanked Vicky before quickly wiping her hands, wishing her a good night, and leaving.

Vicky finished the rest of the work and turned off the lights, just to be sure. She quietly pulled out the drawer in the dark and took the key before rushing off to her room. She had two more hours until midnight. She didn't dare lie down, lest she falls asleep. She sat down huddled on the bed in the darkened room.

While tensely waiting, she wondered whether she could cope with the grand task she was faced with. She kept repeating to herself that things had gone smoothly so far. Still, her premonitions weighed down on her chest with fear and anxiety concerning her son. She was also afraid that the French girl might not help her as promised. What would she do with, herself with a face like this in Europe? She might end up on the street with her son.

It occurred to her that since she'd come here, she had never dared to write to her parents to tell them of the trouble she had gotten into. Although she wrote a letter and put it in an envelope, she never dared to mail it out. For the past five years, her ugly face had held her back and plunged her life in shadows. Perhaps it would be better for her to stay, since Nick came here rarely. The riad was something of a home to them and provided them with a certain degree of safety. Plus, her black djellaba and shawl hid her entire body and face from the outside world.

She had nothing to fear here. In Europe, she couldn't wear this outfit and can't hide her face without attracting people's attention. She was on the verge of leaving the riad permanently within an hour, yet her inner self still hesitated until the very last moment. Hopefully, she could get rid of Nick, yet she would still have to resort to someone's goodwill because of her face.

She thought long and hard about whether it was a good idea to go through with all of this. She only had a few hundred Euros which she got from Nick. She carefully hid the money in a bag and moved it to the bottom of her pocket, still unable to overcome her uncertainty and fear.

You can still go to sleep now, reminded an inner voice. No, no, she mustn't, she couldn't give up on the girls since she'd promised them that they would escape tonight. And Sarhan was waiting for her as well. She couldn't miss out on this chance; there might not be a second time. She tried convincing herself that she had to do this for Antonio's future.

CHAPTER 29

It was midnight. The time had come to move. She shouldered her tiny sack as the sweat glistened on her forehead, and she carefully picked up her sleeping son – whom she previous dressed up – from the bed. She silently turned the key in the lock at the end of the corridor.

"Come on, we've got to go," she whispered.

"Don't make any noise or we're doomed."

The girls nimbly crept out into the corridor. Vicky carefully locked the door to their room. She held on to her sweet burden, ready for the trip which led to her uncertain future.

They silently reached the staircase. Her heart was pounding in her throat since she suddenly recalled the moment, she had experienced a long time ago when she and Pedro were hit by bullets at this very same spot. The sweat started pouring down her forehead in fear. She halted for a moment and almost turned back.

"He's heavy, isn't he?" whispered Yvonne.

"Shh," motioned Vicky with her head, continuing their escape. As they reached the roof-garden, she peeked down into the alley, where Sarhan fidgeted in the shadows.

"We're here," she whispered down to him.

"Hurry up, you can start coming down," replied the man from the street, climbing up to the outcropping to help the girls.

"Go," whispered Vicky to the girls.

The boy woke up. "Where are we going?" he asked sleepily. "Be quiet. I'll explain everything later on." Sarhan quietly urged her from the street. "Dangle your son down to the street."

Vicky leaned over the edge.

"I'll hold you by the arms and let you down next from the roof," she whispered to Antonio, kissing him on the forehead.

"Be brave. Don't say a word, and don't worry. The man will help, and I'm coming right down after you."

"Let go," she heard the man say as he cautiously cradled the boy in his arms before passing him on to Yvonne. "It's your turn," he added softly.

Vicky ascended at once and quickly let go of the ledge, but the man missed her, and she fell on her knee. The pain made her bite her lip, but she stood up with some difficulty.

"Are you OK?"

"Yes," she hissed.

"Then let's get going, we have no time to waste," noted Sarhan, taking the boy back from the French girl. "Don't lag" he warned the others.

"Wait, I'll carry him," Vicky whispered determinedly.

"We have to hurry. Don't worry, he'll be OK. If you can't keep up, you know where to go," replied Sarhan. They dropped the subject and headed off at once.

The girls followed the Arab as a shadow, while Vicky limped behind them as fast as she could. The little group soon disappeared into the shadowy labyrinth of the medina.

Sarhan waited up for the panting, limping Vicky at the Djemaa el-Fna square. "So, you did hurt yourself after all?"

"A little bit, but it's no big deal. Go on, I'll follow you."

Her knee ached, but she bit down on her lip, mustering all her strength, and did her best to keep up with them.

Finally, they reached the hotel. The man turned around.

"We have to go a bit further. The car is close by," he said encouragingly to the group of panting women, hoisting the sleeping boy higher in his arms.

The bluish moonlight shone down to the depths of the alley as they pressed on. Their shadows loomed on the ancient walls as if they were giant ghosts floating on the air. Rats scuttled from the sound of their footsteps. Zoe emitted a quiet shriek as something touched her foot. The Arab turned around and hushed her

"Keep quiet. We don't need any attention. We'll get there soon."

Indeed, a few minutes later they reached a square where a car was parked. "Get in," Sarhan said, opening the door and seating the boy next to the mother on the front seat with the girls in the back.

"Show me your leg. You hurt it badly, didn't you?"

Vicky reluctantly let the Arab examine her aching knee. She winced in pain. "It isn't broken," said the Arab in relief, "but it is swollen. Wait, I'll get you a wet towel that will help the swelling."

When he returned, he bandaged her knee tightly.

"Once it dries out, you have to wet it again."

He stood up when he was done and expectantly rubbed his hands together.

"Thank you," said Vicky. The man nodded.

"Look," he said in Arabic, "you have to pay me an advance." He added in a business-like tone, "I hope you have some money?"

"I don't know. I have to check." She slipped her hands into her pocket, looking for the plastic bag.

"What does he want?" asked the French girl.

"Money."

Yvonne instantly slipped off her bracelet and handed it to the man. At the same time, Vicky handed him all the money she had gotten from Nick. She knew they wouldn't have any money left, but she didn't care anymore.

"This isn't enough," said Sarhan, shaking his head without even counting the money.

"What is he saying?" asked Yvonne, leaning forward on the seat. "The money isn't enough," she said, turning around in fright.

"I gave him all the money I had," she added anxiously.

"I have my credit card. Don't worry, I won't owe you any money," shouted Yvonne in French. "Just take us to Rabat. Once we get there, we'll go to the embassy or the police, since we have no papers on us.

"You better forget that."

"But why?"

Sarhan glared at her in annoyance.

"Fine. I'll take you to Rabat, but I want another thousand. But you do better to trust yourselves to me."

"Why, what's wrong?" asked Vicky ominously.

"Look, the first thing Nick will do is look for you at the embassy or police, since it's obvious he can catch you there more easily," he explained in Arabic.

Yvonne interrupted him.

"What is he saying?"

Vicky was terrified since she had never really considered this possibility. She turned to the girls and related the problem.

"Then let's stick with him. It's better that way."

"It's going to cost a lot," he added.

"Don't worry about that," noted Yvonne at once, turning to the Arab. "How much do you want if we go with you?"

The price was high, yet Yvonne agreed in an instant. Vicky looked back at her in shock, yet didn't dare tell her in front of Sarhan to haggle with the man. The Arab's eyes flashed with satisfaction in the dark.

"Then we are agreed. Don't move until I return," he said, hurriedly turning around and disappearing into the night.

"You should have haggled with him," noted Vicky, turning back to the girls.

"I know, but I don't want to go back there, understand?" They didn't speak anymore, silently sinking into their seats. Most of the city was still fast asleep, and the stars were twinkling in the night sky above.

Zoe sighed heavily and noted, "I hope he'll be back."

"He definitely will," replied Vicky, thinking of the stiff price, yet she also feels uncertain during the long wait. She tightly embraced her son in the cold night air.

"Thank you for helping us," said Yvonne, breaking the silence. Vicky nodded. "I'm also grateful that you decided to help us. We overcame one obstacle, but it looks like the hard part is still yet to come," she noted, thinking of Nick.

"I think you're wrong since we're already free," said Zoe in consolation.

"You know, it was a good thing I hid my credit card," interrupted Yvonne. "If we make it back to Europe, I promise to help you out as soon as I get in touch with my father. We'll go to Paris together," she added, squeezing Vicky's hand.

"Thank you," Vicky whispered awkwardly, also squeezing the hand of the French girl.

Sarhan finally arrived. He spoke up as soon as he got into the car.

"Listen," he said in French, "There's something important I have to explain to you. This trip is far from harmless. I can't even promise that we can make it across the sea in one piece. It's November, and the ocean is choppy. They monitor the sea with a radar on the other side. Still, I'm convinced they won't evict us like the other refugees from Africa if we get caught. You're European."

He paused for a moment before carrying on.

"You can still change your mind," he warned them fairly. He scratched his chin with one of his hand, thinking of the handsome payment and hoping they would stick with him after all.

Yvonne answered him without hesitation,

"Let's get going."

The man gazed at the other blond girl, who leaned forward and nodded. Finally, he looked at the young mother.

"We have no time to waste, so let's get going," said Vicky firmly, clinging on to her sleeping son in her lap. She couldn't back down now and decided to face all the dangers, mustering her reserves.

"Okay, let's go, but I can't assume any responsibility. Do you understand?" he asked, turning around.

He felt bad to think that this little group of people might never make it to the other side. His experience showed that just as many people vanished on the sea as made it over to Europe.

"Well, let's trust in our good luck," he muttered, starting up the motor. "Oh, and one more thing. You must promise not to give my name out to anyone, no matter what happens. I'll help you because you're in trouble, but others might need my help as well. Do you understand?"

"We promise," replied Yvonne impatiently.

"Let's just get going."

"There are some warm blankets in the trunk if you're cold."

"Please, let's go," urged Vicky.

The stars shone palely in the sky by the time they made it to Rabat. Sarhan took the girls to a relative's house.

"We'll stay here until tomorrow evening. Sleep and get some rest, since the following night will be very long. He eyed them frostily for a moment since he doubted whether they were capable of facing the hardships of the crossing – especially the French women, who weren't too promising with their confident, well-to-do attitude.

He would nevertheless keep an eye out for them, otherwise, he could forget all about the reward. He was more interested in the woman who wasn't an Arab and her son. Who could she be? he wondered for a few minutes. Her green eyes seemed familiar from somewhere. Well, whatever, all that counted was the money, he thought, rubbing his hands in anticipation.

Vicky lay her sleeping child down on the mattress. She exhaustedly sat down on the edge of the bed, groping at her aching knee. Yvonne noticed what she was up to. She approached her and silently removed the dry towel, soaked it in water, and bandaged her knee tightly.

"Thank you."

"It's still swollen. It hurts, doesn't it?"

"Uh-huh."

"Well, it's better if we get some sleep."

"Goodnight!" she exclaimed, turning the lights off and lying down on the bed in her clothes. For a while, Vicky laid on her back in the darkened room, thinking of the day to come.

CHAPTER 30

They woke around noon to the knocking of the housewife, who brought them some warm food with a smile on her face.

"Eat," she said in Arabic. They all hungrily sat down on the worn-out ottomans.

"There are no plates," noted the blond girl with a laugh.

Vicky silently removed the conical top of the glazed tagine dish. The food was steaming in the dish, looking tempting and delicious. She broke off a piece of flatbread, dunked it into the sauce with three fingers, slightly lifted the edge of her shawl with her left hand and swallowed the bite. The boy ate just as skilfully as his mother. The girls imitated them, giggling and exchanging glances.

"Different culture," noted Vicky disapprovingly. This silenced the girls while they hungrily devoured the food.

Vicky stood up with some difficulty and returned the empty dish. When she saw the kitchen, she wanted to wash the dish, but the housewife made a dismissive gesture.

"Go and get some rest. Is your leg better?" the woman asked regretfully.

"Yes, somewhat."

Antonio followed his mother everywhere like a shadow. A

few children were, playing on the spacious patio, so he stopped to watch them. By the time his mother returned he was already having fun with the others.

After resting off the adventures of the previous night, the members of the group rested lazily, yet they didn't talk, anxiously looking forward to the next day's events.

The wind battered the window. Vicky limped over to the window to close it but instead stared out at the sea for a while in concern. The sun was setting over the western edge of the huge mass of water, staining the clouds above it red. She sighed heavily and closed the window.

After a while, her son came in and huddled next to his mother. "When will we go home?" he asked, gazing at her with his lovely round eyes, but his mother averted her gaze in alarm. "Why are we here?" he continued his questioning.

Vicky eyed him thoughtfully. The tears welled up in her eyes and she searched for the right answer. Zoe got up and sat down next to them.

"We're here because we're going to a beautiful city called Paris," she explained in a soft voice.

"What's your name?" asked the boy in French.

"My name is Antonio."

"I'm Zoe," she said, holding her hand out.

"You're pretty."

The girl laughed and kissed the boy on his plump little cheek. "Well, you have beautiful eyes!"

"Uh-huh."

"I hope we'll be friends! If you want to."

The boy tilted his head to the side. He slipped his thumb into his mouth, sleepily eyeing the girl without a reply.

"He doesn't speak much French," explained the mother.

"Your hair is very long. It has the colour of the sun," muttered Antonio. Zoe replied cheerfully, "Yes, it's blond." She raised her hand to the back of her head, wrapped her hair into a braid, and tied the ends together with a rubber band which broke. She pouted and laughed with the boy.

"How old, are you?"

"Four," he replied, glancing at his mother, who nodded. There was a knock on the door. Sarhan entered the room. His face seemed troubled.

"We have to stay here for an indefinite period," he explained. "Partly because of the weather and partly because I haven't been able to talk to the right people yet. And of course, this won't work without the right amount of money," he added, meaningfully glancing at the French girl.

"I have to go now, but I'll come back to you as soon as we're to leave. You'll be safe here. If you go into town, make sure you wear a djellaba and cover your face with a shawl. Don't talk in the street so no one would recognize you. If you stay careful, we can avoid any possible problems."

After concluding this advice, Sarhan caressed the head of the boy, who fidgeted, stuck his thumb into his mouth, and stared up at the man with wide eyes. "The bank is close by," he warned Yvonne."You can take care of the money tomorrow morning." He gave her directions and headed towards the door.

Yvonne spoke up.

"I have to go into town tomorrow for the money, but I want to call my father as well. What should I tell him where will we end up if we manage to make it over to the other side?"

Sarhan paused and thought for a moment.

"Look, I can't give you a definite answer, but we'll probably end up somewhere on the shores close to Tarifa," he replied tersely. She could tell that the man didn't want to give away the location of their hideaway.

"Fine. That's good enough for me."

She decided to tell her father to come at once and bring the money. She'd tell him to find a place to stay in the area, and she'd call him as soon as she could. The night set in. The mother lovingly hugged her son after his evening bath and quietly started telling him a story.

The young boy broke free from her embrace and lay on his stomach, propping himself up on his elbow. He supported his chin in his palms, steadily closing his eyes and attentively listening to the story until he dozed off.

Vicky smiled as she eyed her son sleeping in such an odd posture. She cautiously turned him over and covered him with a blanket

"Sweet dreams, honey," she whispered.

The girls were also breathing steadily, fast asleep.

She quietly walked over to the bathroom. Her knee felt much better, so she decided not to bandage it after the bath. She crept back into bed, slightly limping on the way, yet she couldn't fall asleep. She stared into the darkness with open eyes, yet her uncertain future still seemed muddled to her.

The following morning, the housewife invited them to come shopping with her, showing them the bank on the way. Vicky stayed at the house with Antonio, watching over the other children as well. She didn't feel like going out on the verge of her freedom. She kept checking the time and peeking out the window. The wind whipped the white-crested waves in the brisk sunlight, lapping them up on the shore. She didn't dare think about what would happen tomorrow and the day after that.

During her years in Morocco, she'd heard rumours about African refugees, yet she never thought this could happen to her. It would be better for them to go straight to the embassy since it was here in Rabat. Perhaps Nick would be looking for them elsewhere.

Oh, you're so foolish, she warned herself. Nick isn't stupid. She thought of her unrecognizable face and the fact that they couldn't get anywhere without money. They might have to wait for a long time for the papers, but where? Who would give them free lodging and food? Her anxiety increased. Her heart ached since she was afraid of the events ahead of her. What would the future have in store for her? Did she have a future at all? She wondered as she gazed out on the waves.

She knew very well that she didn't have any plans and she wouldn't have any for a long time since her future and perhaps her life was greatly dependant on others. Her only hope was Yvonne, who kindly offered to help. If it wasn't for her, Vicky would be in deep trouble with her son.

The groups of "Arabs" returned around lunchtime, looking tired yet cheerful. Once they entered the room, their good mood was dampened when they spotted Vicky huddled on the bed with tears in her eyes. Yvonne rushed over to her at once.

"I told you not to worry. Trust me," she insisted, caressing Vicky's head. "Listen, I managed to get some money. The ATM accepted my card," she reported cheerfully.

Vicky wiped her eyes with the edge of her shawl, yet it slipped from her face. For a moment, Yvonne spotted her uncovered, repulsive face. She quickly turned away to hide her pity, while unpacking and giving Vicky some time to cover up her face. In the meantime, Antonio curiously showed up in the room. Yvonne stopped him and gave him a chocolate bar.

The boy was about to turn away with his newfound treasure when she said, laughing teasingly, "And where's my kiss?" The boy planted a kiss on her cheek and rushed back to the other kids. Yvonne slowly turned back to face her.

"I bought you some warm clothes because of the bad weather," she explained, adopting a light voice, hoping that Vicky hadn't noticed the previous look on her face.
"Try them on, they might be your size," she said, dumping the clothes on the bed.

"Thank you for taking care of me," Vicky sniffled emotionally. The mood in the room slightly improved. All three of them changed their, clothes and dumped the overused djellabas in the bottom drawer of the closet.

While getting dressed, the girls noticed Vicky's impeccable body. Zoe couldn't stop herself from crying out, "Do you know you have an amazing body?"

Vicky turned away without a smile, clearly not wanting to take notice of this. She slipped on the tight jeans and quickly put on the warm sweater. She kept the black shawl wrapped around her head.

Yvonne squinted and placed a finger in front of her mouth to warn Zoe to stop. Of course, she noticed how to fit Vicky was too, but she didn't say a word. Poor thing, she must have lost a lot when she got injured. A beauty without a face. This bizarre thought made the hairs stand up on her back. She deeply felt Vicky's loss and decided to help her no matter what, otherwise she would be left in the shadows for good. Yvonne had grown fond of Vicky and her child in this short time.

She was amazed that Vicky had given all her money to that Arab man, in the car without hesitation. It seemed she was generous despite her poverty. Yvonne didn't carry on this train of thought, but rather furtively wiped the tears from her eyes and suddenly glanced towards the open door where Sarhan appeared at long last.

"I brought a waterproof coat for your son and a hat," he said, turning to Vicky.
"Thank you very much," she muttered, deeply moved, "but … but … I have no money." Her throat dried out. She had to be strong, and she mustn't cry, she thought in alarm.
Sarhan noticed her reaction and benevolently shook his head. "Don't worry." *Why did she cover up her face?* he wondered. *Who was this, woman and how did she know Pedro?* Pedro had disappeared without a trace, and Sarhan hadn't seen him for at least

five years.

Well, it's none of my business, he concluded.

"It's not a good idea for you to go out into the street in clothes like this," he warned the girls.

"It's better if you put your djellabas back on while you're here."

"I managed to get some money, but not all of it," noted Yvonne. "Once we make it to Spain, I'll call my father at once, and he will bring the remaining amount. If not, then we'll go find the nearest cash point. Is that OK?" she asked, handing him a bunch of bills.

"Fine," said the man intently. "I hope everything will work out." He put the cash in his pocket without counting it. The rest of the day went by uneventfully while they waited for the time to come.

CHAPTER 31

They were fast asleep when Sarhan knocked on the door. Yvonne jumped up from the floor and excitedly opened the door.

"What's wrong?" she asked.

"We have to go at once. Hurry up, because we're running out of time. Get well dressed. As I told you, put on the djellabas over your clothes and cover your heads with shawls," he warned them.

"Once you're ready, come to the car as fast as you can," he ordered the sleepy little group. Suddenly, the room came alive inactivity. Vicky woke her son with trembling hands. He muttered something in his dreams. She shoved the waterproof coat into his bag to slip on later if needed. Yvonne took the bag from Vicky and dangled it from her shoulder.

"I'll carry it. You have your son to deal with," she noted. Vicky gratefully thanked her and quickly scooped up Antonio, whose the head fell onto her shoulder. The groups of "Arabs" approached the car on the deserted street.

"Get in," urged Sarhan, and they took off a minute later. As they left the city, they drove on towards Asilah. The rain started drizzling. The people in the car were shrouded in silence. No one asked or said anything, and the only sound was the monotonous whirring of the windshield wiper, creaking from time to time. The headlights illuminated the deserted road.

The girls slumped sleepily on the back seat. Vicky sat next to Sarhan, clinging on to her son, stonily staring into the distance. She could hardly overcome her nerves. They might be toying with their lives. Although her life wasn't worth much her son's life was dear to her. He still wasn't even four years old, she thought as she pressed her chin down onto his head.

Then she shook her head defiantly. No, enough of this. If she had stayed in Marrakech, Antonio's future would have been bleak at best, since she couldn't rely on Nick.

What would have become of him as an adult?

A porter, a servant, a shoeshine or some street vendor who harangued tourists all day long with his wares for a handful of dirhams. He could have been selling spices from a rickety wooden shack as a trader or God knows what else he would have ended up doing. Not to mention the fact that she would have been a servant for the rest of her life.

No, no, and no.

She counted her blessings for the fact that Yvonne would cover the financial costs of the crossing. She had done the right things by allowing herself to get involved in this dangerous undertaking. Although they would have to blindly trust Sarhan without their papers, perhaps they had nothing to worry about, thanks to the great sum Yvonne had paid the man.

The car slowed down. The man turned off the headlights and leaned forward, staring out into the night-time darkness. He quickly found a narrow dirt road which led to the ocean. He stopped the car close to the shore and tensely eyed the dark mass of water. A few minutes later, he opened the glove compartment and rummaged through it until he found a flashlight. He checked his watch.

"We have to wait," he noted briefly, checking the time again a few minutes later before suddenly flashing the headlights three times on and off. He tensely waited for a reply. In the meantime, he supported both his arms on the steering wheel, intently gazing out into the dark. He was so impatient that he failed to
notice the drumming of his fingers on the steering wheel. The excitement of his anxious waiting caught on to the rest of the group. The man repeated the signalling. Somewhere out in the distance, they saw a light flashing back at them.

Sarhan cried out in relief.
"Finally, you're here," before turning to the women.
"Get out," he ordered them urgently, quickly jumping out of the car himself. He opened the trunk and pulled out a few blankets and waterproof sheeting before backing the car up into the bushes. He locked the car and ran down as fast as he could towards the shore. In the meantime, the mother slipped the waterproof jacked over
Antonio.

The wind was buffeting them, and the tiny group of people clung to each other, helpless in the face of the elements. The clouds gathered over their heads, and the moon occasionally shone out from behind them, palely illuminating the churning Atlantic Ocean.

Sarhan handed the blankets to the girls.
"Cover yourselves."
He walked up to the mother, who desperately clung on to her son. "Follow me," he said anxiously. As they reached the edge of the water, they shivered and waited while the wind cruelly whipped at their faces. Fortunately, it stopped raining, yet the waves kept lapping up on the shore. Vicky kissed Antonio's cold little face. The boy timidly gazed out at the waves.

"When are we going home?" asked the boy. The mother said nothing in reply. They didn't have a home. A few minutes later, they noticed the dark outline of a boat, bobbing up and down, approaching the shore. Sarhan flashed his light towards the water, and the rubber boat drifted ashore with ease.

The man in the boat hurriedly welcomed Sarhan, who dumped the covering in the boat, lifting the boy and seating him in the bottom of the vessel. The unknown man helped the women get in.

"Sit in the middle, on the bottom," he orderly brusquely.
"Let's go," he ordered, and they pushed the craft into the water, with Sarhan nimbly leaping aboard as the boat set out. The mother tightly wrapped one of her arms around her son, holding on to the edge of the boat with her other hand.
"Is Paris far away?" asked the boy, peeking out from his mother's arms.
"Yes, we still have a long journey ahead of us. Hold on to me tightly," she encouraged him with care. The stranger's mobile rang. "We'll be there soon. I can see the lights already," he shouted in Spanish. He quickly pocketed his phone and gripped the wheel with both hands, focusing on the incoming waves.

The dark mass of the water lifted the nose of the craft into the air with ease as they lurched forward. Vicky's stomach churned. Right next to her, Yvonne squinted into the dark and held on tightly to the boat.

"Can you see the lights too?" she asked excitedly.
"Yes. They're getting closer."
At long last, the craft pulled up against the side of the fishing boat. The Spanish man leaned forward, gripping the ropes dangling from the ship, which was fastened to a sturdy metal ladder which the man tied securely to the boat. A dark figure cried down from above; "Hurry up, we can't stay here any longer!"

Sarhan lifted the boy without a word.

"Are we there yet?" asked the boy.

"Not yet, but listen to me: I need your help! Hold on to my neck and promise not to let go until we get up on the boat. Can you promise me that?" asked Sarhan.

"Yes," sniffled Antonio, tightly holding on to the man's neck with his tiny little hands. Sarhan latched him on with a leather strap while the Spanish man held on to them. Sarhan stepped on the first rung of the ladder. He made slow progress with the extra weight, yet they still managed to get on the swaying boat without any difficulty.

"Next!" shouted someone from above.

The mother sighed in relief. At least he's safe, she thought while gripping onto the side of the rubber boat. The Spanish man took her by the arm. "Come on."

Vicky looked up at the ladder running up to the boat, with no end insight.

"Go!" warned the man, helping her up on the first rung. She determinedly clung onto the cold, wet metal and tried pressing forward. She thought she would never make it up to the deck. Her stomach was churning from the swaying, and she felt like she was about to pass out. The Spanish man in the rubber boat impatiently shouted at her, "Get going!"

The rough voice forced her to muster her remaining reserves and press on, finally reaching the top of the ladder. At the same time, someone gripped her hand from above and pulled her up onto the slippery deck. The French girls and finally the Spanish man soon followed them up onto the fishing boat.

"Let's go!" cried the stranger.

The wind howled at them over the waves. One of the sailors was constantly cursing the weather. Sarhan leads the little group across the tilting deck.

"Here's the washroom," he said, pointing at a door next to the cabin before entering a darkened little room.

"It's warm in here. Get some rest, and I'll come to fetch you when the time is right," he explained benevolently, shutting the door behind them. The boat tumbled across the top of the waves.

The fishermen were working hard on the deck in waterproof clothes and hoods pulled down low over their faces. In the meantime, the group anxiously waited, down in the hull in silence. They felt like they were locked inside a walnut tumbling across the top of the waves.

CHAPTER 32

The glare of the light tower flashed at them from time to time. The motor of the boat shut down, with the murmur of the waves as the only sound. The Spanish man with the craggy face told the Arab to fetch the group. Sarhan raced across the deck. It wouldn't be easy to reach the shore, he thought as he looked up at the stars. The moon appeared in the sky before dipping below the rushing clouds.

As he entered, he slammed the door of the cabin shut behind him, turning on his flashlight in the windowless hold.

"We're here, close to the Spanish shores. Come, we have to get back into the rubber boat."

"I have to pee," whispered Antonio to his mother, who quickly took him to the restroom. She took care of his needs before returning to the cabin, shivering in cold.

In the meantime, Sarhan produced life jackets from a chest behind the door. "Strap them on and hurry up," he urged them, putting one of them on the boy. It was too big for him, but this made no difference whatsoever.

"Don't be afraid," he said encouragingly. "Everything will be alright, but you have to prove you're brave again, understand?"

"Yes," replied the boy timidly. He quizzically glanced at his mother, who quickly covered his head with his hoodie "Don't let go of the man's neck," she warned him excitedly. The Arab man picked up Antonio and again strapped the boy to himself with a belt.

"Let's go. Bring the blankets," he said and quickly took off. The cold of wind whipped at their faces on deck. The Spanish man draped the previously bundled-up waterproof sheet from his shoulder and climbed down to the lowest rung of the ship ladder before standing into the swaying rubber boat. He tied the two ends of the sheet to the rope dangling from the lip of the boat.

"I'm ready; you can come down now," he shouted. They worked like a fine-tuned duo, both knowing the exact thing to do. Sarhan started descending at once. As he reached the lowest rung, the Spanish man helped him into the boat with a steady hand.

"Next!" he shouted up to the deck.

Vicky stepped onto the uppermost rung of the ladder without hesitation, yet it still seemed like an eternity for her to reach the boat, where she held Antonio tight.

Once the girls found their way down to the boat, the Spanish man warned them;"Hold on tight to the ropes at the edge of the boat and don't let go!"

Then, with the help of Sarhan, he covered them with the waterproof sheet. "Hopefully, this way you won't get wet," he shouted and quickly loosened the rope from the ship. He pushed the boat away from the ship with his muscular arms and started up the motor. Sarhan busied himself with the other end of the waterproof sheeting for a while.

We should have stayed in Marrakech, thought Vicky.

She tightly squeezed her son to her body as he slowly slumped in her lap.

"Are you cold?" she asked, but the boy didn't reply. His hand was cold and he clung on tightly to his mother's clothes. She did her best to cover him up warmly. She was getting cold as well since the wind blew at them from somewhere. It was a good thing she'd kept the djellaba on herself. She could finally get rid of it once they reach the shore, she thought. The waves spattered onto the top of the sheet, producing a frightening sound. Antonio started crying. Vicky desperately pressed his head closer to her chest.

"Don't cry, honey, we'll reach the shore soon."

Yvonne slightly lifted the sheet, and her pale face was illuminated by the moon for a moment as she leaned over the side to retch.

"Honey, hold me tighter," she warned Antonio quickly. She pressed down with her legs and tried clinging onto her son. She gripped the rope tightly with one of her hands while instinctively reaching out for Yvonne with the other, as the girl lost her balance when the boat tilted.

"Good God, hold on!" she cried in terror, pulling her back. Yvonne cuddled up to her, trembling. "Do you feel better now?"

"Not really. Thanks for helping me. Who knows what would have, happened otherwise..." she sobbed.

"Come on, everything will be fine," Vicky consoled the girl. She was terrified as well, but she was most worried about her son.

"Hold on tight!" cried the Spanish man suddenly as the noise of the boat rose in the air and then suddenly plunged as the next wave crashed over them. Somehow, they managed to make it through. Sarhan quickly produced a plastic bucket and used one hand to bail the water out from the bottom of the boat.

Suddenly, a powerful gust of wind ripped the covering off from the women, who waited for their moment of judgment, yet somehow this avoided them.

Vicky stretched out one of her numb legs.

"Where is Zoe?" she cried in terror. The girl had been sitting in front of her a moment ago.

The Spanish man killed the motor at once and cried something incomprehensible to Sarhan. His flashlight died, and he cursed as he spat into the water. They all stared out into the dark waters. Sarhan gauged the situation and turned around.

"We can't do anything. The waves have swallowed her for good, but we have to go on or we'll go right after her."

Vicky suddenly screamed as she touched Zoe's hand, which was desperately clinging onto the boat.

"She's here!" Vicky yelled and grabbed hold of the ice-cold hand.

Sarhan turned around. "Let go, I'll get it," he ordered, taking hold of the arm. "Take care of your son," he warned her and managed to pull the poor soul back into the boat. Zoe's long hair was caught in the ropes, and that had saved her life. Sarhan tried untying it, but he couldn't make any progress.

"What's the matter?" cried the Spanish man.

"Have you got a knife?" he asked.

"I do," he replied anxiously. He nudged Yvonne and handed the knife to her. "Pass it on."

Sarhan cut off the long strand of hair with the knife, causing the soaking wet body to sink to the bottom of the boat.

"Turn her on her side," shouted the Spanish man anxiously, starting up the motor. He desperately accelerated. He knew they had no time to lose, and he hoped that the unfortunate young woman would survive. He recalled a similar incident when he fought for the lives of an old man and two women over the churning waves of the sea. He only managed to save a girl at the time, but he almost lost his own life as well.

Yvonne sobbed as she tried shaking some life into Zoe's rigid body.

"Hold on tight, or you'll end up like her," Sarhan ordered, anxiously forcing Yvonne into a sitting position. Her skin looked deathly pale in the moonlight which suddenly spilt out from behind the clouds.

The man pushed her head down. Despite his harsh actions – and much to their relief – Zoe finally started throwing up. A few minutes later, he wrapped a seemingly dry blanket around her before helping Yvonne lift the trembling girl next to her. Vicky's iron grip on Antonio didn't relax. She restlessly thought that the same thing could have happened to her. Out on the right, from a fairly close distance, they spotted the flashing of a light tower.

"We'll make it to the shore soon," reported the Spanish man to shake some life into the shivering passengers. The leaden clouds raced across the sky. The wind ceaselessly whipped up the tips of the waves while everyone anxiously waited, under the soaking blankets for them to hit land.

The Spanish man spotted the faint outline of the sandy beach, so he killed the motor. The bottom of the boat finally scraped on the sand. The man instantly leapt out from the boat into the knee-deep water. They quickly pulled out Zoe and carried her to the shore while the water slowly washed the boat away from the land.

"Help!" cried Yvonne desperately.

The Spanish man looked back. "Take her," he said, letting go of the girl's legs, which splashed into the water. He turned back at once and managed to get a hold of the boat before it drifted away. Sarhan dragged Yvonne onto the beach before rushing back into the ice-cold water. Together the two men pulled the rubber craft ashore.

"Stay here," said the Spanish man to Sarhan before picking up the boy and carried him out onto the beach and turning back at once. Suddenly, a sneaky wave crashed over the top of the boat, soaking everyone in the process.

"Get out!" cried Sarhan, spitting water as he eyed the women. "Hurry out to the shore before the next wave comes in." He waited for the Spanish man, and let go of the boat. "Have a safe trip," he noted in parting and tried to get ashore as fast as he could. He turned around from time to time to keep the next wave from hitting them.

The knee-deep water was icy cold, yet the hope of escaping gave the women a burst of energy since the shore was right in front of them. Sarhan looked back and faintly saw the Spanish man clamber back into the rubber boat. By the time he turned back, Yvonne had reached the shore, but he couldn't see the other woman as a wave knocked her over.

The icy water which pushed her out towards the beach had a shocking effect on Vicky. She stirred up the sand with her writhing arms and legs, yet she couldn't stand up in the shallow water since the next wave pushed her back down while she coughed and swallowed salt water. Although she was wearing a life jacket she was helpless against the force of the waves. She gripped the sand with her hands, yet it trickled through her fingers as the cold water slowly put an end to her struggles.

Sarhan spotted the dark shape in the water nearby. He dove into the water, gripped the end of the djellaba and dragged the terrified woman ashore with Yvonne's help.

He leaned over her on the beach. "Are you okay?" he asked in alarm, tenderly slapping some sense into her. Suddenly, the moon illuminated her ravaged face. So, that's why she hid her face, thought the man.

"Come on, it's all over now. We made it," he noted in exhaustion, eyeing the boy and calling him over to his mother's side. In the meantime, the Spanish man was far out on the sea, approaching his fishing-boat. His mouth twisted into a smile. He was satisfied that the soaking wet group had managed to make it ashore.

CHAPTER 33

Vicky was still lying on the beach. She was terribly cold and trembling all over. She felt completely spent.

"You have to help," said Sarhan to Yvonne. She nodded and took hold of Zoe's legs as Sarhan reached under her armpits and they carried her off to the dunes.

The mother heard the sound of her son crying next to her. He squeezed her trembling hand. This shook some strength into her, and she sat up with effort.

"Don't cry, everything will be better now," she assured her son, hesitantly standing up. "Come on, honey, we have to go after them somehow," she said, panting. They supported each other and slowly took off after the others. Sarhan stumbled towards them in a hurry. He picked up the boy with one hand and wrapped his other arm around the mother, pressing on together.

"You must get yourselves together since we have to reach a house nearby where you will be safe and can sleep in a warm bed."

"You can't leave Zoe behind!"

"Don't worry, of course, I won't leave her here, but first I need to get some help and will come back for her at once," he explained, nervously looking around.

"Go, I will stay with her until you return," interrupted Yvonne, wrapping her arm around Zoe's trembling, wet shoulder.

"Fine. I'll be back soon," agreed Sarhan. A car approached from the distance, its headlights illuminating the deserted road.

"Get down," cried Sarhan anxiously. "It's probably the coast guard." He perked up once the noise passed them.

"See, I was right. It was a police car."

Vicky listlessly spoke up. "Can we go now?"

"Not yet. Up to the right, the road comes to an end, so the car will soon come back." Indeed, he was right again. A few minutes later, the car slowly drove past them and the surroundings were covered in darkness again.

"Let's go," said Sarhan in relief, picking up the boy.

The sand stuck to Vicky's wet clothing, hands, and face, but she didn't mind. She senselessly moved on, her leg aching. She moved almost automatically, blindly following the man. They passed down a narrow path lined with bushes before stopping in front of a gate.

"Come on," he said, taking her by the arm. "Only a few more steps and you'll be safe," he encouraged her. She ascended two flights of steps and found herself on a patio. Sarhan set the boy down and knocked on the door, entrusting the refugees to the woman who welcomed them. He had a few words with the host and hurriedly disappeared with him into the night.

The embers were still red-hot in the fireplace, casting a pale glow into the room. The housewife didn't turn the lights on. She handed the trembling Vicky some dry clothes; quickly helped the boy get undressed and dressed again, and put the two of them down to bed.

Vicky felt so weak that she didn't even have the strength to thank the stranger for her help. She held her son tight, and everything disappeared around her. Antonio fell asleep under the warm blanket as well. The door opened again, and they brought Zoe in, followed by Yvonne staggering into the room. They dropped the French girl down on the sofa.

The housewife rubbed down the lifeless body and wrapped her tightly in a blanket. Finally, Yvonne ended up in a warm bed as well. After the troubled night, a reddish light glowed on the eastern horizon.

The Spanish woman quietly got up and peeked into the room of the refugees. She lay a hand on the boy's face and sighed in relief. Then she checked the woman's feverish forehead and shook her head in alarm. She brought a damp cloth at once and spread it over Vicky's forehead before dealing with the French girls. One of them was fine, but the blonde's face was also hot, even if it wasn't as bad as the other woman.

Once she was done with her tasks, she tiptoed out of the room. Later on, she called up the doctor. She asked him to hurry since she had some relatives who are in a rather bad state. One of the women had a very high temperature. The doctor promised to come as soon as he could.

Yvonne appeared in the doorway, gingerly taking step after step. She quizzically gestured to see if she could make a phone call. The housewife nodded.

"*Numero?*" asked the girl. Sarhan appeared from somewhere.

"I want to call my father," she explained.

"Wait, let me first give you the directions," he explained, writing down the name of the village on a piece of paper, along with a phone number.

"If something comes up, tell him to call – I'll be here."

"Thanks, and again, thank you for everything," she repeated, still remembering the horrors of the night before.

Sarhan nodded. Her fingers trembled as the dialled the number."Dad, it's me," she said before going on in a sniffling tone, relating the most important information and giving him the phone number of the house.

"Please, hurry up."

"I'm coming right away," her father said. "Are you okay?

"I guess, but please, hurry up," she repeated. "There's a girl with us and her son. You have to help her. I'll explain everything later on."

"Fine," replied the father tensely. "I'll get going."

Thirty minutes later, the doctor entered the house.

"Sorry I couldn't come sooner," he explained apologetically.

"Still, thank you for coming. Right this way," said the woman, showing the way. The doctor knew where the room was since this wasn't the first time he'd come here. He also knew what kind of relatives he was dealing with, but that was none of his business. He had to help, regardless of who they were and where they came from.

"That relative of mine is very ill," she said, pointing at the woman lying next to the boy. Nevertheless, the doctor examined the boy first.

"Don't worry, I won't hurt you," he said, resting his hand on Antonio's forehead. Once he was convinced the boy was okay, he turned to face the woman. He removed the shawl from the fiery hot face and recoiled in disgust.

"Jesus," he cried absently in shock.

The almost bald red hair of the girl ringed a fiery red, repulsive-looking face. The injury was probably caused by a gunshot and probably healed without treatment, he determined. He replaced the shawl in pity and examined her with a stethoscope

Vicky opened her eyes for a moment, blankly staring into space. She instinctively fidgeted with the shawl before closing her feverish green eyes. The doctor didn't ask much since the situation was obvious. He prepared and gave her an injection to fight off her high fever. However, he sadly, acknowledged that there wasn't much hope for the girl as he glanced at the charming little boy. Next, it was Zoe's turn. She was somewhat better off than the previous patient. He gave her an injection as well.

"Get some rest," he said. Finally, he examined the last girl and found everything in order with her. Once he was done with the examinations, he left some medicine.

He instructed the housewife; "If the woman's fever doesn't go down in an hour, she has to be taken to a hospital. Still, try calling first."

He often visited the house for matters like this, but he never thought about reporting the incident. It was none of his business, and he was just helping those in need – if he could. Most times there was nothing he could do.

He moodily stared ahead while driving down the road. After Tarifa, he turned onto the dirt road that led him home through the cork wood. He thought about the poor woman again and her repulsive face, but those green eyes – which he'd only seen for a minute – seemed familiar.

PART 2

CHAPTER 34

She could barely open her leaden eyes. Her gaze rested on the grey hair of the stranger who was driving the car. Yvonne was sitting in front of her. Vicky lifted her head based on the dashboard display, it was past ten o'clock. She squinted at the woman sitting next to her whose face she couldn't see since she turned away while sleeping. She only recognized Zoe when she leaned in close.

Vicky felt tired, terribly tired. The warmth of the car felt pleasant on her skin. Still, she pulled the blanket tighter around her. She dozed off for a while, occasionally opening her eyes. Barcelona, she read on the blue sign above the highway when they stopped at a gas station. Suddenly it occurred to her to wonder where her son was. She excitedly sat up and grabbed hold of Yvonne's shoulder.

"What's wrong?" Yvonne asked, turning around in her seat.

"Where is Antonio?" Vicky asked ominously, noting how Yvonne awkwardly averted her gaze. "For the love of God, say something!" she shrieked in a thin voice.

The grey-haired man looked into the rear-view mirror. "Relax, I'll tell you everything," he assured her, stopping the car.

"I want my son," whimpered Vicky. "He's dead, right?"

The man turned around and shook his head.

"No, he's not dead. The day before yesterday, when you were unconscious with a high fever, a man arrived and took the child. All he said was that he was the father and he was taking him back to Morocco where he belonged.

The mother turned to Yvonne in despair.

"Who took him?"

"An Arab man."

"An Arab man?" Nick didn't look like an Arab at all, she thought quizzically. She was so stunned that she didn't notice the shawl slipping from her face.

"I want to go back," she muttered in a barely audible voice.

"That wouldn't make much sense since you wouldn't get far without a passport" advised the man. Vicky didn't cry or scream, merely stared blankly into space. She couldn't believe that she had lost her son. On their way, the man kept looking back at her through the rear-view mirror. He didn't like her silence or her stony stare. He had a suspicion, yet they had to wait until they made it to Paris.

The sun was setting, so they spent the night at a hotel. The following day, in front of the doctor's summer home in Nice, Yvonne eyed Vicky with concern and carefully adjusted her shawl.

"Come on, we're here," she said awkwardly, blaming herself for what happened. Why didn't she shout? Why didn't she call for the owner of the house or Sarhan? The whole thing happened so fast that by the time she came to her senses, the stranger had picked up the boy and hurried out of the house while the mother was lying in bed with a fever.

Vicky felt like a puppet. She uncertainly moved along next to the man who took her by the arm, letting him lead her. As they entered the house, the plastic surgeon took her temperature.

"Fine," he muttered. "It's not so high anymore. Still, she has to take medicine." In the meantime, Yvonne took care of Zoe and fixed a few sandwiches.

"Eat," she said, leaning over Vicky, who didn't react. Yvonne quizzically eyed her father.

"It's better if you get her to lie down."

Yvonne tenderly wrapped her arm around the mentally and physically devastated women and led her over to the guest room. She guiltily thought of Antonio as he gazed at his mother with his chocolate brown eyes. It's my fault, Yvonne thought, blaming herself again and anxiously leaving the room.

"Did she fall asleep?" asked the doctor.

"No."

"Did she have anything to eat?"

"No. Dad, I didn't have a chance to tell you about her yet. You have to promise me something."

"What is it? You know I'd do anything for you."

Yvonne looked up at him gratefully.

"Vicky is the reason why I escaped and that I'm alive at all. I have to make it up to her somehow. I promised her in Marrakech that if she helps me escape, I'd help her too. You could see for yourself how awful she looked."

The man considered the situation for a moment.

"You know very well that I have to examine her first. I might not be able to do a lot for her. But that's further down the road."

"What do you mean by that?"

"I feel she has to get better first since she's mentally broken. Once she gets out of this we can start worrying about her face. Nevertheless, it won't be a short run."

"Time is not a problem I'll take care of her. She deserves it – I owe her a lot." Suddenly she started crying as she recalled that awful moment when she helplessly fell over towards the waves. If Vicky hadn't caught her, she surely wouldn't be here, she thought in shock.

Dr Siran tenderly caressed her head.

"Don't cry," he consoled her, noticing that her thoughts had strayed off. "You know, I was very worried about you while I was driving to Spain. It's great to have you around again. Don't worry about her, I'll do everything I can for her since I'm a doctor."

The man fell silent for a few minutes before turning to his daughter with concern.

"Yvonne …"

"Yes?"

"Please tell me how you ended up in this situation in Marrakech."

"I swear to God, Dad, I don't know. We went down to a local bar for a drink at night, where we had a few cocktails. A good-looking man brought us a third cocktail, saying he didn't want to drink alone, and he introduced himself. He seemed like a decent guy, so we started to chat. I remember, later on, he invited us to a disco next to the hotel. When we went out into the street, he told us to wait for a moment while he went back to the reception for something. It still doesn't make sense, it happened so quickly," she explained excitedly.

"As we were waiting in front of the glass doors to the hotel, two Arabs suddenly took us by the arm and yanked us into a car parked at the curb and took us to a riad in the medina."

"Did they hurt you?"

"No. They took us to a room and locked us inside. That's where I met this poor woman who was working as a servant at the riad. When I started begging her, she decided to help us escape."

The father felt it better not to ask any more questions.

"OK, that's enough for today. I'm tired, and you need some rest, too. We'll get back to this subject later."

Yvonne looked up at him with teary eyes and kissed him on the forehead.

"Goodnight, Dad. I love you."

The doctor remained in his chair for a while. It was hard for him to get over the fact that his daughter had ended up in a situation like this. He decided to pay more attention to his family from now on. He stood up and called his wife.

"We will most likely arrive in Paris tomorrow," he explained sleepily. "I'm bringing a guest as well."

In the morning, they continued their trip. Vicky was still sullenly sitting on the back seat without moving. They had no idea what she was thinking about or whether she had any thoughts at all. They drove Zoe home late that night, and their long journey finally came to an end.

CHAPTER 35

They took Vicky to the doctor's apartment in Paris, providing her with a room on the upper floor. Yvonne gave her a glass of water and some fever medicine.

"Sleep well," she said quietly. She was deeply upset by the whole unfortunate ordeal. She thought that Vicky was probably quiet because she was distraught.

The silent woman stayed in bed for another week. Although she slowly recovered physically, it was obvious that she wasn't showing much improvement mentally. She had meals with the family but never asked them a single question. Most of the time, she just stared into space.

Yvonne made sure Vicky took all her medicine. She talked to the woman for hours on end, telling about what had happened and what she was up to during the day. She often read some passages, but Vicky never reacted to anything.

Lately, Yvonne's father had started visiting her as well. Usually, Vicky sat still in the armchair in front of the window with her hands kneaded together in her lap. The doctor sat down on the chair opposite her and started telling her about himself and his family, and how hard he studied when he was younger and struggled to realize his dreams and establish his current living conditions.

"Life isn't easy for anyone, but we have to overcome our obstacles. If we're going through a bad period we have to focus on straightening out our thoughts. We have to overcome our uncertainty, darkness, weakness, and fear. Life is short, so we have to appreciate every moment of it. We mustn't waste our time licking our wounds. Trust me," he explained in consolation. "Don't forget, there's someone out there waiting for you, someone who needs you." For the first time in three months, the blank eyes stared at the doctor with unspeakable pain as the tears welled up in the green orbs.

The doctor knew he had managed to stir up her memories. It was true that he didn't make much progress, yet he was still pleased that perhaps he managed to shake her up from her deep depression. He warned himself to go slow. That's enough for the time being, he thought, standing up.

"Look, I believe that all of your problems will be solved. Trust yourself. Let me remind you of an old saying: You are what you make of yourself," he added quietly, silently walking out of the room.

Vicky's condition improved within a month, yet the sadness was still there in her eyes. Although her sadness slowly dissolved, she never initiated any conversation. She lacked interest in the rest of the world. The family surrounded her with patience and love, bringing her closer to her recovery every day, rekindling the hope that she would find her son.

One day, Dr Siran felt the time had come to act. She told her daughter to bring Vicky to his clinic at six in the evening. "Well, let's see," started the doctor, slowly removing the black shawl. Vicky always wore to cover her features. Vicky instinctively grabbed the shawl.

"Don't worry. I'm a doctor, remember? It's my job to help you," he lectured her firmly. She closed her eyes. Tears flowed out from behind her thick eyelashes, while her fingers dug into the armrest of the chair. Her forehead grew moist in shame as the doctor illuminated her face – the face she had hidden for years, which had plunged her life into shadow. The doctor handed her a tissue.

"Wipe your tears away and don't worry about a thing. Trust me," he assured her, setting aside all his emotions and taking a serious, thorough look at her damaged face. He made recordings of its surface. One operation wouldn't be enough, he determined at once. He squeezed her hand once the examination was concluded.

"That's enough for today. You can take her home now," he said to his daughter. The doctor thought about the damaged face for days. It promised to be a difficult task. The girl was incredibly lucky when she was shot that her jaw wasn't injured at all; only two of her teeth were damaged. Whenever he had a moment to spare, he went over the recordings again and again until he finally set a date for the first operation.

"We'll start next week," he told Vicky, who listened to him with an alarmed expression, sweat running down her face from her pent-up anxiety.

"Look, you have to be strong, and we have to cooperate to let you have a new life. I can't promise you it will be painless, but the result will be better than your current condition," he concluded. He intentionally left her alone so she could prepare for the changes that would take place.

"Thank you for everything," muttered the young mother, covering her face back up with trembling hands.

CHAPTER 36

Over the next eight months, Vicky underwent three plastic surgery operations. Finally, she sat in the doctor's office after the last operation, waiting for the results. Yvonne sat next to her, holding her hand, perhaps even more anxious than her girlfriend. She couldn't shut up while they waited.

"I'm sure it was successful. My father knows what he's doing." Still, she couldn't deny that she was nervous about the result as well.

The door finally opened, and the doctor asked Vicky to come in. Yvonne flashed a pleading look at her father behind Vicky's back so he would let her in too. The man faintly nodded and asked his patient to sit down as he turned on the lights. Yvonne hovered in the background.

"Well, let's see." He slowly removed the bandages and cautiously removed the stitches. Finally, he swivelled the magnifying glass in front of him and furrowed his eyebrows as he studied the scabs. In the awkward silence, Vicky squinted due to the strong light as she eyed the doctor, who suddenly rose while pushing his chair back with his legs, causing the chair to fall over to the floor.

"It's done. That's all I can do," he said in a serious, considerate tone. "Come," he said, leading the terrified girl to a mirror. She didn't dare look up to see herself. The doctor winked at his daughter, who nudged Vicky from behind.

"Come on, open your eyes. Get to know your new face," she suggested. Vicky gazed into the mirror and saw a stranger looking back at her.

"The awkward red lines on the edges of your nose, mouth, and chin will grow lighter in time, and then I can release you with a good conscience, but first we have to repair your damaged teeth. Yvonne will ask for an appointment with our dentist. Oh, you can throw your shawl away now," added the famous plastic surgeon.

He was deeply satisfied with his masterpiece, and it was a great feeling to replace a repulsive face with an acceptable one. He looked down at his hands, which gave him the power to make others happy. This case was entirely different from the times when rich men and women visited his clinic to undergo surgery to correct unnecessary faults.

Before dinner, they opened a bottle of champagne with a bang and filled the glasses with the fine liquid. "I wish," said the doctor, rising for a toast, "for you to have a better life. I hope you will find yourself and be very, very happy."

They clinked glasses, and their eyes misted over when a hesitant smile played across Vicky's lips.

"We're visiting the dentist tomorrow," said Yvonne, "so try not to laugh too hard until then." Her girlfriend suddenly covered her mouth with her hand, giggling in the process. Vicky glanced at the doctor. "Thank you for everything. I don't know how to reciprocate the fact that I can now go out into the street without attracting stares."

"You already paid for this by saving my daughter's life," he explained lovingly. Vicky blushed awkwardly. "Anyone would have done the same thing," she noted emotionally.

For a long time, she couldn't believe that she could get rid of the black shawl with which she had been covering her revolting face for years. She stood in front of the mirror in her room for a while. As the doctor told her, the faint red lines grew fainter in time and became barely noticeable.

They could easily be covered up with makeup. In the meantime, she managed to get some papers with the help of the family. She changed her name from Vicky López to Sandra López.

She decided to drop the Vicky name for good because of her bad memories. She would hide her real self, perhaps for good. Her plans were ready. She wanted to return to Marrakech as soon as possible – she had to get her son back. Her now-charming complexion gave her newfound confidence. The formerly grey, insignificant girl turned into a princess. Her life underwent a huge change. She was stirring and felt full of hope and energy.

She started surfing on Yvonne's laptop for hours on end since she wanted a job as soon as possible. She didn't want to be a burden for the family, even though she knew they loved her dearly.

With her good looks and confident attitude, she quickly landed herself a job at a five-star hotel and started learning more of the trade. After she received her first paycheque, she parted with the family. She rented a penthouse apartment in one of the rambling streets of Montmartre. Yvonne helped her get settled in, which wasn't too difficult since she practically had no belongings at all. Apart from a few books and the clothes she had, she got everything from the family. All of her stuff fit into a sports bag with ease.

"Call me whenever you need something," Yvonne said as she left. "While you're in Paris, we can help you with anything." She placed an envelope on the table. "Only open this once I've left," she ordered her with glittering eyes, quietly closing the door on her way out. Sandra picked up the pink envelope and opened it. She emitted a quiet shriek in surprise since it contained a check for ten thousand Euros and a note:

"Good luck with your new life. Don't try paying this back or I'll never get in touch with you again."

Her throat ached as her emotions welled up inside of her since she hadn't expected this. She dialled a number on her phone at once.

"Dr. Siran," said the man over the phone.
"It's Vicky, or, um, Sandra here," she stammered, sniffling.
"Thank you for everything, the money and …"
She started sobbing over the line.
The man discreetly cleared his throat with a cough.
"I'm greatly pleased that I could help you sort out your life, but I don't want to hear you crying again. Agreed?" he chided her lovingly.
"Don't forget, we're expecting you for dinner this weekend. I have to go now. Take care."

The doctor thoughtfully stared out the window for a few minutes. He had grown fond of this respectable young woman who had suffered so much. She had lost her face, her son, and God knows what else. He was proud of his work and that he could restore her face and get her going in life again. The happiest moment for a plastic surgeon is when he can turn an ugly face into an acceptable one, or even a beautiful one. Yes, he gave birth to a lovely girl, he smiled with satisfaction.

CHAPTER 37

Things changed in Sandra's life once she got rid of her shawl. Her long red tresses, which had grown over the recent months, nicely framed her lovely, freckled face. Naturally, she was thrilled that she didn't have to hide anymore, yet she still wasn't at ease. She cried herself to sleep over Antonio every night. She knew she didn't stand a chance against Nick. She didn't have anyone to rely on, apart from Yvonne and the doctor.

She thought of her parents a lot, but she didn't have the confidence to seek them out after six years of absence. While her face was a mess, she felt so ashamed of herself that she didn't want to nor didn't dare face them. How could she prove it was her since this was her third face now? she wondered in terror. She was practically convinced that they wouldn't believe her shocking tale. Yet she couldn't stop thinking about getting into a car and visiting them unannounced since she wanted to be with them again.

It was a beautiful sunny day in the autumn when she aimlessly wandered down the Champs-Élysées. Her thoughts were elsewhere. For some unfathomable reason, she felt certain she would leave this bustling city once she concluded her studies. Passing by a travel agency, she spotted a cheap offer for a weekend in Marrakech. She decided then and there that she would revisit the city. Maybe she could get some information from her son.

The reddish houses in Marrakesh – the colour of the Sahara – hadn't changed much. She paused in the Djemaa el-Fna square amongst the crowds staring at the dancers, absently covering her face with a shawl but then removing it at once. She smiled and re-minded herself that she had nothing to be afraid of and was free to show herself off.

No one suspected who she was. She had a strange feeling as she played with her unusual incognito. One person with three faces and three pasts. The three-faced woman, she thought, savouring the words. Still, the third one had only just begun. Anyone could become anything, and it was up to them how much of their past they wished to reveal. Yvonne was the only person who knew her, yet she didn't know her full story either.

She recalled the way and turned down the alley which twist-ed and turned and eventually led her to the hotel. She excitedly entered the building. She noticed two Arab men at the counter. She could hardly believe her luck since one of them was Sarhan, whom she approached at once.

"Can I speak with you for a moment?" she asked, trying her best to hide her excitement. She wasn't mistaken since she recognized his beaklike nose and flashing dark eyes. The man searchingly eyed the strikingly beautiful red-haired woman.

"Come," he said readily, leading her in the direction of his office. "Have a seat," he said, politely pointing at the plush armchair.
"Tea?"
The stranger nodded. Sarhan disappeared, only to return a few minutes later.
"How can I help you?" he asked curiously.
"Sandra López," she said, holding out her hand.

The man introduced himself and comfortably stretched out in the armchair behind his desk. He had no idea that the woman had known him for a long time. She loosely kneaded her hands together and patiently waited.

The servant brought in two glasses of mint tea, set them down on the table, and silently left the room.

"I love mint tea," she noted politely.

The man didn't fail to notice that the stranger lifted the glass for a sip in an Arabic manner, slowly sipping the hot, amber liquid. Sandra cautiously got to the point.

"About a year ago, you helped two French girls and a woman with her son cross over to Spain. Do you remember?"

Sarhan cried in astonishment.

"Who are you and what do you want from me?"

"Please, you can trust me," she added hastily. "I just want to know what happened, to the boy. The mother was my sister, who died" she said, covering up the truth. "I would like to find Antonio, who was brought back to Marrakech by Nick Winkle," continued Sandra, letting the sentence trail off. She felt that perhaps she had said too much already, yet she still paused before continuing.

"I would be grateful if you could help me since I can't find him on my own." The man fell silent. He remembered the group and their crossing well. He could still recall the woman's feverish, repulsive face. He remembered Yvonne as well, and the story of how a man in Arabic garments had shown up to claim the boy.

It took an incredible effort on behalf of the young woman to mask her feelings.

"I must find him," she said in a trembling voice.

"Fine, I'll do my best," agreed Sarhan.

"Thank you," she panted in relief, with a sparkle of hope in her eyes. She produced the hotel's stationery from her bag and jotted down her room number on it. "I have to return to Paris in two days. I hope you won't let me leave empty-handed?" she noted, meaningfully eyeing the man. She hesitantly wrote down her phone number, reached into her bag, and pulled out an envelope which she slid across the table to the man.

"I would like to pay you in advance since I'll be leaving

shortly."

"Don't, only when I find out something."

"Put it away, it's not important. I trust you will help me out."

The man shook his head. "I can't promise that. But I will do my best."

"Thank you so much," she noted in a trembling tone. She stood up and kindly said goodbye.

"Do you need any help? Do you know the way out of the medina?" asked the man in parting. The woman waved the matter off without turning around.

"Thank you, I can cope on my own."

She adjusted her thin shawl and mingled amongst the locals. She was caught up in her memories, doing her best to find her way out of the medina. The alleys twisted and turned in an unruly yet familiar pattern. The tiny shops were filled with thousands of goods. Sandra thought of the riad yet didn't dare approach it, since she was afraid of Nick's revenge.

She flattened herself out next to a wall as a scrawny donkey approached, heavily loaded with gas canisters. Its tongue dangled from its mouth in exhaustion, and its mouth foamed while it spread its front legs apart and trembled as it came to a stop. Nevertheless, its young owner did his best to urge it to move on by hitting it with a stick.

"Why are you hitting that poor donkey? Can't you see it's about to collapse from all the weight you loaded onto it?" she scolded the boy in Arabic. He stared at her for a moment. The donkey moved on, and he left without a word.

Next, a filthy sticky-looking dog appeared, searching for food. A bit further away, a woman was sitting on the ground, holding her hands out, begging for some money. There was an ugly scar on one of her cheeks. Sandra instantly touched her face and sympathetically handed the woman a bill. Once she had done the same thing when she was in a tough situation, she recalled in shock.

The woman, surprised, gratefully thanked her.

The phone rang on her final evening at the hotel. Sandra quickly answered it.

"Hello?" she said excitedly.

"It's a Sarhan. All I could find out is that Nick Winkler took the boy to a boarding school in England. I need more time. I'll get in touch when I have more information," he said, quickly ending the call.

She stared at the corner of the room, clueless. She hadn't expected this to happen. So, it seemed that Nick was taking care of Antonio since he'd sent the boy to school in England. She should be pleased about that, regardless of the events.

It was past eight o'clock. She got herself together and went down to the restaurant to have dinner. She sat down to a free table. The smile was glued to her face as she kept thinking about Antonio. *What is my dear son doing now? Is he studying diligently? How much has he grown? Does he remember me?* She wondered in anguish.

"Can we have a seat?" asked an older-looking businesswoman.

"Naturally," Sandra replied, snapping back to the present-moment. The strangers kindly chatted with her. During their conversation, it transpired that they came from Marbella and were looking for investment opportunities in tourism and real estate sales.

"There was a time when I worked in that field," Sandra mentioned.

"Oh? That's interesting," noted the woman, perking up.

"I'm going to return to Marbella shortly," said Sandra, startled by her claim.

"Look, I might be able to offer you a great job. Think about it and get in touch, if you're interested," concluded the woman in a business-like tone, handing over her business card.She thanked her for the unexpected offer and sleepily returned to her room.

CHAPTER 38

Spring touched down in Paris, but Sandra didn't take much notice. She routinely and precisely did her job at the hotel while diligently studying. She met up with Yvonne in her limited free time. Their friendship blossomed. They went to classical concerts as well as visiting the opera, the Louvre, and other galleries. Sometimes they accompanied Dr Siran to promising auctions where the prices quickly skyrocketed while the little hammer kept beating down on the stand.

Indeed, it was springtime, yet love evaded both of them. Whenever a good-looking guy approached during their walks, they sighed and giggled. Sandra had other reasons to sigh at night in her hotel room since she was futilely waiting for her Arab contact to call. She kept asking herself what she should do now. Time was going by, and she hasn't made any progress at all. She often cried and wondered at night if perhaps she had lost Antonio forever.

After she finished her studies, the spring turned into summer. She called up Yvonne to meet at the terrace of their favourite café. Her friend eventually showed up at their little round table late.

Sandra started the conversation.

"I want to go to Portugal for at least a week."

"Portugal?" asked Yvonne in surprise. "Yes, Algarve. Have you ever been there before?"

"No, but I heard it has beautiful shores."

"That's right. Want to come with me?"

"Sounds good to me."

Sandra looked at her anxiously. "I have to visit my parents – I don't want to put it off anymore."

Yvonne stared at her in shock. "You never told me about your parents and that they live so close! I thought you were all alone without any relatives at all," she said quizzically. "How could you do such a thing? Why didn't you say something? Why did you wait for so long?"

"I wanted to write to them, but I didn't because of my face," she protested, raising her voice protectively.

"Yeah, but now you have no reason to hide your cute little face," Yvonne mocked her heatedly.

"Yes, but I'm still afraid they won't recognize me. That's why I waited for so long, don't you understand?"

"No, I don't!"

"Think about it – how could I prove my story? Answer me! You can see for yourself that I'm not the same person. My cute little face changed a lot after that gunshot," she noted self-mockingly, "and I can barely remember my old face. I don't even have a picture of myself," she whispered.

Her old memories surged to the surface from the past. It was true that her conscience had been tormenting her for some time. Her throat constricted from the painful thoughts, and she kept biting at the lovely curve of her mouth which the surgeon had created for her.

After the way, her girlfriend hostilely attacked her, she sadly hung her head and retreated behind her defences.

Yvonne fumed in silence until she started to understand Sandra's agony. She felt a sense of fear coming over her.

"Sorry," she sniffled. "I'll go with you, just please don't shut me out," she promised, rummaging through her bag for some tissues.

CHAPTER 39

They arrived in Albufeira in early July. They rented a place in the upper part of the town for an indeterminate time. After settling in, they went walking down the zigzagging streets, making their way down to the picturesque bay. The waters of the Atlantic Ocean barely stirred.

"It's amazing," exclaimed Yvonne enthusiastically.

"I told you so."

"I'm just sorry that I didn't bring my easel."

"You can come back here again some other time," Sandra said, thinking of her parents and the villa in Gale.

They continued their stroll down to the main square, which Sandra thought had changed a lot over time. The town was full of tourists who were looking for nothing else than swimming, sunbathing, eating, drinking, and of course partying.

"I can't remember exactly when I came here the last time, but I remember old people sitting in the shade of huge trees, chatting and gazing at the sites of the small town," she recalled nostalgically.

"I like it this way. The bay is so quaint!"

"I guess. Walking down those tight little alleys, you can still sense the town's peculiar atmosphere, but the square filled with bric-a-brac isn't my cup of tea."

It was getting late in the afternoon. Sandra glanced at her watch. The tension she had been coping with since they arrived here remained. She kept on walking around instead of rushing off to see her parents, even though they lived so close by. Suddenly, she made up her mind.

"Come on," she said to Yvonne, "I'll show you the villa. Perhaps …"

"Are you sure you want to go see them right away?" Yvonne asked. "Wouldn't it be better for you to wait a few days?"

"No. They're the reason why I came here," Sandra noted firmly.

"OK, if that's what you want, then let's get going." She slowly manoeuvred her car down the familiar roads where so much had changed over the last years. They'd built a marina under the cemetery, surrounded by colourful apartment buildings.

Gale was also more fully developed, yet the old sandy road hadn't changed at all. She slowly drove past the back of the domed villa.

"See, that's it."

She stopped the car. She got out and peeked in over the gate, yet didn't see any signs of life. The hedge running along the fence densely masked all sight of the house. Sandra sadly got back into the car and parked on the shore.

Yvonne glanced at her in concern.

"Please, try to get yourself together."

"I'll try."

The waves gently lapped at the sandy shores in the familiar bay. It seemed like only yesterday that she was sunbathing on these shores. The two friends slowly walked up the narrow path that ran along the top of the rocks.

"Look, you can see it from here," Sandra said, pointing at the villa. She was starting to get incredibly anxious about her parents, whom she hadn't seen for ages. Her heart urged her to go to the villa regardless of the consequences. She had to get back to where she'd spent all those wonderful years. The memories buried deep inside of her suddenly burst to the surface like a volcano. How could she do such a thing? She should have written them a letter, she scolded herself. Yvonne was well aware of her girlfriend's agony and self-blame, as her face blushed from her pent-up excitement.

"Come on, let's go back, and you can ring the doorbell. We'll figure something out." Sandra gratefully glanced at her.

"You're right, let's go."

CHAPTER 40

All her courage seemed to disappear as they stopped in front of the entrance. Yvonne stepped up to the gate and firmly rang the doorbell, but they didn't hear or see any motion, so she rang the bell again.

The heavy chestnut front door finally opened, and a woman with the composed face slowly approached the gate.

"I'm coming. How can I help you?" she asked kindly through the metal grate.

"We're looking for Vicky," noted Yvonne tensely.

The blood drained from the woman's face, and she stared at them in shock.

"Unfortunately, my daughter isn't here," she said in a faltering tone. Sandra turned away, lifting her hand to her throat as she almost choked from the suppressed emotions. She breathed heavily to stifle her excitement.

"How do you know my daughter? She disappeared years ago, without a trace." The woman intentionally avoided saying that she died.

"We were good friends in the past," explained the French

girl in English. The woman opened the gate while furtively eyeing Sandra, who glanced at her mother with alarm in her eyes. She could barely stop herself from hugging her.

"Do you know anything about her?" the mother asked hopefully.

"No, unfortunately, we don't."

"Well, you can still come in. Maybe you can tell me something I don't know," said the woman, unsuspectingly letting the strangers into her house.

"It's a beautiful villa," said Yvonne, admiring the building. The woman nodded acknowledgement.

"Have a seat. Can I get you some coffee or tea?"

"Yes please," replied Yvonne.

While her mother was in the kitchen, Sandra emotionally looked around her old home. Nothing had changed in the spacious living room over the years. She spotted a few pictures on the bookshelf. She went closer to take a better look. She saw a teenager looking back at her from one of the pictures. On another picture, her father was swimming in a pool with a red-haired girl.

"My husband and my poor daughter," explained her mother, coming over to her. Sandra couldn't hold her emotions back anymore. "Where's daddy?" she asked anxiously, afraid that he was no longer with them.

"Excuse me?" asked the mother, glancing at the unknown young woman.

"Mommy, it's me, Vicky.

The woman stared at her at length.

"No, you don't resemble her."

"Trust me, it's me," she cried hysterically as her emotions gushed to the surface. Yvonne tried saving the situation and quickly intervened.

"Ma'am please, believe me, Sandra, or rather Vicky, is your daughter," she assured her, discreetly walking out into the garden and giving them some time to themselves since she couldn't bear to watch the scene anymore.

The woman didn't believe her story.

You couldn't have changed so much," she cried, perturbed.

"But I did. I have been using the name Sandra for some time now. My surname is still López," she sobbed achingly.

"No, you're not the same," repeated the mother stubbornly.

Sandra wiped her tears away with her palm and spoke up in a changed tone.

"You're right, ma'am," she said, explaining herself. "Why would you believe me, since it looks like I can't back up my story with anything. I don't want to impose on you anymore." She left a note on the table with trembling hands.

"Here's my mobile number; perhaps you'll change your mind and give me a call," she added in anguish and turned to Yvonne.

"Come on, let's go. There's no sense in bothering the lady anymore," she explained, passing by the barbecue, descending the steps, and walking out the gate.

The mother was left standing motionless, watching them leave. Her heart was pounding, so she slumped down on the sofa in confusion. Her husband arrived shortly after, baffled with the confused look on his wife's face.

"What happened?" asked the husband when he came home.

"Is something wrong? Are you okay?" he asked, but his wife didn't reply. He crouched down, put his hand on her shoulder, and gently shook her.

"Answer me, what happened? Tell me!" he repeated. The woman glanced at him with alarm and suddenly burst out in tears. The man sat down next to her, pulled her close, and patiently waited for her to say something. Once his wife told him everything, he walked over to the table and picked up the piece of paper. He dialled the number at once and introduced himself, inviting the unknown woman over.

"Please, come back tomorrow."

When she heard her father's voice, Sandra hopefully answered him at once. "I'll be there," she promised, with hope finding its way into her heart.

CHAPTER 41

The following day, she excitedly approached the wrought-iron gate of the Villa Tamariscus and excitedly rang the bell, terrified of losing her parents forever. The front door of the house opened almost instantly. Her father hurried over to the gate and opened it with some difficulty. Sandra was so emotionally charged that she couldn't say a word. She noticed that since she last saw him, his hair had become grey and his shoulders slumped.

The man scanned the young woman with uncertainty. *This isn't my daughter,* he determined at once.

"Come in," he said coldly.

She felt an icy grip on her heart due to the cold welcome. *How would I convince them?* She wondered hopelessly.

Once they entered the living room, her father offered her a seat. In the meantime, her mother appeared and nodded reservedly before sitting down opposite her. They searchingly eyed her in the awkward silence. Sandra glanced back and forth between them with a look of terror in her eyes.

"I know it sounds absurd," she said finally, breaking the silence, "but what I'm about to tell you is a hair-raising, incredible tale."

A heavy silence set in, and then she started telling them all the details. After her lengthy confession, she expectantly eyed her parents. The stunned parents exchange perturbed looks, and the mother finally spoke up.

"Take off your sandals," she ordered strictly. Sandra glanced at her mother in surprise but didn't protest. "Put your left leg on my lap," the mother said and put on her glasses. Sandra quizzically followed her order.

The woman picked up her foot, lifting it and taking a good long look at her sole. She prodded the scar caused by a piece of broken glass many years ago. She repeated the motion several times before turning pale and hoarsely speaking up.

"It's her," she said to her husband. "See for yourself."

The father also carefully checked the barely noticeable scar and awkwardly eyed his daughter. He was left speechless in surprise and unexpected joy. Tears welled up in his eyes.

Sandra felt the joy of acceptance and buried her head in her mother's lap, tightly holding on to her waist. She was glad to get them back. The pain accumulated and holding back for many hopeless years suddenly mixed with joy which blotted out the past.

"My dear daughter, we thought you were dead. We had given up on our hopes after all those years."

Sandra moved into the villa that very same day with her girlfriend. However, the father still had some doubts. Thus, the following day, he asked them, "Why don't you go for a bath in the swimming pool?"

"May we?"

"Sure, that's why we have a pool."

A few minutes later, while Yvonne was enjoying the cool water of the pool, he asked his daughter anxiously, "How come you don't go swimming?"

"Maybe I will later on."

The mother felt uncertain again and gave her husband a meaningful glance. She decided to go inside. Later on, she watched from the domed, round-shaped dining room as the "lovely young girl with red hair" swam with even strokes in the water. The girl swam laps and laps for at least a half-hour. Finally, she climbed out of the pool, feeling refreshed. She wiped herself down and comfortably sprawled on the deck chair on her stomach.

She supported her head on her arms and absently stared out at the ocean. The mother relaxed as she recognized her daughter's habits and sat down next to her, lovingly caressing her back. She was still looking for one last confirmation. Her eyes were searching for something. When she spotted the tiny birthmark under the girl's left shoulder blade, she was finally convinced that indeed it was her daughter who had returned.

She gladly winked at her husband, who sighed in relief, went inside, and returned a few minutes later with a bottle of champagne. The cork bursted out of the bottle with a bang and landed in the pool, so Yvonne fished it out. The man motioned for her to come out of the water, and he filled the glasses with champagne.

"To your return," he said emotionally to his daughter, quietly clinking glasses. The father turned to Yvonne.

"My wife and I are very grateful for everything you did for our daughter, not to mention your father. Whenever you are in need or would like to have a vacation, you are welcome at our house. The door will always be open to you. Please give our thanks to your parents. I would love to meet them and invite them over, whenever it's convenient for them. I'm sure they're remarkable people, just like you."

"I hope they can find the time to visit you," replied Yvonne, thanking him for the offer.

CHAPTER 42

`Sandra's mobile suddenly rang.

"It's a Sarhan. I couldn't call you any sooner. I finally found out the address of the boarding school in London. Write it down!"

"One second," she replied, digging out a pen and a notepad from her bag. "I'm ready," she urged the man, writing down the address provided with trembling hands.

"Could you spell that for me?" she asked excitedly, carefully checking the address. "Fine. Thank you very much," she sniffled gratefully.

"You're welcome. Good luck!" said the man and hung up.

Due to her work, she couldn't make it over to London until October, when she visited the boarding school at once. Much to her surprise, however, Antonio was no longer there. According to the principal, the boy had been taken to another school by his father.

"Please, give me the address."

"I'm afraid I can't do that."

"At least give me the contact information for Winkler," she begged him in anguish.

"Unfortunately, I can't. It's against school regulations."

Sandra's plan was foiled again. She headed back to her hotel feeling hopeless. The rain was pouring down on her, mourning her failure. Her heart was burdened by her series of failures, and her hatred for Nick grew inside of her even more.

Her alert nature and readiness to act only heightened her anger. Who could she turn to now? what lawyer could she hire from which country, since she didn't even know where the boy was? Antonio had been born in the riad. During the hardships of childbirth, she had been accompanied by a single midwife who disappeared namelessly after giving birth. It suddenly hit her that she couldn't even prove she had a son. The joy that had seemed to be within her grasp suddenly evaded her. Her happiness slipped through her fingers again, and she glumly returned to Paris.

Yvonne felt sorry for her. Whenever she visited, she didn't dare to ask any questions. She extended invitations to numerous events, yet Sandra never felt like attending them. Yvonne could barely get a few words out of her friend, who was usually sitting sadly in the corner of her sofa.

"What are your plans for the holidays? Are you staying here, or will you visit your parents?" Yvonne asked her one day.

Sandra shrugged indifferently.

"If you're staying, you know we would love to have you over." Sandra's eyebrows fluttered, yet she didn't say a word. She hung her head since she wanted to be left alone.

Yvonne felt it better to say goodbye. She was worried about her girlfriend since she could never forget the fact that she was responsible for the loss of Sandra's child and the depression that followed.

Sandra gazed sullenly out the window. The final rays of the sun illuminated the rooftops of Montmartre, with the grey pallor of dusk creeping through the streets below. She turned away and donned her coat, shouldered her bag, and locked the door. Once she'd descended the narrow, steep flight of stairs, she opened the gate and walked out into the street. She pulled the shawl tighter around her neck.

The street lamps came to life, and lights appeared behind the windows. She didn't know where she was heading as she aimlessly wandered through the city before getting on a bus. The city was awash in the night time glow by the time she got off the bus in the city centre. She drifted through the crowd of people hurrying home after work. She stared at the glossy shop windows before heading over to a cinema to forget her sorrow. She watched a film, but she couldn't pay attention to the plot.

After she returned from her lengthy stroll, she removed her clothes in exhaustion and headed over to the bathroom. She filled the battered tub with warm water before lying down in it and supporting her head on the rim of the tub. She enjoyed the warmth of the water, yet her heart remained icy cold. She recalled the time when her face was ruined and she felt miserable, yet at least she had her son at her side. *I was born to be sad,* she sobbed out loud.

After a thorough cry, she got dressed and put on her warm flannel pyjamas. She brushed her teeth and combed her red hair, creamed her face, and finally went to bed. *Where should I look for my long, lost son?* she sighed in despair. She pulled the sheets over her head and sleeplessly tossed and turned.

The months went back monotonously. Almost every day after work, Sandra strolled down to the bus stop and let the crowds sweep her away. Since she didn't feel like going anywhere, she visited a bar instead. The place was filled with people, but no one paid attention to another beret-wearing woman who approached the bar and asked for a Campari. While waiting for her drink, she slipped her unruly locks of hair back under her hat.

It was too early for the bubbling Parisian social life to get started, but the mood of the people chatting around her was on the rise. Sandra listlessly sipped her drink while deciding to leave Paris for good and return to Marbella.

"Can I get you a drink?" asked a young man, hoping for a one-night stand. His hungry eyes feasted on the sight of the lonely woman. Sandra finished the rest of her drink and left without a word.

CHAPTER 43

The following day, she welcomed her colleagues as she arrived at the hotel and went up to the office to go over her evening duties before burying herself in paperwork.

"The boss wants to see you," said one of her female co-worker peeking into her office.

"Thanks, I'll be right with him," Sandra said, picking up a few letters and heading over to the manager's office.

"Good evening," she said as she entered the room.

"Have a seat," said the man, sizing her up and telling her that because of her diligent, reliable work, he was promoting her to a higher position.

"Thank you for your trust, but I can't accept the offer since I intend to leave Paris soon."

"But why?"

She faintly shrugged. "I'm going back to Marbella to be closer to my, parents."

"Fine," said the man, raising a bushy eyebrow. "If you must go, I will let go of you, albeit with a heavy heart."

"When am I free to go?"

The man flipped through the calendar on his desk.

"Is the first of December acceptable?" he asked, looking her in the eye.

"Yes. Thank you – you're not mad at me, are you?"

"You'll leave whether or not I'm mad at you, so it's better to part in friendship, right?" he said, standing up from his chair.

"Come, let's have a drink downstairs so I can get over the shock of your announcement," he suggested.

She silently followed her boss downstairs without a smile on her face. "The usual?" asked the mixer as he glanced as his female colleague.

"Whatever."

The pianist was playing a familiar tune. The good-looking mixer made a big show of shaking the cocktail flask while picking up a glass behind him which he filled with an emerald-green liquid.

"Enjoy," he said, sliding it over to her. "It's almost the same colour as your eyes," he added. Ever since she started working here, he couldn't keep his eyes off her.

Sandra faintly smiled at him and clinked glasses with his boss, discussing the matters of the hotel and the plans for the future. Her boss briefly glanced at his watch and quickly finished off the rest of his drink.

"I have to go now, you know, it's the family," he said, winking as he got up and left. Sandra stayed but took no notice of all the people surrounding her. A range of uncertain reasons clouded her mind, yet she couldn't come up with any decent explanation.

"Would you like another one?"

"No, thank you."

The good-looking mixer wanted to keep on chatting, but the bar was filled with customers.

She was about to get going when a company of people arrived who were clearly in a good mood. Not too far away from her, she heard a familiar voice ordering a round of drinks, expecting the mixer to get down to work.

Sandra didn't take particular notice of them. She'd had to deal with carefree people like them who were wealthy. However, the man noticed her perfect figure and her beautiful long red hair. As he stood next to her, he could only see her profile, but that was enough for him to get interested. And he wanted to have fun.

"I would like to buy you a drink," he said, lightly touching her arm.

Sandra slowly turned around.

"Are you talking to me?" she started, but she was left speechless as she found herself face to face with Nick. For a moment, they looked at each other in the eye.

"Yes, if you don't mind. It's my birthday today, so please don't turn me down," he explained, nodding towards his friends.

"Am I right?"

"Right!" cried the group resoundingly. Nick smiled broadly at her as if he is undressing her with his stare. The redhead blushed and fell silent, yet joy was twinkling in her eyes. She felt incredibly lucky. This was the moment she'd been waiting for. I have to make good use of this opportunity, she thought, doing her best to steady herself.

"Well?"

She smiled and shrugged, at ease.

"Sure, why not?"

The mixer eyed his beautiful, desirable colleague in surprise. She'd seemed unapproachable until now. The man grinned in satisfaction and introduced himself.

"Nick," he said confidently.

Sandra's hand slipped into his palm, causing her to shudder in surprise as she introduced herself. They clinked glasses.

"Happy birthday, Nick," she said kindly, barely sipping her drink. Just be careful and cautious, she warned herself. The man's elegant clothing, charming appearance, and fine speech were worlds apart from his behaviour at the riad.

"Are you staying here?" he started sneakily.

She shook her head.

"I work here," said Sandra calmly.

The man thoughtfully eyed her for a moment. "What's wrong?" she asked with concern, worried that perhaps he recognized her.

"Oh, it's nothing, it's just that your eyes seem so familiar as if we met somewhere before," he laughed temptingly.

"Perhaps in some long-forgotten story," replied Sandra. If you knew who I am, I'm sure you wouldn't be laughing, she thought, averting her gaze. She covered up her excitement and tossed her red hair back.

At that moment, Nick had something completely different in mind, so, he got right down to business.

"Do you know you're exactly my kind of woman?" he purred warmly.

"Your red hair and fine face look just perfect – I won't mention the rest since I don't want to scare you off."

She suddenly turned serious. She remembered everything – her son, the bitter memories of the riad – and the hatred kindled inside of her. She stared at him coldly, finally flashing him a smile at the very last moment.

"Oh, don't exaggerate," she said, leaning close to him as the anger raged inside of her. *She's just like all the other easy prey,* thought Nick, imagining the night ahead of him.

"I suggest," she said, slightly lifting her head, "that you do not think of me like the rest of your girlfriends," she whispered, walking out on him. *Oh, I'm such an idiot, I've gone too far*, she screamed inwardly. *I ruined everything with my cockiness!*

Nick, however, wasn't the type to let a woman lecture him and walk right over him. This momentary failure hurt his sensitive pride. Indeed, he was usually a popular person. He could seduce women with ease, and he let them seduce him as well. But he couldn't just let someone walk out on him like this in front of his friends, who were already giggling behind his back.

"It's my birthday," he cried, running after her.

By the time, she pressed the elevator's button, he had caught up to her. "Wait!"

A satisfied smile played around her lips.

"What do you want from me?" she demanded, turning on him.

"Well, let's say I'd like to have lunch or dinner with you tomorrow." He wanted to get in bed with her right away.

Sandra hesitated. She wasn't prepared to face such a landslide, yet she had to nonetheless. She gazed at him with innocent eyes.

"I don't even know you."

"It's alright, you'll have plenty of time to get to know me. Surely, you're not surprised by such an offer after living in Paris, right?"

She blushed.

"Unfortunately, I don't have time for things like this," she said, her eyes throwing sparks as she stepped into the elevator. Nick shook his head and furrowed his eyebrows as he stared quizzically at the elevator door closing in front of him.

The next morning, Sandra checked the man's room number. He would be here for five more days, she realized from the data on the computer. Much to her surprise, he had come alone, which wasn't typical of him. What should I do? She wondered uncertainly since she had missed out on this unexpected opportunity already. She noticed a bunch of red roses left next to the phone. She leaned over to smell them.

The receptionist approached her. "They're yours," she said.

"Mine? Well, that's odd."

"Well, they are," replied the receptionist with a laugh. "There's the card with the flowers."

It wasn't hard for Sandra to figure out who sent them. *Perhaps my time has come, after all*, she thought, envisioning her revenge. This time, she wouldn't make any mistakes. The girl standing next to her suddenly plucked the card out from amongst the flowers.

"Read it," she urged her playfully.

Sandra laughed. "So, you're getting involved in something that's none of your business," she said with a smile, reading the card.

Nick pulled all the stops for this enticing fling. He invited the redhead for every single lunch and dinner, yet made no progress at all. It seemed to him that she was toying with him. The last day of his stay, Sandra disappeared. He felt he had failed, and he was forced to leave without saying goodbye. Yet he couldn't stop thinking about her. *I have to have her*, he thought, longing to see her again.

He was surprised that he wanted to talk to her and be with her. He simply couldn't stop himself from thinking about her. He'd had no idea that love was capable of such things. This was an unknown sensation for him. *You idiot,* he cursed himself. *You're surrounded by women, so why make a fuss over this one?*

As the days and weeks went by, his feelings remained the same. He couldn't find peace, and due to his restlessness, he kept drumming with his fingers on his knee or the table or any other surface. Even his legs started shaking, so he crossed them to quit the habit. *They might think I lost my mind,* he scolded himself.

His business dealings were faltering, and thus he had to hastily travel to Hong Kong. It was the perfect place to satisfy his emotionless desires. However, once his craving was settled, he longed for the redhead even more. He tried calling her several times but never managed to get a hold of her. Due to his work, it was four weeks before he could return to Paris. However, Sandra was no longer working at the hotel. After he asked around at the bar, the mixer gave him a hint. He mentioned that she probably went to Marbella.

I have to find her, he thought, emotionally charged.

He was angry at himself and everyone else for letting the redhead go. She still attracted him like a magnet. Thus, he soon returned to his villa in Marbella.

CHAPTER 44

After almost ten years in Paris, Sandra started working at the hotel in Marbella in February. She was pleased with her new job since she loved the city and this way she was closer to her parents. She spent the holidays with them and felt full of energy as she looked forward to the new year.

She dearly missed Yvonne, so they kept chatting over Skype at length. She continued to live a lonely life, although she often thought of Nick. It was a shame she had ruined everything. Because of her foolishness, she wouldn't be getting closer to her child. Her plan hadn't worked. Thinking back, she couldn't deny that the man's charming looks affected her, oddly mixed with her hatred of him.

It seems she couldn't handle men. She couldn't schmooze, charm, lie or allure them. Perhaps that's why she was always alone. Still, she longed for love. She thought of Pedro; she loved him dearly, but unfortunately, she'd lost him for good.

Where is my man, when will I meet him? She wondered as she tossed and turned in her bed. However, coincidences do happen, yielding a series of surprises, joy, and sorrow.

Another year went by. As the summer rolled in, the heat increased. The real dog days set in. She finally made it down to the beach by the late afternoon hours. She closed her eyes under the parasol and enjoyed the bliss of recreation. She occasionally watched the teeming masses on the shore or went into the water to avoid the heat. Her soles were burnt by the hot sands, urging her to pick up her pace.

She swam into the deeper waters before heading out with even strokes. When a wave approached, she enjoyed letting it rock her closer to the shore. The tides weren't as strong here as in the Atlantic Ocean. Nevertheless, she kept an eye open, just in case. One wave stronger than the others could treacherously pull anything under. She suddenly remembered the winter crossing from all those years ago, when a numbingly cold wave knocked her over and pulled her down.

The thought made her quicken her pace to get out of the water. She felt the sand under her feet and quickly moved to the beach. She was on the edge of the water when she was knocked over by the blast wave. She stood up, sneezing and fuming and covered with sand, and so she went back into the water. She was still clumsy, but the water was divine.

A yacht was bobbing up and down on top of the churning waves, anchored near the shore. A suntanned man dove into the water and started swimming towards the shore. He had only returned to Marbella a few days ago, after his regular month-long vacation with his son, whom he left in London to continue his studies. Once he'd finished his studies, he would bring the boy here. That is if he wanted to come. He wouldn't force anything.

For years, Nick had silently accepted the fact that he had a son, but he couldn't provide the boy with a home. He had sent him to expensive boarding schools to comfort himself and lull his conscience. Many years ago, he had carelessly separated the child from his mother in anger, yet he'd never really accepted his fatherhood.

Back on the beach, Sandra sat back down under her parasol. She bent her head to the side, running her fingers through the wet sand. The man coming ashore came her way with great strides. Suddenly, they noticed each other.

"I can't believe how incredibly lucky I am!" exclaimed the man in joy. Sandra was slightly startled and surprised to see him.

"It's a small world," she said, sharing a laugh with the man. The water trickled off of Nick's suntanned lower body, yet he still hopped down next to Sandra. He leaned in close, nearly pressing his lips to her face.

"How about dinner?"

"Not so fast," replied Sandra teasingly.

"Oh, don't protest. We have to celebrate this odd coincidence."

"Fine, OK," she said, giving in with a laugh. She couldn't deny that she was pleased to see him. At that moment, the past and even her sense of revenge seemed like distant memories.

From that day on, they met frequently. The man wanted to know everything about her. Sandra, however, was always cautious and careful with what she said. She craftily asked Nick if he had a family, but he shook his head in denial. Her endless stream of questions often piled up inside of her – where is Antonio, what is he studying, how much has he grown – yet she knew, full well that she might never be able to ask him these questions. She had to wait for him to tell her himself about the boy, she thought hopefully.

At night, she tossed and turned restlessly, since she couldn't come up with an idea. She didn't trust the man and she was afraid of him, yet she still seemed to grow fond of him. Her sixth sense often warned her that she'd end up back in the riad when he got bored with her. She didn't want to end up like those other girls. At the same time, however, when she was with him, she almost forgot her concerns, since she constantly felt his attentiveness and kindness.

Nevertheless, she stayed alert, since she had to do everything she could for the sake of Antonio. Her positive and negative thoughts gave her mood swings. Their glances often met, and one night the unavoidable moment happened. Their long pent-up emotions were unleashed. Nick couldn't get enough of her. You must be crazy, he kept telling himself, but he didn't mind since he had fallen deeply in love with Sandra.

CHAPTER 45

After a romantic dinner, Nick presented her with a tiny box. He regarded Sandra closely and slowly slipped the box over to her across the table.

"Open it."

Sandra obeyed him with sparkling eyes and cried out in surprise. "It's beautiful," she whispered, blushing, yet she didn't touch the ring. The man took the ring out of the box and slipped it on Sandra's finger. Perhaps for the first time in his life, he blushed like a little boy.

"Please, be my wife," he said awkwardly.

She bowed her head, overcome with emotion, but didn't dare answer him.

"Do you remember the first time we met, I said you were my type?"

"Yes, I do."

"I was telling the truth."

Sandra was overjoyed, yet also apprehensive of this sudden turn of events.

"Well?" prompted the man.

She avoided the question and asked for some time so they

could get to know each other. "I can wait, but I must remind you that I'm not the patient type."

She wondered for days what would be the best solution. If she said no, she would lose her son for good; if she agreed to get married, she might be able to get closer to him or at least find out what had happened to him and where he was. She knew very well that she would be involved in a dangerous game since she mustn't fool around with Nick.

Yet if she played her cards right, her secret would never be revealed. She didn't have to worry about her parents. Yvonne was the only other person who knew something about her past, and she perfectly trusted her friend.

Sandra wished she could tell everything to Nick, but after all the years she'd spent at the riad, she knew what kind of person he was. She decided to cover up her secrets and mask them in silence. However, she wasn't indifferent towards the man either. *So, you fell for him, huh?* she wondered, and that was a question she didn't dare to answer. He did so much harm to her, yet she thought that perhaps he had changed after all these years.

They got married two months later. They went to Kenya for a honeymoon, where the endless savannah sprawled out in front of them with the promise of a wealth of rich experiences. They spotted the Kilimanjaro through the vibrating heat in the air. It majestically towered in front of them, clouds basked in silvery light circling its flat peak like a ring.

The Land Rover jolted and bounced underneath them as they raced across the Savannah. The driver kept looking back at them through the rear-view mirror, especially when she cried out in fear from time to time. At such times, the black man flashed a row of impeccable white teeth, steering the car ever closer to the wild animals they spotted. During their thrilling safari adventure, they spotted the great beasts of Africa and were captivated by the rapture of the moment and the proximity to unspoiled nature. Sandra was amazed by their experiences and the beauty of the unknown continent. She was simply captivated by Africa, yet as a tourist, she never encountered the continent's dark side.

CHAPTER 46

Sandra's life changed completely. After she and Nick returned from their honeymoon, she moved to his villa in the Las Chapas district of Marbella, a hundred metres from the sea. He didn't want her to work, saying that he had enough money to support her.

Spring was fast approaching, and she often went down to the sandy beaches. She loved the sea and frequently went for long walks or cycling. When Nick was home, he would join her. As they strolled along, they discussed many things, including their life and their future. Nick explained that he dealt with the purchase and sale of antiquities and rugs, so he had to travel a lot.

It seemed like he took their marriage seriously – and indeed, he did. He hurried back home as soon as he could to devote all his attention to his new wife. He loved spending time with her. He furtively eyed her long red hair and immaculate figure at length, as well as her freckles and gestures. He had indeed been with many women in his life, but none of them got as close to him as this little redhead, his angel, for whom he wanted to change his ways. He dumped his former girlfriends and ended all of his affairs.

Nick quickly realized that his wife was a trustworthy person. Her cold, reserved personality and elegant looks masked the fire inside of her that showed during their intercourse, and so her proximity made him want to win her over again and again. Still, as time went by, Nick had the feeling that there were secrets between the two of them. He didn't press the matter and never asked any questions since he had just as many things to hide which he never shared with anyone.

Sandra didn't learn much as time went by. Occasionally, she cautiously questioned her husband about his past, his possible relatives, and any possible children. At times like this, the man's face hardened. He briefly replied and shook his head, unable and unwilling to say anything. Once, Nick invited one of his friends over – a man called David who scrutinized Nick's new wife. He often gazed at the noticeably beautiful red-haired woman who kindly chatted with his wife.

Naturally, Sandra quickly noticed the attention she was getting from him. Accordingly, she often turned her back to him and assured herself that there was no way he could recognize her. She often felt awkward in situations like this, since somewhere in the shadows, Vicky lurked with her dark, faceless past. Her secret was a heavy burden which she was forced to bear silently. At night, she often cried for her long-lost son. Sometimes she was on the verge of admitting the truth to Nick, yet she always backed down at the very last moment. She couldn't find peace in the summer either when the man regularly disappeared for a month. At least she could visit her parents at this time.

Lately, it seemed to Sandra that Nick had changed. He was often away on business. He had been away for a long time, she thought to herself suspiciously.

The phone rang in the afternoon.

"I'll be home tomorrow around six," Nick told her.

"I invited some guests over in the evening, so take care of things. Make sure we have some champagne in the fridge."

"Where are you? I've been waiting for you for over a month. You could've at least called."

"I'll be home tomorrow," he noted briefly.

"Why didn't you say something earlier, and what kind of guests should I expect?"

"I didn't have time. David and his wife are coming over," he stated before the line went dead.

"I don't have much time, but I'll sort it out," she noted, accepting the situation. She didn't like surprises. She simply couldn't understand Nick's behaviour. Fine, she wouldn't get in his way, if this made him happy. She could put up with everything except lies.

She went shopping in the morning before swimming her regular fifty laps in the pool. She had a bite to eat and a good cup of coffee. Then she busied herself with preparing everything for the evening party, except the barbecue and salad, which she wanted to make fresh. She put the marinated meat in the fridge and wiped down the kitchen counter. She looked around the kitchen one more time and thought she would get herself in order by the time Nick arrived.

She had a comfortable bath and washed and dried her hair. Once she was done putting on a faint layer of makeup, she looked into the mirror with satisfaction. Her green eyes were just as sparkling as always, yet she still sensed some sort of tension.

Suddenly, the front door opened, making her shudder. Nick peeked inside the house. For a moment, he gazed at his wife appreciatively.

"I came early. How much more time do you need?"

"I'd like to get dressed if you don't mind."

"But I do mind," he said, spanking her bottom.

"It will only take a few minutes."

"Hurry up, because we already have a guest waiting for us

down on the patio."

"Who is it?"

"You'll see. It's a surprise," he said, mysteriously winking and pulling the door shut. Sandra was pattering around in the wardrobe. Who did he bring with him? she wondered as she donned a floral dress.

An unknown young man was waiting out on the patio. Nick heard his wife's footsteps approaching.

"Come on, I want to meet someone," he told her eagerly.

"The surprise?"

"You could put it that way."

"What does that mean?" asked Sandra quietly.

"You'll see, he's sitting out there on the patio."

"Who?"

"Patience," laughed Nick cheerfully. I should have done it sooner, he thought.

The young man was leaning back in one of the reed armchairs, thoughtfully gazing out at sea, but once he heard the approaching footsteps, he quickly stood up. He took a few steps in their direction. He smiled faintly and held his hand out to the woman. "Antonio."

Sandra staggered. The guest pulled his hand back at once.

"Are you okay?" asked Nick.

"I'm fine, I just slipped," she said, practically stammering. Her face grew pale, and her heartbeat in her throat. Her mouth was shut, yet she was rapidly breathing through her nose. She bowed her head and let her hair fall, over her face. This way, she hoped, they wouldn't notice her reaction.

Nick didn't notice anything since he winked at Antonio.

"My son," he said, resting his hand on Antonio's shoulder. "And she's my wife, but I'm sure you recognize her from the photo I showed you earlier."

"Yes, I remember. I'm sorry you didn't invite me over earlier."

"Slow down," grinned Nick.

She was so shocked she still couldn't say a word. Her throat constricted from her suppressed emotions. Her tears were about to burst forth, but her joy helped her hold them back. She swallowed hard as she glanced up at the sky. *God, thank you for finally having mercy on me,* she thought.

"Pleased to meet you," she said with some delay, hugging Antonio. *What happened to my little boy?* she wondered suppressing a sigh. He is practically a young man now.

Nick disappeared in the kitchen and returned a few minutes later with glasses and a bottle of champagne. He opened the bottle with a bang and quickly filled the glasses with the bubbly liquid.

"The family is now complete," he said with a peculiar feeling. "To the three of us." Antonio lifted his glass for a toast. Nick quickly refilled the glasses.

"Don't forget, we're on a first-name basis, OK?" he added cheerfully.

"OK. Hi, Mom," replied the boy kindly, planting a kiss on her face. Nick picked up the empty bottle. "I'll get another one."

"There's no rush," said Sandra.

"You still have the barbecue to finish off."

"Oh, we'll do that later," Nick noted happily, hopping down into the armchair. He fumbled with the cork, which shot out of the bottle with another loud bang.

Antonio furtively glanced at his new mother, loving her looks and appearance. It was great to look her in the eye since he felt sympathy and even love emanating from her eyes. Strangely enough, he was attracted to her at once. *You're imagining things since that's impossible,* he told himself, *but her eyes somehow reminded him of his real mother.*

Sandra was thrilled, since the dream she had given up on years ago, had now suddenly been realized. Although she had missed out on many years of her son's life which could never be replaced, he had now resurfaced in his life. She pinched her arm and realized that it was true, she wasn't dreaming.

"Why did you keep it a secret?" she asked Nick reproachfully. Suddenly she felt like sinking all ten nails into his face.

"I didn't want any rivals around," he laughed evasively. "It's a long story." Antonio eyed his father with grim seriousness. Nick suddenly glanced at his watch and got up from the armchair.

"I'll go get the fire started," he said. "David and his company will be here any minute now. You can get to know each other in the meantime." They silently, searchingly eyed each other until finally, the young man broke the silence.

"I'm pleased to finally meet you."
"Me too."
Sandra wanted to hold him tight as she had in the past, but she couldn't. She had to keep her secret, perhaps for a long time, perhaps forever. However, the heavy load she had been carrying until now suddenly felt much lighter.
"So, tell me about yourself," she asked.
"What would you like to know?"
"Everything."
"I've been studying in London since I was a little boy, but because of Dad's business, I'm going to attend university in New York. I'm going to study medicine, and I want to be a dermatologist. I'm interested in tropical diseases as well, so I'm keeping my eyes on you," he said with a laugh.
"Why? Is something wrong with my skin or my face?"
"Of course, not, I was just kidding!"
Sandra felt a twinge in her heart since poor Pedro had been a doctor too. During their conversation, she carefully inspected Antonio to see who he resembled. His nose, his build, and his hands reminded her of Pedro. Even after all these years, she could still see her beloved in him.
"I'm sorry we didn't meet sooner."
"Trust me, I feel the same way," said Sandra, unable to take her eyes off him. "Where is your mother, does she live with you?"
"She died, unfortunately," he replied sadly. He couldn't carry on, since Nick returned and sat down next to them.
"You remembered to marinate the meat, right?" he asked, interrupting their discussion.

"Yes, it's in the fridge."

"Our friends are late," he added, glancing at his watch and reaching for the bottle to fill their glasses with the leftovers.

"*Salud,*" he said with ease.

CHAPTER 47

The doorbell rang.

"I'll get it," said Antonio, readily standing up, yet his father rushed after him as well. The young man shook hands with David. In the meantime, Nick welcomed Carmen, leaning close and whispering something in her ear, making her laugh out loud.

"Long time, no see," Nick said, turning to face David.

"That's not my fault. I tried getting through to you about a month ago, but your mobile was dead."

"I had some travelling to do. Sorry."

"Don't worry about it," David said, waving the matter off and handing Nick a bottle of wine. Nick checked the label. "Sounds good, but I'm not familiar with it. Well, thanks, we'll have to taste it later on."

"It's some great Spanish wine," David explained before welcoming their hostess. "What a lovely evening."

"Indeed," replied Sandra coldly. She turned to Carmen, who seemed to follow Nick around. "Glad to see you again," she noted, leaning close to the woman and lightly touching her face.

"Oh, me too. I brought this for you," Carmen said, handing Sandra a box of chocolates.

"Thank you, that's very kind of you."

"Okay, enough of the formalities," interrupted Nick.

"Let me introduce you to my son," said Nick, pushing Antonio ahead of him.

"Ooooh … where did you find this strapping young fellow, if you don't mind me asking?" asked Carmen, touching upon a delicate subject. Nick coughed but didn't say anything in reply. Sandra flashed him an angry look.

"I didn't know you had a son," said David in surprise.

"Only a handful of people knew about him. Come on, have a seat," he suggested, fending off the awkward subject.

"What a good-looking young man. You should be proud of him instead of hiding him from us."

"He's been studying in London, and we've been travelling for a month at a time during his holidays. That's why you couldn't get through to me. This was more important for him. Right, son?" he explained, glancing at his wife to signify the reason for his absence.

"True," nodded Antonio. "I've seen a lot of beautiful places and learned a lot during our travels. I'm glad you gave me a chance to get acquainted with the culture, art, and traditions of other people, even if for a short time."

"That's true," noted David. "Seeing the world, travelling, and cramming as many experiences as you can into your short life can expand your horizons, and even change you in the process. It makes you wiser, more considerate, and more confident."

"At least you'll have something to remember when you'll be old farts," interrupted Carmen, laughing annoyingly. She failed to notice that no one appreciated her inappropriate joke.

Nick lifted his glass to the others while pushing his chair back to stand up and check on the fire.

"Please, bring the meat," he cried to his wife.

Sandra went over to the kitchen and fetched the tray from the fridge. She looked out through the window for a moment. She was satisfied and felt peace in her heart – her son was here she'd gotten him back. Nothing bad could happen to him anymore.

"Vicky?" said David, standing in the doorway. She shuddered and closed her eyes for a moment.

"What?" she said, turning to face him.

"Oh, it's nothing, it just slipped out of my mouth. You know, from this angle, you look just like someone I knew in the past. Even your hair is red."

"A lot of people have red hair," she noted dismissively.

"But not this kind. You know, she's still a cherished memory for me."

"Why should I know about that?"

David shrugged. "I don't know. I'm sorry."

"I guess she must have been close to you," she noted in a gentler tone.

He waved it off. "It was a long time ago."

"What happened to her?"

"It's a mystery. She suddenly disappeared."

"Did you go looking for her?"

"Yes, I tried for a long time, but I simply couldn't find her."

"I'm sorry."

Nick showed up in the doorway.

"So, where's the meat?" he asked a bit crudely.

"It's coming. Make sure you don't burn it, okay?" she warned him. "The last time we did this, it was delicious," she added, handing him the tray.

Nick grinned. "I just opened your bottle of wine," he said to David, "so, we could get the dinner started." The two men headed out to the patio together to put the meat on the grill. She fixed the salad. She felt awkward; David had spoiled her joy. He kept looking at her the last time he was here, she recalled. She was a bit alarmed by his confession.

Ah, there's nothing to worry about, she assured herself. She carried the salad and the side dishes out onto the patio before sitting down next to her son and striking up a conversation with him.

The rest of the night went by uneventfully. The dinner was delicious, the candles burned down low, and the guests left. Antonio sleepily headed off to his room. Nick wrapped his arm around his wife in bed, but she drew away from him.

"What's wrong?" he asked.

"Why did you hide Antonio from me? I'm sure you remember how many times, I asked you whether you had any relatives, and you never admitted to it."

"He was studying. I thought it better if I didn't force the matter. He's here now. So, what do you think of him?" he asked to avoid the incoming storm.

"He's a very kind young man," Sandra said emotionally.

"Are you just saying that to be polite, or can I hope that you'll like him?"

Sandra replied cautiously, "I guess it won't be hard for me to like him."

Nick fell silent. *Could it be that she doesn't like him?* He wondered. He would have to wait and see. Antonio would be spending a month with them.

"What happened to his mother?" she asked indifferently while gripping her pillow. Nick held a lengthy pause.

"It happened a long time ago," he said slowly. "Antonio was still a little boy when his mother died."

"So, I'm your third wife then?"

"Wrong. You're my second wife."

"But then …" she noted without finishing her thought. She fell silent since she knew the story well.

"I have an old house in Marrakech," explained Nick suddenly. "It's in pretty bad shape. I should get it renovated. If you're interested, I'll take you there once they're done renewing the place. Well, the whole thing started there. I spent some time with a girl. I don't remember her, she only slept with me once. The next day, she had an accident and her face was damaged. After her recovery, I took her in, since I got her pregnant. She wore a black djellaba – you know, one of those long, flowing robes, with her face covered up, while living in the house like a shadow. She did her work like all the other Arab women and raised her son. Finally, she died. End of story. It happened a long time ago, so let's just forget about it," he begged before planting a kiss on his wife's forehead.

"Goodnight, darling," he muttered before turning in, yet he couldn't fall asleep.

He stared into the darkness with his eyes wide open. He tried recalling the fling and the face of the girl, yet he simply couldn't remember her after all these years. He'd slept with many girls before and after her. They'd dragged her onto his yacht because of a mistake one of their new members made. They mistakenly assumed that Lucy told something to an unknown girl. Lucy was already in Marrakech at the time, so this way at least she would have some company, he'd thought at the time, putting off his decision. He toyed with her for an hour.

He was out having fun somewhere the next night when the girls disappeared. Although his men caught Lucy, the other girl made the mistake of returning with Pedro. The two idiotic goons thought after the relationship soured that the men from Casablanca had returned. That's why they fired at them.

The girl stayed at the riad, but Pedro somehow managed to slip through their hands, even though the guards told him that they wounded him as well. He made them take the girl to the hospital at once. In those days, things weren't going as smoothly as they were now, and he quickly left with Lucy because of the gunshots.

Antonio must have been around four years old when the French women escaped with his mother. Thanks to his connections, he quickly found out where they were hiding. In his momentary rage, he got one of his men to take care of the matter, and he brought the child back and told him that the mother had most probably died.

Sandra knew that Nick was still awake, yet she decided not to ask him any more questions. The memories and her previous life came back to her, as they had so many times before. The last time she had seen him, Antonio was still a little boy, but now she had him back. Several times she tried to find out where is her son. But now, she was thrilled and overjoyed. For perhaps the first time in ages, she slept in peace.

CHAPTER 48

Nick went away. This pleased Sandra since she could devote all her time to Antonio. They chatted at length in the house, on the patio, in the swimming pool, or down on the beach. They walked for hours on the sandy beach. They were never bored, and they always found something they were both interested in.

"I want to look around Marbella a bit and see all the sights," said Antonio. "There's going to be a concert," he explained one day. "Fine, go ahead, have fun, and meet some people," she told him encouragingly. On his way, Antonio's thoughts kept straying back to his stepmother. He was instantly attracted to her. He'd always imagined his mother to be like her, even though she'd been absent from his life for all these years.

That evening, Sandra was sitting outside on the patio by herself. She started reading a book, but after a few pages, she shifted her focus to the garden and the flowers instead. Tomorrow, I'll do some gardening, she decided.

Suddenly, the doorbell rang.

"I'm coming," she cried out loud, picking up the keys on her way.

"Good evening," said an unknown man before she could open the gate.

"Can I help you?" she asked openly.

"I'm Robert Grey," said the stranger, holding out his hand in welcome. "Detective."

"Detective?" she asked in surprise. He smiled when he saw the surprised look on her face. "I'm looking for Nick Winkler," he told her.

"I'm afraid my husband isn't home. He left."

"Where to? And when is he coming back?"

"He didn't tell me." The man eyed her incredulously.

"Did something happen? Is this about a speeding ticket or an accident?" she asked. It never occurred to her that it might be something more serious."

"Oh, no, it's nothing. When did he leave?"

"A week ago. But I'm expecting him to return any day now." The man's engaging expression didn't reveal a thing.

"Sorry for intruding. I'll stop by some other time. I'd appreciate it if you'd give me your number."

"Is the home number alright?"

"Sure," said the man, pulling out a notepad and jotting it down. "Thank you. Have a nice evening," he said politely and then slowly walked away. Sandra quizzically watched him walk off before returning to the patio. In the meantime, the sun had set, and the shadows were growing longer. It was a warm summer evening. The sea behind the pool in the distance had changed to a dark, murky colour.

She silently slipped into the water and swam for a long time. Later on, she did some chores around the house. As always, she recalled her past and her ravaged face, which she still couldn't completely get over. It was true that since she'd married Nick, she had nothing to worry about. However, lately, he had been away more frequently. She usually didn't ask him where he was going and what he was up to. Perhaps that was why things went so smooth. She was

thrilled that her son was finally by her side. That's all she had wanted for a very long time.

Later that night, the phone rang. *Maybe it's Antonio,* she
thought as she picked up the receiver.

"Hello?" she asked, yet there was only silence on the other
end. "Hello, hello?" she repeated, yet the line was disconnected. She
glanced at her watch – it was half past midnight. Who was it and
why didn't he say something? She wondered for a while, before
sleepily closing her eyes. She fell asleep, breathing evenly as her
soul wandered off to some distant region.

She stirred from a bad dream. She was standing on top of a
cliff with the sea churning below and the sky turned to black in the
distance. She saw herself in old age. She wore a black, hooded robe
which the wind nipped at. She eyed the sea as if she were waiting for
someone to appear, before getting cold and turning around, slowly
heading over to a nearby house, her back bent over in old age. It was
her home. She grasped a gnarly old staff in her left hand which she
used to support herself.

The wind grew stronger, so she had to stop from time to
time. Her eyes were blurry from tears, yet she managed to push
through. Still, she couldn't get closer to the house.

Awoken from the dream, she turned the lamp on. The antique grandfather clock struck two o'clock. She produced a tissue
from her drawer and wiped her eyes and blew her nose before turning off the lamp. She stared into the darkness with her eyes wide
open.

Where was Nick and why didn't he come home? She wondered. She had grown accustomed to his presence, and she had
become somewhat attached to him. She managed to find it in her
heart to forgive him since he raised her son, provided for Antonio's
schooling, and took care of the boy in his fashion, even though she
was left out of this. Had they stayed in Marrakech, Antonio would
have never become a doctor. Both of them paid a great price for this.

He surely missed the love of his mother and the warmth of a family home, she thought emotionally.

Sandra knew that fate could be unpredictable, since love, pain, change and odd coincidences can bring drastic changes in one's life.

CHAPTER 49

They had breakfast on the patio.

"So, was it a good concert?" she asked, breaking the silence.

"It was fine."

"You seem sleepy."

"Yeah, a bit," he quipped. He was sleepy since he had been walking until late at night. He spread a thin layer of butter on a slice of toast and put a piece of ham on his plate, which he quickly gobbled up. He started working on his second slice of ham, yet he still didn't say a word. He picked up a spoon to stir his coffee.

His mother furtively eyed him.

"Will you have lunch with me?" she asked the sullen young man.

"Sure."

"Are you mad at me?"

"Of course not. What makes you think so?" he asked with surprise, looking her in the eye.

"You seem troubled and pretty quiet."

Antonio faintly smiled before awkwardly glancing at her and falling silent. Once they were done with breakfast, Sandra reached across the table and squeezed his hand.

"You know, your eyes are full of unspoken questions. Or am I mistaken?" she asked, standing up without waiting for an answer.

"Please, don't leave."

Sandra sat back down and tensely waited. Antonio bowed his head and waited for a moment before finally getting to the point.

"No, you're not mistaken," he said, shaking his head.

"Then get to it. Tell me what's on your mind."

"Ever since we first met," he began slowly, "you seemed familiar to me and a bit mysterious."

"Me?" she exclaimed in alarm.

"Yes, you." Antonio responded.

She anxiously picked up her cup and took a sip, but she didn't dare look him in the eye.

"It's true that we only met two weeks ago, but I still have a feeling that I've known you for a long time." Sandra sighed deeply.

My dear son, if you only knew that I've known you since the day you were born, both of us would be a lot happier, she thought.

"Can I ask you something?" asked Antonio, leaning forward.

"Sure, anything."

"The first time I saw you, you reminded me of someone."

"Who?" she asked, growing pale.

"My mother." He answered, unflinching.

"Me?" she asked, her heart pounding in her chest.

"Yes, you. Ever since I got here, I could hardly get any sleep because of this. Look, I know it's nonsense since I can faintly remember that my mother's face was always covered up. I think that she was injured somewhere and somehow, but we were still very close – I loved her dearly. Even your voice is like hers, but your eyes – I swear to God, they're just like hers."

Sandra felt so confused that she knocked her cup over. She opened her mouth to tell him the truth, but she couldn't speak since an inner voice stopped her from doing so. She picked her napkin with trembling hands to soak up the coffee she spilt. She knew she couldn't say anything since she was afraid of Nick's revenge. Even her son might call her to account for all the years she didn't say a thing.

Antonio continued.

"Perhaps you heard that I grew up in Marrakech for a while. I faintly remember anxiously huddling in a boat with my mother, soaked by a wave as we trembled in the cold." He closed his eyes for a moment.

"You won't believe me, but I can still feel the way she held me tight to protect me from any harm." He brushed his forehead with his right hand as his expression turned grim from the old memories. "Only now can I understand what I must have meant to her."

He fell silent for a while and flashed a faint smile. "I still remember the spanking that I got at the riad sometimes."

"You must have been a darling little boy," she whispered emotionally. Antonio failed to notice her reaction and kept on reminiscing about his memories.

"I'm sure Dad told you that I threw a lot of tantrums and kept bawling since I always wanted to be with my mother. That's probably why I was spanked."

"I'm sure she was very tired," she said protectively with a serious look in her eye.

"Yes. I think she must have been working a lot."

"You know, little kids don't understand that their mother has a thousand things to do during the day. I guess when she finished her job, she was always with you."

"That's true."

"And where does she live now?" she asked accidentally. "Oh, I'm sorry, you already told me."

"Yes, she died," he noted with a mysterious look in his eyes.

"What happened to her?" she asked.

"All I know is that she was lying motionless in a bed next to me. Then someone picked me up and whispered that he was taking me to my father." He fell silent, wiping his eyes with the back of his hand.

"I'm sorry," noted Sandra, feeling crushed, squeezing her

son's hand.

"It's okay. This happened many years ago. The bad memories become fainter, but I'll never forget her." A silence set in for a moment. After a while, he looked up at his stepmother. "There's something else I have to tell you."

"I'm listening."

"Although your face is beautiful and you have nothing to hide, your eyes have reminded me of my mother since we first met. She was the only one who could look at me with such love a long, long time ago."

Her throat went dry, and she could barely hold back her tears. She encouragingly squeezed Antonio's hand again.

"I promise you'll never be disappointed again. I'll do everything I can to have a good relationship and to somehow make up for your mother's loss," she assured him, stirring the liquid in her cup with a spoon to cover up her emotions.

This made both of them smile.

"Thank you," said Antonio, missing the love of a mother, which he'd had to go without for so long. "You know, I swear that your hand is just like hers too. Of course, I think she never used nail polish, and I surely can't think that these are her hands," he said, squeezing her hand.

"Still, if it would be true, I'd be the happiest person in the world."

"Don't worry, since I am your new mother now – that is if you accept me," she sniffled.

"I accepted you at once."

"I hope we'll remain friends for a long time, and that you'll keep on sharing your thoughts with me. Don't forget, whatever happens, you can always count on me."

She stood up and kissed the top of his head before hurrying up to her room. She had to somehow put an end to this teary conversation, since her heart ached and throbbed behind her ribs.

As much as she wanted to tell her son that she was his mother, she knew she had to keep her secret. She rushed up to her bathroom, grabbed her towel, and buried her face in it to unleash the emotions pent up inside of her.

Later on, she went down for a swim, since that always managed to wash her bad thoughts away. She was convinced that water had healing powers. Once she got out of the pool, she noticed that her son was gone. He'd left a note on the table.

Sorry, I had to go. I won't be back for lunch.

CHAPTER 50

Antonio disappeared with increasing frequency, and thus their intimate conversations grew few and far between. Perhaps he's angry at me for some reason, she thought anxiously. She was also worried about Nick who still didn't return. Where was he for so long? she wondered with concern. The phone rang, and Sandra quickly answered it.

"Hello?"

"It's David."

"Yes?"

"I don't mean to be pushy, but I'd like to ask you a question."

"Go ahead."

"Do you have any sisters or twins?"

"Oh, please, don't get started again. I don't have any siblings, and please stop asking me questions," she said, hanging up. She was convinced by now that David had a hunch, or perhaps he recognized her. She decided to avoid him in the future.

Nick finally arrived at noon. A bit later, Antonio returned as well, thus, preventing Sandra and Nick from having the fight that was brewing between them.

Sandra glanced at her son and noticed an odd smile playing on his lips. Something must have happened to him.

"May I take you out for dinner tonight?" Nick asked his wife, in order to make up to his family after his lengthy absence.

"Whatever you want," agreed Sandra sullenly. "But you're only getting a salad for lunch then," she noted, pausing and adding, "...with some smoked salmon."

"Okay, sounds good to me," said Nick with a faint smile, turning to Antonio. "You haven't said anything yet."

"Lunch sounds great as well as dinner, but wait a few minutes" he noted, blushing all over before running out to the patio, where he chatted on his phone at length. Nick rubbed his chin while narrowing his eyes as he scrutinized Sandra.

Antonio returned with a smile on his face.

"Dinner is good if I can bring someone with me."

"Oh, what a surprise. Can I ask who that certain someone is?" asked Nick meaningfully.

"Don't be rude," interrupted Sandra.

"It's no secret," said Antonio, shaking his head. "I don't know much about her, since we only met a week ago."

"Really?"

"Come on, Dad! Don't forget, I'm leaving soon. It's probably only going to be a summer friendship."

"Whatever. Just be here at nine. Oh, not here, but at the restaurant," he added, giving him the directions to the place before striding out to the patio with a can of beer in his hand.

Antonio followed his father, hopping down on the nearest armchair and striking up a conversation with him. Sandra watched them from the living room for a while. She lifted one of her hands to her face in concern. She was always hesitant about whether Pedro or Nick was the real father. But now as she watched her son bow his head, his resemblance to Pedro was uncanny.

At that moment, she felt she might never be able to rid herself of her secret. The fear of Nick figuring this outweighed down on her heart. As they finished their lunch, Antonio helped clear off the table. He planted a kiss on his stepmother's face and said goodbye to his father.

"See you tonight, then," he said in a level-headed manner before leaving in a hurry.

They rested during the siesta. Nick hugged his wife. She looked at him in the eye before asking, "Why do you always leave me?"

"I have to, that's just the way my work is."

For the first time, he seemed concerned. "I'm sorry," he whispered, burying his face in Sandra's fragrant hair.

Late that afternoon, he went for a swim in the pool. As he saw his wife stepping out of the house, he motioned for her to come over.

"Come on, the water is fantastic."

"I'm coming," she called out, lifting her arms busying herself with her hair before taking a shower at the end of the patio. She turned around under the running water for a while before slipping into the pool, which was lukewarm from the lasting heatwave. Nick was already sitting on the steps. He lazily leaned up against the edge, occasionally glancing at her. Sandra swam up to him.

"What would you say if I wanted to start some kind of business?"

He glanced at her in surprise before silently submerging and swimming over to the other side of the pool under the water and calling back to her from there, "Why, are you bored?"

"Not really, but I want to spend my time in a useful manner."

"Have you got any ideas?"

"Maybe I do."

"And what would those be?"

"For example, I could continue to work at a good hotel, or maybe I could start up a real estate agency." She furtively glanced at her husband, scrutinizing his gaze.

"You know, I have plenty of time on my hands," she added. "Especially when you're not around, and that happens often lately, right?" She glanced at him reproachfully.

Nick wasn't thrilled by the idea, yet he didn't want to put up a fight. He knew she was right since he had to go away often because of his far-reaching dark dealings and thus didn't spend much time with her.

Actually, I approve of her idea, he thought to himself.

"Well, if you feel it suits you, I'll gladly help you out," he said in consent.

"Oh, I didn't mean it that way. You know I have my own money to get me started."

Nick shook his head. "You're my wife. You can spend as much money as you want," he said, thinking of the Swiss bank account where his funds were growing.

"Thank you, then we've agreed," said Sandra joyfully. She never discussed financial matters with Nick, and thus she had no idea how much money he had. He always took care of banking matters. When they got married, he gave her a credit card and encouraged her to spend as much as she liked. This had always been the case since she was his wife.

"Naturally," he replied. "If you're still interested in hotel work, David can surely help you out."

"I'm not sure. Perhaps. I still haven't completely figured it out. I need some time to sort things out. I just wanted to let you know," she added quickly. She decided at once that the hotel work was out of the question because of David.

"Good. Let me know once you've made up your mind," he said, getting out of the water, drying himself, and lazily stretching out on a deckchair. She continued swimming without any thoughts on her mind for the time being.

CHAPTER 51

Amy's black hair was tied up in a knot. Her kind oval face, gentle gaze, intelligence, and reserved personality had captivated Antonio from the moment they first met. She was different than all the other heavily mascaraed teens in London. Her natural beauty, relaxed conversation style, and discussions on a host of interesting subjects simply blew the young man away. Even though he'd only known her for a week, he couldn't stop thinking about her.

"Come on, we still have some time, so let's go for a walk."

They slowly walked down Marbella's crowded seaside promenade, hand in hand. Antonio looked at her from the corner of his eye and reflected that he would have to leave soon. They might not see each other again.

Amy suddenly glanced at him, but when she noticed he was eyeing her, she blushed and turned away. Antonio faintly smiled and glanced at his watch. "They're expecting us at nine."

"So, tell me about them. What are they like?"

"They're pretty normal. They aren't difficult and don't ask too many questions." He didn't tell her that this was also the first time he'd come here. I've only recently met my 'new' mother."

He suddenly wondered why his father had kept his marriage a secret for such a long time.

"And what do you think about her?"

"She's intelligent, elegant, and thoughtful," he laughed, suddenly kissing the tip of her nose.

Amy pulled her head away. "Okay, Okay, but I think it's very important for her to like you."

"I think I managed to do that."

"And what about you? Isn't that important for you, too?

"I would say I'm fond of her as well," he said, glancing at Amy ambiguously. He stopped for a moment, let go of her hand, and wrapped his arm around her shoulder.

"You'll be surprised to see how lovely and smart she is."

"I can't wait."

"I bet she's curious to meet you too."

"Me?"

"Yes," he noted teasingly before changing the subject. "So, how long are you staying?"

"I'm not sure. All I know is that my mother has to fly back to Rio soon."

"And that means you're going with her too. Right?" he asked sullenly as an odd feeling suddenly swept over him.

"Yes. That's right."

They'd avoided this subject until now, yet their thoughts kept straying back to it again and again. Amy's home was in Rio de Janeiro, and she only came here on vacation, whilst Antonio had to go to New York, since the university semester was starting in a week – a fact of which she wasn't aware.

They spotted an empty bench. A multitude of people was strolling down the promenade. A woman was holding a tiny Yorkshire terrier puppy in her arms. The dog listlessly stared at the masses, its long hairs tied together on the top of its head with a red bow.

"Sweet, isn't it?"

They both laughed and sat down on the bench.

"Amy."

"Yes?"

"I have something to say."

"I'm listening," she said attentively.

"Perhaps you've realized by now that I like being with you. You could say I've been thinking a lot about you since we first met."

Their gazes locked, and their mouths spontaneously touched. The people walking by couldn't take their eyes off them. Some people smiled and some eyed them longingly. An elderly couple approached and stared at the youngsters.

One of them sighed deeply. "Do you remember?"

"Yes. It's as if it was only yesterday," said the old lady to herself.

"Oh, yes, it was ages ago. Half a century ago," said the man.

"Any regrets?"

"Not at all. If I could start all over again, I would head down the same path," muttered the seventy-something old man. They clasped wrinkled hands more firmly before quietly recalling their memories.

The youngsters gave their seats up to the elderly couple and held onto each other tightly as they disappeared into the crowd. The sun reached the edge of the horizon. The sea was shimmering in front of them, and the summer night was fast approaching. Antonio checked the time.

"We've got to go." He spoke up again as they reached the car, hand in hand. "I have to tell you something." Amy turned to him expectantly with a sparkle in her eyes.

"Next week, I have to go to New York."

Amy swallowed hard. "And I have to go to Rio," she interrupted with an awkward smile.

"I'm just starting university," continued the young man, "but hopefully I'll find a way to visit you. What do you think, is this going to work?"

"We can give it a try."

Antonio was so thrilled that he suddenly kissed her.

"Then let's forget about such serious matters," he said, cheering up. Time will solve everything, he thought as he started up the car. Neither of them spoke a word as they drove to the restaurant. Once they arrived, Antonio could barely find a parking spot. "We have to hurry up, I'm sure they're already here."

Amy laughed.

"What are you laughing at?" asked Antonio.

"I'm hungry," she said quickly, changing the subject.

"Me too," he added, grinning, taking her by the hand and running off. Nick soon noticed them and waved. After a quick round of introductions, he pushed over the two empty glasses on the table.

"So, do you think we can give her some?" asked Nick, making a face.

"Thank you," interrupted Amy, cutely rolling her eyes. If Mom were here, I'm sure she would hit me on the head, she thought guiltily. Nick poured a little bit of liquid into the blushing girl's glass.

"To our encounter," he proposed, in a slightly ironic tone. Perhaps for the first time, he thought about how time was running by. Sandra silently and inconspicuously eyed the girl. She liked Amy's reserved looks at once. Her dark eyes free of makeup, her high forehead, her curly black hair tied into a knot, and her classic South American beauty gained Sandra's approval.

"So, I heard you're on vacation with your parents," said Nick suddenly.

"That's right."

"Is this the first time you've come here?"

"Yes. Or rather, it's the first time for my mother and me, but my father is Spanish. He lived here in Marbella many years ago."

"How did he end up in Rio?"

"I don't know. I have to admit, I never asked that from him."

"How about your mother?"

"She's a genuine Brazilian," Amy explained with ease.

"Stop questioning her," interrupted Sandra when the waiter brought them their menus.

"Why don't you choose something delicious instead? I'm sure you're hungry," she suggested encouragingly. "Hungry like a wolf," growled Antonio in a funny tone.

"The truth is, we're both famished. For example, I haven't had anything to eat since noon." He winked first at his stepmother and then at Amy. Sandra caught herself gazing at them at length. The boy has become a young man, and this kind girl seemed like a truly lovely person. For a moment, they both smiled at her, and Sandra returned the smile. They were so cute. A little curly-haired angel, she thought.

When Amy went to the washroom, Antonio was quick to question them.
"So, you like her too, right?"
"She's a lovely girl," replied Nick.
"Slow down," cautioned Sandra humorously. "I like her too. What do you know about her parents?"
"Not a lot, but I don't think that's too important. Her father is a doctor. Her mother doesn't work," he added quickly since Amy was approaching them.
"Let me guess: you were talking about me," she said, making a face at Antonio, who shared meaningful looks with the others.

The kids said goodbye after the delicious dinner and the pleasant meeting.
"I hope we'll see each other again?" asked Sandra kindly.
"I hope so too," replied the girl politely before they walked off hand in hand.

Nick wrapped his arm around his wife's shoulder. "Time is running by," he noted in a melancholy tone. "Unfortunately, no one can stop that. They say the soul is ageless and never grows old." He squeezed his wife's hand.

CHAPTER 52

Nick's macho appearance hadn't changed much over time, and he was always surrounded by women, yet he remained faithful to his little red-haired wife. Perhaps it was because of the calm home that awaited him on his return. The villa was like an island of peace from which he could exclude his dealings, which seemed to get increasingly worse.

He was captivated by his wife's cold behaviour, beauty, calmness, and the way she handled their marriage. He sometimes wondered whether that was what he loved about her.

Sandra was perfect for him in all regards. He didn't even mind when she hatefully asked him recently, "So where were you? I'm sure you're seeing someone! Don't try telling me again that the business isn't going well." During arguments like this, she often said, "If you want to leave, I won't hold you back, but don't lie to me. Face it – it's a spineless thing to lie and fool the person you're living with."

At times like these, he fell silent and agreed with her.

Perhaps she'd never trusted him, but that was no wonder since she wasn't familiar with a big part of his life – the reason why he was away so often. Still, he was entirely sure that he would never tell her about that. His dealings in Marrakech had come to an end. Although he hadn't sold the old riad yet, he hadn't been there for years.

He squinted at his wife, who was sitting in an armchair, deeply engrossed in a novel.

"Tomorrow is going to be very hectic," he noted abruptly. "I don't know when I'm coming home."

She eyed him reproachfully.

"And what's new about that?" she quipped, seemingly focusing on her novel while her wrath seethed inside of her. In the morning, he promised to come back as soon as he was done. He leaned over and planted a kiss on his wife's forehead while she was still stirring in bed.

Antonio got up late since he'd come home around midnight last night. He was sleepy, yet he still got under the shower on the patio. The cold water stirred him up, and he turned off the faucet before jumping off and landing in the pool.

Sandra was busying herself in the kitchen. The coffee was ready. She loaded the tray before going out to wipe down the table outside. "Breakfast is ready," she shouted to the young man busy doing laps.

He quickly dried himself off and left to change his wet swimming trunks. In the meantime, she set the table with a healthy spread. "Well, good morning!" he exclaimed as he returned with a fresh smile on his face.

"Good morning to you too, son," she welcomed him lovingly, handing him a plate of thinly sliced ham. "Have some."

"Thank you," he said with a grin, getting down to breakfast with a voracious appetite. The mother lovingly watched him and waited for him to speak up.

"I'll probably come home late tonight," he said.

"Aha. I noticed the same thing happened yesterday."

"We only have a few days left, so we want to spend them together," he explained guiltily.

"Naturally, I understand," she said, thinking back to the old days.

The love of parents is an important thing for a child, yet her son hadn't received much of that. She often thought back to their bleak existence in Marrakech. She'd hardly had any time for the little one with all her work. Without a real home, money, and father, he hadn't had much of a family to speak of to give him an impeccable upbringing.

She thought back to their eternally cold room, where they barely had any personal belongings and lived in a spartan style. She worried a lot about this, and the child sensed her worries, even though he surely didn't understand them and often cried and threw tantrums. Perhaps that's why she was impatient with him so often. Still, their relationship had been based on love. They had nothing else to claim as their own. The highlight of their monotonous days always came at night, when she took her son in her lap and told him of their seaside home, her parent's house. *It was so long ago*, she sighed.

She looked up at her son, who was now starting on his own life. All it took was a girl showing up for the parents to be sidelined. That's just the way life is, she thought, stifling a sigh.

Antonio finished his breakfast and awkwardly stood up. "Well, see you here tomorrow," he said with feigned ease since he felt a bit guilty for thrusting his stepmother into the background because of Amy. He rushed up to the bathroom to collect his belongings for the beach.

"We're going down to the beach," he noted in hurry and headed out, only to turn back at the end of the patio. "Phew, I almost forgot my swimming trunks," he noted, running back to fetch them. Finally, he waved to her and hurried off.

CHAPTER 53

He and Amy were sunning themselves on the beach when Antonio's mobile rang, forcing him to focus on his father. "You said you wouldn't be coming back for a few days."

"Yes, I did, but the plans have changed," said Nick, "and I'll be back this evening. Tomorrow I want to take you out for a whole day of sailing."

"Wait a minute." He hesitantly turned to the girl.

"My father wants to take us out for a longer sailing trip."

Amy happily nodded. "But wait, let me call my mother first," she said, digging out her mobile.

"We would be glad to go," he said to his father. "Just wait a minute, she has to ask her mother's permission," Antonio explained with a grin. "When are you coming home?"

"I don't know, around seven. It depends on the traffic."

"Okay then, see you tonight."

Amy motioned that it was OK – her mother agreed to their plans.

"They let her come, so she has permission," explained Antonio, forwarding the news to his father.

"Great, then plan on leaving tomorrow at ten."

"Thanks," Antonio said, turning his phone off and leaning back on his mat, laughing.

Amy lifted her thumb to her mouth for a moment before turning to Antonio with her hand in the air. He suddenly rolled away from her, and her weak blow only hit his back.

"You're cheeky."

"Me?" he said innocently, turning on his side and laughing at her.

"Yes, you, you're making fun of me because of my mother."

"Oh, come on, I'm just happy."

"You didn't mention you had a yacht."

"I don't, but my father does."

"That makes no difference."

"Maybe, but it's still not mine."

"So, what is it like?"

"It's not that big, it's just a sailboat. It'll be just big enough for all of us, but if it isn't, you can stay at home," he noted, cheekily grinning at her. "You're always fooling around," she said peevishly, yet not angrily.

"We have an old worn-out tub at home, too. My father always manages to fix it up every year, and he carefully paints its sides. He loves it a lot. And so, do I," she added. Antonio was pleased by her natural, non-poised behaviour.

"Come on, let's go for a swim. It's really hot," he said, holding out his hand to her as he jumped up from his chair. She instantly took him by the hand, and they rushed off towards the water.

"Phew, the sand is really hot," she cried, rushing over the scalding surface while screaming, much to the delight of the people on the beach.

The young man picked her up and ran into the water with her in his arms as a wave crashed over them.

"Br…, it's so cold," cried the girl with a giggle.

Antonio swam out into the water with great arm strokes.

"Come on," he said, waving to her and urging her to come out further. Amy floundered her way over to him and clung onto his shoulder. He wrapped his arm around her for a moment, but she suddenly pushed him away, causing her to slightly sink and then swim out to the shore, awkwardly sitting down on the sand at the edge of the water.

Antonio quickly followed her.

"What's wrong?" he asked as he reached the shore.

"The water is cold," she replied evasively, staring at the churning sea, sensing some tension before they lay back down on their mats. They remained silent for a while.

"Two days to live," said the young man, breaking the silence. She mischievously turned towards him. "Merle?"

He stared at her quizzically for a moment and then cheerfully shook his head. "I wasn't thinking of the book, but of us," he replied with the smile fading from his features. "You know, we only have two days left."

There was a mysterious glow in Amy's eyes as she awkwardly started packing.

"It's getting late, I should head home now," she noted in a barely audible tone. "Tomorrow?"

"Yes, tomorrow, as I promised." As she glanced at him, she bit her lip to hide her smile. "I'll come, but parents' rules are rules. Plus, you know, they already let me go as they always do. They trust me," she added, sticking her tongue out at him.

"It's early, so what's the rush?"

"I've got to go; my parents have some plans."

"Fine. Then see you tomorrow at ten."

"Okay, I'll be on time," she noted, standing up and planting a light kiss on his face before disappearing amongst the people on the beach. Antonio stayed at the beach for a longer time than strolling down the promenade on his own. The lights slowly came on in the city. The lido was teeming with people.

Couples walked in front of him, hand in hand. The elderly sat on the low stone wall which separated the sandy beach from the promenade, chatting and admiring the view. Groups of boys and

girls approached and passed him by. The bars and cafés in the neighbourhood filled with people. The city came to life in the evening
glow. He'd soon be flying off to New York.

He would miss Marbella, his parents. and of course, Amy.

He was glad to have met her, and he hoped their summer
love would prove to be lasting.

CHAPTER 54

Nick routinely started up the yacht. He always felt free at such times, like a bird which could fly any way it wanted to. He'd been driving boats for ages. He knew well how strong the waves could be and the dangers of the silent waters. He loved the sea; he thought of it as a kind of challenge.

He enjoyed the salty fragrance and the freedom of it all. He didn't mind when the wind whipped through his hair from time to time. He loved watching the agile dolphins accompanying the smaller boats in the water as if guiding them somewhere. He loved the long nights under the starry sky when the whales eerily cried out somewhere close to him under the waves. If the sea were still, he sometimes even lay down on the deck in the middle of the night, gazing up at the stars.

They slowly distanced themselves from the Puerto Banus harbour. He guided the ship west with the nose of the boat evenly dividing the huge mass of water, leaving white-crested waves in its wake. Antonio stood next to him, leaving Amy in his stepmother's company.

"Come on, take it over from me," Nick suggested to his son, who gripped the bulky wheel with pleasure. Nick had already given him a few lessons. He put his arm on the young man's shoulder again while explaining the rules to him.

Sandra was sitting in the back with the girl, chatting at ease. She had taken a liking to Amy since the first time they met. Amy rummaged through her bag and produced a picture which she handed to Sandra.

"A picture from Rio with my parents," she explained.

Sandra glanced at the photo and her heart almost stopped in surprise. "I assume you're the little girl in the picture," she managed to finally say.

"Yes."

Antonio suddenly tugged the wheel to the right, so they both leaned to the side. The wind nipped at their hair, and the girl cried out in laughter. Sandra failed to notice how her fingers opened, and the photo flew away. Amy watched the photo fly off in surprise. The wind lifted it for a moment before tilting and plunging it into the water. Sandra stuttered as she spoke up. "I'm … I'm so sorry, that's so clumsy of me." She dashed away and tumbled down inside the hold.

Amy quizzically watched her leave before regretfully gazing out over the waves. Antonio looked back and saw Amy sitting all alone. He told his father to take over the helm so he could join her. In the meantime, Sandra painfully winced down in the cabin.

"Why, why does something so unexpected and terrible always happen to me? Why are these odd coincidences haunting me?" she cried hysterically as she rummaged through her medicinal drawer without remembering what she was looking for. Finally, she slumped back down on the narrow sofa.

"What did I do to be punished this way?" she muttered as her thoughts turned increasingly dull. Her heart was beating out loud and her head was tingling and she suddenly fell backwards, unconscious.

"Where's Sandra?" cried Nick to the kids.

"She went down to the cabin. Maybe she fell asleep," replied Amy unsuspectingly.

"I'll take a look," shouted Antonio before striding down the steps in ease. Noticing Sandra's motionless body, he checked her pulse at once. It seemed erratic. "Dad, come quick!" he shouted with some excitement in his voice.

Nick stopped the boat and hurried down below the deck. As he spotted his unconscious wife, he cried out, "What happened?"

"I don't know."

"Is she dead?"

"No, but you've got to turn back at once while I call an ambulance. I have a feeling it might be her heart ..." he noted, glancing at Amy, who shuffled her feet at the top of the steps in shock. She held tight to the railing with her hand, staring down at the pale face of the woman. Nick didn't even hear the end of the sentence. He slightly pressed the girl up against the railing to get past her. He quickly started up the motor, turned the boat around in a wide arc, and headed back to the marina at full speed.

Antonio finished the phone call and turned back to his stepmother, whose eyes were open by now.

"Are you okay?" he asked. Sandra eyed her son with unspeakable pain through her teary eyes, looking deathly pale, yet didn't say a word. Antonio poured her some water and made her drink it.

"Don't get up. Just rest," he warned her. He faintly motioned for Amy to follow him back up to the deck. "I saw you two happily chatting a moment ago. What happened?"

"Yes, that's right. Trust me, I don't understand what's going on. I just showed her a picture of my family and somehow it flew out of her hands. Then she got up and walked out on me."

"I'm sure something happened. No one faints without a reason," he said, searchingly eyeing her before turning his back on her and peevishly joining Nick.

"Sandra came to," he said.

"Good, I'm pleased to hear that," said the man in relief.

"I'll go down to be with her until we reach the shore. I don't like it that she's so pale."

"Good idea," nodded Nick, gripping the wheel tighter.

"Trust me, it's not my fault," said the girl, but Antonio walked by her without an answer. She sat down on the stairs, feeling puzzled, thinking over the whole thing again.

"When I handed Sandra the picture, she turned grim." Amy recalled. The next thing I saw was the photo flying out into the sea while she stumbled down to the cabin. Yes, she seemed to move hesitantly, but maybe that was because of the boat.

They soon reached the port. The ambulance was nowhere to be seen. Antonio nervously eyed Amy.

"Come on, I'll call a taxi," he said.

"No need to. I know where to find one." She hesitantly leaned over to him, barely touching his face. "Bye," she said lethargically.

"I'll call," he cried out to her as she walked off before he headed down below deck. Sandra was still lying motionless, yet her eyes seemed alert.

Nick sat next to her, asking, "Are you in any pain?"

"No," she replied faintly. Only my heart is broken, she thought sadly.

"Then I'll go back upstairs. They might be coming already."

As he stepped away, he muttered with annoyance, "You can curl up and die by the time they get here."

When they reached the hospital, Sandra was taken to an examining room. In the meantime, the men waited in the corridor. After quite some time, a doctor finally appeared.

"What happened to her? Please, even the smallest details might be important."

"It was nothing special, we went out sailing," replied Nick in puzzlement. Antonio interjected with his suspicions.

The doctor listened and then told them, "I have to run a few more routine tests. It was probably some mental strain." He slipped his hand out of his pocket and glanced at his watch. "Hopefully I'll know more by tomorrow."

"Her pulse missed a beat," noted Antonio.

"I never noticed she had any problems," interrupted Nick.

"I'm sure she didn't suffer any shock since she was still laughing a few hours ago."

Antonio thoughtfully recalled the image of his stepmother again. When he first looked back, she and Amy were both chatting with smiles on their faces, which pleased him.

"I hope it's nothing serious, right?" insisted Nick.

"We hope not," the doctor replied. "Nevertheless, she needs a thorough check-up. Unfortunately, I've got to go now," said the doctor in parting.

An hour later, they took Sandra over to the ward, and she quickly fell asleep on her bed.

The men went home. They silently sat on the patio with long faces for a while. Nick suddenly stood up, grabbed a bottle of whiskey in the living room with two glasses, and walked outside. He unscrewed the cap and filled the glasses.

"Not too much for me," warned Antonio.

"Cheers," said Nick wryly. Antonio didn't drink regularly, and he raised the glass mostly for his father's sake, emptying its contents and shuddering. He didn't like whiskey, yet its effect certainly helped him ease up.

CHAPTER 55

The following morning, Sandra was lying on the bed with her eyes open. She remained silent and didn't look at the two figures standing next to her.

"Please, tell me what happened," said Nick, holding her hand. Sandra, however, didn't reply.

Antonio stood up. "I'll go find the doctor."

"Wait, I'll go with you."

"It seems to me that her condition has gotten worse."

"I've noticed that too," said Nick in despair. The doctor stepped out of the elevator. "We were just on our way to see you," Nick said, holding his hand out.

"We brought my wife in yesterday."

"Yes, I remember. As I said, she must have experienced some kind of shock. It was possibly induced by a former depression or a bad memory. There could be many reasons. She had a slight haemorrhage," he added, glancing at Antonio and then back at Nick. "If her condition doesn't improve in a few days, then her recovery, which is still in doubt at the moment, might be extended indefinitely."

Nick interrupted, "I don't understand what's going on."

"Look, let's hope for the best. She might be able to go home in a few days. The human body can be unpredictable."

"What is that supposed to mean?" perked up Nick.

"Nothing in particular. Hopefully, I'll be able to tell you more tomorrow or the day after. I'm still waiting for two test results. But please, come with me, I have a few more questions to ask."

In the meantime, Antonio returned to Sandra. She was lying in bed with her eyes shut as he caressed her hand and planted a kiss on her forehead.

"Goodbye. I have to fly off to New York for university, but I promise to keep in touch. I want you to get better," he said, squeezing his stepmother's cold hand. "I love you." The patient's face remained expressionless.

His throat ached. He glanced at his watch and saw his time was up. He kissed her face again in parting and walked out of the room. His father hurried over to him. "Come on, we've got to go or you'll miss your flight." They parted company despondently at the airport in Malaga.

"So, your New York credit card is safe and sound, right?"

"Yes."

"Be careful once you get there. I'll send some money to your account from time to time as I always did. Call me if it's not enough."

"Thank you. I'm sure it will be enough," he replied before they embraced one more time. "Take care of yourself."

"OK, and you take care of yourself and Sandra. I'll call."

When Antonio reached Madrid, he got on another plane after a three-hour layover, which crossed the heavens towards New York. He stared out the window cheerlessly. The clouds billowed in a silver haze beneath them. The steward brought him his dinner, but he only poked at it with no appetite. Later on, he closed his eyes and listened to Mozart on his headset. His thoughts wandered off to his stepmother before he thought of Amy.

He hadn't had a chance to say goodbye to her with the way things turned out. He called her before the plane took off, but they only spoke a few words. Finally, his thoughts strayed off to New York, the university, and his new life.

CHAPTER 56

Her memory was perfectly intact. However, due to the medication, she frequently fell asleep, which undoubtedly brought her closer to recovery. Sleep is gold because it shuts off the brain's overburdened thoughts.

Once Sandra woke, suddenly everything was clear to her. She recalled the way Amy handed her the photograph of her family. She could still feel the way her fingers feebly spread apart and see the picture with Pedro smiling back at her flying out over the rippling sea.

The man she'd thought dead for a long time was alive, and she was glad to know that. It had all happened a long time ago, and both of their lives had changed. Their short-lived love was but a precious memory by now. However, her joy couldn't last for long. She turned grim when she thought of Antonio, whose father was almost definitely Pedro.

What should she do, since it was clear for all to see that the kids were in love?

"But they're half-siblings!" she cried out in despair. Once again, she was in an irresolvable situation, one that seemed impossible to unravel. She felt an icy grip on her heart and her hands trembled as she picked up the bottle of water from her nightstand. It slipped through her fingers and fell to the floor.

She gasped for air and helplessly sunk back down on her pillow. Her hand hesitantly groped for the buzzer.

Fortunately, the nurse noticed through the open door that she was in trouble. She called for the physician on duty, who covered her face with the mask. Later on, they gave her an infusion. The liquid slowly dripped from the suspended bag and flowed down through the transparent tube into her vascular system. She woke a few hours later. Her eyes slowly fixed on the empty infusion bag. While she was asleep, the nurse had shut off the tap and freed her arm. Her thoughts were clearer now, and she hoped she would soon recover, unlike the last time in Paris.

For some reason, she thought of Yvonne. They hadn't seen each other for years. She felt ashamed of herself since she hadn't even bothered to call. Suddenly, she missed her friend dearly and felt it would be good to have Yvonne at her side.

The following day, Sandra finally spoke up, much to Nick's delight. She slowly fixed her gaze on him.

"Sorry," she said quietly.

"Don't say that, since it's not your fault," he replied, sitting down next to her on the bed. He squeezed her chilly hand, yet she soon closed her eyes. He felt she wanted to be left alone, so he decided to leave the room and seek out the doctor.

"Although your wife's condition has improved, she might relapse at any time, as she did yesterday," the doctor noted, sharing the most necessary information with Nick. "Make sure she doesn't get too anxious," concluded the physician, going over the results in his hand one more time.

"I might even release her two days from now," he added, slightly tilting his head. He didn't like sharing negative facts, and he always left room for hope. Nick thanked him for the information and left, feeling clueless.

CHAPTER 57

The shadows drew out and not a leaf rustled, with the man's fierce arm strokes emanating from the pool as the only sound in the air. The water felt best in the evening, he thought. He went inside once he was done swimming.

The house seemed hollow and empty. Suddenly, he didn't know what to do with himself. He reached out for a bottle of booze and had a glassful. What should he do? He had to leave in a week because of his business, even if it wasn't entirely clear. He was stuck since he couldn't leave his wife on her own in such a condition.

He slipped on a T-shirt and headed down to the shore, where he walked at length over the dunes. The crowds were getting sparse on the beach, and people were collecting their belongings and heading home. The steel-grey sea barely moved in the half-light.

"Hi!" exclaimed Carmen, still in her bathing suit. She gently patted his back with her rolled-up mat. Nick turned around.
"You come down to this beach a lot?"
"Usually when David is working at the hotel," she said

meaningfully while donning a flimsy outfit. Nick turned away and walked home. Carmen joined him, uninvited, and started chatting about nonsensical matters. She just wouldn't shut up.

As they reached the front gate, he glanced at her.
"Want to come in for a drink?"
"Sandra?"
"She isn't home." Carmen's eyes flashed.
"I'd love to," she said at once. As they entered the house, he headed straight over to the kitchen. He filled two glasses with ice before pouring whiskey into them. The woman leisurely dumped her bag and expectantly stopped next to him. She was pleased by this sudden opportunity. She smelled adventure in the air. She had been watching for a chance to get close to this good looking macho for quite some time now.

Nick silently handed her one of the glasses. He scratched his chin in boredom and they both quickly finished off their drinks. Carmen comfortably sprawled over the armchair opposite him, crossing her legs in the most advantageous posture. Her short beach shirt left little to the imagination. She levelled her eager, beguiling gaze on the handsome man. She raised her arms, slightly stretching and leaning back. She ran her tongue along the edge of her mouth, unmistakably signifying that she wanted something.

Nick squinted at her, clearly understanding her body language. The mischievous woman leaned forward towards him.
"Where is Sandra?" she asked, while her thoughts focused on something far more exciting.
He poured them another drink. They sipped their drinks before he also sprawled on the sofa. He morosely related the incident without looking at her at all. She noticed how sluggish he was. She walked over to him and sat down right next to him.
"I want some more," she purred, pushing her glass up to the bottle. The man mechanically filled her glass. "Well, I hope she'll get better soon," Carmen noted regretfully, lifting her full glass. She could sense the drink kicking in, and her instincts drove her on as

she urgently moved closer to Nick. She leaned on the sofa with one arm, carefully stroking the back of his neck.

"Don't worry," she whispered as her other hand slowly coursed down his chest. She lifted her head with her mouth half-open, offering herself up to him. Nick had just enough booze to relax his poise. He understood what she wanted without any words and pulled her onto his lap as she giggled in satisfaction.

"The siren has left," he thought an hour later, making a face. Their hasty intercourse had left no impression on him whatsoever. It just happened. His past was littered with similar liaisons.

The women kept coming and going with no end in sight, yet none of them truly belonged to him – except Sandra. *But then why did you do it?* He asked himself, unable to come up with an answer. He turned on the table lamp and rolled a joint. Once he was finished, he comfortably leaned back and took a puff, blowing the smoke up towards the ceiling. He gazed at the rings of smoke drifting upwards with a dull consciousness. He felt lighter and grinned as he stretched out on the sofa, maybe even dozing off.

He went down to the beach bar on the shore around eleven. The sound of quiet Latin music played in the background.

The owner stood behind the bar, humming the tune as her fat body swayed to the beat. She squinted at Nick and spoke up.
"What will it be, darling?" she asked.
"Whiskey with a fistful of ice," he said brusquely. He sat on his own at the bar for a long time. After the third glass, he didn't even notice that he was thoroughly wasted.
"Hey dude, long time, no see," said one of his old friends is welcome. Nick shot a glance at him before yawning. His head felt heavier due to all the booze. "So how are your old pals? What's up with Rodrigo?"
"Hell knows, we split up."

"You don't work together anymore?" pressed the man in surprise. "You heard me."

"Well, that's hard to believe."

Nick didn't bother to reply. He motioned to the fatty that he wanted the tab and then disappeared into the night. He stumbled home at a late hour. While standing at the gate under the light of the streetlamp, he noticed that the mailbox was stuffed with letters. He dug out his keys from his pocket. He cursed out loud when the key didn't want to fit the hole of the metal box, yet he finally managed to complete the seemingly daunting task. As he entered the house, he tossed the letters on the table.

CHAPTER 58

He woke with his head buzzing to find that the phone was ringing. He sleepily answered it.

"Hi, honey. It's me, Carmen." *Well, there goes my day,* he thought. "Do you want me to come over in the evening?"

"I'm busy," he said, brushing her off and slamming the receiver down. He peevishly loafed around for a while before heading over to the bathroom. He looked into the mirror and saw his face looking neglected. He took a shower with cold water, which almost helped shake him up. He brewed some strong coffee in the kitchen, had a hearty breakfast, and stretched out in satisfaction, forgetting his slip from last night.

He leaned over to pick up the scattered letters. One of them was addressed to Sandra. He turned it over in his hands for a while before finally opening it.

I'll be in Marbella on the sixteenth and I'll be staying in town for a while. We haven't met in ages. I want to know what's happening with you. Call me because I couldn't get through to you. Yvonne.

There was a phone number included at the end of the letter. Nick glanced at the calendar. It was the seventeenth. He dialed the number at once.

"Hello, Yvonne?"

"Yes?"

"I'm Nick, Sandra's husband."

"Hello there. Where's Sandra?"

"She's sick. That's why I'm calling. I'm just about to head over to the hospital. You can come with me if you'd like to."

"Sure, I want to," the woman said, quickly explaining where she was staying.

"I'll be there in half an hour."

"Thank you. I'll wait for you in front of the hotel. Oh, my hair is brown, and I'll be wearing a blue dress."

Nick got there a bit early. He parked the car with a view of the entrance. He had the ulterior motive of entrusting the care of his wife to this stranger of a woman, who arrived punctually. He hurried over to meet her, and they introduced each other.

"Come, my car is parked nearby," he said in a friendly tone, taking the lead with his sluggish strides. On their way, he explained to her what happened to Sandra.

"The doctor encouraged me and said that he might release her."

"I hope it's nothing serious?"

"The doctor feels she must have suffered some kind of shock, which I don't think is the case."

"Shock?"

"Yes, that's what he said." He looked at Yvonne for a moment. "He also mentioned that perhaps it might be because of a previous illness or depression, which I don't think is the case either since it happened so suddenly and unexpectedly. The whole thing puzzles me. She's never been sick since I've known her."

Yvonne turned pale, recalling the time when they arrived in Paris with Vicky and she slowly recovered from her depression after many long months. *It was hard to believe that she'd relapsed after such a long time,* Yvonne thought in alarm.

When they reached Sandra's hospital room, Nick politely let the Frenchwoman walk ahead, while tensely biting his lip due to yesterday's affair.

"Oh, honey, it's so good to see you. Are you feeling better?" asked Yvonne, rushing over to the bed as tears welled up in her eyes. Sandra lifted her head and cried out in surprise.
"Yvonne? Is it you? You won't believe me, but I was just thinking about you. See how strong my sixth sense is?" she cried as they embraced. Nick leaned closer to his wife and planted a kiss on her forehead.
"I'll leave you two alone while I talk to the doctor."
"Please ask him when I can go home."
"I'd like to know that too," Nick mumbled, disappearing with great strides. The girlfriends eyed each other their hands tightly gripped.
"Vicky, honey, I haven't seen you in ages."
"Hush. I'm Sandra, remember?" she warned her quietly, glancing towards the door. Yvonne looked back at the door.
"OK, darling. I'll keep that in mind," she added, sitting down on the edge of the bed. "So, tell me. What happened to you?"
The joy vanished from Sandra's face at once and she slowly turned her head away.
"That was a foolish question, forget it," Yvonne quickly added. "If you don't want to talk about it, it's fine, just don't turn away, since we haven't seen each other for so long," pouted Yvonne. Sandra turned back and nodded with a slight smile.
"That's true, we haven't seen each for a long time."
Nick came back an hour later. "You can go home on the weekend," he noted. He didn't stop by or make any calls after his visit and only took Sandra home on the day of her discharge. She quickly noticed her husband's cold, sullen behaviour.

CHAPTER 59

After Sandra was released from the hospital, Nick quietly drove the car home. In the meantime, Sandra was busy with her thoughts. She was upset that her husband didn't bother to check up on her in the last few days.

As she entered the house, she recoiled from the heavy, stale stench of booze in the air. The counter was littered with dirty glasses and dishes, which she always kept clean. On the coffee table in the living room, she spotted a half-empty bottle of whiskey and two unwashed glasses, one of them knocked over. The floor was littered with empty bottles and cans of beer, while the sofa was covered with crumpled pillows. There were stubbed out cigarette ends in a small plate. She opened the window to air out the room.

Nick eyed her with annoyance for a while.

"How about I call your girlfriend over? She can stay here as long as she wants to." Sandra nodded, yet her heart was full of suspicion and doubt. It seems like one and a half weeks were enough for him to grow distant from me. He didn't even bother to excuse himself for the mess, she thought, deeply offended. She went up to the bedroom in silence. Nick knew very well what was bothering her, yet he didn't feel like explaining himself or arguing. He wanted to avoid any awkward conversations, so he called up Yvonne and told her that if she would like, she could come over to his house for the sake of his wife, who would be glad to see her.

He quickly scooped up the garbage and took it out to the bin. He filled the dishwasher with dirty glasses and dishes. He adjusted the pillows on the sofa. He opened the window in the hallway so that the house would air out by the time their guest arrived. He had no reason to worry about thieves since he would be back soon and the windows were covered with grates. Once he was done tidying up the place, he got in his car to bring the Frenchwoman over.

In the meantime, Sandra came downstairs for a bottle of water. She was surprised to see that almost all of the mess was gone. She eased up when she saw the dishwasher was in use. Perhaps she had been mistaken.

Yvonne gladly accepted the invitation, and Nick felt much better now that he had taken care of this great burden. Now his wife wouldn't be alone while he went away for an indeterminate period. That evening, he packed the car in front of the supermarket with readily purchased food and left the following day.

On Friday, Yvonne headed down to the local store. When she reached the gate, she found a daringly dressed woman about to ring the bell. The stranger welcomed her in surprise.

"Is Nick home?" she asked grimly.

"No, he isn't. He left."

The woman blushed and her eyes filled with rage. She stormed off without saying a word. Yvonne decided to wait and tell Sandra about this later. Down at the store, she bought fresh bread, fruit, and a few other missing items. She returned to the house and spent the rest of the day with her girlfriend, who often lapsed into sudden sleep from the medication.

Sandra was still resting, but she didn't dare think of tomorrow. She knew that the danger had momentarily been averted since Antonio was in New York and Amy was in Rio. *It's a great distance, and if I'm lucky, they'll forget about each other,* Sandra hoped, somewhat comforted by the thought.

CHAPTER 60

At the end of September, the Mediterranean summer was still in full force. Yvonne brought her painting tools and sometimes went down to the shore in the late afternoon. That's when the colours were the prettiest. Various stretches of long, sandy beach filled with vacationers. Still, it wasn't hard to find a quiet spot where she could mix colours in peace.

When the sun disappeared behind the western horizon, she picked up her belongings and headed up to the villa, since she didn't want to leave Sandra alone for a long time. She washed off the sand clinging to her feet in the garden's shower. Later on, she prepared some sandwiches, filled glasses with chilled orange juice, and took it all up on a tray to the patient's room. Sandra was sitting on the edge of the bed.

"I think that's a bit too early for you," Yvonne noted with concern.

"No, I need some exercise."

Yvonne smiled. "OK, come on, I'll help. It'll be easier together," she said, putting her arm around her friend. "Steady now, let's go nice and slowly. Do you hear me?" she joked.

"I hear you, but don't let go. Don't treat me like I broke a leg," said Sandra impatiently. Still, she sat down in the armchair after a few steps, since she was feeling dizzy. "Don't worry, I'll get better," she nodded a bit hesitantly. "I want to. I have to."

"Of course, you'll get better," Yvonne replied quickly.

"Can I get some water?"

"I brought you some orange juice, but you'll have to wait a bit if you want water."

"Thank you, the juice will be fine," she said, accepting the glass held out to her.

Yvonne was glad that her girlfriend wanted to get better, as opposed to that time in Paris, many years ago.

"Here you are, here's your sandwich," she said, handing her a plate.

"You know, I'm not hungry."

"Come on, eat it."

Sandra took a bite of the meat sandwich. "It's good."

"See," Yvonne said, suppressing a smile.

"When will Nick be coming back?" Sandra asked suddenly.

"I don't know. Maybe a few days," Yvonne said, turning grim. She wanted to tell her that a woman was looking for him in the morning, but since she noticed the concerned look on Sandra's face, she decided to ask what was wrong instead.

"Please, promise me something," Sandra said.

"You can trust me," Yvonne assured her.

"I would like you not to talk about things that happened in the past. Promise? This means a lot to me," she said, anxiously looking the other woman in the eye.

"Definitely," Yvonne promised.

"If that's what you want, so be it."

"Good," she whispered, visibly relieved. She got up, walked back to the bed lay down and closed her eyes. They both fell silent. Yvonne stayed for a while and then left the room since Sandra appeared to be asleep. However, she wasn't. She was trying to sort through her scattered thoughts. She knew full well that her girlfriend only knew part of her secrets.

She never saw Nick back in Marrakech, so she couldn't identify him. She only knew Antonio, who was kidnapped by an Arab man after their crossing. Sandra was simply unable to tell her friend that the main reason she married Nick was to get Antonio back. Yvonne would laugh at her if she said that she'd grown fond of Nick over time. Not to mention the hair-raising tale of Amy and Antonio. No. She couldn't bear to share her secrets.

Yvonne arranged some fresh fruit on plates. Today was the first day she'd noticed Sandra eating with a hearty appetite.

"Would you like anything else?"

"No, thank you," Sandra said, placing the empty plate on the nightstand next to the bed. Yvonne paused for a moment. "Sandra."

"Yes."

"I didn't want to bother with you with this until now, but …"

"Go ahead," Sandra said, interrupting her.

"Where's your son? Did you manage to find him?" Sandra bowed her head.

"Perhaps you remember that this was why I went to Marrakech and London, but I never made any progress," she explained, turning her head away since she didn't dare tell the truth. It was too late for that. The secrets of the three faces of her eventful life formed a tight link. If she shared her secrets, she might lose Yvonne's friendship. She didn't want that to happen since she loved her friend dearly and had much to thank the woman for.

"I'm sorry to bring up such a painful subject."

"Oh, I'm not angry. Yvonne please, if you don't mind, I'd like to get some rest now," she said, suddenly turning head away because she felt she was about to start crying.

"Naturally, of course," Yvonne said, standing up with a start, slightly puzzled by her girlfriend's behaviour. "Get some rest, and in the meantime, I'll go get some fresh strawberries and whatever else we need." She picked up the tray and quietly closed the door on her way out.

CHAPTER 61

She opened the garden gate when she returned from her rounds. She headed up to the house alongside the tall hedges. She could barely slip the key into the lock because of all the packages she was carrying. However, the door was open. She unpacked in the kitchen and peeked into the living room on the way to her room. She recoiled in surprise, since Nick and the woman she once saw at the gate were in each other's arm, making love while leaned up against the sofa. Yvonne covered her mouth with her hand while the woman mockingly glared at her for a moment.

She hurried into her room at once and quickly closed the door. If Sandra came down, she would surely faint. Poor thing, she'd suffered so much in her life already. What a scumbag of a man. At least he could do it somewhere else, especially while his wife was home, she thought indignantly.

She composed herself and silently hurried upstairs so Sandra wouldn't come down. As she entered the room, she noticed Sandra was sleeping. She sat down in the armchair in relief. She thought of how they'd made their acquaintance, their dangerous crossing, the time spent in Paris, the months of recovery, and her plastic surgery. She'd had such a long, hard journey so far to make it back to living a normal life.

Yvonne decided never to say anything about what she just witnessed. It's true that sometimes in life you're forced not to tell some things to your best friend or close relatives. She couldn't break Sandra's heart, she thought. Or could she?

What would a true friend do? she agonized in confusion. If she didn't say a thing, she'd spare her the pain. But if she doesn't?

Sandra opened her eyes.

"You're here?" she asked in surprise.

"Yes, I'm taking care of you and watching over you so I can keep your happiness safe and you can dream in peace," she said. She felt a twinge in her heart when she thought how true her words were.

"Oh, come on." *Poor thing, if she only knew that this was no laughing matter.* Yvonne leaned over and caressed her friend's face.

"I'm glad that I can spend some time here with you."

"Me too," Sandra said, gratefully looking her in the eye. "So, what do you say we walk down to the sea together?"

"No, not yet," Yvonne said in alarm. "Why?"

"It's still very hot outside. I might want to go down to paint because you know, the colours are sharper later on."

"Sure, sure, you might be right."

"I brought a few newspapers so I could read something in the meantime."

"How kind of you."

Yvonne started leafing through the paper.

"Here, listen to this: 'Famous flamenco dancer Patricia Gomez and pop star daughter Lucy, who just returned from London, will be performing together in Marbella."

"When?" asked Sandra in surprise.

"It doesn't say. If you're interested, I can look into it."

"I would be, but …"

"Do you know them?"

"Yes."

"Look, here's a photo of them," Yvonne said, showing Sandra the paper. Lucy looked fabulous. Sandra hadn't seen her since their failed escape attempt when she disappeared from behind her all those years ago at the Djemaa el-Fna square. The years showed on her, but they played to her advantage. Sandra sighed deeply.

Her girlfriend continued flipping through the paper.

"Police expose drug ring in Barcelona,'" she read.

Sandra's sixth sense stirred. Perhaps Nick was involved since he often visited the city. *No, it can't be,* she protested inwardly, yet the doubt remained in her mind. Time went by fast, and the sun had set behind the carob tree by the time Yvonne finished reading.

"I'll be back at once," she said, jumping up and hurrying down the stairs.

The ground floor seemed deserted, and she didn't see Nick or that despicable woman on the patio. She peeked inside the garage, but his car wasn't there. She walked back upstairs, feeling reassured.

"We can get going now," she suggested. "If you don't mind, I'll bring my easel, since I want to make some adjustments to my last painting."

"Fine. I'll carry the towels and whatever else you need."

"One is enough since we won't go in the water anyway, right?" Sandra smiled but didn't say anything in response.

By the time they walked out into the street, the heat had subsided. Yvonne cautiously looked around to see if Nick was nearby. She failed to notice a man standing next to the hedges. He headed in the opposite direction when he spotted the women. Sandra did notice the man and was sure that he was the same one who'd previously come looking for Nick, a visit she'd forgotten to mention to her husband. She was scared as she thought of the newspaper article. It would be awful to get involved in this dirty dealing. Perhaps that's why Nick had changed so much lately. She was worried about him since after all she still loved him.

"The air is marvelous, isn't it?" asked Yvonne.

"Yes, it is," Sandra said, stirring from her dark thoughts. "I love the late afternoon hours since there are fewer people on the beach."

"If you want, we can come down again tomorrow, and you can even go swimming if you want to."

"I can give it a shot," said Sandra, scanning the long stretch of shore in front of them.

"Should we carry on?"

"A bit further."

"Let's sit down instead. You need some rest," Yvonne suggested. "I'm not tired." Sandra answered.

"I know, I know, but all at once, " she started without finishing a sentence, as Sandra dropped down on the sand, pulled her legs up, clasped her arms around her knees, and silently stared at the sea, watching the waves gently lap on the shore.

Yvonne unpacked her belongings and critically continued and adjusted her painting from the previous week until the sun sunk beneath the edge of the horizon.

Sandra watched a young girl happily playing with her dog.

"It would make me very happy," she began.

"If?"

"If you could stay with me for a long time."

"You're being selfish. I've got a life too, but I can stay a while longer," said Yvonne who lovingly hugging her. "Come on, look at my painting. I've finished it," she said, holding her hand out. Sandra critically scanned the picture.

"Lovely. I like your pastel colours and that you don't apply the paint too thickly on the canvas, so there's no glare."

She complimented. "Congratulations."

"That's kind of you," Yvonne replied, packing up her belongings.

"I don't like darker colours and shiny oil paints. I want to put an exhibition together in Paris before Christmas. Dad is keen on it. I'll send you the date," she explained.

"Come, if you can."

"Maybe, perhaps," she replied, thinking of Antonio, who would hopefully spend the holidays here. But that's a long way away, she thought.

"Come on, it's time to go back. See, the sun has set, and the night is fast approaching."

"I'm not blind."

"What's wrong with you?" Yvonne glanced at her in surprise. "You're acting like a mother. You're treating me like I'm a little girl."

Yvonne smiled. "I'll buy you a pacifier tomorrow."

Sandra suddenly clung to her, and they sank to the sand while laughing at ease. A few belated seagulls circled above them, squawking in the air. The long sandy beach was deserted. The sea adopted a steel-grey tint with the darkness fast approaching, rolling in over the waves. As they returned to the house, Yvonne turned the lights on above the patio.

"Nick still hasn't returned," Sandra noted with concern.

Yvonne eyed her searchingly, yet didn't say a word. *She loves him,* she thought sadly.

"I hope he'll come home today," Sandra added, mostly to herself.

Nick walked into the room late at night.

"Are you sleeping?" he asked quietly.

"No, not yet," she whispered, feeling reassured, turning the lights on. "I just wanted to say goodbye, since I'm leaving early in the morning. I didn't want to wake you," he explained.

"You're leaving again?" she asked, just to say something. *They'd been sleeping in separate rooms since she came home from the hospital so they wouldn't disturb each other. It didn't make much difference since he wasn't home anyway,* she thought listlessly.

Nick noticed the reproachful tone lurking behind her indifference. "It's a week at the most, I don't know yet. I'll come back as soon as I'm done."

"It's always the same thing."

Nick didn't react to her remark.
"I'll call," he said, hesitantly leaning closer and kissing her on the forehead. "Goodnight."

CHAPTER 62

He packed his most necessary belongings into a sports bag. He knew he'd made another mistake. He felt sorry about this afternoon, which left him feeling hollow again. Thus, he wanted to disappear for a while again as soon as possible. Carmen was a burden for him. He was fed up with the way she was hounding him, clinging onto him like a leech.

He met Rodrigo this week, which came in handy. A new deal, with a lot of profit to make, yet far from secure. He had to urgently fly off to Rio de Janeiro tomorrow for a rather sizeable shipment.

He tossed and turned in bed for a long time. He went down to the kitchen when he got thirsty. He took a can of beer out of the fridge and finished it off at once. He noticed that the lights were on at the pool, but he didn't feel like going outside. It made no difference. He'd turn them off tomorrow, he thought sleepily.

His alarm clock went off. The pale light of the dawn streamed through the window. He quickly got ready without having anything for breakfast. I'll grab something at the airport, he thought. He quietly locked the door to the house turned off the lights at the pool and hurrying out to the garage. The highway ahead of him was deserted. It was only him wandering down the lanes in the early morning hours as the fog billowed around him from time to time, forcing him to slow down. As soon as the road cleared out in front of him, he slammed down on the accelerator. He turned on the radio and listened carefully to the news and the weather.

He left his car in the long-term parking lot near Malaga Airport. A a few minutes later, he was on a van taking him over to the departure lounge. He was sitting on the plane when he thought, with a bad taste in his mouth, that he hadn't even bothered to tell his wife that he was heading off to Rio. He'd take her somewhere once he got back. They could both use some rest. Then he thought of his long-deserted house in El Palmar. Somehow, when he divorced Lucy, the keys stayed with her and in the hiding place.

Their unspoken agreement was for him to keep the villa in order, although he never really bothered to check up on it. He had no idea why he never took Sandra there. He'd forgotten all about it and didn't have time for the place anyway. He passed through from time to time on business, but he never took Sandra with him. He didn't want her to get suspicious or start asking questions. *It's better if I keep the house a secret,* he thought.

Now that I'm back with Rodrigo, I might just need a hiding place again. Back in the day, he'd given Pedro a substantial loan to buy the seaside house. From that point on, they often went there together. They became friends. Later on, their ways parted, since Nick didn't want to share his business secrets with Pedro. He simply didn't trust the man.

He knew that Pedro would choose the straightaway. Usually, they thought in opposing terms. Nick couldn't recall the time they'd seen each other. Their relationship broke down for good after the incident in Marrakech. It was only when he married Lucy that he found out that Pedro went to Rio de Janeiro. Old pal, he thought. If he'd known the address, he would have paid a visit.

His trip to Rio was short. Nick met the liaison and, after taking care of the usual inspection, set up appointments and left the dubious neighbourhood as soon as he was done with his tasks. He kept his eyes open and didn't make any friends, only taking care of business in a brief, precise manner. He took care not to attract the attention of the police. He was always cautious; perhaps that's why he'd managed to stay in such an uncertain trade so long without any problems.

On the other hand, he did like a challenge, and he could make good use of the sizeable profit. He paid special attention to the current delivery. Despite the constant threat of being caught, thanks to his routine and good appearance, he took care of everything without any trouble. Once he'd finished his work, it was finally time to leave. He stepped into the elevator with his small suitcase. He paid the bill and ordered a taxi.

A few minutes later, the driver approached him.

"Are you ready, *Señor?*"

"*Si,*" Nick replied with a nod and quickly followed the Brazilian man with dreadlocked hair.

They'd hardly reached the first intersection when a few police cars passed them by, sirens wailing, before screeching to a stop in front of the hotel. The traffic light switched to red, so they were forced to stop. Nick had a bad feeling. Perhaps they were looking for him? He tensely looked back just as the taxi finally took off. Traffic was heavy. He impatiently glanced at his watch. At this rate, he'd miss his plane, he thought nervously. When they reached the airport, he rushed to the check-in desk at once. He frequently wiped his sweaty brow as he stood in line. Finally, the woman behind the counter smiled and handed him his boarding pass, focusing on the next passenger in line.

Everything's going to be alright, he comforted himself as he hurried towards the designated gate. He glanced at his watch.

It was departure time. The majority of the passengers had boarded the plane already. He strode down the narrow jet bridge, making his way to the door of the plane, where he was politely welcomed by a lovely dark-skinned stewardess. He looked for his seat, sweating from the rush, then sat down and pretended to focus on reading his paper, intently waiting for the plane to take off.

After an anxious wait, they finally taxied out onto the airstrip. A few minutes later, the plane lifted off into the air. Nick glanced out the window in relief.

CHAPTER 63

Nick silently entered the house. *Sandra is surely asleep,* he thought. He tossed his jacket on the sofa and headed over to the cabinet filled with drinks, yet halted on his way. *I have to finish it first,* he warned himself. He quietly went up to his room.

He thoroughly checked the contents of his bag. He ripped every suspicious bit of evidence into pieces, including his boarding card. He got changed and stuffed the pieces of paper into his pocket.

He walked out in front of the house. There was no one around, only a stray dog running across the street. He calmly and leisurely walked over to the other side. He walked by a trash can into which he suddenly tossed the fistful of papers. Once he reached the bar down by the shore, he got rid of the rest of the evidence, dumping it into the stuffed garbage can. Finally, to provide himself with an alibi, he entered the nearly deserted bar and asked for a drink. He was on his way home when his mobile rang.

"Talk," instructed the familiar voice.

"Everything is fine, but we must meet."

"I'll be in the usual place until the morning. It's better if you get going at once," said the other voice on the phone.

"I just got back," Nick noted with annoyance.

"It is urgent, you'll have to come anyways."

Nick pondered for a while before silently heading back upstairs. He stuffed his dirty clothes from Rio into the closet. He dumped his most necessary belongings, including a few sets of clean clothes, into his sports bag. He quietly locked the door and started up the car a few minutes later.

As he left Algeciras, he felt exhausted. A truck suddenly appeared on the winding road. It skidded over to the opposite lane, unstoppably sliding closer to Nick's car. Nick had no time to avoid it and was unable to do so. All he saw was the vehicle approaching him, as if in slow motion. Miraculously, the truck slipped over to the other side of the road right in front of him.

Nick turned pale. His life had been dangling from a hair; he thought as the perspiration gathered on his forehead. A ditch ran along the edge of the road and a car, was following him from behind, so he couldn't stop. He ran his trembling fingers through his hair, barely able to compose himself.

"You're tired, man, but you've just been incredibly lucky," he said out loud. Finally, he reached the seaside villa. He stumbled across the pitch-black grounds to the house. A minute later, he collapsed on the bed in his clothes, feeling dead tired.

In the morning, he visited Rodrigo to tell him about his trip.

"Did the police catch the wind?" Nick asked with feigned indifference. The man glared at him.

"Not really. What makes you think so?"

"I don't know, I'm just asking. Forget about it."

"This might be the last shipment. We might not have to deal with Rio again."

"Whatever," Nick said, picking up the cash and leaving. He wanted to temporarily leave the cash in a safe place before having a can of cold beer. He wiped his mouth with satisfaction and smiled that his adventure was fortunately concluded.

Soon after this, he walked down to the shore with ease to relax for a while. The water was cold as always, yet the sun was still shining warmly. He swam into the water with fierce strokes before turning back and enjoying the waves, the sandy beach, the people on the beach, and the carefree life. He lay on his stomach and dozed off as he listened to the murmur of the ocean. He thought of the late-night near-car-crash again.

I could have been lying in a body bag, he thought peevishly. He grew hungry, so he headed over to the local inn before heading back to the house after a few hours. He pulled out his mobile and deleted all the suspicious phone numbers and calls. Once he was done, he sleepily rested at length through the siesta. It was dusk outside by the time he woke up and sat out on the patio with a bottle of whiskey. He kept on drinking alone until the darkness blanketed the house and quiet neighbourhood.

A million stars shone from the sky above him. The full moon which cut the waters in two with a long, silvery stripe mysteriously illuminated the ocean and his drunken complexion as his head grew heavy from all the booze he had consumed. Hours later, he stirred from some noise and hesitantly stumbled inside the house, taking the bottle with him. He neglected everything and even left the door open. After a few steps, he crashed down onto the worn-out sofa, still fully dressed.

CHAPTER 64

Yvonne left a week later. After a lengthy period of waiting, Sandra received the permit she had requested months before. With Nick's help, she could finally open her new real estate office. She hired a woman to take care of the administrative work and advertisements and deal with the clients. Sandra searched for new markets, took photos, and signed contracts to expand her website. All her duties made her more cheerful, and she finally had a will, goals, and decisions. Thanks to her good appearance and level-headed nature, things went smoothly, and business slowly picked up. However, the real estate market was in a slump, and it was almost impossible to sell anything. Prices plunged.

This made her nervous, and thus it was no wonder that she was looking forward to the approaching holidays.

At Nick's suggestion, they surprised Antonio for Christmas by heading over to Mexico together. After a pleasant dinner, Nick asked him about Amy and whether their relationship still going strong. Antonio briefly told him that they were still exchanging letters. Sandra anxiously listened to him. Her sixth sense warned her about possible future problems. After the unforgettable weeks they spent together, they said goodbye to Antonio and flew home, full of rich experiences.

In February, Nick installed heating for the pool, thus allowing them to use it all year round. Nick was bored and asked his wife when she came home late and tired, "Do you have to do this?"

"Why?" she asked, perking up in surprise and pouring herself a drink. "Because you simply don't need to work, plus you're never around, and we hardly see each other. You're always busy," he complained, raising his voice.

"Oh, come on, you're joking," she retorted sarcastically. "You've been wandering off God knows where for years and leaving me all alone, right?"

"Yes, but when I came home, you were always there for me. That's what I miss."

"I have to admit, that's true," she said, reproachfully looking him in the eye.

"Now you're not happy that I found my calling and I've got something to do. You're just selfish." He wants to keep me for himself like an expensive car which he can start up whenever he wants to, she thought indignantly. Or what's even worse is that he might miss me because there's no one to serve him.

"No, don't get me wrong. I'm glad you found what you were looking for. The problem is that we've grown distant. Am I right?"

"Really?" she asked, flashing her eyes at him.

"So, you disagree?"

Sandra fell silent for a while, unwilling to get worked up.

"I didn't grow distant. I'm just the same as I was before." Nick couldn't continue their discussion due to her cold, dismissive attitude. He stood up and went out onto the patio. He knew their previous heated conversation was pointless. He still hugged his sleeping wife in the morning, and she hugged him back. Later, they silently lay next to each other in their customary manner. Nick went back to sleep.

Sandra cautiously slipped out of bed. She got dressed and quietly went outside, locked the gate, and slowly headed down to the beach. The sun was just starting its ascent across the sky, repeating its countless days. The morning air was fresh and slightly chilly. She loved running, swimming, and riding a bicycle since it allowed her to get a fresh start to the day.

Further up the shore, she sat down panting. The stretch of beach in front of her was still wet from the evening tide. Nearby, a fishing boat puffed black smoke into the air over the gently swaying sea. Once she got back home, she had a quick shower in the bathroom downstairs.

By the time, she reached the kitchen, she heard Nick singing in the bathroom upstairs. This always made her smile, since he wasn't exactly a true talent with his flat voice. She'd grown fond of him over the years and they'd gotten used to each other, and somehow, the memories of the past had faded. She often felt that he was devoted to her in his way, and this comforted her.

She hummed a tune as she brewed some coffee and fixed breakfast. By the time, he came out of the bathroom, the table was set, full of treats, on the table outside.

Nick grinned. He loved mornings like this, giving his day a good start. "Do you have any plans for the weekend?" he asked indifferently. She shrugged.

"I don't, but if you do, then let me know."

"We could invite David and Carmen over, and anyone else you want." Sandra turned grim and searchingly eyed him. She was about to say something, but then she changed her mind.

"Whatever."

She wanted to stay away from David since he once called her Vicky in the kitchen. Although she didn't like Carmen, who seemed to be nice with her, they never got close and they'd never really befriended each other. When they met, Carmen usually talked about tacky things or the gossip in Marbella. Recently, she noticed that whenever they met, Carmen always seemed to lurk around Nick.

Am I jealous? But David often approaches me as well, she recalled. This made her smile.

"What's so funny?"

"It's nothing special, it's nothing," she noted evasively.

"You don't sound too keen."

"That's right," she said, standing up. She filled the tray with the remains of the breakfast and carried it over to the kitchen. She quickly tidied up the counter and picked her bag up in a rush.

"So, should I call them?" asked Nick.

"If you want to."

"Saturday night?"

"Sounds good to me."

"When?"

"It makes no difference, whatever's good for you. I've got to go. I'll be back the usual time," she said, leaving in a hurry.

CHAPTER 65

She carefully drove down the road. As she reached the office, she started by checking her emails. Nothing interesting, she realized. Or maybe not, she wondered, clicking back on the previous letter. A client wanted to make an appointment for buying a house next week, she read.

Great, she thought.

At the same time, her desk phone rang.

"Home Real Estate," she said in a business-like tone.

"Good morning," said a welcoming female voice. "We're looking for some real estate."

"How about today at five or tomorrow at ten?"

"Thank you, I'd prefer today, if possible," replied the stranger.

"What kind of real estate are you looking for?" she asked in an upbeat tone.

"A place that's in a well-frequented spot, with a nice view of the sea, that's all," replied the stranger.

"What's your ceiling price?"

"Four hundred thousand."

"Okay, I'll see you at five, then..." said Sandra in parting in a professional tone. She spent the rest of the morning taking care of phone calls and arranging appointments.

She returned to the office after the siesta at five. It was half-past five by the time she headed out with the client. The number of cars on the road was picking up, and they ended up in a traffic jam. Fifteen minutes later, the long line of cars still wasn't moving. She nervously called the seller to tell him they would be late and turned off her motor. The man sitting next to her impatiently opened the car door and walked ahead for a while before returning in annoyance.

"What happened?" asked his wife. "I don't know."

A police car raced past them down the opposite lane of the street with sirens blaring, followed by an ambulance.

"It must be an accident," said Sandra, tensely tapping the steering wheel with her fingers. The long line of cars finally shuffled onwards after another half hour. A few hundred metres farther, they passed the critical point. The ungainly heap of an overturned truck lay crushed in the ditch running alongside the road. The alarming sight of a passenger vehicle laying under it, damaged beyond recognition, made them shudder.

After a silent ride, they finally reached the house. The location, the silence, and the proximity to the sea made the married couple exchange hopeful looks since the view was truly stunning.

"The plot is exceptionally well-positioned, the neighbourhood is superb, and with a decent investment, you can easily turn it into a villa." she explained.

"It's nice," they said in praise of the house, yet they decided to take a few days to think the matter over. The following day, the man called, saying they'd like to take a look at the house with an architect.

"Naturally," replied Sandra politely.

The prospective clients suddenly left, promising to get in touch soon. *So much for your sixth sense,* she noted mockingly. It was late by the time she drove home, feeling exhausted.

It was getting dark and the lights of the city came on. She advanced sluggishly through the traffic. She pulled out her mobile and called Nick, but he didn't answer the call. *He's off doing something again,* she thought. *But then again, why would he sit around at home, doing nothing waiting for me?*

As she entered the house, she turned the lights on and was pouring herself a martini when she noticed an open envelope on the table. She read the letter. It was a brief note from Antonio, explaining that everything was doing well for him. This comforted her. He would become a doctor, just like his father. She wondered whether Pedro still thought of her after all these years. *Of course, he doesn't,* she decided, brushing off this weird question.

I'm sure he forgot me a long time ago. Yet still, a sentimental sigh slipped through her finely lined lips. He had married and had an adorable, smart daughter who with any luck would never see her son again. If she did, Sandra would have to take matters into her own hands. Siblings can't fall in love since that would be incest, she thought, as a shiver coursed down her spine. *Take it easy, you always assume the worst,* she scolded herself. Still, she was hopeful that the time and distance would overcome them.

CHAPTER 66

They had a cold lunch with some beer and rested during the afternoon siesta. They went down to the kitchen around six to fix something for dinner. She greatly appreciated Nick's habit of never asking what to do but rather getting to work on his own. Preparing salads and fruit was a time-consuming task. Sandra was already busying herself with fixing the starters.

Nick poured some red wine into glasses and silently slipped one of the glasses over to her.

"You know, it heightens your sense of taste," he said frequently. Sandra smiled at him. She wiped her hands with a paper towel and raised her drink to a toast. "Salud!"

She took a sip of the pleasantly tasteful wine.

"It's delicious. Where did you get it?" She exclaimed.

"I discovered a new liquor store," chuckled Nick, thinking about the other, bottle. Sandra planted a light kiss on his face.

"Is everything alright with the barbecue?"

"Yes."

"Okay, then go and get yourself ready. I'll finish soon."

Later on, Nick set the table and was making some final adjustments to it when Sandra showed up. His gaze lingered over her for a moment. Her slim shape, long red hair, emerald green eyes, and classic feminine beauty still seemed undeniably attractive.

Her elegant outfit was never too racy or daring. She hardly used any makeup—just a hint of eyeliner and no mascara—yet her lips still seemed full and tempting. She wore a single golden earring, which he once bought for her. He was certainly delighted by the sight of her.

She placed some flowers on the table. She arranged saucers on a tray in the kitchen and finally placed a few bathing towels on the deckchair. *Perhaps someone might want to go for a swim,* she thought. Nick was already sitting in the armchair, sipping his regular dose of whiskey.

"Would you like anything?" he asked, turning to face her. Sandra shook her head. "I'll wait for them to show up."

The guests arrived sometime after eight. Carmen wrapped her arms too tightly around Nick's neck when she welcomed him. She stepped too close to him while giggling something into his ear. Sandra unintentionally witnessed the scene, which ruined her good mood. She felt they were playing dirty. She recalled the name of a song. *Love Is a Losing Game.* She loved living simply, although she knew that infidelity was an everyday thing in this day and age. She always tried to distance herself from this kind of lifestyle and naively expected Nick to be faithful as well.

She didn't like double-dealing. She occasionally mentioned that she would let go of him if he wanted a divorce. She knew this had nothing to do with jealousy. If he wanted to go, so be it, she wouldn't hold him back. Still, she felt an ache in her heart that resonated with humiliation, bitterness, and shame. At the same time, however, her pride surged forth, protesting against the way a woman like Carmen, who offered herself up in her flimsy outfits, would make fun of her like this or make her regret having such a fickle husband. *Nick had always been a womanizer,* she recalled. *Why did she ever think, he would change?*

David also watched the scene with an ashen look on his face and suddenly glanced at Sandra, who bit her lip in annoyance. When they exchanged glances, he was practically convinced that they both had the same thought in mind.

Later on, the mood improved. Nick brought out a bottle of a special beverage before dinner. He opened it with masterful motions and poured everyone a hit from the dark green sphere-shaped bottle into a couple of special glasses prepared for the occasion.

"You have to down it all at once," he warned the others.

"What is it?" asked Carmen, standing right next to Nick, resting her hand on his shoulder as if he belonged to her.

"It's a special Hungarian drink called Unicum, which I bought at a recently opened liquor store," he explained, turning to the others. "Actually, I wanted to surprise my wife," he continued, brushing off the leech. He picked up two glasses and held out one of them to Sandra. He suddenly leaned closer to her and whispered in her ear, "You drive me crazy." She blushed and awkwardly turned away.

How dare he say something like that after chatting with Carmen moments ago? The drink burned her throat, yet the bitter taste proved to be a pleasant aperitif, and thus they quickly finished off the round of *tapas* awaiting them on the table. The embers glowed without any flames, producing a thin greyish outer layer. Nick put the meat over the grill. Carmen stubbornly stood next to him. There was no doubt that she was clinging to him. David peevishly and absently chatted with the others while openly admiring his wife. He kept looking back at Sandra, even though he wasn't entirely sure why he did so. *It's as if she's been avoiding me all night,* he thought. They hadn't said a word to each other apart from their welcoming words.

It turned dark. The evening lights grew sharper in the pool and on the patio. Quiet Latin music resounded from the living room. Sandra brought out some candles. She put two on the table and four on the flagstones of the patio before returning to the kitchen. She quickly fixed the salad and carried it out onto the patio with the side dish. In the meantime, the meat grew tender over the grill, filling the air with its spicy aroma.

They were in a great mood as they sat down at the long table which was decorated in fine colours on the final Saturday of May. Nick placed the delicious roast meat in the middle of the table and brought out two bottles of red wine which he'd opened previously, passing one of them around.

Carmen sat down opposite Nick. She mischievously eyed him and wouldn't take her eyes off him. However, he continued to ignore her, just as he walked away from her when she joined him, telling her to leave him alone. Still, Carmen wouldn't give up. She extended her leg under the table and unmistakably rubbed her feet on his inner thigh.

Nick angrily glared at her, yet Carmen licked her lips and daringly stared him down before repeating her erotic motions. Nick simply hated it when women latched on to him like this, and thus, he slightly leaned forward and, inconspicuously, reached under the tablecloth, fiercely twisting her prodding foot, making her wince in pain. After dinner, the discussion headed in the direction of a delicate subject.

"My neighbour was in trouble," began Maria, "because of the man working for he asked for more money than they previously agreed on and thus, she didn't pay him the hundred Euro difference."

"Good for her," noted Nick.

"So, what do you think about honour?" asked the forty-something Carlos humorously, sitting at the end of the table. He and his wife were also, old friends of Nick. Since no one said a thing, he turned to David.

"What do you think?" he repeated his question.

Carmen deceitfully eyed Nick.

"Well, it seems like you've cornered me, pal," he said, before pondering and answering the question. "It's a bit hard to sum it up, but I'll do my best." He raised his glass and drank the rest of his wine.

"Well," he started with some difficulty, wiping the edge of his mouth. "An honourable man does the utmost to always observe the social rules and laws. To limit the scope of discussion, I think honour is about always giving unconditional trust to the people living with us and around is. I mean to say that the word should have weight. This includes business matters our, life, marriage, our parents, and our friendships." He reproachfully glanced at Nick and then Carmen, who wouldn't look at him.

"We gain trust by not lying, not using others, and not making promises we can never fulfill."

"So, honour is tied to love as well, correct?" asked Carlos' wife. "Not necessarily, but to a certain degree, yes. I think this leads to another subject. I couldn't separate the matter since if I think that one half of a married couple is unfaithful, they will inevitably be forced to lie since they must lie to the other person. That's part of honour as well."

"Does that mean it isn't just be really difficult to be honourable, but perhaps there won't be any honourable people at all?" noted Carmen cynically. "What are your thoughts on this?" she asked, sarcastically glancing at Nick. The question made him uncomfortable. Still, he nonchalantly shrugged it off.

"There are many moments in life when we don't think about honour," he explained evasively.

"Go on," encouraged David attentively. "Well, you're right about the subject you've brought up, it's hard to unanswer. Oh, it's nonsense, I don't want to go into it."

"No, go on," interrupted Carlos.

"I think this is a far-reaching subject, since it involves morals." Carmen laughed sharply. "What is this nonsense about morals? We're living in the twenty-first century," she interrupted daringly.

"Indubitably," noted Sandra, who had remained silent until now. "This is precisely why you mustn't forget that there's no need to lie to each other nowadays. We no longer have any social rules against hiding our varying feelings. Thus, there's no sense in fooling the other person either," she rubbed it in. "Divorce is no longer a complicated legal procedure, yet as far as I know, there are still a lot of people who like living double-dealing lives."

"Oh, that's just what jealous people complain about," retorted Carmen, a bit too harshly.

"Settle down, now. Exactly what is jealousy?" cried Carlos, clearly enjoying the discussion. He stood up, grabbed the wine bottle, and filled everyone's glass, while silence settled over the table.

"Salud," he said to take the edge off the discussion.
He wiped his mouth and sneakily looked around.
"Well, come on, can't anyone give me an answer?" he forced the matter with a grin. David broke the awkward silence again.
"Another tricky answer. Let's say, if a man and a woman love each other, it's only natural that they're jealous when a third person shows up and approaches their beloved partner. That much is clear, right?" he asked, quizzically glancing at the others.
The others nodded and hummed. Nick morosely gripped his glass. "Let's move on. A jealous person clings onto the other and won't let go even if they love someone else. They always follow them around, watch their every move, and do all they can to mess things up. However, you can't call someone jealous who notices that their partner is looking for something else and who takes every opportunity to latch on to someone else. Perhaps they catch them in the act. Since that's unacceptable, they ask the classic question. Why don't we break up if I don't mean anything to you anymore?"

He paused for effect and glanced at his wife, continuing, "If someone is capable of saying that, it's clear that they already made up the mind. It's better to get a divorce than to be treated off-handed, laughed at, or felt sorry for. No one likes being pitied."

Sandra glanced at Nick, who glanced at the pool in boredom, clearly unwilling to discuss the awkward subject. He knew all of this well, yet he still didn't care what other people thought of him. His primary intention, apart from making money, was to satisfy his desires. Morals meant nothing to him. Life is such that if you want a woman or perhaps grow fond of her (he glanced at Sandra for a moment) you try to get her.

If you get bored with her -he thought of Carmen- you try to get rid of her. So much for morals. The morals of nature – which let feelings flow and which weren't invented by old men wearing wigs who tried tying life down with rules – control our behaviour and actions. He wouldn't let anyone tell him how to live his life.

David quietly continued. "Once you forgive the other's slip, they will soon do it again, which cannot be accepted with common sense. Thus, it's better if they part ways." He picked up the bottle and filled his glass. "If you have a sense of pride you will want to clear the air. And maybe I need to clear my head after all this wine," he chuckled to himself, concluding his lengthy discussion.

Sandra stood up.
"Let's change the subject. The water is lovely, come on, let's take a dip," she said, dissolving the depressed group and going inside to change.
On her way out, she added, "There are some swimsuits and trunks on the sofa." Nick appreciatively eyed his wife, admiring the ease with which she'd ended this depressing conversation. The mood improved. Soon, the host dived head-first into the water after his little redhead.
"David, please fill the glasses for me, won't you?" he cried as he swam after his wife. He slipped up next to her and noted, "Good thing for intervening. The subject was boring."
"Oh, really?" she asked, glancing at her husband without surprise. "Well, I guess I'll just have to believe that coming from you," she added sarcastically and swam away from him.

He was infuriated by her cold mockery, but by the time he turned around, Sandra was already walking out onto the patio without looking back at him. She wrapped the towel around herself and stormed inside to change.

Carmen used this opportunity to hurry into the water, eyeing Nick as he swam across the pool with fierce strokes, waiting for him as a well-planned coincidence. "What a stupid subject, huh?"

"Yeah. I was bored."

"Me too." She cautiously looked around before quickly caressing his rump. "Do you think David suspects anything?" She glanced in the direction of her husband.

"I don't care, so please, leave me alone, okay?" he hissed with flashing eyes, swimming away from her.

As he reached the other end, he held onto the edge of the pool and pulled himself up onto the rim with ease before wiping away the water from his face with annoyance. He grabbed a towel, rubbed his muscular figure until it was dry, and went inside to get changed. He saw no sign of Sandra. On his way back, he dangled a bottle from one hand and three round cognac glasses from the other.

"Salud," he said, raising the glass. He thoughtfully eyed David, whom he'd known for a long time and whose considerate nature always had a reassuring effect on him. He felt uncomfortable having an affair with the man's wife, but that was over now. This sudden, shallow affair was a mistake. His glance wandered over to the pool. Nick had no idea that Carmen was already scheming the revenge that was just unravelling.

She couldn't stand losing and the fact that Nick had simply dumped her. What happened to him? Only last week they were still making love. At that moment, she even forgot whose wife she was. She coursed through the water with fierce arm strokes until she finally held onto the rim of the pool. Her treacherous gaze fell over the men standing close by.

"David, why don't you come in? The water is delicious," she cried alluringly.

"I'm not in the mood. Come on out, it's time to head home."

Sandra didn't show up to say goodbye. The guests slowly left. Nick continued drinking cognac on his own before he pulled out some of the white powder. His mind felt numb after the last line. He didn't feel like staying at home or going up to the bedroom where Sandra had surely fallen asleep by now. Lately, he was getting annoyed by her cold behaviour and the fact that she was constantly busy. He was used to being thronged by women.

His wife never adored him. Her embrace rarely felt truly devoted. Perhaps that's why he ran into the arms of strangers and unknown women, but the flings never made him any happier. At times, such as this, he always resorted to booze or drugs.

As he had many times before, he felt an animal-like rage building inside of him. He suddenly threw his glass away. It landed on a bush and slowly slipped down onto the lawn, but it didn't break. He stood up, closed the sliding door to the patio, and stumbled up the stairs. He burst into the bedroom with a crash. He threw his clothes off and lay down next to where she lay motionless in bed. He violently turned her towards him. Sandra silently cried, but Nick paid no attention to her and perhaps didn't notice this at all. He quickly and selfishly did what he wanted before falling onto his back and dozing off to sleep. She stared into the darkness with her eyes wide open. She felt herself alone.

CHAPTER 67

She was puttering around in the garden when she heard the sound of the mailman's yellow scooter in front of the gate. He spotted her and cried out in welcome, handing her an envelope through the fence. It was a letter from Antonio.

She hurried inside and curiously opened it. In a month, despite her hopes that he would come home for his extended vacation, he would, in fact, be heading over to Rio to visit Amy, who turned pale as she read the letter. It seemed that platonic love had turned serious. She laid back on the sofa, lost in thought. She didn't notice that the letter slipped from her fingers and fell to the ground as she stared out at the garden. Somehow, she had to get Amy's address.

But how? She couldn't write to Antonio that she wanted to go to Rio de Janeiro with him. That would be absurd. It was an oppressive feeling to keep secrets from others. For days on end, she thought about what she should do to prevent her son's trip. She had headaches from the futile pondering. She couldn't bear this agonizing feeling for long.

She squeezed her hands into fists in her momentary help-lessness before pressing her fingers down on her throbbing temples. She picked up the letter she'd dropped to the ground and hesitantly moved it to a desk drawer. At that particular moment in time, she couldn't think over or handle this delicate subject. After her lengthy, fruitless pondering, she slipped into her swimsuit. A few moments later, she started doing laps in the pool.

She pushed herself onwards in a fierce tempo, hoping to wash her filthy thoughts clean with the water. What could she do if she managed to make it over there? she wondered for a while, becoming increasingly anxious. At first, she kept counting the laps, but later on, she simply kept swimming and swimming until she was exhausted.

Nick suddenly arrived. He sat out on, the patio with his usual drink, waiting for her to notice him. He didn't want to disturb her. He morosely eyed her for a while before he grew bored and went inside to refill his glass. He talked on his phone at length, which made him rather annoyed. When came back out again, his wife was still swimming. She's been in the water for almost an hour, he thought. He suddenly stopped and noticed that something was wrong with Sandra. Her arms moved feebly and automatically in the water. Her legs didn't flutter. She floundered in the centre of the pool, and it was clear that she wouldn't make it to the edge. Perhaps she didn't want to. Her red hair floated unfurled in the water, covering her face as she slowly sank to the bottom of the pool.

He removed his shoes and jumped into the water, fully dressed. His powerful arms gripped the exhausted body, and he kicked them both up to the surface before reaching the steps and laying her out on the edge of the pool. She quickly came to, since she had only been under the water briefly.

"Okay, honey, everything will be okay," he said nervously. He quickly shrugged off his soaked clothes and ran inside, yanking two towels out of the closet. He spread one of them out on the sofa before bringing Sandra inside and gently laying her on the towel. He used the other towel to thoroughly rub her body down. He felt odd as he brushed the red hair matted to her face to the side with his palms. I've neglected her, he thought guiltily. He poured a shot of brandy and lifted it to her lips. "Drink this, it will do you good."

They'd grown distant lately, perhaps because of her reclusive nature, but he was particularly annoyed by her work. He kept telling her to stop it since the real estate market had been lying dormant for years. Those who previously purchased real estate on a mortgage were forced to market it sooner rather than later due to a growing number of defaults. This increased the real estate on offer, and the prices plunged drastically, yet there were few potential buyers. The solvent clients offered ridiculous prices for the chosen real estate.

There was no sense in sitting in an office all day long, hunting for clients. She did not need to do so. It was true that he never told her that he had a lot of money, yet he was convinced that this wouldn't impress his wife. After all their bickering and arguing, she'd finally given in and gotten rid of the office.

Nick was glad that his little redhead was around the house again. However, his joy wasn't long-lived, since she'd grown increasingly remote. He searchingly eyed the woman lying in his arms. He had the feeling that she was still silently rejecting him. This was true since Sandra stubbornly closed her eyes. She couldn't bear to explain herself.

A week after the incident, Carmen suddenly appeared. Her hair was bleached to a honey-blonde colour. Her face looked smooth and rested, yet her heavy makeup and blood-red lips seemed just as daring as always. She flaunted herself in her low-cut top. She openly showed off her undeniably beautiful brown stomach as her hips erotically swayed side to side. Her tight white pants revealed the outlines of her briefs and well-shaped posterior.

"Long time, no see," Sandra welcomed her in a reserved tone. "Well yeah, that's true. But now I'm back. I stopped by to ask if you'd like to go out on the sea this weekend. Nick could hoist up the sails as he did in the past," Carmen said sneakily, forcing a friendly smile onto her face.

"The weather is divine, so let's make good use of it, right?"

Carmen hated Nick since he broke up with her. She didn't like the way he dropped her like a rug when he grew bored of her. Of course, she might be someone who offered herself up to men and looked for adventure wherever she could. Yet the lust for revenge burned hot inside of her. Sandra thoughtfully eyed the woman.

"I'll mention it to him," she noted coldly.
"Is something wrong? You seem so melancholic," asked Carmen attentively.
"Oh, no, it's nothing, I just didn't sleep well last night," Sandra replied, concluding the conversation and slowly heading towards the exit. She didn't like Carmen, but she didn't hate the woman either, even though she noticed Carmen had been constantly hounding Nick. She didn't know that at their last party her husband did everything he could to avoid Carmen.

In the past, Nick and Carmen had always lagged from the others while chatting, Sandra recalled. They craftily hid her back, which was rather annoying. She simply felt better than this daring woman, who was also David's wife. She'd known David for a long time. She felt sorry for him since it seemed as though his second marriage would sooner or later end up in a divorce, just like the first. Of course, Sandra's marriage wasn't too far from falling apart either.

She was undeniably annoyed by this situation with Carmen. She increasingly despised her husband for his weak character. Perhaps sometimes she even hated him – not just because of Carmen, but also because of the suspicious trips he went on, over the years they'd been together. Nick noticed all the women around him. Whenever they went somewhere, he loved standing behind her back to freely gaze at the members of the fairer sex. When it came to women, he stopped at nothing, whether it was a relative, a friend, or an acquaintance, and thus he didn't have any real friends – except David.

Her bitterness increased, but she couldn't do anything about it. She simply felt weak, bored, and increasingly remote. *Perhaps my whole life is a compromise,* she thought again for the umpteenth time.

CHAPTER 68

Lately, Sandra was pleased when Nick went away for weeks. She had been increasingly thinking about how to take care of herself without him. She often decided that she had to do something, but how? *Tomorrow*, she thought. Tomorrow turned into today, today became yesterday, and nothing happened. She knew she was verging on depression again – or perhaps she had already fallen into it. One thing she knew for sure: she wanted to be far, far away from there.

At night, Nick silently slipped into bed and tenderly wrapped his arms around her, causing her to stir and tamely push him away. He turned the light on with an annoyed expression.

"I want to know what's wrong, what's bothering you," he said. "Why don't you open up to me? What is it that I can't know about? Why don't you realize we can't go on like this!"

She remained silent. She clenched her mouth shut, closed her eyes, and lay motionless amongst the tangled sheets. Nick angrily glared at her and suddenly realized that there was no sense in questioning her since she would never open up to him.

"Fine, I won't ask any more questions, just tell me what you would like to do. What do you want from me?"

She still didn't say anything.

"Why won't you answer me?"

"I want to go somewhere else. I need to be alone," she noted at long last, determinedly.

He looked at her in surprise and didn't say anything in reply for a while before giving up. "Fine. That's okay with me, you can go somewhere if that's what you really want," he noted listlessly, quickly getting dressed and leaving without a word. Sandra started crying. Even though she had everything, she felt she had nothing.

In the morning, she walked over to the bathroom, had a shower, and carefully applied what little makeup she wore. She brewed some coffee and checked the mail. She found an envelope in the mailbox. It was from her son, who had indeed gone to Brazil. He would most likely be staying in Rio for a month. His address was on the envelope, and the letter included his new phone numbers.

She made up her mind without wasting another moment. She sat down at the computer and made a reservation for the next flight. The plane would depart from Madrid the following day, late at night. *The die is cast*, she thought. She quickly packed her most necessary belongings into a small suitcase before finally writing a short letter to Nick.

I'm sorry for causing so much trouble for you. I'll be away for a while. I need some time alone. I'll be in touch.

She called a taxi and headed off to the airport in Malaga. She made it to Madrid by the evening. She found a place to stay for the night close to the airport. The hotel was quiet, yet she still couldn't fall asleep. Everything had happened so fast. Yesterday morning, she hadn't even known she was going to leave, let alone go on such a long journey. She couldn't stop thinking about Antonio. She knew she had to keep something from happening between the kids at all costs since they were siblings. She might already be too late, and then what would she do? She wondered in confusion.

She had no firm plans and no solution in mind, yet she knew she had to solve this awkward issue at all costs even if she had to reveal her murky past, which terrified her. She could still clearly remember the photograph she had dropped into the sea.

She was terrified of the thought of appearing out of nowhere and relating horrifying tales of the darkest period of her life. After all, Pedro was a stranger by now, and perhaps he didn't even remember her. She couldn't understand why fate punished her so often like this. It could be nothing other than destiny. Yet she made up her mind to fight it, mustering her strength from some reserve.

CHAPTER 69

She waited a few hours at the Madrid airport before checking in. She found the gate designated on her boarding pass and found an empty seat, indifferently eyeing the people around her. The lobby was slowly filling with passengers, and the gate to the jet bridge opened. She found her seat on the plane and gave in to the excitement of travelling. She was glad she could finally get rid of the suffocating pressure of her home, yet she still didn't dare think of what was ahead of her.

After a brief period of waiting, the aeroplane taxied out onto the runway. The motors whirred to life, and a moment later, they were in the air. She loved take-off because it helped her imagine she had wings. She felt free, leaving all her troubles behind on the ground. The plane sliced its way through the air, beginning its lengthy flight towards South America.

She'd never been to Brazil before. She never thought she would make it to Rio de Janeiro. She looked around. The passenger space was full. On the other side of the narrow aisle sat a man whose face looked familiar.

The stranger eyed her attentively yet not pushily, nodding at her in a barely perceptible manner. Sandra reciprocated the nod before pulling a magazine from the holder in front of her and engrossing herself in a lengthy read. The stewardess started serving drinks. She asked for red wine. She took a sip and glanced over at the man for a moment, and he kindly lifted his glass for a toast. After dinner, she closed her eyes for a while to get some rest.

Later on, the man sitting on the other side of the aisle addressed her. "May I?" he asked, pointing at the vacant seat next to her. Sandra raised an eyebrow.

"Sure."

"I hope you have no objections? It's going to be a long and boring trip. Perhaps we could have a chat if you don't mind. I'm Robert Grey," he said, holding his hand out to her.

Sandra was surprised, yet his open, vigorous handshake radiated a kind of trust to her. She didn't feel like he was being intrusive at all. Thanks to his direct and open nature, it was like meeting an old friend or acquaintance.

"I'm sure you're thinking I'm looking for some kind of adventure. Please, just try to forget about that. If you want to, we can talk. I would certainly, like to." He smiled mischievously. Although you probably don't remember, we've met before."

She gazed at him, trying to recall that earlier meeting. She said, "OK, I won't put up a fight. You're right, it's going to be a long trip. So, what do you want to know?" she asked, turning to the stranger.

"Ask and I'll do my best to answer." Suddenly, she did remember him – he had come looking for Nick once. Fine, if he wants to play, then I'm ready, she thought. The man was satisfied with her answer.

"There's nothing I want to know. I see what I see, and that's enough for me." Sandra felt reassured. She knew that this temporary acquaintance meant nothing. People usually opened up in situations like this and might say something about themselves that, under normal circumstances, they wouldn't share with their closest friends.

"Can I get you a drink?" he asked.

"Sure, why not." He sure is a pleasant companion, she thought. It simply felt good to move out of the boring, monotonous rhythm of her life.

"Will you let me pick a drink?"

"Sure," she replied with ease.

The man shortly sat back down next to her. A few minutes later, the stewardess politely brought them their drinks. They clinked glasses and continued to chat. They talked at length, never asking anything personal from each other. Later on, they sat silently next to each other, watching a film and even dozing off for a time.

After a long while, the pilot finally announced they were preparing for landing. The warning signs went off, indicating that passengers should fasten their seatbelts. The plane descended, the engines disengaged, and finally, the plane landed with a slight jolt.

Sandra's tension and problems suddenly returned as she hesitantly waited for her suitcase. When she saw it on the conveyor belt, she wanted to snatch it up, but her new friend got ahead of her before they hesitantly said goodbye.

Sandra looked for a taxi.

However, the stranger kept an eye out of her, and thus they bumped into each other in front of the entrance.

"Can I help?" he asked, noticing that no one came to pick her up. She eyed him hesitantly.

"I'm not sure, I'm looking for a quiet hotel somewhere downtown." Sandra answered. "That means you don't have a hotel reservation?" asked Grey in surprise.

"No, I don't."

"Then let me take you into town. Please, wait here. I'll get my car from the parking lot and take you to a small hotel if that's fine with you." She could tell from the look on his face that he was hoping for a yes. Sandra uncertainly nodded, and the man turned around and hurried off.

In a few minutes, a sports car pulled up in front of her. Grey nimbly moved her suitcase to the trunk and opened the door for her. He held a hand out to her and humorously bowed. "Please, get in."

"Thank you," she muttered in a reserved tone, feeling uncomfortable as always when she was forced to accept the favour. Her motto was always 'do it yourself', or at least pay for it, but never accept anything for free and never ask for anything. If you're forced to accept something, then you're indebted to the person in question. However, unforeseen situations often arise in life.

Some like asking for favours which they never reciprocate. They latch themselves onto the people they deem to be their friends, like a leech. Simpletons make the same mistake again and again, but if you have some common sense, you can avoid people like this in the future.

A few days ago, one of her girlfriends had sadly reported that someone visiting from a foreign country had latched onto her husband and got him to invite her over. The woman had stayed with them for weeks, during which she managed to get them to take her out for trips in the neighbourhood. She never so much as buying them a bottle of wine or anything else in return. Even when her girlfriend had a birthday, the uninvited guest didn't bother to buy her a thing; meanwhile, she greedily drank up their champagne.

The whole matter was a one-sided, freeloading invitation.

CHAPTER 70

They raced down the road towards downtown Rio de Janeiro. The man glanced at his passenger for a moment.

"Don't worry," he assured her, "I know the city well. I have a feeling this is your first time here – or am I mistaken?"

"No, you're right, this is my first time. What about you?" she asked, turning to the man.

"I've lived here for a long time, but currently I'm working in Spain. Still, I have a few things to take care of here. For example, I have to sell this car and then say goodbye to this beautiful city for good."

She didn't ask him what kind of work it was since she suspected that he must be a private eye or a lawyer. Then it occurred to her that he might be a detective. As they reached the busy downtown district, they slowly edged along the streets until he parked the sports car in a lot of an old, well-established building. "Come on!" said her new friend, directing her to the reception desk.

"*Hola!*" said the man behind the counter, welcoming his old friend."Long time no see."

"Indeed."

"On your own?" he asked before catching a glance of the strikingly beautiful woman at the man's side. *"Buenas Tardes!"* welcomed the stranger nervously.

Sandra reservedly reciprocated the welcome and turned away. "Yes," said Grey in Portuguese. "Please get the lady a room. She's dear to me, so I'd like to entrust her to your care," he added, glancing at the woman, who reached out for the map on the counter.

Sandra made a face since she couldn't help but overhear their discussion. The men had no idea that the redhead spoke Portuguese.

"She's a beautiful woman," said the desk clerk.

"Okay, I'm not blind, but cut that out for a change. I'd appreciate it if I could have her as my friend. Understand? Please, keep an eye out for her."

The receptionist nodded and turned away to check the computer. "Yes. I have a nice room on the third floor." Robert nodded in satisfaction. He turned the woman and authoritatively spoke up.

"If it's suitable, I'll come to pick you up tomorrow at eleven. Would that be okay? I'll show you the city so you can be familiar with the place. I'm convinced you're going to need this."

Sandra was startled for a moment, yet she still managed to smile. "Thank you, that's very kind of you," she said, heading towards the elevator. She didn't appreciate the fact that he wanted to show her around. She also wasn't thrilled that he wanted her to waste her time on him.

The spacious, comfortable room offered a spectacular view of the city, Sugarloaf Mountain, and Guanabara Bay. She stood in front of the window as the dusk settled in, truly enchanted by the view of Rio de Janeiro. Back on the plane, she read a caption about this unparalleled beauty:

"The Lord created the world in six days and added the seventh day as a gift." In the bathroom, she stood under the shower at length to wash off the exhaustion of her trip.

By the time she finished, it was dark outside, and the city was flooded in lights. She opened her suitcase and dug out her pyjamas but didn't unpack the rest. She went straight to bed.

The following morning, she woke feeling fresh and rested. She locked her suitcase in a hurry and went downstairs to have breakfast. Shortly after breakfast, she paid for her stay and called a taxi. The man standing behind the counter quizzically raised an eyebrow. However, she ignored him completely.

"Perhaps you're leaving because you weren't satisfied with the room?"

"No, no. The room is beautiful, but I have to go."

"Where can I take you?" asked the driver. Sandra handed him the envelope she had received from her son, with the address legibly spelt on it.

"Do you know the place?" she asked in Portuguese.

"Sure, it's on Copacabana beach. Come!" he said, picking up her suitcase. They'd almost reached the exit when the man behind the counter motioned to the driver.

"Where are you taking her?" he asked, nodding towards the woman. The taxi driver answered him in a hurry before opening the door for the woman, getting in and driving off. Sandra attentively eyed the traffic on the street before glancing at the driver's bulging hands. He wore a thick silver ring on his pinkie.

His confident motions showed that he'd gone down this stretch of road millions of times before. She glanced at her watch. It was almost eleven. She smiled faintly. She was satisfied with herself that she had brushed off her new acquaintance with such ease since she wanted to deal with this awkward issue on her own, even though she still didn't have a definite plan. Nevertheless, she firmly made up her mind that she couldn't wait any longer and had to deal with this delicate matter now.

"We're here," said the driver, turning back to her before slowing down and stopping in front of the block of apartments. "Here's the entrance," he said, pointing at the gate.

"Would you like me to show you inside?"

"No, I don't want to get out, I'd like you to find me a quiet little hotel somewhere nearby, something like the previous place," she asked him.

"Well, wait a minute. Let me think," said the driver, furrowing his dark bushy eyebrows and falling silent for a moment.

"Oh, I know just the place," he said, snapping his fingers. He turned his indicators on and headed out, slowly edging along before coming to a stop at the next corner.

"This is a rather old, reputable hotel, mainly used by foreigners. Wait, let me ask them if they have any vacancies."

"Thank you for helping me out."

"That's only natural," said the Brazilian man with a broad smile on his face. The man returned after a few minutes. He leaned over and told her through the window that everything was good. He took her suitcase from the trunk, and a young porter took it from him at the door. "Thank you again," she said politely before paying the driver his fee.

CHAPTER 71

After settling in, she walked out on the street and excitedly headed over to the block of flats. She stopped in front of the reception and gave the man Antonio's name.

"I know him. He's only been here for a week. The gentleman isn't in at the moment. He usually heads out in the morning," the man said in a friendly tone. "Can I help you with anything?" he asked the timid woman.

"That's okay, thank you. I'll call or stop by again," she replied hesitantly before turning around and walking out the gate. She smiled at the way the Brazilian man referred to her son as a gentleman. For a while, she aimlessly wandered through the crowds of people rushing and walking by on the street. She stopped from time to time to admire the shop windows or gaze at the people on the street, but she quickly grew tired, so she headed back to the hotel.

She kicked off her sandals, slipped out of her dress, and took a shower. She dried her hair and comfortably lay down on the bed. She rested for a while before dialling a number.

"Hello?"

"Hello!" she said excitedly over the phone.

"Oh, it's so good to hear your voice!" she exclaimed in relief as she recognized Antonio's voice.

"What a surprise! I should have known that you would call me once you get my letter. I hope you're both doing okay? What's going on at home? Is Dad around?"

"No, he isn't. Can I see you sometime?"

"Excuse me?" he said in surprise.

"Can I see you sometime?" she repeated slowly.

"Sure, why not," he continued playfully, assuming this was some kind of game. "The distance might be problematic, though, since Marbella is a bit, far from Rio de Janeiro."

She cheerfully laughed and played along.

"I see, but I'd still like to see you if you don't mind."

"Oh, I'm at your service," chuckled the young man.

"Please, come down to the hotel on the corner," she said, getting serious and giving him the address. Antonio's jaw fell open in surprise. "Sure, I'll be there right away," he said, quickly hanging up.

Fifteen minutes later, they warmly embraced.

"How did you get here?" he asked in surprise. She shrugged in reply. "Is Dad here?"

"No, he isn't. I came alone."

The young man eyed her quizzically.

"Aren't you happy to see me?" she asked.

"Come on, of course, I'm happy, I'm just surprised, that's all. I'm sure you had a good reason to come all this way, right? Is something wrong with Dad?"

"No. Nothing's wrong with him. Why are you asking so many questions? Are you thinking about working as a reporter?"

"Come on, tell me." Antonio said, letting Sandra know he's not feeling the playful banter.

"Hopefully nothing bad has happened yet," she replied.

"Then?"

She shrugged. "I needed to go somewhere on my own. I've been dying to come to Rio for ages, that's all. When I read your letter, I thought at once that if you don't mind, I'd like to join you, but if you don't have time, I won't be bored since it's such a beautiful city."

"Oh, come on, I'm glad you're here," he said, clearly moved.

"At least I can discuss our plans with you, even if Dad isn't here."

"What plans?" she asked ominously, with the cheer suddenly disappearing from her face. "You know, I want to marry Amy."

"Oh no," she blurted out, "not so fast," quickly finishing her sentence.

"I think this has nothing to do with age." Antonio answered defensively.

Sandra furrowed her brow. Her forehead creased and worry crossed her face. "You're not even twenty. Perhaps you should finish your studies first. Enjoy life a bit and then start worrying about serious things like this," She said.

"What's wrong?" he asked, eyeing her quizzically, noticing her anxiety. She didn't look at her son and was simply unable to answer him. He wouldn't take his eyes off her.

"Please, tell me." The young man begged.

"Not now. Perhaps I'll tell you everything tonight, that is," she said hesitantly, "that is if you want to have dinner with me."

"Sure, there's just one little twist." Antonio said. "I'm going, or rather, we're going, to Amy's parents' tonight." He offered to Sandra. Her face surprised. She was not expecting that.

"No, that's out of the question," she protested, turning pale. "I don't want to go," she excused herself in a louder tone.

"But why? I would like you to come or rather I'm asking you to come because this is going to be our engagement dinner." Antonio added. Sandra jumped out of her chair as if she was stung. She rushed to the window before turning back.

"But … but you didn't tell us about this."

"I wanted it to be a surprise," he said unsuspectingly. *She's being protective as if she were my mother,* he thought emotionally.

"Well, this is just perfect," she said, feeling an ache in her throat. "Aren't you pleased with the news?"

If I tell him now, I'll never see Pedro, she thought. I have to talk to him first. The old memories suddenly burst forth, and she trembled at the possibility of the upcoming encounter as the panic seized her.

Would she have the strength to look him in the eyes after all these years? She turned to the window again to somehow get a grip of herself. She felt the landslide was about to begin. There was no way back now, she had to see him.

"You know, things work differently nowadays, most people just move in together without telling their parents," explained Antonio uncertainly. She fell silent for a long time before giving in and answering him.

"Fine," she said, glancing at her watch. "When would you come to pick me up?" she asked.

"Seven."

"I'll be waiting. Go now," she said, spontaneously caressing his head and planting a kiss on his forehead. Antonio trembled. This motion, this gesture felt so familiar to him. He eyed his stepmother warmly before turning around and hurrying off.

He recalled his mother from his muddled memories. A long, long time ago, perhaps it was just a dream, this was just the way his mother used to caress him and kiss him on the forehead. Once he was out on the street, it occurred to him that he couldn't explain the reassuring feeling and attraction he felt when this woman was around. He'd felt the same way when they first met, and he kept thinking about it again and again. Yet today, she seemed unusually uptight, and her odd behaviour had an alienating effect on him.

CHAPTER 72

They met at the arranged time. "You look great," he said, appreciatively looking at his stepmother.

"Thank you," she replied, accepting the compliment without a smile, with her tense thoughts revolving around Pedro.

"You seem young and fresh," continued Antonio. *And her hair is simply amazing! No one would be able to guess her right age,* he thought proudly. Indeed, Sandra's hair had lost none of its natural reddish tints, giving an unruly frame to her kind face dotted with light freckles. "Why didn't Dad come with you?" he asked suddenly.

"I needed some time alone," she replied curtly, in a nearly dismissive tone. Antonio felt he shouldn't ask any more questions and thus dropped the subject and eyed the back of the cab driver for a while. The traffic was fairly heavy.

"If I'd known you were coming, I could've picked you up at the airport."

"It was no problem, plus it was a spur-of-the-moment idea. Once I got your letter, I managed to get a seat on the next flight, last minute. That's all." Antonio incredulously swayed his head, yet he was still pleased that this mysterious lady was at his side.

"There's a guest room where I'm staying, so I'd like you to stay at my place while you're here."

"Oh, no, I don't want to get in the way."

"I wasn't saying it to be polite. I'm taking your stuff over tomorrow." He glanced at her demandingly. Once he saw her nod in agreement, he added, "Well, consider it done then."

"This is such a beautiful city," she noted.

"Yes. When the time is right, Amy and I will show you all the sights." She turned pale and her mouth trembled. She quickly glanced out the window so her son wouldn't notice how upset she was.

The young man excitedly warned the driver to stop at the next gate. "We're here," he noted happily. He paid for the ride, took his stepmother by the arm, and reached the gate after a few steps.

The flushed young man pressed the buzzer, which chimed somewhere faintly in the distance. Amy jumped up at once and hurried over to the gate with ease. Her face glowed with joy, yet when she spotted Sandra, she froze in surprise. She sensed at once the tension or unrest that vibrated between the two of them. She instinctively felt that something was wrong from the serious look in the woman's eyes.

Sandra nodded coldly and glanced at the girl in passing. Amy thought for a moment that Sandra wasn't behaving the same way she did when they first met. *She seemed cold and distant. Perhaps she even hates me,* Amy thought in alarm. They welcomed each other reservedly. Sandra dug her nails into her palm and reluctantly eyed the two other individuals who appeared at the door to the house as they unstoppably approached them. She felt like turning around and running away.

Don't worry. She encouraged herself. Your face isn't the

same, so he won't recognize you. They quickly concluded the introductions as she stealthily sized up Pedro. The face she hadn't seen for so long seemed more masculine, yet basically, his physique was the same, she thought as she quickly looked him over.

Long-forgotten memories involuntarily burst to the surface. During the evening, she mostly listened to the others, carefully avoiding any discussions with the girl. She kept looking for an opportunity to talk to Pedro in peace, yet she soon realized that she would have to give up on that. She simply couldn't do anything in this situation.

Long-forgotten memories stirred for Pedro too as soon as he saw her. Her eyes and voice reminded him of someone who was long gone. However, he didn't have a chance to ponder this at length. He ran his fingers through his hair and glanced at the kids. He raised his glass for a toast: "To your happiness," he said, and four glasses clinked together. The fifth remained silent. Sandra quietly withdrew from the others. Pedro eyed her quizzically for a moment and then decided to ignore her.

Antonio was startled by his stepmother's behaviour. *Something must have happened to her,* he thought with concern. Pedro exchanged concerned looks with his wife, who bit her lip before breaking the awkward silence.

"I'll bring the food," she said, jumping up from her seat while her eyes flashed with hatred for a moment. She went out to the kitchen, where she muttered an ancient African curse she had learned from her great grandmother. Then, suddenly remembering the woman's recent illness, she took it all back.

Fortunately, Amy noticed nothing of this, since her glance mostly rested on Antonio. The icy mood wouldn't thaw, and thus everyone except the kids looked forward to saying goodbye. Nevertheless, Pedro politely offered his business card to Sandra, adding that if she needed anything, they would both be at her disposal. Sandra awkwardly coughed and reluctantly shook hands with him.

She felt the warmth of the man's hand, which had embraced her in the past. Their gazes locked for a moment. Here he was, standing in front of her with no idea of how close they were to each other in the past. *I should tell him that I want to speak with him,* her inner voice said forcefully, yet she kept her mouth firmly shut. She felt like crying out loud, demanding to know how she should carry on since this was an impossible situation, she couldn't cope with. As the pain ached inside of her, she yanked her hand out of the man's palm and sadly turned away.

What am I doing here when he loves someone else now? We both love someone else. They had grown apart, yet these odd coincidences intervened. The youngsters' attraction had brought them back together, she thought bitterly, hastening her pace towards the exit.

At the gate, Antonio and Amy hugged in parting. Sandra halted. "Please, let's go," she said to her son, scared to death.

Amy turned around without a word and hurried back inside the house. Pedro quizzically eyed his daughter and watched the red-haired woman walk off before closing the gate. He furrowed his eyebrows and strolled back inside after his wife, as memories oddly surfaced again.

He was glad that his wife and daughter were busying themselves in the kitchen since this way at least he had a chance to think over this unpleasant evening, which he simply couldn't explain. He poured himself a glass of cognac and sat out on the darkened terrace. He thought back to a long-forgotten period of his life and remembered how out of place he'd felt in Marbella after the incident in Marrakech. At the time, a Brazilian friend unexpectedly invited him over here. The new surroundings, the friendly people, and their lifestyle had a positive effect on him. For some odd reason, he stayed here for good. After a few years, he met a kind woman, who became his wife, then Amy...

"What are you doing, sitting here in the dark?" asked his wife in surprise as she walked out onto the terrace. She turned on the lights and searchingly eyed her husband.

"You two were busying yourselves in the kitchen. It's nice out here in the evening, making it the best place to relax for a while. Come on, sit over here next to me," he invited her evasively. "You must be tired," he added with concern.

The woman gently smiled at him.

"Would you like another drink?"

"Oh, no, no. That was plenty for today," he said, putting the empty glass down on the table. "Where's Amy?"

"Somewhere around here." She turned to the door and called out inside. "Honey, where are you?"

"I'm coming," replied Amy from the bathroom. After a few moments, she appeared at the open door. "I'm going to bed, good-night," she said in a surprisingly curt manner.

"Don't you want to come and sit with us? The evening is so lovely."

"I know, but I'm exhausted from this day and want to go to bed instead," she explained apologetically and disappeared back inside the house. She tossed and turned in her bed, unable to fall asleep, still feeling Sandra's cold, dismissive glance on her.

CHAPTER 73

They sat silently in the taxi. Antonio thought of Amy and didn't care about the rest. *His new mother would surely accept things after a while,* he thought.

Sandra thought of Pedro.

It seemed like things had become even more complicated since she couldn't find a chance to talk to him all evening. There was no sense in her going to the dinner tonight since she had just spoiled the mood. As they reached the hotel, her son said goodbye.

"I'll come to pick you up tomorrow. If you need anything until then, let me know," he said with a long face. Sandra tensely nodded and disappeared through the entrance. She was distraught. She looked around the hall, feeling clueless. In her desperation, she headed over to the bar instead of the elevator. She ordered a cocktail. She quickly emptied her glass, so she glanced at the mixer and asked for another one, which she thoughtfully sipped.

Then she asked for a third.

"Put some more ice in it," she told the young mixer.

"I think you've had enough."

She slowly turned around. "Oh, it's you again," she slurred, eyeing him with boredom.

"Yes, it's me, Robert Grey, from the plane," he noted reproachfully. "I must admit, you did a good job of getting rid of me." Sandra giggled.

"I remember you well, and I haven't forgotten the time you came looking for my husband in Marbella, either.

"Oh, you're too kind," muttered Grey sarcastically.

"What do you want from me? How did you find me?"

"I already told you I don't want anything from you if that's what you're thinking."

"How do you know what I'm thinking?"

"It was just a figure of speech, I hope you don't mind," replied the man a bit awkwardly.

"Well, maybe," she noted morosely. "So, how did you find me?" she asked again, in a hostile tone.

"Oh, it wasn't too hard. The taxi driver, who was working for the hotel, told me everything. Not to mention that I don't take well to being stood up or for someone to make a fool out of me. I'm sure you understand."

She smiled since she'd heard those words before. She thought of Nick. "You ran away from me so fast that it makes me think you're up to no good with that pretty little head of yours."

"Don't make a pass at me."

"I had no intention of doing so."

Sandra tilted her head to the side as if accepting his viewpoint. In the meantime, the mixer put her third cocktail down in front of her. Sandra picked up the glass. "Salud," she said.

"Want to have a drink with me?"

"I'm not in the mood," said the man, shaking his head without a smile. The heady cocktail kicked in, making her feel giddy. She leaned on the bar at ease, as if forgetting all about Grey standing next to her. "So why did you run away from me?"

Sandra looked up at him in surprise before quietly chuckling. "Are you interrogating me?"

"Of course, not. I was just asking because I felt at the time that you needed my help. It's not wise to go strolling off in this city on your own. So?"

"Oh, well, then let me thank you for your gracious help. Still, I want to be alone. I don't need your support," she said dismissively. He suddenly came to his senses.

"You must know that you have no reason to be afraid of me. I already told you I don't want anything from you," he said in a low voice. "That's all I wanted to say. Goodnight." He turned around to leave the mysterious redhead to her own devices.

"Wait," said Sandra, changing her mind. She supported her head on her hand, causing her red hair to slightly falling over her face. Grey turned back. "What was that?" he asked, perking up.

"You heard me, didn't you?" she asked with a mischievous look in her eyes. The detective knew it was the booze talking. He acted carefully. He knew how people could be since, after all, he was a detective. He also had a degree in psychology, which helped him a lot in dealing with people.

She finished off her cocktail, pushing her agonizing memories and problems into the background for a while. Robert stealthily picked up her tab. "Come," he said dully, taking by the arm the lady whose clever comebacks and mysterious behaviour increasingly intrigued him. As they reached the elevator, he pressed the button for the third floor.

"Fetch your card."

Sandra awkwardly rummaged through her bag and finally, she dropped it, spilling its contents onto the rug. He leaned over to gather up everything back into the bag except the card, which he slipped into the slot above the doorknob. The intoxicated woman took a few steps before crashing down onto the bed. Robert politely stooped to remove her high-heeled sandals before quietly backing out of the room.

Sandra sat on the bed for a while and then fell on her back and started sobbing. She mourned her bitter life, which was a constant source of problems, never giving her any rest or respite.

CHAPTER 74

She sleepily opened her eyes as the phone rang.

"Hello," she said listlessly into the receiver.

"It's me, Antonio. I can only make it over by two o'clock, and then we can have lunch somewhere. Would it be okay with you?" he asked in a rather brusque voice.

"Fine. I'll be waiting for you."

She picked up her wristwatch from the nightstand. It was past noon. "So, I overslept," she realized with a start. She quickly got up and hurried over to the bathroom. Her son showed up as soon as she was ready.

"Wait a minute," she said, walking over to the closet. She quickly gathered up her clothes and stuffed them into the open suitcase. Antonio silently watched her. What happened to her? he wondered. She had been so different in Marbella.

Sandra glanced at him, explaining herself. "I have to wash them out anyways," she noted, pulling up the zipper. After a few minutes, they reached her son's rental flat where she sized up the living room. It had a friendly atmosphere.

"You're in a bad mood," said Antonio, breaking the silence, since she still hadn't said a word.

"No, nothing's wrong, I'm just a bit hungry," she explained evasively. She didn't even have breakfast, she remembered since she slept in late after last night's boozing.

"Well then, come on. You can unpack when we get back."

After a short walk, they reached the restaurant on the shore they were looking for. "Anything to drink?" asked the young man grimly.

"Just a glass of mineral water," she said, thinking of last night. Her son curiously looked at the menu. "Can I pick something for you?"

"If you want to," she replied, shrugging as if she weren't hungry at all. "You just said you're hungry."

"Yes, please, choose," she said, suppressing a yawn while crinkling up the corner of the tablecloth. "It looks like a nice place," she said impassively just to say something.

"This food is the best," encouraged Antonio, ordering lunch. After half an hour, the waiter finally brought them some delicious roast meats with salad. Sandra clicked her tongue. "It looks good," she squinted eagerly and they laughed for the first time. She picked up her fork and took a few bites, just prodding at the rest, since for some reason, she'd lost her appetite.

"Don't you like it?"

"Yes, I do, it's delicious, but my head hurts," she replied timidly, gazing out at the ocean. The sandy beach was beautiful. A bit further away, a few brown-skinned boys were busy playing volleyball. One of the serves hit the net, causing the left pole to fall over. They were forced to stop playing, and they cried out as they ran into the water. For some reason, the sight cheered her up.

The waves lapped up on the shore again and again, unstoppably repeating their eternal movement.

"Come on, let's go for a walk, it might help you shake off your headache" suggested Antonio.

"OK," agreed Sandra. She put on her straw hat, and they

silently headed out. Antonio felt uncomfortable. He glanced at his stepmother occasionally and finally broke the silence.

"What happened to you? Something is bothering you, right?" he asked at length. Sandra swallowed hard. She knew she couldn't hold back the growing tension for long, yet she still felt unable to say a thing. She simply couldn't get started.

"Please, if something is wrong, I must know about it," he said, thinking of his father. At the same time, he thought of the time when Sandra suddenly blacked out in the summer and ended up in the hospital. The tides increased, and the ceaseless pounding of the waves resounded in the air.

Sandra suddenly sat down on the sand.

"Come on, sit down next to me," she ordered him forcefully before finally getting started at length. "If I'm going to ask you something that will surely shock you, will you still tell me the truth?"

"Yes," replied Antonio at once.

"I have to know ..."

"What?"

"Has anything happened between the two of you?"

"What do you mean?"

"I mean, have you slept with Amy?"

Antonio looked at her in shock. He couldn't believe what he'd just heard. Sandra's eyes flashed. "Tell me! But tell me the truth!" she demanded sharply. He bowed his head. He gripped a fistful of sand, but the tiny particles slipped through his fingers.

"No. Nothing of that sort has happened between the two of us." Sandra was visibly relieved, and her eyes already seemed to smile, as if she'd changed completely.

"That girl, you must forget all about her," she said, stressing the last four words. Antonio perked up in surprise.

"But why? What do you have against her? She's a decent, well-meaning girl and we love each other. You can't stop me from marrying her. Do you understand?" he said, blushing in the process.

"But I will."

"I want an explanation. I have the right to know." Antonio said, almost angrily. He doesn't mean to sound disrespectful but he needs an asnwer.

"Face it, I'm not going to settle for such a short answer. I want to know the reason"

"I can't tell you that, but you must trust me."

"How can I trust you if you always keep secrets?" he yelled, so his voice would rise over the crashing of the waves.

"I'm sorry, but that's all I can tell you," she reiterated, standing up. She patted her rump to shake off the sand from her clothes.

"What did you say?"

"I said that's all I can tell you. Let's go," she said, practically taking off in a run. Once she reached the sidewalk, she sat down on a bench. She took off her sandals and nervously tapped them together. She brushed off the sand clinging to her feet and put the sandals back on.

Once they reached the flat, she sank into an armchair, but only for a moment. Her suddenly rising fear made her disappear to her room without a word. She could tell that all hell was about to break loose, and she couldn't stop it. She desperately sought a way out, her thoughts muddled. It was as if she stood in front of a dark corridor which possibly had no end to it. She was simply unable to tell her only child the truth. She didn't want him to find out about his past amongst such circumstances, along with his mother, a woman he thought was dead and gone.

Antonio suddenly entered the room without knocking.

"Please, I would like you to tell me why you're opposed to our relationship. Amy is a trustworthy girl. I feel we would get along just fine in the long run. Look, I know we're young, but marriage is a long way down the road. Only once I finish university."

"You can't marry her, and that's it," she said, jumping up and pushing her hair to the side with trembling hands. She started madly pacing back and forth, nearly breaking into a run. Antonio anxiously stopped her. He took hold of her hands while impatiently looking her in the eye.

"But why? Explain it to me. I want to know the reason," he demanded. She started hysterically crying, yanking her hands-free from his grip and running out onto the balcony.

The young man followed her.

"Please, calm down," he tried reassuring her, slowly wrapping his arm around her and taking her back inside the living room.

"Fine, if you don't want to, you don't have to, but it would be better for both of us if you would tell me what you have against her." She broke down, eyeing him with teary eyes.

"There's nothing wrong with her, don't you get it?"

She whimpered.

"You can't marry her because, because, she's your sister."

Antonio recoiled and eyed her incredulously.

"That can't be true," he said in a faltering tone, yet as he looked her in the eye, he knew she told him the truth. He pressed his hand down on his throbbing temples before running out of the room without another word.

Panic swept over Sandra. She had been caught up in her misery until now, but it suddenly dawned on her how much pain she had just caused her son. She laid down on the bed and cried for a long time before finally falling asleep. It was dark outside when she woke up, and Antonio was nowhere to be found. Her eyes scanned the room and spotted the bottle of alcohol her son had bought for Pedro, which he'd left behind.

She slowly walked over to it and unscrewed its cap with some effort. She picked up a glass and poured herself a decent dose, which she downed in a single gulp. She shuddered and retched, yet still refilled the glass. The drink numbed her perfectly. Why had she come here? She only caused trouble. She lethargically felt that whether or not she told the whole truth, this overwhelming landslide would sweep away everyone – Antonio, Pedro, Amy, and herself. Not to mention Nick – and she just couldn't stop it.

It would have been better to remain in the shadows for good.

Why was she born in the first place? Ever since she turned twenty, one misfortune had followed another. During the long recent years, she had been forced to drag along a heavy bag full of troubles. A blurry image of Pedro appeared in front of her. She had been so sure, he was dead. No, she was simply unable to process all of this in her right mind. She was trapped and simply couldn't avoid her destiny. She sobbed hysterically. Her tears washed away her makeup, and her body turned numb. Her temples throbbed as if someone was hammering on them with a mallet.

She blinked long and hard, unable to think straight. She stumbled around, searching for her bag, but tripped on the edge of the bed and fell. The room swayed around her, and she was unable to find a single stable point. She reached out with her hand and finally managed to grab her bag. She uncertainly reached inside it but couldn't find what she was looking for. She urgently dumped the contents of the bag on the bed. She spotted Pedro's white business card amongst her belongings. It occurred to her that she could call him up, but then she found what she was looking for.

She grabbed the half-empty bottle and went to fill her glass, spilling the booze. She leaned closer and tried again, and then she dumped the contents of the small plastic bag into her drink. She hazily watched as the pills dissolved in the liquid. She stirred it with her index finger before taking a deep breath and swallowing the whole thing. The glass finally rolled away on the floor. After a while, she had to support herself on the edge of the bed, but she had no strength left to lie down. She slowly slipped back down onto the rug, where she stared into nothingness with her eyes wide open.

Her body slowly tilted to the side like a rag doll.

"The soul is trapped in a body in the material world, but when it breaks free, it rids itself of all mortal ills."

CHAPTER 75

The nearby beach bar was empty on the deserted beach. A single wind chime was left behind, tinkling in the wind, uselessly announcing the approaching storm. The red disc of the sun had long disappeared behind the building.

Dark clouds gathered in the distance.

Antonio wanted to be alone, yet he simply couldn't get over the terrible situation his stepmother had put him in. He futilely wandered up and down Copacabana, walking over the sand at length. The secret revealed and the eerie coincidence utterly upset him.

"Why! Why!" he cried out loud.

His voice was lost in the murmur of the waves. He sat down on the sand and rested his arms on his knees, which he pulled up close to his body. He sadly drooped his head. He didn't move for a long time. He didn't stir when his tears rolled down his cheek and pattered on the white sand below. His temples throbbed, so he began massaging them round and round to ease his headache, hoping he could chase away his agonizing thoughts. He blinked and stared out at the towering dark mass of waves when his mobile rang.

"Hi, it's Amy. Want to meet up tomorrow?" she asked in a carefree tone. "No. Not anymore." He answered coldly.

"What happened?" she asked in surprise.

"It's better if you never find out."

"Why, I have a right to know the reason!"

"I can't tell you, do you understand?" he cried, beside himself. Actually, he wasn't angry at her, since this was none of her faults, but rather he was angry at fate, life, and odd coincidences. If Amy hadn't sat next to him at that concert in Marbella, they would have never met.

"No, I don't understand. Please, I want to see you," said Amy in a thin, anxious voice.

"Trust me, there's no sense in doing that. It's better if we just stay as far away from each other as possible," he said, ending the conversation.

However, the annoying ringing started again a moment later, it didn't want to end, so he turned the phone off. The rain started drizzling in the humid air. He stood up and headed off towards the promenade. The wind buffeted him from behind and the clouds fast approached from the ocean. Behind him, the waves began hammering at the shore, as if eager to catch up to the morose suitor.

The lights on the shore glowed faintly in the drizzle, yet he continued wandering down the streets. As he came home, he dug his keys out of his pocket, wondering what he could say to his step-mother. He glanced at his watch. It was almost midnight. She was probably fast asleep, he thought. He turned the lights on and entered the living room, where there was no sight of his guest. He took a shower and quietly headed off to his bedroom, yet he instinctively stopped in front of the door to the guest room, as if someone was forcing him to peek inside. He knew it was rude to disturb someone so late, yet he still quietly knocked on the door.

He waited for a while before repeating the knock. Silence settled over the house. She's sleeping, he thought, walking past the door. An inner urge made him turn back.

He quietly pressed down on the handle.

The room was faintly illuminated by the lights streaming in from the street. The bed was untouched, but the cover was pulled aside. He had an odd feeling as he turned the lights on. The room seemed deserted. He found the whiskey bottle on the floor. The window was open, so he went over to close it. As he turned around, he spotted her on the floor in an odd pose, leaning up against the nightstand, slightly tilted to the side.

He was petrified by the sight of the motionless body. He rushed over and anxiously shook her, and Sandra's head lifelessly tilted backwards. He spotted the glass lying on the floor with something white at the bottom. He quickly checked her pulse, which seemed very faint, but it was still beating. He called an ambulance at once before pulling the unconscious body up on the bed.

The contents of her bag lay in front of her, so he picked it all up. He picked up the glass and found a few pills scattered on the ground, which he dumped in his pocket along with the empty packet of medicine. At the hospital, he gave the pills and the empty medicinal box to the nurse, who got to work at once.

"It was a suicide attempt," said the duty physician later on.

At dawn, he sleepily nodded off sitting next to her bed. Who was this woman? He hardly knew her, apart from the fact that she was his father's wife. He searchingly gazed at the motionless pale face. How could she know a secret which could turn his entire being upside down? He wondered again.

I have to talk to Dad, he realized. The female doctor entered and interrupted his pointless pondering. "She'll make it, right?" he asked anxiously.

The doctor raised an eyebrow. "It seems her time to leave this world hasn't come yet. She took some sleeping pills, in a big dosage, and washed them down with a lot of alcohol. Unfortunately, we don't know how much of the medicine her system absorbed. We can't know for sure how the body will react and how much will she has to stay alive, so to speak, but we'll know more by tonight." She glanced at the sleepless, broken young man.

"I suggest you go home," she added. "You could use some rest. If anything, changes, I promise to call you."

She pulled out a notepad from her pocket and expectantly glanced at the young man, who came to his senses and gave her his mobile number. Once the doctor left, he approached the bed. He picked up the hand resting on the sheet, which was bandaged for the infusion.

"Everything will be fine," he whispered and left.

CHAPTER 76

In the afternoon, he had some urgent matters to attend to. He tried calling his father but couldn't get through. There was a knock on the door. He opened it in a hurry.

"How can I help you?" he asked, quizzically eyeing the stranger. "Detective Robert Grey," said the forty-something man in the introduction. "And you are?"

"Antonio Winkler, medical student," he said mechanically. "How can I help you?" he repeated his previous question.

"Can I come in?"

"Sure, of course, come inside," he said, pointing at the sofa. Grey didn't sit down. He didn't waste time and got right to the point.

"Does this mean anything to you?" he asked, showing him a crumpled letter. Antonio glanced at the envelope. He recognized his handwriting at once.

"Yes, I wrote it. How did you get a hold of this?" he cried in surprise. This is ridiculous, he thought. He'd never done anything to make a detective sniff around after him. "The red-haired woman left this envelope at a nearby hotel," he replied.

"She's your mother, correct?"

"Stepmother," Antonio replied.

"I see. Do you know where she is currently?"

The young man nodded with a glum expression on his face. Grey gazed at him piercingly, noticing how dejected he was.

"Something happened, correct?" he asked ominously.

"Yes, but can I ask why a cop is looking for my mother? Oh, I'm sorry, I didn't mean it that way," he apologized awkwardly.

"No problem," said Grey calmly. "She got involved in some dubious business, correct?" he continued his routine questioning.

"I can assure you, she did not, at least I hope not," Antonio said in a faltering tone. "Could you tell me why you're looking for her?"

"Naturally," said Grey, pondering before carrying on.

"A few days ago, I made the acquaintance of your stepmother on the plane to Rio. We accidentally bumped into each other two days ago, late at night. I wanted to see her again today, but she left the hotel."

"How did you end up with my letter?" asked Antonio, suspicion racing through his mind.

"The answer is simple. In the hotel room where your mother was staying, I found the maid busying herself, and she gave me the letter she left there. That is why I was looking for her, so I could return it. But I can give it to you, too." Antonio mechanically reached out for the envelope. "Thank you."

"What happened to her?" asked the detective again.

"I don't know either," he replied curtly.

"Is it serious?" answered Grey.

"I hope not." He answered with worry in his tone.

"An accident?"

"You could put it that way."

"Tell me. When did it happen?"

"Last evening, or night." Grey was getting nervous from the way he had to wrench every single word out of the young man.

"Where did it happen?"

"Here, or in her room. I don't know exactly."

"So, that means you weren't around, or am I wrong?"

"No, unfortunately, I wasn't," he whimpered quietly, guiltily staring at the ground.

"Where were you?"

"Down on the beach."

"With whom?"

"But," he left the sentence unfinished. However, when he looked up at the man, he replied at once. "I was alone."

"Is her life in danger?"

"I don't know yet. She took sleeping pills."

"Which hospital did they take her to?"

"Unfortunately, I don't know the name," he said, doing his best to explain where it was located. "I hope you know that if there's something else behind all of this, you will need an alibi."

"What?" asked Antonio in shock. "Do you have one?"

"I already told you, I was down on the beach." He suddenly realized that he couldn't prove himself. He uncomfortably eyed the stranger. "No. I don't think I have one."

Grey eyed him with a strict look for a few breaths before suddenly speaking up. "That will be all then," he said, moving to the door. "If something occurs to you, give me a call," he added, handing the young man his business card.

"I'll be here for another week, but then I'm flying back to Marbella. Give my regards to your mother."

"I already told you, she's not my mother. She's my father's second wife."

"I'm sorry, that slipped my mind." Antonio nodded and opened the door. The stranger headed over to the elevator. As he reached the foyer, he asked the receptionist what he knew about Winkler's mother.

"Not much, since she only came here yesterday. An ambulance took her away last night." Robert kept on questioning him.

"Do you know which hospital they took her to?"

"Unfortunately, I don't."

He stopped his questioning and left, looking troubled.

Robert Grey was a man who knew how to find people, so a few hours later, he was walking into Sandra's hospital room. He slowly approached the woman lying on the bed, staring at the ceiling. "I found you again. It looks like you just can't run away from me," he said, trying to adopt a light-hearted tone.

The patient didn't seem to take notice of him. Her thoughts were wandering far away above the clouds. The painful past and the muddled present were plunged into obscurity. "I'm Robert," said the man quietly, taking her hand. She shuddered at his touch. "Please, at least look at me. I'm your friend, I just want to help, if I can," he said quietly, unconsciously sighing heavily.

It was always hard for him not being able to help someone out. Sandra's hand fluttered again and her mouth silently opened, as if wanting to say something. He squeezed her hand tightly.

"Please, I would like you to say something. I know you said you wanted to be alone and you don't need my help."
"Perhaps some other time." whispered the patient in a barely audible tone. He leaned over to her in relief and caressed her hair. He slipped his business card into her bag of toiletries on the nightstand.
"Call me if something comes up. I won't bother you anymore, just rest." He silently left the room and hurried down the corridor. He visited the doctor to find some information.

"I am practically certain that the patient experienced some unspeakable grief or event. We can't know for sure whether she'll attempt it again. I have the feeling that she's no longer attached to anything on this planet. It seems like she wants to leave for good – unless someone intervenes to shake her up from her apathy."

Grey thanked the doctor for the information and left in a hurry. *Did she want to commit suicide? Or perhaps someone tried killing her?* He thought about it for a while. He didn't like this confused tale at all and thought of Nick Winkler, who got away from him. At the same time, his wife flew here to Rio. And what was his son doing here? Grey didn't like the way she always brushed him off, specially after she was so kind and open with him on the plane.

CHAPTER 77

Antonio got up from the armchair, feeling exhausted. He thought of length about what he should do now. He decided to fly back to Marbella with Sandra since he couldn't let her go on her own.

The following day, his stepmother was peacefully sleeping in her hospital bed while he was walking up and down the corridor, thinking about how Amy could be his sister.

Perhaps Nick and Pedro's current wife had an affair? he wondered in confusion. Still, he no longer had any reason to stay in Rio. He would return to Marbella. He tried calling his father, but his mobile went dead. He thought of his previous unsuccessful attempts at calling Nick and superstitiously thought that if he started the day with something unsuccessful, he would surely experience a series of misfortunes.

As he sat in the corridor, staring at his dusty sandals, the doctor he met previously approached, welcoming him and sitting down next to him.

"The patient's condition is uncertain," she started with some difficulty. "We should be careful since we don't know exactly what happened to her. It's best not to ask anything from her. She'll talk when the time is right," she warned him briefly.

Antonio shamefully realized that this hadn't occurred to him. Why did she want to die? If Nick is the girl's father, then why did she do it? If Pedro Gomez is his father he still didn't understand a thing. How could his stepmother know of such secrets?

Perhaps she had something to do with all of this, he pondered futilely. Sandra didn't fit any of his theories. But then why did she want to throw her life away? He shook his head. He simply couldn't make any sense of his muddled thoughts. He realized he had to wait, as the doctor said. He returned to the room and sat down next to the bed.

Sandra was lying on the bed with her eyes closed. Her face looked pale. She knew her son was nearby, yet she didn't have the strength to talk to him. Her thoughts were cast into obscurity. She didn't want to remember anything. She simply wanted to rid herself of all her earthly concerns and troubles. Her life had been a series of misfortunes so far. She was always unfortunate, and she always lost someone. She'd ruined her son's life, and thus, she couldn't look him in the eye. She was so hopeful that things would get better. She didn't want to live anymore. She hated this cruel world which always mistreated her. Her heart ached in pain, and the tears rolled out from behind her closed eyelids.

Antonio didn't witness this, however, as he had gone home.

CHAPTER 78

A note was slipped under the door.

"Please, come see me. I'll be waiting for you at the usual spot at 6 pm. Amy." Antonio nervously slammed the door shut and crumpled up the note before changing his mind and ripping it up into tiny shreds.

Suddenly, he practically hated Amy, even though the poor girl knew nothing of the shocking secret. He angrily walked out onto the balcony and scattered the bits of paper into the air.

"It's over," he said, wiping his hands.

Luckily, nothing happened between the two of us, he thought to comfort himself. He felt somewhat relieved as he turned around and went inside, closing the door to rid himself of this depressing feeling. He comfortably leaned back on the sofa, propped his legs up on the table in front of himself, and turned the TV on. He watched a Brazilian football match to chase away his painful memories.

Two days later, Sandra managed to compose herself and sat on the edge of her bed. Perhaps it was due to all her sleeping, but her condition had greatly improved.

"I'm glad you're feeling better," grinned Antonio. "I brought you some sweets." He set a little package on her nightstand.

"Thank you, son." She glanced at him with tender, motherly love. Her grim thoughts seemed to fade from her.

Her will to live returned. Antonio trembled faintly since these words rang so familiar in his ears. He lovingly gazed at Sandra. Her face was flushed, and she was no longer as pale as she was in the last few days. Millions of questions piled up inside of him, but he remembered the doctor's warning to wait patiently.

For quite a while she would need peace to recover, he thought.

"Oh, I brought you a few magazines."

"Thank you. At least I'll have something to read."

Antonio nodded. "I'll go look for the doctor."

As he returned thirty minutes later, he happily slipped the prescriptions into his pocket.

"Come, let's go for a walk so I can see if you've regained your strength," he invited her with a grin. He tenderly helped her slip into her robe, and he took her arm as they walked down the winding corridor.

"I have some good news," he said.

"The doctor is letting you go home."

"Then why are you making me walk?" she asked in annoyance. "Because I wanted to see for myself whether you've truly recovered. You know, I need to hone my medical practice skills," he noted cheekily. They shared a smile.

"I'm not a lab rat."

"And I'm not a veterinarian."

"You could use a little slapping in the face."

Antonio went over to the closet to pack her belongings in her bag. "Don't, I'll do it."

"But …"

"No buts."

"Are you hiding something from me?"

"Yes. A bunch of cash," she noted, gently hitting him over the head with the magazine.

"Help, my mom is beating me!" He glanced at her with a boyish look on his face. "It'll get worse if you keep it up."

"I promise to behave," he said, ending the teasing.

"I'll go out in the corridor while you get dressed. Let me know if you need anything. I'll be right around the corner."

"Go," she motioned with her hand.

"I'll let you know when I'm ready." She pulled out her clothes and got dressed. She gathered what little belongings she had into her bag. As she searched for a comb, she came across Grey's business card in her toiletries.

She read it before crumpling it up and tossing it into the wastebasket. However, a few minutes later she changed her mind. She dug out the crumpled card from the bin, slightly smoothed down the edges, and put it away. She applied a thin layer of lipstick to her lips while thinking of the man.

Antonio peeked inside.

"Why didn't you say you're ready?"

"Oh, come on. If you want to, we can get going."

The young man hung the bag from his shoulder with ease, taking his stepmother by the arm and walking over to the elevator. They both felt they belonged together. Antonio spoke up.

"Yesterday I looked for your ticket since I decided to go with you. It's better if we both get out of here. I want to get as far from Rio de Janeiro as possible. We have to leave the day after tomorrow," he concluded his speech, while he looks at Sandra with confusion.

"Are you satisfied with me?"

"Fine, that's the smartest thing you could do."

"I tried calling Dad recently. I wanted to tell him what happened to you, but I couldn't get through to him."

Sandra grew pale.

"Please, let's keep this our secret. I wouldn't be thrilled for him to find out what happened or what I told you previously."

"You mean about Amy?"

"That's right."

"Fine, if you want me to, I'll keep quiet."

He thought of the doctor's warning and decided not to force the delicate subject.

CHAPTER 79

As they reached the flat, Sandra headed off to her room.

"I want to get some rest," she said with a grim face.

"Okay, I'll go and get something to eat in the meantime." Antonio suggested. He was getting hungry. With a lot going on, he barely have the time think about eating.

"I'm not hungry." Sandry sighed. She still feels tired after all that rest at the hospital.

"Look, you don't have to eat much, but you have to eat. Doctor's orders. Do you hear me?" Said Antonio in a stern voice.

"Of course, I'm not deaf, Mr. Future Physician."

"You'll see, I'll get something delicious, and we still have the cakes left," it occurred to him. He mischievously glanced at the package, licking his lips. Sandra smiled with exhaustion.

"Based on the look on your face, I don't think there'll be any leftovers." she said, almost sounding amused.

"We'll see. What would you like? Not now, later," he added quickly. Sandra doesn't feel like eating but she needed something inside her system.

"Well, some yoghurt and a slice of fresh, crusty bread would be nice," she said, eyeing him lovingly with a hint of sadness in her eyes. Antonio laughed.

"We've recorded your order. Fresh and crusty," he added humorously, just to cheer her up. "I won't be away for long. Get some rest in the meantime," he added, heading out of the flat.

An hour later, he was busying himself at the kitchen counter. Since Sandra still didn't show, he went inside his room. He pulled out his suitcase and carefully folded and packed all his clothes.

In the meantime, he kept thinking of what to write to Amy in parting. He didn't want to meet her. He pulled out an envelope and some letter paper. He didn't write to her that he was her brother; all he wrote was that they had to give up on having a life together. He was very sorry, but their ways had to part for good. He knew well that the letter sounded corny, but he wrote the truth. He folded the letter up, slipped it into the addressed envelope, and glued it shut. He glanced at his watch. It was late, so he ran down to the concierge.

"Please, I'd like to ask you to mail out this letter for me. I have no time to do it myself." He left some money on the counter with the envelope.

The concierge was surprised but thought that we all have our troubles to deal with. He shrugged and nodded and slipped the easy cash into his pocket. He glanced at his watch. He would be relieved in ten minutes. He slipped his hand back into his pocket where the money was.

"I could have a few beers at the bar on the corner," he muttered cheerfully. Antonio cautiously peeked inside Sandra's room once he was done. He saw her eyes were open, so he sat down on the edge of the bed. He took hold of her wrist and found her pulse, which seemed to throb in order.

"I'll bring in your dinner," he said, heading off to the kitchen. He fixed the sandwiches and put the light meal on the tray.
"Wait," said his stepmother, walking up behind him.

"I'd like to eat here with you instead," she said, sitting down on the high chair next to the counter. She never took her eyes off her son, who carefully set the table. Her appetite returned as she eyed the delicious food. "It looks good."

"Wait till you taste it," he said encouragingly. "You'll see how delicious it is," he added, pushing the plate over to her and quickly gulping down his first sandwich before opening a bottle of beer.

"You're not getting any of this yet," he noted humorously.
"Here's to you!" he cried, drinking half of the beer, eyeing the remaining sandwich. "Do you want it?"
"Oh, no. That's for you," she said, holding back her smile. My dear son, she thought. She was glad he was here with her and that they had gotten over the hardest part.

As they finished their light dinner, she disappeared into the bathroom. Antonio washed the dishes and wiped down the counter. He watched a bit of TV while Sandra was reading. On their final day, they walked up to the summit of Sugarloaf Mountain and reached the top of Corcovado Hill, where they admired the unparalleled view of Rio de Janeiro under the huge Christ the Redeemer statue.

Finally, they had dinner on Ipanema Beach. As they came home, Antonio spoke up. "Well, get yourself in order and go to bed. I'm sure you're tired, and we're getting up early tomorrow. I'll go pack your suitcase. Just tell me what you want to wear."

"Perhaps my long black slacks and that green blouse will be the best for the trip. Leave me my blazer out as well, since it can get cold on the plane." She checked her most important belongings, her passport and papers, one more time before going for a bath. Soon, the suitcases were lined up, locked and ready in the living room.

Sandra slipped into her bed. "Come here, please."
Antonio turned around.

"Stay awhile. Sit down." He told the young man.
I have something to tell you," she said invitingly.

"Yes, I'm listening."

"I've been wanting to tell you everything for some time now, but this is a long and old story," she began, as her voice shifted.

Antonio noticed his stepmother's frantic glance at once, so as much as he was interested in the secret, he stood up instead.

"No, don't say anything. We can do that later, just rest. There's no sense in working yourself up again. Listen to me. I believe you, that's why I'm going back to Spain with you. Please don't forget that."

Tears welled up in Sandra's eyes.
"Fine. You might be right, some other time, then," she conceded, calming down.
"Goodnight, sleep tight," he said quietly.
"Goodnight," she whispered, "my dear son."
His love, care, and devotion brought back her will to live. A smile played around the edges of her mouth as she dozed off.

CHAPTER 80

The restful night quickly came to an end. The red glare of dawn gave the sea a golden sheen on the edges of the horizon. Sandra took one last glance at this amazing bay. She sighed heavily and slowly moved away from the window, leaving someone here for good.

They both flew off to Madrid. Antonio occasionally glanced at his stepmother. He was satisfied to see that she was deeply engrossed in a magazine.

"What's wrong?" she asked, perking up suddenly.
"Nothing. How are you doing?"
"Thank you, I'm fine," she replied briefly, caressing his arm. "Thank you for everything, including saving my life, although..." she let the end of the sentence trail off. She emotionally turned her head away and gazed out the window. Antonio sadly spoke up.
"Everyone would have done the same thing, but don't say although. Don't forget, I'm here with you, and there's Dad as well." Sandra's eyes filled with tears. Her mouth opened. She licked her lips.

"Look, there's something I have to tell you before we get home, which I tried telling you a few times before, but something always came up. But you have to promise to keep my secret."

The stewardess kindly approached them and interrupted her sentence. "Anything to drink?" Antonio quizzically eyed Sandra.
"Is red wine good?"
"Perfect," she said, quietly chuckling. She thought about how something always seemed to thwart her plans. They clinked glasses. For the first time, her son attentively asked her to go on.

"It's a really old story," she began slowly.
"You know, my life was full of strange coincidences. Do you remember that seaside house, your mother always used to tell you about?"
"How do you know about that? My mother died ages ago." Sandra sadly bowed her head, losing the courage to carry on.
"Why won't you answer me?" he urged her. Her face turned pale and her mouth opened, but she simply couldn't admit to him that she was his mother. Antonio gripped her arm and then realized at once that he'd gone too far.

"I understand. You don't have to go on."

He nervously bit his lip and glanced at the passengers seated in front of him. He ran his fingers through his hair, which covered his forehead. He suddenly stood up and stumbled over to the toilet. The stewardess was busying herself nearby.
"Can I help?" she asked the good-looking young man.
"No." He shook his head dismissively and entered the narrow toilet. He tensely pressed the faucet with one of his hands while doing his best to cool off his face with the other. He pulled out a paper towel while glancing into the mirror with concern. He didn't understand what was going on.
"If she has more secrets, and she does, then why won't she share them with me?" he asked his mirror image. A few minutes later, he composed himself and sat back down.

"Forgive me for my previous outburst," he said peevishly.

"It's alright," said Sandra mechanically. She was getting cold, so she pulled on her blazer with trembling hands. "I know it's not easy for you, but I hope that one day you'll understand me. As you can see, I tried sharing a few important things with you, but I just couldn't do it. Believe me, I thought about sharing my secrets with you many times, but somehow I just didn't have a chance."

Antonio laughed out loud.

"I guess that's why you came after me to Rio. Right?"

"That's true, but I had no other choice than to come and somehow prevent this absurd relationship."

"And you did," he noted reproachfully. Sandra glanced at him in alarm. "Trust me, it was a coincidence. My whole life is a series of odd coincidences."

"I've heard that before. But why didn't you say so before? How could you live this way, keeping such a secret?"

"I wanted to, but I didn't have the chance. You'd already left by the the time I came to the hospital in Marbella."

"That's true. I'm sorry."

"Coincidences happen," said Sandra guiltily.

"That's true as well," he said, thinking about the way he'd met Amy, which was also a coincidence.

"For a long time, I've been forced to carry a heavy burden. I lived the way I could. I had no other choice, only the sleeping pills could help me, or rather they would have helped me if you hadn't prevented that from happening," she noted reproachfully.

Her son turned to face her in grief. He felt like asking her why she did it, but he didn't dare. He knew this would push the conversation in the wrong direction.

"No, that's not what I meant," he explained himself quickly, squeezing her trembling hands. It suddenly occurred to him that Sandra might be involved in all of this.

Yes. He felt there was some other secret in the air.

"It's still hard to believe that she's my sister," Antonio added quietly.

"I know son, I know, I'll tell you my whole story at a more suitable time," she concluded the subject, fastening her seatbelt, since the plane was starting its descent.

PART 3

CHAPTER 81

They got in a taxi at Malaga airport. As they reached Marbella, Sandra exhaustedly pulled out her keys. She was glad to be back home. As they entered the house, quiet music was playing in the living room, and the door to the patio was open. Her sixth sense warned her, as always, that something was amiss, so she went straight up to her room. There was something she didn't want to see which her subconscious self was signalling to her. Antonio followed Sandra, barely able to drag up the two suitcases to the hallway upstairs.

"You know where your room is, right?"

"Sure. On the left, next to the bathroom," he grinned.

"Once you're ready, have a drink, and I'll be down soon. I'm sure Nick is home, so say hi to him too."

Antonio dragged his suitcase to his room, threw down his bag, and hurried down the stairs to see his father. He froze in the doorway when he saw Nick kissing a woman out on the lounge chair. Sizing up the impossible, he blushed and turned back at once. However, the man noticed him. He pushed the woman away and hurried after him. "What a surprise!" Nick said reluctantly.

"Well yeah, it is quite a surprise," Antonio replied in a distraught tone. Nick didn't react to his sarcastic remark.

"Why didn't you write or at least give me a call?"

"Would that have changed anything?" Antonio retorted sharply. Nick laughed. "Oh, come on, let me introduce you to my ex-wife," he said, moving over to the surprised woman. Antonio, however, turned around and walked away.

Nick hurried after him. "You were rude, you know that?"

"Oh yeah? You always pay attention to insignificant things, but never to the things that matter." Antonio responded.

"What's wrong with you? This is my business, and it doesn't mean anything." said Nick. He doesn't like having a confrontation with his son but with how the situation is, it seems like he needed to respond.

"So? Isn't Sandra your business as well?"

Nick was surprised by his son's sharp tone.

"Yes, indeed she is, but it's none of yours. Do you understand?" He said sharply, but he doesn't sound as stern as he usually do.

"You're right, it is none of my business. Just let me ask you one question. Did you forget you have a wife? And not just anyone."

Nick was startled by the unanticipated remark, yet he didn't feel like getting involved in a delicate argument.

"Why won't you answer me?" asked Antonio indignantly. He wasn't ready to let go of the conversation either. "Or perhaps you think that has nothing to do with this?"

"This is a different matter," replied Nick listlessly.

"So, she didn't mean anything to you either?" Antonio glared at his father angrily. The man eyed his son with an ashen look on his face. "OK, enough of this," he finished their exchange, turning his back on the young man.

"Sandra almost saw it too. It was a pretty close call," he shouted after him. Nick suddenly turned around and looked at the young man in surprise. "Where is she?"

"You should know the answer to that,"
Antonio retorted hostilely.

Lucy comfortably stepped between the men.
"Can someone tell me who this good-looking young man is?" she asked with a mischievous smile, interrupting the unpleasant situation.

"My son," blurted Nick reluctantly.
"What? That's incredible, I've never seen him through all these years," she wondered in surprise, taking a good long look at the cute young man. Antonio, however, didn't feel like chatting at all, so he disappeared into his room, leaving them alone. Nick got noticeably anxious.

"Pack up your stuff and let's get out of here quick. You have two minutes," he warned her quietly as he scrutinized the living room through the open door. "Let's go somewhere, like your place. I don't want any more uncomfortable arguments," he urged her, toning down his voice.

Lucy blinked treacherously since she was enjoying the situation. *Things are heating up around here,* she thought a bit maliciously, but finally, she shrugged without a word.
"We can get going whenever you're ready."
He quickly picked up his bag. *So, she came back, after all,* he thought, jotting down a few lines on a note while omitting where he was going before they quickly left the house.

CHAPTER 82

Nick roared the motor because of his tense mood.

"What's wrong?" asked the startled woman. "This is so unlike you."

"Don't worry about it," he growled at her nastily.

Lucy grimaced lightly, and a malevolent smile creased her lips. She never worried about all the scandals she caused due to her countless relationships. Whenever she had some free time, she just went with the flow. She seemed to enjoy the mess she caused. Now she'd bumped into Nick again. He meant nothing to her anymore, yet she felt a kind of sweet revenge since she was no longer the slave of the man she'd idolized in the past. She knew he was married, but she had no idea who was his wife.

"Where are you going, don't you remember the house? You should have turned around here," she cried, shaken up from her thoughts.

"Oh," he muttered absently, quickly turning around at the next intersection. "Is your mother home?"

"She isn't. She went to Madrid."

"Then I'll come inside."

A sarcastic grin appeared on Lucy's face. She clearly remembered the time Nick was sleeping with her mother and she spied on them once as they were making love. You never forget something like that. Ever since she was a little girl, she'd undeniably adored him, yet she couldn't explain her attraction to him for a long time. It's no wonder she simply swooned in his arms back in Marrakech.

During the first few months of their abrupt marriage, she was always tensely waiting for him to come home, yet she soon realized that Nick was only good as a lover, not a husband. Of course, she quickly learned the secret of living an easy life at his side.

They got divorced soon after the baby's death. She moved back for a few months with her mother, who never forgave her for the way she'd married Nick. There was always some tension between the two of them. Her well-assuming mother knew nothing of the booze, the drugs, and her countless affairs. Lucy was good at covering up her tracks. She used her big, innocent eyes to ward off uncertainty and smoothed over her lies and her mother's suspicions with crocodile tears. Her mother was far too biased, as always, despite their differences. She was well aware of this and made good use of this fact. Lucy soon turned into an incredibly wily, deceitful person. Her unloving, vain, and selfish being longed for nothing other than sex and money, which always slipped through her fingers. She couldn't accumulate any savings. Whenever she had financial problems, she fawned and flattered and made her mother feel sorry for her. Once she got the help she was looking for, she left at once, abandoning the woman. This caused a lot of grief for her mother. It also made Patricia think more and more about changing her will and donating all her fortune to charitable causes.

She soon got a new contract and thus stayed in London. Back in the past, her career had always been on the rise. She often toured throughout the world, and her private life became increasingly tempestuous. She undeniably enjoyed her go-as-you-please irresponsible lifestyle, yet her straying thoughts suddenly jolted her back to reality. She thought of Antonio as she lay in Nick's arms. He's very handsome, though Lucy, so she wanted to meet him somehow. After their lovemaking, she propped herself up on her elbows and asked, "Why did you hide him from me?"

"Who?"

"Your son."

The man silently stared at the ceiling before speaking up. "He was staying at a boarding school in London. I thought it would be better to leave him be," he explained briefly.

"Who's the mother?"

"No one special. She's long dead."

"You're a strange person, you know that?"

"Maybe."

"I have an idea."

"What?"

"How about making it up to him by inviting him over for dinner? Let's go somewhere together, okay?"

"That won't work. Maybe some other time," he noted dully, thinking about today's argument. He pulled his arms out from under her head and walked over to the bathroom, naked.

Lucy jumped up at once. She cautiously searched through his bag. She found his mobile and quickly searched for Antonio's number, which she jotted down before leaning back on the pillows in satisfaction.

Shortly after, Nick sat down on the edge of the bed, all dressed and strapped on his sandals.

"I'll call you," he said in a flat tone, knowing that it was over. He kissed his still attractive ex-wife on the forehead in farewell.

Nick got in his car. It was late, he thought as he glanced at his watch. He didn't want to see Sandra and explain himself. He was glad she'd come home, but it was too late to change his current plans. He'd left her a short message on the kitchen counter telling her not to wait up for him. Had he known she was coming back he would have arranged things differently. It made no difference now. He was picking up Carmen an hour from now and taking her to Marseille. He was almost certain that he wouldn't come back for a long time, especially after his exchange with Antonio.

CHAPTER 83

The following day, Lucy woke at noon. She felt rested, so she picked up the receiver, hoping for a crazy night.

"*Hola!*" she said in a flattering tone. "I'm Lucy. We already met briefly yesterday."

"Oh, I remember now, the ex-wife," taunted Antonio.

"I'd like to see you," she explained, letting the previous remark pass unnoticed.

"Me?" he laughed sharply.

"Yes, you. I can't explain it over the phone, but it's really important. Please, come to the club tonight, I'll be waiting for you," she explained, giving him the address.

Antonio reluctantly promised to go. A triumphant smile appeared on Lucy's face, since she'd managed the lure this cute boy into her web.

She lazily rested for a few hours. As the night rolled in, she took a bath and carefully put on some makeup, which took a long time. She slipped on a pair of incredibly thin nylon stockings, which were sexily strapped to her thighs with an elastic fixing. She slipped into a blood-red dress. The thin fabric perfectly fit her figure. She put on a pair of expensive high-heeled sandals.

As she reached the club, an enticing smile played along her lips. She sat down at the bar, waiting for her next victim. Most of the men took notice of her shapely legs, crossed in front of her.

Antonio approached with firm strides, touching the woman's shoulder.

"Good evening," he said.

"I'm glad you came to see me," she purred, turning to the mixer, lifting her empty glass and raising two fingers. Lucy directed her attention at the lovely young man. The mixer made a face and a big show of preparing the cocktail before serving it in two previously prepared glasses.

She gently slid one of the glasses over to the young man.

"*Salud*," she whispered chummily. "You know what? You can call me Lucy, so bottoms up." Once they finished off the pleasant-tasting drink, she leaned over to him and planted a fine kiss on the edge of the young man's mouth. This was followed by another and yet another cocktail.

"Why did you want to see me? What was so important?" asked Antonio, getting tipsy.

"I'll tell you later. I'll promise you'll find out today. Come on, let me take you to a nice little place. But first, we could have something nice to eat. I'm hungry. Aren't you?"

The boy-toy blinked and shrugged.

"If you want to," he said, leaving the matter up to her. He lost his inhibitions and let his gaze linger on the beautiful woman. He couldn't determine her age, but he wasn't interested in it.

After dinner, they went dancing in a packed disco. The woman kept cuddling up to him under the flashing lights with a beguiling smile on her face, before distancing herself from him. She knew how to tease a man. They somehow ended up in each other's arms.

"Let me get you another drink, at my place. How about it?" she asked with an innocent look on her face.

The sudden invitation made Antonio grin. There was no doubt about it, he was getting increasingly infatuated with this experienced woman, but he didn't mind at all. He instantly accepted the invitation. He liked this uninhibited woman.

"So, what are we waiting for?" she asked with a giggle. "Come on," she invited him, tagging on the young man's arm.

The lock quietly clicked as it opened. Lucy crossed the pleasantly furnished living room and headed straight over to the bar. She half-filled two-round tumblers with cognac.

"Come on, I'm sure you can use another sip."

Antonio fended it off. "If I drink that, I'm going to pass out"

"I won't let that happen," giggled Lucy.

The drink burned his throat as he eyed the woman, who started teasing him.

Lucy spun around. "Please, pull down my zipper."

Antonio took a big breath and was barely able to complete the task entrusted to him. The ruby-red dress to fall to the floor. The woman stood in front of him stark naked with her back to him. He lifted his arms to embrace her, but she tiptoed off to the bathroom.

The young man sank on the sofa. While anxiously waiting, he noticed a photo album lying open on the table. He flipped a page and suddenly leaned closer to take a better look. He quizzically stared at a picture of Nick and Pedro laughing, of course from years ago.

"I'm back," said the woman, standing behind him, tenderly caressing Antonio's neck.

The young man coughed awkwardly.

"What's wrong?"

"Who are these guys?" he asked, pointing at the picture.

Lucy looked down at the picture and laughed in ease.

"I'll explain later, but you know one of them well. Go to the bathroom now," she said with a promising look on her face.

At the moment, his lust was stronger than his curiosity, so he quickly slipped out into the bathroom and soon returned. Since she was making a lengthy phone call, he lay down on the bed with a spinning head and he fell asleep at once.

Lucy eyed the boy-toy at length in the light of the lamp. He slept so sweetly that she didn't dare wake him up.

It was dawning outside when he woke up. He turned on the lamp and leaned up in the dim light, fixing his chocolate brown eyes on Lucy.

"What is it?" she stirred suddenly.

"Nothing, I was just thinking about the photo."

"Now?"

"What is that photo doing in the family photo album? Of course, I know Nick was your husband, but what have you got to do with the other men?"

"We should go back to sleep instead," she rubbed at her eyes sleepily.

"Please."

"It's a long story," she said with a huge yawn. "If you want to know, I'll tell you all about it later on."

"I would like to hear it now. We have plenty of time. Please, I'm really interested."

"Okay, fine, I'll tell you. Pedro is my mother's brother. At one time, he was Nick's best friend."

"And?"

"Something happened between them a long time ago and the friendship came to an end," she cut the story short since she was sleepy.

"Why?"

"I don't know exactly, but shortly after that, when Vicky died in Marrakech, Pedro took a job in Rio and stayed there."

"Who is Vicky?" asked Antonio, sobering up at once.

"Pedro's girlfriend. I think they were very close. She was a nice girl with a freckled face and boyish red hair, but the poor thing died."

"Freckled face and red hair?" muttered the young man in shock. "How did she die?"

"She was shot."

"She got involved in something?"

"I don't think so. She was a decent girl."

"How do you know she died?"

Lucy continued with a grim look on her face.

"I know. I saw her bloody face myself, shattered by a gunshot. She laid there in front of me on the tiles of the riad. Phew, I still get the shivers when I think about it, even though it happened a long time ago, you better believe me. Nick took her to the hospital at once. That's where she died."

"Do you know for sure?"

"Yes. Nick told me himself back in the days," she concluded the story, sleepily falling back on the bed.

Antonio was excited by the news he'd just heard, since the red-haired woman kept popping up. She was there in his childhood memories, she was there in Pedro's life, and now she was here in his father's house. He still couldn't see things. He recalled the few times his mother's shawl slipped aside and he saw her ravaged face. She had red hair too. She was called Vicky too. All he could remember of her was a faint image of her black shawl and her eyes. Suddenly, he seemed to remember that his mother had freckles on her face.

He slipped his arm under his head and started thinking. He was so caught up in his thoughts that he didn't notice that the woman lying next to him had fallen asleep.

He couldn't stop thinking about Pedro's lover, his faceless mother, and Nick's current wife. This was simply absurd. *There was no way this could be a coincidence,* he thought, suddenly remembering what Sandra said: *"My whole life is a series of odd coincidences."*

He simply couldn't sort through his muddled thoughts. Images clogged up his mind in a disorderly mess. Was Sandra his mother? If that's true, then why didn't Pedro recognize her in Rio? No, Sandra couldn't be his mother. Nick wasn't his real father, but then why did he take care of him? He couldn't place Amy anywhere in this mess. The countless ill-fitting combinations boggled his mind. He eyed the sleeping woman. Perhaps she was a relative if Pedro was truly his father. It's a good thing she fell asleep and nothing happened between the two of them. *She's just another coincidence, like Amy,* he thought in confusion.

He had the feeling that he was surrounded by far too many hair-raising coincidences. Thus, he cautiously slipped out of bed, quietly got dressed, and silently slipped out of the house like a thief.

He wandered down the deserted streets with his hands slipped into his pockets. He felt cold and bunched up his shoulders since the morning air was chilly and the first rays of the sun were just flittering across the city.

CHAPTER 84

Sandra woke up later, rested from her travels and feeling great. She quickly noticed Nick's brief message on the dining table: "I went to Barcelona. I'll get in touch." she read sadly. She crumpled up the piece of paper while absently sipping her coffee. So, she was right to think that he was home, yet he'd left again without even welcoming her. She hoped they would resolve all their matters. She even thought they could go sailing or for a longer trip, but it looked like not even Antonio meant enough to him. *This marriage kept getting better and better. They hardly make any contact at all,* she thought peevishly.

"Good morning," welcomed her son sleepily.

"Hi, honey," she replied, watching her son closely. "You look a bit worn out."

"Possibly," he shrugged, pouring himself the rest of the coffee.

"You want me to brew you another cup?"

"I'd appreciate that."

Sandra stood up and headed over to the kitchen.

"I'll help," he offered drowsily. "Did you find his letter? I left it yesterday on the table."

"Yes, I just read it," she said briefly, mechanically loading the tray with coffee and milk, toast, ham, and butter before handing it to her son. She carried out plates filled with fresh fruit. "Here's a dose of vitamins. This will help you get back in shape."

After a hearty breakfast, Antonio felt better.

"Thank you. That hit the spot."

"You're welcome." Sandra knew he was out last night, but she didn't ask any questions. He would tell her himself if he felt she was worthy to know, she thought. He's practically a grown man. She furtively watched his every move. She was glad he was sitting with her on the other side of the table and that she had her son back. This was her true joy.

"Are you staying home tonight?"

"Yes, I think so. Why?"

"We could go out for dinner if you want to."

"Fine," he agreed, eyeing her at length.

"If you're not up for it, we do it some other time," blinked Sandra hesitantly.

"Come on, I love eating out with you," he replied in a more refreshed tone.

"Fine, then we'll meet up tonight, but I have to go now." She got up and left the morose-looking young man. From the look of his concerned face, she was sure he was brooding over something again.

It was dark by the time they walked down to the shore. They sampled the catch of the day at a nearby chiringuito, yet they hardly said a word to each other. They were both caught up in their thoughts. Sandra awkwardly glanced at her son. She decided she wouldn't wait any longer with her confession.

"Should I lock the door?" asked Antonio when they arrived.

"If you're not going anywhere, then yes."

"Not tonight."

"Put the key in its place," she said, leaning back on the sofa, as she anxiously looked for the right words to say. She didn't want to wait any longer. She simply wanted to rid herself of her long-guarded secret.

"Come here, sit down next to me."

Antonio eyed her expectantly, with a thousand questions coursing through his mind, yet lacking the courage to ask any of them.

"Perhaps you remember," she began her confession, "that a long, long time ago, your mother often told you about a seaside house which was the home of truly happy people."

Antonio perked up and eyed her expectantly. He was so anxious he forgot to answer her question.

"Do you remember?" she repeated.

"Yes, you already mentioned it on the flight back. But how do you know about this? As far as I remember, my mother didn't talk to anyone," he said in a low voice. He bowed his head to hide his sadness.

"Your mother isn't dead," she said in a pure, ringing voice.

"She isn't?" cried Antonio, jumping up in surprise. "Then where is she and why did she leave me?"

Sandra couldn't bear to answer his question. Instead, she told him about their escape from Marrakech and their crossing, the way she lost her son, and her long years in Paris. She told him how she was sick for a long time and that perhaps this sickness was still with her to this very day. She mentioned her recovery and plastic surgery. She mentioned that she returned to Marrakech twice to find her kidnapped son or at least find some lead. She gave a broad description of her meeting with Nick, her marriage, and her long, fruitless waiting. However, she didn't mention Pedro.

Antonio stared at her with eyes wide open, listening to her lengthy confession in shock.

"My dear son. You have no idea how much this means to me," she said, emotionally bursting into tears.

"I can't believe what I'm hearing. Is it you? So, you're not dead. If that's true, I'm a lucky man," he cried. He sat closer and wrapped his arm around his mother and they wept together, crying tears of joy.

For a moment, he thought about last night, and it seemed like Lucy's story was true. "You know, oddly enough, when I took you to the hospital in Rio, I subconsciously knew that there was something between us." He looked at her face with teary eyes, recalling the way that ever since they first met, he always felt a kind of love, sympathy, and in fact, devotion to her whenever he was around her, feelings which confused him at the time.

She stood up and practically ran over to turn on all the lights in the room.

"Come here. Take a good look at my face." She picked up her hand and gently felt out the three faint scars on her face. "See?"

"Barely. I never noticed it before. I must say, the operation, or rather the operations must have been carried out by a professional."

"That's right."

Antonio respectfully kissed her hand. He faintly recalled the image of his mother's scabbed face, and now here she was, changed and standing in front of him, reappearing in his life.

"I love you," said the mother quietly, hugging her only child. "I'm so happy that I got you back," she cried in joy. Suddenly, she felt unspeakably happy to rid herself of her heaviest secret, which she had been forced to carry and hide for years.

Antonio grinned and wiped his eyes. "We have to celebrate this with some champagne."

"Go, there's a bottle in the fridge," she urged him, watching her son busy himself at the kitchen counter.

The bang of the cork, the bubbling of the liquid, and the quiet clinking of the glasses unleashed rejoiced sighs and never-before-experienced joy into the air. The joy spread throughout the mother's heart. She could barely believe it was true.

Antonio started asking questions at once. "So, am I right to think that Pedro and not Nick is my father?" he asked, eyeing his mother quizzically.

She seemed to hesitate for a moment.

"Yes, he's your father," she replied hesitantly. However, to this very day, she still didn't know the truth herself.

"Why did Nick adopt me?"

Sandra turned pale. What should she say to that?

"I don't know," she whispered. "All I know is that he took you away from me."

She didn't dare to tell Antonio that she slept with two men in one week. How could she explain her muddled past to him? After all, that little joyful time she spent with Pedro was only their business, she thought as the joy drained from her face.

"Why didn't you tell Pedro in Rio?"

"I wanted to."

"Yet you didn't."

"You forgot something again."

"What?"

"That he loves someone else now. That he has a wife and a beautiful daughter, who's your half-sister."

"Then why did you come to that dinner with me?"

"I didn't want to. You asked me to come, so I couldn't say no. Then I wanted to talk to Pedro in private, to tell him the truth, but you know I didn't have a chance to do that. Is that so hard to understand?"

"No. It's not hard at all."

Sandra was relieved. "Still, the fact that I saw him again deeply upset me. Perhaps that's why all those other things happened to me," she added in a perturbed tone.

"No. You mustn't focus on anything but your joy now," said Antonio, fending off the dark thoughts mustering in his mother's mind.

The happiness slowly welled up again in Sandra's eyes. "Do you know that the seaside house I told you about isn't just a fairy tale, but a real story? I'd love to show it to you over the weekend, unless Nick shows up by then," she added, as a shade passed over her face. "You can meet its benign inhabitants, who don't know yet that I got you back."

"I'd love to go with you. I still have time."

"What do you mean by that?"

"Before I continue my studies at the university, I would like to spend some time at a hospital. I want to work. It doesn't matter if I'm just a porter since I can still see, learn, and pick up things. As we were coming back from Rio, I sent an email to a friend, asking for help."

"I appreciate your determination."

"You know, if you hadn't come after me, then …" he glanced at his mother anxiously.

"Then what?"

"The truth is that I was thinking about breaking off my studies, but now I see things differently. I want to continue learning."

"I'm really happy to hear that. Creating a stable basis for your future is more important than anything else. Without studying, you might be thrown about and forced to struggle your whole life. Never trust in luck; it might raise you from time to time, but usually, it avoids you altogether."

"You might be right. But please, tell me about your parents."

"Your grandmother and grandfather," she continued in an instructive tone, "are still living in that seaside house."

"I'm interested in them."

"They're kind, decent people. The rest you can decide for yourself."

Antonio raised an eyebrow. "I'm already glad to have them and that I'm no longer alone."

"Secretly that was what I was hoping for. Okay then, it's a deal. We could probably head out after tomorrow.

"We have to get out of here before Nick returns," he warned his mother with care.

"Well, you don't necessarily have to think of him that way. After all, he raised you, you're using his name, and he's paying for your education. That's no laughing matter. I think he loves you in his way. You mustn't be ungrateful. Don't forget, he's my husband too."

"I know that." His voice was tinged with sarcasm as he recalled the scene on the patio. "However, I never had the chance to feel the love of a family and the warmth of a family home," he admitted sullenly.

Sandra was fully aware of that. "Please don't say that I don't like hearing that," she said grimly. She lifted her glass to cover up her sadness.

"Now it's my turn to say we should be happy, okay?" Her thoughts raced off to the distant past, thinking about all the things missing from their lives. "Never forget that I am now irrevocably back with you," she said out loud. "You can always count on me."

She lovingly caressed his head before walking over to the phone. She called her mother to tell her she would be visiting after tomorrow and would be bringing a huge surprise.

She happily went up to her room and puttered around for a while. She imagined how happy her parents would be to finally meet their grandson. Her son would surely love the seaside house and the people living there. She suddenly remembered the other house on the sea which emerged from her memories from time to time, the place where she was very happy with Pedro. *Unfortunately, that's lost in the past now,* she thought sentimentally.

She looked into the mirror and adjusted her hair. Lately, she's been at odds with Nick. She knew he would leave sooner or later, or she would leave him. She'd had enough of his dirty little trips. This house had felt alien to her for a long time now; perhaps it was never really her home. She never felt safe at Nick's side. Her sixth sense always warned her that something wasn't right between the two of them. She wasn't a vengeful person to reciprocate all of this. Travelling to Rio was her way of warning him that she could survive without him. All she could do was love or not love.

She often thought about how corrupt the world was. Love might disappear from the world for good. Sex was all that counts. There was hardly any difference between human sensations and animalistic instincts. Nowadays, faithfulness was an old-fashioned, outdated thing, at least in the eyes of many people. But then why were there so many divorces? she wondered. When she was younger, she always avoided the womanizing type of men, who seduced girls with their handsome looks. *Yet I still married Nick,* she thought mockingly.

She was convinced by now that her husband was the same type. She didn't understand how he could live this way, constantly lying to her face. Her hatred was now stronger than her love. A long time ago, she read these words somewhere: "You can live your life the way you want to. You can squeeze out all the joy you can from it, but don't forget there's someone up there who expects you to pay for all of this one day."

She thought of Carmen, who was always following Nick around. She knew David to be a decent, straightforward man. Unfortunately, men or women like him often made poor choices of companions.

Sandra was fully aware that ever since she met Nick, strange, hair raising things have been happening to her. She recalled the time when David took her to that seaside house many years ago, where she first met the charming man who undressed her with his piercing gaze. She sensed at once that Nick was eyeing her up sexually, and it made her feel deeply uncomfortable at the time. Yes, the eyes reveal it all: interest, boredom, hate, love, sex. The eyes never lie.

CHAPTER 85

It was two o'clock in the afternoon by the time they crossed over the seemingly fragile bridge into Portugal.

"Let's change places," Antonio said. "You could use some rest since you've been driving since early morning."

"I'm not tired. I like driving, but I can stop at the next gas station if you want."

After topping up the car, she invited him to the bar. "Come on, let's have a *bica*."

"What?"

Sandra laughed. "That's what the Portuguese call a shot of coffee."

Antonio was glad to see that his mother was happy. The sadness had vanished from her fair features as if she was a different person.

"The *bica* tastes a lot better than Spanish or English coffee. Still, the Italian might be better. I'm not sure."

The waitress gave them a couple of white, tiny cups containing the fragrant liquid.

"Hmm, this is delicious," said Antonio, licking his lips.

"I love it too. I never miss it when I'm here."

Antonio soon started up the car. "I love driving," he told his mother.

"Me too, but I hate parking in tight spots. To this very day, I still can't master it. Can you imagine, I saw on TV a driver parking between two cars in a single motion, with just a short span left in front of and behind the car."

Antonio laughed and changed the subject.

"Since this is the first time I'm here, I wonder what the Portuguese are like and how they live."

"Good things come to those who wait."

"Tell me something about them."

"The rooster is their symbol," she said happily. "Their national dish is the grilled sardines, at least here in Algarve, which I think is one of the most delicious types of fish. What they're most famous for is *fado*, a peculiar type of music, which is almost always sad. The words are usually about poverty, the sea, and life. As far as I know, *fado* is now part of the list of their cultural heritage. They're also famous for their complex, light-blue imagery painted on tiles, which spread throughout Portugal in the fifteenth century. They often decorated the inner and outer walls, ceilings, and even floors of houses and churches with these tiles. The southern part of the country, Algarve is a Mediterranean region, the loveliest stretch of beach in Portugal and I think maybe the whole of Europe. People here are usually kind and peaceful. You can always see old people playing dominos and cards or just chatting and watching life go by as they sit under the leafy trees on the quaint squares of the town. Interestingly, only men take up this habit. Who knows where the women gather to chat?"

Antonio started laughing.

"My parents, or rather your grandparents, have been living in Algarve for a long time and I grew up right next to the ocean."

Antonio rubbed his forehead in concern. "I'm worried whether they'll accept me or not."

"Come on, don't be silly," she said, glancing at her son for a moment. "Open-hearted people quickly understand and grow fond of each other."

Traffic picked up and they talked less.

"I'm going to put on a CD. Do you like Latin music?"

"Yes," said Antonio with a smile.

"I simply love Brazilian, Cuban, the Latin music, including Argentinean tango, but of course, classical music still comes first." Then she put on a CD and they both hummed the tune of Cesaria Évora's superb voice as the car steadily headed towards their destination.

"Poor thing, she died along with her great voice. I never saw her live, but I watched a concert of hers on TV. It was amazing," said Sandra.

For a while, Antonio said, "I hope everything will be fine." He undoubtedly felt tense to meet close relatives he never knew existed in the first place or that he belonged to them. *I finally have a family*, he thought. This was unlike the old days when he spent years in boarding school, often during the holidays as well. Though his father, or rather Nick, visited him regularly and went travelling with him for a month during the summer vacation, he always felt the absence of belonging somewhere and the warmth of a family home. All he had was his cherished, faded memories of his mother dressed in black, and he adoringly eyed the beautiful red-haired woman at length, his mother, sitting next to him.

"Don't worry," she encouraged him, catching a glimpse of him.

"You know, this isn't easy. Perhaps it's because of my roommate, Sean, once told me that his mother didn't like his father's parents.

"You can't force love or pay for it with money, but it's sad if this is missing and leads to the family falling apart. We carry good or bad traits from our parents in our genes. The word family isn't just about the belonging between husband and wife and their children. It extends to the grandparents as well. Today, you're the head of the family, tomorrow your child will be and the next day, you grow old as well."

"Yeah, But Sean didn't tell me the reason behind all of this.

"Well, son, there can be many reasons. But if no one deals

with the situation, the situation will remain unresolved for a long time.”

“I agree.” Then he stopped for a rest.

Sandra turned to Antonio. “This is what I think, so please pay attention to what I’m saying. If a mother sees that her son is happy with his wife, then she has to accept that. It’s his life, he chose it for himself. However, if they are mistaken in some way, she must warn them, if necessary. There’s no sense to hate. If you will end up doing this eventually,” she glanced at him seriously, “I’m sure you will lose me, and then I’ll move as far away from you as I can. I’ll even do my best to forget I ever had a son.”

Antonio glanced at her in alarm and squeezed her hand. “But that will never happen, do you understand?”

“I hope not,” said Sandra, thinking for a moment, how her heart will break if she would be in such a case. She continued after a brief pause. “Those who are bad, they will never reconsider since they’ll always, be treacherously plotting something.”

“You are right.”

“Son, if you become a father, that is means you have to continuously teach your child of love, goodness, morality, and decency. Let’s say if the parent is indecent, malicious, and deceitful, then what could we possibly expect from a child who grows up in this atmosphere seeing, hearing, and imitating everything they see day after day. You can befriend them, but they mustn’t think they can get away with everything. Don’t serve them. Teach them how to be independent. Otherwise, they’ll learn to use you. I’m sure that one day you’ll be a father, but you must never hide behind your wife if you know she’s wrong. You must have to set an example so your child will look up to you.” Sandra concluded her lengthy discussion and started the car.

Her words of wisdom were deeply ingrained in Antonio. “I’ll follow your advice. You’ll never be disappointed in me,” he promised emotionally.

Sandra furtively wiped away a tear from her eye. “I love you,” she said, and this magical word encapsulated everything she had to say.

"I love you too, and I'm really happy I got you back."

"Honey, you'll see how great it is, sharing a laugh with your family, which is something we had to do without for a long time. How about telling me something more cheerful about yourself and your life?"

"As I think back, there was hardly anything cheerful in my life," he admitted ironically.

I could say the same thing, she thought. "My experiences show that we'reforced to tolerate a lot of things," she told him. "You're still young, and you have your whole life ahead of you. But watch out what kind of people you surround yourself with. Never trust girls who use too much makeup and dress too daringly, sexily selling themselves off, since they're like reeds that bend whichever way the wind is blowing. A more modest girl is better for establishing a long-term family. Trust me, this is still true in the twenty-first century," she concluded, involuntarily thinking of Amy. Their fate cruelly got in the way. *But he's still so young,* she thought.

CHAPTER 86

They turned left and approached the ocean.

"We're here," she said excitedly, leaving her grim thoughts behind and parking the car near the gate. Her happiness was bubbling forth, so she playfully honked the car's horn.

"Nice surroundings," said Antonio, curiously looking around.

"Yes, I love this place too. Don't forget, I grew up here."

The gate opened. Her mother approached them with a beaming expression on her face. Her father soon joined her in the entrance. They all hugged each other while Antonio silently fidgeted a few steps further away.

"Who is this good-looking young man?" asked the old woman, kindly eyeing him.

Sandra grabbed Antonio by the hand and pulled him closer. "Allow me to introduce you to my son, my long-lost son, your grandson. He's my surprise, or rather my present to you."

Sandra's mother glanced at the young man in surprise. Antonio felt uncomfortable from her look. He had no idea what to say or do.

The woman suddenly spread her arms apart and hugged her grandson.

"So, that means I'm a grandmother?"

"Yes," giggled Sandra in joy.

"Well, welcome both of you. Perhaps we should go inside," suggested the grandfather, taking the young man by the arm.

In the days that followed, the villa was filled with happiness and a family atmosphere, which it hadn't witnessed for a long time. They gladly asked questions and told stories, wanting to know everything about each other.

Mother and son often walked down to the nearby sandy bay. When the tide was out, they wandered amongst the cliffs or the slippery rocks, covered in green algae, which protruded from the shallow, translucent water. They searched for tiny crabs, black sea urchins, fish, and the rest of the ocean fauna. When the tide rolled on, they swayed on top of the waves or ran screaming to the shore, where they stretched out and basked in the sunlight. Even the grandparents came down to the beach at the foot, without ever taking their eyes off their beloved family.

Antonio looked back from the edge of the water and saw that his grandmother, his granny, kept wiping away tears from her eyes. This made him emotional as well. *I'm so lucky,* he thought, *to belong to such a great family.*

"What's wrong?" asked the old man of his wife, who was oddly quiet as she sat under her parasol.

"Oh, it's nothing, it's just the wind blowing the sand in my eyes," she whispered evasively.

He could see that she was moved, just as he was. He looked down at the youngsters again, who moved along the rocks, twisting this way and that. He didn't say much since he didn't like talking about his feelings. Later on, he coughed and spoke up. "Well, it is a nice present for us, isn't it?"

"Yes," said his wife. "The best present you can ever get from your life. You know, I could never accept the idea that Vicky died. I never believed it, and I was waiting and waiting for something to happen. Of course, it was a long time, and sometimes my hope was wearing thin. But now, my joy is even greater that my grandson is here as well."

He knew full well that his wife often cried into her pillow, which she tried hiding from him. He wrapped his arm around her shoulder.

"Do you remember when Vicky was little and she was running up and down the sand like a crazy little puppy? Sometimes, she fell over and was covered in sand. She loved the sea and screamed in delight when I took her into the water."

"And do you remember those long walks we went on, searching for shells? Once she even cut her little finger."

"Of course, I remember, it's as if it was only yesterday. You know, the great thing is that we'll have these memories for the rest of our lives," he sighed heavily. "But now even our dreams have come true."

"That's right," sniffled his wife.

Sandra waved to them. "We're going for a walk," she cried, disappearing behind the rocks with Antonio.

They headed over to the nearby, several-kilometre-long stretch of the shoreline, where the waves lapped up far inland. Antonio enjoyed the Atlantic Ocean and the amazing shore, and he quickly grew fond of the house, the garden, and his grandparents. This is exactly how he'd imagined the seaside house in his dreams, which his mother had told him so much about. They rested on the sand for a while sitting next to each other, silently watching the rumbling waves.

"Do you like this place?"

"I do."

"So, do you think we could live here?"

"I'd love to."

"Then let's stay. Once you finish your studies, I think you could easily get a job at the hospital in Albufeira or Faro."

"That's a long way away, but it sounds like a great idea. That means you want to leave Nick, right?"

"Yes, I've been planning to do so for some time now," she replied hesitantly.

"We can give it a shot, but what will your parents say?"

"What did you say?"

"Sorry, I mean Grandma and Grandpa."

"That's better. I don't think they'll have any problems. Well, that does it then, I mean we've agreed."

"Okay, but talk to them first. Don't forget, I have to go back to New York in September, and I still have quite a few years left."

"That's true. But I hope you'll spend the holidays with us?"

"I'd love to."

Sandra laughed happily. After what felt like an eternity, the pressure bearing down on her heart had vanished. She felt they would be able to manage to start a life of their own and finally leave the oppressive shadow of their past behind them.

CHAPTER 87

The following day, Antonio headed down to the shore again and went for a long walk along the edge of the water. He felt hot, so he found a suitable spot and stabbed the end of the parasol into the loose sand, rolling his mat out underneath it. He took his shirt off and ran into the cold water. Later on, he gazed out at the shoreline as he lay on his stomach. He enjoyed the beautiful beach as he listened to the murmur of the Atlantic Ocean, which eased up his thoughts.

The tides started rolling in. The waves grew stronger and stronger as they crashed ashore. He grabbed his mat and pulled it further up on the dunes. In the distance, the beach disappeared into the haze. There were a lot of people walking on the edge of the water or the amber sand, enjoying the carefree idling under the colourful shades. Two girls kept on sunbathing near the shore. Their white skin grew red under the heat of the sun. *They were probably from Northern Europe,* thought Antonio, looking at them.

Suddenly, a powerful wave washed ashore and soaked the girls in seconds. They screamed and jumped up, lunging for their belongings, which the water pulled back into the deep. Finally, they came further in from the water, close to Antonio, who chuckled as he averted his gaze.

In the meantime, Sandra talked with her parents.

"Mom," she began quietly, "what would you say if my son and I would move in with you?"

The unexpected question made the parents exchange surprised looks. Sandra fell uncertain as she saw the shock on their faces.

"Please, you don't have to answer me at once, just talk it over first," she said, standing up to leave them.

"Sit back down. There's nothing to discuss," interjected her father. "This has always been your mother's secret dream."

"Yes," confirmed the grey-haired woman. "My dear child, we would love to have you, but could you tell me what made you come to this decision?"

Sandra looked up at them gratefully with teary eyes.

"Well, thank you for your trust and consent. The truth is," she said as she sat back down, "that unfortunately, my marriage is in shambles. I don't think it can ever be restored. And I've given up on my husband ever changing his ways. I've lost hope, and there's no sense in wasting any more words on this."

"We thought you had a good life. You never complained."

"I intentionally didn't complain. Trust me, I didn't say anything because I foolishly hoped that things would get better. Perhaps I still do," she thought as her heart quivered.

"But what happened?"

"Well, I have the feeling that he's strayed far off the well-beaten path. Of course, I never snooped around after him. I don't deny the fact that I married him to get my son back since I always had the feeling that he took him away from me. I had to marry him first, and unfortunately, I quickly fell in love with him. But that's my problem."

"Oh," sighed the mother.

"No, don't worry, everything will work out just fine. Antonio will soon return to New York for his university. I think we should give it a shot. I hope we can get along. We'll take care of the financial matters along the way. Would that be okay with you?"

"There will be no financial matters," said her father sternly.

"No, Dad, I naturally have to pay for the utilities, food, and additional expenses, too. I don't want to use you. I have a friend who keeps complaining to her parents to get some money out of them, whilst her family doesn't show any love for them at all. I don't think parents are there to just give."

"Honey, you're different."

"That's right. You helped me enough until I came of age, now it's my turn. If necessary, I'll always be here, and I'm sure my son, your grandson, feels the same way."

"Fine, we'll discuss this later," concluded the mother emotionally.

"Once Antonio finishes his studies," continued Sandra, "I hope he can soon get a job at the nearest hospital. And I'm sure I'll come up with something as well, but first I have to size up the situation here. I have some money to get me started," she concluded the most important subject.

"When are you planning all of this?"

"As soon as possible," she promised. She had no idea that this would only remain a dream of hers.

She was pleased by her decision and that her parents said yes at once, but she was particularly pleased that they both accepted their grandson, her only son, whom they only met a few days ago. Still, he wasn't hard to accept, since he turned out to be a rather open-minded, sincere, and moderate person. Antonio never made any demands and wasn't greedy at all. Life had taught him that things don't always happen the way we want them to. Despite his young age, he suffered a major blow from life when he lost his mother. He'd had to go without parental care and the warmth of a family home since, four years of age, which he hardly got any of for many long years.

CHAPTER 88

They returned to Marbella two weeks later. The house was empty and deserted. Nick was nowhere to be seen. The mailbox was stuffed with letters. Most of them, however, were merely bills. They spent the next few days sorting through their belongings.

"So, when do you think we can get going?"

"As soon as I'm done with my official matters. It only takes a few days."

"Perfect."

She glanced at him.

"Something's bothering you, right?"

"No, it's nothing, I was just thinking about Amy."

"Amy?" she repeated her question in surprise.

"Yes. What's so surprising about that?"

"You have to forget all about her, you know. She's your half-sister."

"I know, I remember every word you said. You can't forget something like that," interrupted Antonio impatiently.

"Trust me, you must forget her," she said in a calmer tone.

"There's no need to convince me. I understood it the first time around. Yet I still feel that you should somehow tell Pedro that

I'm his son, don't you think?"

"Yes, you're right, but I'm already too late for that."

"You could have asked me for his phone number, right? That would have spared everyone an uncomfortable situation. Or am I mistaken?"

"No, you're not," she said, hanging her head, feeling shocked. "You did, however, forget one thing which I mentioned to you before," she added sadly.

"What?"

"That after all these years, I felt I didn't have the courage or the right to get involved in the life of a family."

"That's true, but then why did you leave him at the time, since I assume you were the one who left him," he asked reproachfully.

"Well, you're wrong."

"Then how about informing me? I would like to know what happened between the two of you. I might have a right to know, even though this is your business."

"Naturally, you have the right to know the truth."

"I would like to know. Please, start – or rather finish – the story."

The tension settled in between them again. Sandra nervously started pacing up and down the room. She tried to composing her thoughts and recalling the long-forgotten period. "We'd only known each other for a short time," she began slowly. "The whole thing started with his niece's disappearance. I had just got back from El Palmar when the doorbell rang and two Arabs carried me off to a yacht. That's how I ended up in Morocco."

Antonio glanced at his mother in surprise. This was the last thing he expected.

"Good God, you were kidnapped? But why, and where was Pedro?"

"Yes, it was kidnapping, but I still don't know why to this very day. Fortunately, or rather, unfortunately, Pedro finally found me in Marrakech and tried to get us out of the riad."

"Us?"

"Pedro's niece Lucy and me."

He tensely listened to the story. He grew pale from his mother's confession. "Go on," he asked with growing anxiety.

Sandra related the story of their botched escape and how they returned to the riad with Pedro to free Lucy somehow and take her with them, but things turned out badly. The memories made her nervous.

"Pedro was shot. I thought he died, and suddenly, I was shot as well," she explained in a perturbed tone.

"But who did this to you and why?" cried out Antonio as the blood drained from his face.

"I don't know. I simply couldn't figure that out," she replied emotionally.

"It's better if you stop right there. I think I've heard enough," interrupted Antonio with concern.

"No, let me finish. I'm sure you remember the bullet scars I was forced to live with for a long time, right?"

Her son nodded anxiously.

"I will never forget that abandoned feeling when the nurse covered my face up with a shawl at the hospital exit. *It's better if you keep this on,*' she said in pity. That's how I ended up on the street. I was alone, without a passport, papers, money, or a face. I namelessly found myself surrounded by a foreign, Arabian world."

She didn't want to tell him how many weeks she spent wandering through the medina in a dirty, hungry, and thirsty state. She spent most of her time begging in the Djemaa el-Fna square, where she always got some leftovers in the evening. That's when she learned how hunger can rule one's actions. She spent the night huddled up in some entrance way. Her bad memories made her shudder, yet she still carried on.

"Fortunately, Nick took me in, for which I had to be grateful." She fell silent.

"That can't be true," cried the young man, jumping up from his seat, forgetting all about his mother's condition. "And?" he urged her again.

"There was no 'and.' I was pregnant. We lived in the house in Marrakech after you were born. That was our home. You know the rest."

"You didn't tell me on the plane why Nick adopted me," he asked his mother, hoping to get a satisfactory answer.

Sandra was cornered. What could she say to that? How could she explain the events that took place in a single week?

"Please, tell me," he pressed her.

"I don't know," she whimpered. She was so nervous that she grew cold and started shivering all over. Most people who are forced to cover up a secret or lie start trembling in the cold when cornered. Their forehead starts perspiring, and their skin gets goose-bumps all over, she thought in fright. Yet she still couldn't reveal her secrets and her doubts, especially after she had separated him from Amy. Thus, she decided to fend off her son's questions by questioning him herself. "Do you remember the riad?"

"Barely. But I do remember the times you sat me in your lap and told my stories."

Sandra smiled. "Yes. Sometimes I couldn't finish the story because you fell asleep in my arms. In the morning, you always asked me to continue, but I didn't have time, which always made you throw a tantrum." This led to a lot of fights with Nick, but she omitted that detail. "I'm sorry, honey, that I couldn't do more to show my love for you at the riad. My life was very hard at the time."

"Oh, don't say that."

"I was afraid of Nick, so whenever you started crying and threw a tantrum, which happened a lot, I gave you a spanking."

Antonio laughed. "Children can be naughty. I'm sure I deserved it. But let's stop fooling around. You've completely confused me with your sad story."

"It's not me, but life itself."

"I cried a lot for you."

"Me too."

"Tell me more."

"There is no more."

Antonio took hold of his mother's hand and didn't let go of it for a while.

"What else do you remember?" she asked. "Oh, that was a foolish question, since you were barely four at the time."

"I ended up in London after I lost you. That's where I went to school. I lived in a boarding school under strict rules. Unfortunately, I can't recall exactly the way we were separated, only that I looked for you futilely. I already told you about this."

"Honey," she said, swallowing her tears, "I want you to know that I wanted to get you back at all costs. Nick disappeared at the time, but I didn't dare pick a fight with him. I looked all over London for you, but it was no use since you'd left by then. Things slipped through my fingers. Then …"

"Then?"

"I got lucky after a while. I was working at a hotel in Paris, where I accidentally bumped into Nick, who grew fond of me and perhaps even fell in love with me, and thus we soon got married."

"Did he recognize you?"

"Of course, not."

"Did you love him?"

"Well …" hesitated Sandra for a moment.

"How could you marry him if you didn't love him?"

"Well, son, it was the only way I could ever hope of finding you. I had no other choice. Do you understand? I couldn't tell him I was your mother. I was afraid of him. You don't know what he's like. Since then, I've been very cautious, making sure he wouldn't find out anything." She continued after a brief pause, "In the end, I grew fond of him, and I might still love him. I don't think I made a bad decision since I got you back. Right?"

"Yes, and I'm really glad about that. I missed you, do you know that? Sometimes I dreamt of you, but your face was always hidden behind that black shawl, which didn't even give me a glimpse of your eyes. You were just a shade, yet I still knew it was you."

Sandra blinked profusely.

"Please, tell me," he asked, looking deep into his mother's eyes.

"What?" she asked anxiously.

"Why you took all those sleeping pills in Rio."

She awkwardly averted his gaze. Her thoughts were straying to and for. What could she say to her son? she wondered, exhausted by the lengthy confession. She eyed him tenderly. "Because I regretted going with you to Pedro's house and the fact that I couldn't talk to him and find any solution," she explained, closing her eyes for a few minutes.

"You know," she continued finally, "I could hardly hold back my tears during dinner when I secretly eyed Pedro. The truth is that I wasn't brave enough to expose myself. That woman seemed happy, as well as Pedro. You must understand that I felt lonely at the time since I was clueless and couldn't find the way out, especially after we went home and I told you that Amy was your sister. You ran away and left me alone, and then suddenly, something broke inside of me. I thought I'd lost you for good."

"Dear mother, don't worry about that. I'm still here for you," he said consolingly, caressing her hand.

"Yes, but my conscience is still bothering me for the fact that you were forced to break up with that nice young girl because of me, even though I liked her. Trust me, it took a great deal of effort to be so cold with her that evening."

"I understand you now." He fully sympathized with her grief and her dark past. "Mom, I would like both of us to push these painful memories behind us. Let's give it a try, shall we?"

"Fine."

"I hope that we'll both be happier in Gale," added Antonio with a mischievous sparkle in his eyes.

"I hope so too," nodded Sandra, since she still had issues with her husband to resolve.

Antonio headed off to the kitchen, where he puttered around for a while and finally returned with a bottle of champagne.

"We have some celebrating to do," he explained.

"That's a bit too early for you."

"Why? I came of age. Mom, why can't you see that I'm an adult by now?" he asked, opening the bottle with a bang and quickly filling the glasses as the foam dribbled down onto the counter.

"I think you still need more practice to do, you 20-year-old adult," she noted with a wry smile, lifting her glass to a toast. "To a better future. I hope you'll find the girl you will truly come to love as soon as possible."

"No, I don't want any more of that. Please. Amy is still vividly alive in my memories."

Sandra respected her son's feelings.

"Forgive me," said Sandra. She knew well what it was like to love someone.

CHAPTER 89

Antonio checked his email. As he read the message, his face lightened up, and he rushed over to his mother's room at once.

Sandra eyed him quizzically. "Did something happen?"

"Yes. My friend wrote that the hospital in New York where he's working would be willing to hire me for some temp work. I can work a few hours a day while studying at the university. What do you think? Isn't it great?"

Sandra sighed heavily and nodded. He will be leaving me again, but his studying and his progress are more important than anything, she consoled herself. I think you better sort out your ticket as soon as possible," she warned him.

"I'm sorry, but in this case, our summer plans are ruined. I can't go to Gale with you."

"Cheer up. You're the one who's responsible for building your own life. You no longer need my help," she encouraged him with a smile, yet her eyes revealed her sadness.

"That's not true. I need you, and it would be great if you could visit me or stay there with me."

Sandra started laughing. "Who knows, I soon might be going there myself!"

"That would be great. Well then, I'll go sort out my ticket." He nodded and turned around.

The phone was ringing.
"Hello, Sandra, is that you?" It was her mother calling.
"Yes, Mama, what's going on?"
"I was just calling to find out approximately when you will be arriving."
"Unfortunately, I can only come next week, without Antonio," she said, explaining the situation.
"We're sorry. Still, I must say we're pleased with the same time. I trust you feel the same way?"
"Yes," she sniffled.
"When is he leaving?"
"I don't know yet, he's just taking care of his ticket."
"Once he leaves, it would be good if you would come here."
"I'll do my best."
"You're dealing with some problems, right?"
"No, I'm not. I just need some time to take care of everything. That's all. I'll get going as soon as I can."
"Sure, I understand. We'll be waiting for you. Tell Antonio we wish him a safe trip. I hope he'll take care of himself in that huge city and come visit us for Christmas."
"I'll let him know. See you on Tuesday or Wednesday."

Sandra wanted to go get some air, so she rushed upstairs. She combed her hair back and braided it. Don't worry, she thought, looking into the mirror since things are going smoothly. In a few days, you can say goodbye to Marbella along with Nick. She tried to overcome the negative feelings she was having. She left a note for her son that she went down to the beach, telling him to come after her if he wished.
Antonio joined her an hour later. He took his shirt off and lay down next to her on his stomach.
"So, what did you manage to arrange?" she perked up.
"I have to go."
"When?"

"Tomorrow."

"So soon?" she asked with a quivering heart. That was a sudden change of events. *It would have been great to spend the rest of the summer with him,* she thought, *but such is life.*

"Yeah, tomorrow."

"I'm not that thrilled, son, but working on your future is the the most important thing."

They both fell silent for a long time.

A group of good-looking girls were sitting close to them, chatting and laughing. Sandra glanced at them and was satisfied to see that her son was eyeing them attentively as well. *That's better,* she thought with relief.

"Oh, before I came down, I called up Grandma and Grandpa and said goodbye."

"Good for you. I'm sure they were pleased. You know, it's the little things like that which multiply love."

A few hours later, they went up to the house. They finished packing and had dinner at a nice restaurant.

"Are your financial matters sorted out?"

"Yes. Dad, or rather Nick, always takes care of that."

"Well, if you have any problems, just let me know. You know what my plan is. You understand, right?"

"Don't worry," he said, whilst assuring himself that things wouldn't come to that since he'd be working during his studying. He didn't want to rely on his mother or make use of anyone.

In the morning, she drove Antonio to the airport in Malaga.

"Take care of yourself," she warned him with teary eyes.

"Don't worry. Say hi to Nick for me."

"I will," she blinked at him emotionally. "Call me when you get there."

He nodded and flashed a youthful grin. After he checked in, he turned around and waved back to his mother before getting serious and heading inside the terminal.

Sandra simply couldn't shake off her bad feelings. It was late afternoon by the time she got home. She got her bicycle out and went for a long ride through the quiet streets of the neighbourhood. She checked her email in the evening. Her girlfriend had sent her a message from Paris. She was moved as she read that Yvonne's father had died. She called her up at once.

"Is that you? It's Sandra here."

"Yes," she heard Yvonne's voice over the phone.

"My condolences. I'm sorry for your loss. He was such an exceptional man."

"Thank you, but that doesn't change the fact that he's gone," Yvonne sobbed into the phone.

"Don't cry. I don't want to ask any questions. Please, visit me if you can."

"Maybe," Yvonne said briefly.

"Come. I miss you, and I'm sure you could use some time out. I want to take you to Portugal with my parents. If you can get your mother to come with you, we would love to have her, too."

"That's very kind of you. Maybe next month," Yvonne sniffled faintly.

"Fine. Call me if you can come to Gale," she said, giving her friend the phone number of her parents. "I'll probably be on my way to see them."

CHAPTER 90

Sandra finally took care of everything in the morning. It was hot, and the summer was still in full force. She had a bite to eat and strolled down to the beach. She loved the sea, which was no wonder since she grew up next to the ocean and always felt close to it. Although she was next to The Mediterranean at the moment, which was a few degrees warmer, it wasn't nearly as clear as the Atlantic Ocean.

She spread her towel out on the ground. She stabbed the end of the parasol into the sand and comfortably lay down on the beach. She closed her eyes and listened to the gentle murmur of the waves mixing with the noise of the people in the water.

David noticed her and walked over.

"*Hola*, long time, no see," he said, sitting down next to her.

She nodded in surprise. "Indeed. How are you?"

"I'm fine."

"You seem worn out. Are you having problems?"

"No," he replied.

"Well, I don't want to pry, but you seem fairly shaken. Perhaps I'm mistaken," she added with a shrug. "It's fine if you don't want to talk about it."

He sighed awkwardly. "But you're fresh and youthful as always."

A faint smile crept onto her face. *Always the gentleman,* she thought.

"You're not mistaken," David admitted. "Carmen left me. We're getting a divorce."

"Seriously?" she asked, sitting up with a start.

"Dead serious."

"When did you make up your mind? I take it you were the one who made up your mind, right?"

"Yes. A month ago."

"Don't worry, Nick disappeared a while ago as well, I have no idea where he is. He might still be in Barcelona, as he wrote on the note he left me."

"I don't think so."

Sandra turned to him in surprise and her heart sank.

"Where do you think he is?"

"They're somewhere else."

"Oh, yeah? You mean together?"

"I think so. Come on, I'm sure you noticed something too. Or are you that naive?" He glanced at her incredulously.

"Maybe. I never thought it would come to this."

"I know what you're thinking, but I'm not blind. For a long time, I hoped things would get better. Yet she still did it. I have to face it that I still don't know much about women. She's the second woman who left me," he noted, hanging his head.

"Don't be sad. It seems like I'm in the same situation. Still, I'm fairly certain, we'll survive." She blinked profusely, turning away.

"That's kind of you," he said, squeezing her hand.

Their conversation stalled. They were both concerned with their thoughts, yet somehow, they felt tied together by an invisible bond of friendship.

David glanced at Sandra. "Okay then, I'll take your advice. We don't have to mope around and be sad, since this happens to countless people, day in and day out," he noted, eyeing her searchingly. "We've known each other for a long time, and since we're both on our own, I'd like to ask you to have dinner with me so we could cheer each other up a bit.

She didn't answer him.

"Don't worry, I won't bite off your nose," he joked, thinking about the old times.

Sandra smiled.

"You know," he began in a flat tone, "ever since you've been Nick's wife, I can't stop thinking that we've known each other previously. I'm practically convinced you're the same woman I knew in the past. Of course, your face is different, yet you still resemble that kind young girl I met and dreamed about before she disappeared from my life."

Here we go again, thought Sandra awkwardly. She didn't want to expose herself. David was no doubt a decent, kind man, but he was just a friend. He was good-looking and trustworthy, but love is something entirely different. Not to mention that Nick was still lurking out there somewhere. She wanted to get away from him regardless of the recent developments.

"I'm sorry, but I don't understand. Every time we meet, you keep telling me the same thing."

"You're right. I'm sorry, but whenever I see you, I keep thinking of that kind young girl. Forgive me, I can't help myself."

"Are you kidding?"

"No, it's no joke. You can't convince me."

"You can think whatever you want to," shrugged Sandra.

"Trust me. Whatever happened to you, I promise to keep your secret."

"I have nothing to say. I'm not the girl you're looking for," she concluded the subject dismissively.

"Why aren't you sincere with me?"

"Let's finish this awkward conversation, okay?" she said, gathering up her belongings and standing up in annoyance.

"OK. Wait." He grabbed her wrist. "Fine, forgive me for my pushy questions. Please, give me another chance."

"What do you want?"

"Let's meet tonight so I can tell you the rest of the story and why I keep harassing you with this subject."

"Fine, if that's what you want, but don't expect anything …"

"Nothing at all," interrupted David with a cheerful smile.

Sandra was puzzled by his hint, but she didn't pay much attention to it. She'd always liked David. He would be a fine companion if she could love him, but she couldn't.

"Please, sit back down and enjoy the sun, but not for too long," he warned her. "Watch out for your nose, or it will get red."

"I'll come to pick you up at nine," he added and strode off. His eyes were filled with joy. He smiled as he drove off, thinking back to the kind red-haired girl, he'd met a long time ago.

CHAPTER 91

He picked up Sandra that evening. They didn't talk much on their way. As they reached the hotel, David drove down into the parking lot.

"We're here," he said, opening the car door for her.

"Where did you bring me?"

"You surely know this place," he blurted.

Sandra didn't reply. She felt awkward. She knew, of course, she knew, where he'd brought her. This was the site of their last date many years ago. She recalled the long-forgotten time.

"Okay, I don't want to force it. Come," he said, taking her by the arm.

There were quite a few people in the restaurant. They sat down at the reserved table. David motioned to the waiter, and he brought his boss a menu at once.

"Hola," welcomed an old friend, searchingly eyeing Sandra. "It seems like you found your long-lost dream," he noted in a friendly tone.

Sandra blushed. She averted her gaze to hide her confusion. She recalled the charity night that took place many moons ago. The place hadn't changed much over the years, she thought as she looked around. The waiter uncorked the bottle as he reached their table. He filled the glasses with some quality red wine before setting the bottle down on the table and silently hurrying off.

"Salud," said Sandra kindly, tasting the wine. "It's delicious," she noted.

David reached into the inner pocket of his jacket and produced something from it. He rested his clenched fist on the table and thoughtfully looked at Sandra.

"Does this mean anything to you?" he asked, slowly opening his fingers.

Sandra turned pale in surprise. Her long-lost bracelet was there in his palm. She reached out for the glass with trembling hands to somehow cover up her confusion. Her eyes mysteriously glowed from her emotions. The bracelet had been a present from her mother for her twentieth birthday; the coral heart dangling from it, a memento from Gibraltar, was added by David. The memories brought tears to her eyes. She wanted to take what was hers, yet she couldn't.

"It's beautiful, but this is the first time I saw it," she lied in a veiled voice.

David sensed that he was opening deep wounds from the memories of the past and that she was hiding a lot of things from him, yet he was forced to accept her silence. *If it's a secret, it should stay a secret,* he thought.

"Fine," he said. "Still, I'd like to give it to you. Please, accept this from me."

She opened her mouth to say something.

"No," he stopped her, "don't say anything. You might tell me not to expect anything from you," he added, fending off the awkward situation with a joke.

"The bracelet belonged to a kind young girl who closely resembled you. That's why I'm giving it to you."

Sandra nervously laughed.

David reached over the table, gently took hold of her hand, and simply slipped the bracelet on her wrist. He felt satisfied. He happily picked up the bottle and poured them some more wine.

"It's beautiful, thank you," said Sandra emotionally. The joy clearly shown in her eyes.

"You're welcome." David felt she was eager to find out how the bracelet ended up with him. So, he started relating the story without any further prompting. "You know, many years ago, I went on a trip and found it on Nick's yacht, slipped amongst the seat cushions. I knew at once that it was yours … or rather, Vicky's, who disappeared without a trace. So, I pocketed it at once." He quickly changed the subject, since he could see her turning pale. "What are your plans for the future?" he asked with a constrained smile.

"I … I don't know yet," she stammered. "What about you?"

"If possible, I'll request a transfer to somewhere else, as I already did before," he laughed sarcastically. "Yes, I left London at the time because my first wife left me, just like my second wife."

"Did it happen a long time ago?"

David was a good sport.

"About twenty years ago, but shortly after I meet a nice girl."

"Okay, here comes the old story," laughed Sandra mysteriously.

He let the remark pass and continued.

"She had a freckled face like you and red hair, too." He paused for a moment and furrowed his eyebrows, meaningfully glancing at her. He saw that she didn't want to react, yet he continued. "You know, at the time, I thought I fell in love with her."

"And did the redhead know about this?" she teased him cheekily.

"Perhaps."

"What happened to her?"

"I don't know. I futilely searched for her, but simply couldn't find her. However, now..." he began, but when he saw the look in her eye, he left the sentence trail, off.

"However now what?" asked Sandra curiously.

"However, now I might have found her again," noted the man, quickly finishing off the rest of the wine in his glass.

She fell oddly quiet and didn't encourage him with a single word. She finished off her wine as well and spoke up.

"David."

"Yes?" he perked up hopefully.

"There's something I want to make clear. You've been nagging me with this subject a lot, right?"

He nodded in resignation.

"Please, I kindly ask you to stop if you don't want to risk losing our, friendship. I know that you're an exceptional man, which is a rare treasure nowadays," she added warmly. "I would love to join you, but I would never become your woman. I'm sorry for stating this so bluntly, but I don't like playing games. I'm your friend as long as you want to have my friendship. Please, accept this from me. If that's not good enough for you, I can live with that and I'll get up and leave."

"Fine," he replied hoarsely. "As you wish, let's stay friends."

Sandra glanced at him in relief.

"I hope that third time's the charm and you'll find your real woman," she said kindly.

"I gave up on that by now."

"You must have faith, but don't be so eager to find her. Suddenly, when you least expect it, happiness will find its way to you. At least, that's what people say." She reached over the table and squeezed his hand. *However, the years run by and we might never find the person we've been looking for all our lives. Or if we do, we lose them when we least expect it,* she thought, thinking of Pedro.

Suddenly, their serious conversation came to an end as the waiter brought them their dinner.

"I think I'll disappear for a while as well," hinted Sandra.

"Perhaps that's the best solution," agreed David.

They finished their dinner and emptied their bottle of wine, and David morosely paid for the meal.

He took her home in silence, and Sandra planted a light kiss on his face in parting.

"Farewell, and thank you for the present."

"Wait," he said, stopping her for a moment. He pulled out an envelope from his pocket. "This is yours as well."

“What is it?”
“Open it when you get home.”
Sandra shrugged.
“Thank you for everything,” she repeated, slipping the envelope into her bag.

David watched her walk off at length until she disappeared into the night. He couldn't stop thinking that he had lost his old dreams for good.

CHAPTER 92

She busied herself by taking care of everything over the next few days. As she opened her bag, she came across David's envelope, which she had forgotten to check. Much to her surprise, it was an old picture from Gibraltar which showed a carefree young girl staring back at her. Her short red hair bristled in the air. She emotionally groped at her face with a twinge in her heart before slipping the photo into a pocket on the side of the bag. She'd show it to her parents and her son at the right moment. She smiled as she daydreamed since this was the only photo she had of her past. She packed everything into her suitcase and pressed down on her folded up clothes. She suddenly changed her mind and decided to continue packing the following day and leave the day after that.

However, things played out differently. An hour later, Nick suddenly appeared and probed her.

"You seem pretty happy, did I miss something?" he asked edgily.

"No, nothing happened," she replied with her heart pounding in her throat.

"You won't even ask me where I was?"

"Your smug question makes me laugh. In case you haven't noticed, I've gotten over this a long time ago," she retorted with bated temper.

Nick wasn't used to someone brushing him off. He wouldn't tolerate his wife doing this either. His vanity took hold of him, and anger flashed in his eyes.

"Something happened, right?" he repeated his question coldly, as he sensed her growing distant."

"I already told you, nothing happened. Are you deaf?"

He ran up the stairs without a word and flung open the door to the bedroom. He halted for a moment as he spotted the open suitcase packed with clothes. He realized at once that Sandra was going to leave. He didn't touch a thing. He turned around and hurried back down the stairs, heading straight over to the bar. He picked up a bottle of whiskey and a glass before hopping down on the sofa on the patio. He unscrewed the cap and filled his glass, downing the contents at once. He filled the glass again. The glass was soon half empty. Something made him get up again, and he headed off to the kitchen, where he confronted his wife.

"You want to leave, right?"

"Why, do you mind?"

"Maybe I do."

"But you always left me, so why are you surprised by my decision?"

"I won't let you go," he said hoarsely. He still held on to his glass, which he raised to his mouth and swallowed the booze.

"I'm afraid that won't work out," she whispered.

"You have to stay, do you understand? You're my wife."

Sandra sharply laughed out yet didn't answer him, since she didn't feel like arguing. She realized that her husband couldn't account for his actions.

She turned away to get out of his sight, but Nick suddenly grabbed her wrist and forcefully pulled her close.

"You're mine, and you'll stay mine for the rest of my life," he hissed with the boozy breath.

They stared at each other for a moment.

"You're wrong," she snapped, bending back hatefully and punching him with her fists to get rid of him.

"We'll see," he replied with a twisted tongue.

"Why do you insist on me if you've never loved me? You just kept me as a trinket at your house, like a work of art which belongs to you which you can put up on a shelf and gaze at from time to time before neglecting it."

Nick stared at her oafishly before pushing her away. "What the hell are you talking about?"

"If you can't understand it, just forget about it."

"Whatever I do, it's never good enough for you," he shouted suddenly.

"Keep it down or the neighbours will hear you."

"See if I care!"

"If you would act as normal people do, perhaps things could have been different, but unfortunately, you're not like that. If I want something, you surely want just the opposite. You're the one who's full of opposition. If I dare to complain and tell you to stop lurking around other women, you go ahead and do it again and again. It's like you enjoy hurting people or annoying them in some way."

"Me? That's nonsense. You always had a twisted view of things."

"Right, it's always the same thing. Am I mistaken about Carmen as well?"

Nick didn't answer her. Despite his dazed condition, he knew she was right. The truth was, he could never resist temptation. Nevertheless, he loved his wife in his fashion and was devoted to her, which is why he didn't want to let go of her. He needed a stable point in his life, a home which he could wander out of whenever he wanted to.

"What do you think, what kind of woman would put up with this from a man? I'm fed up and I want to leave," she said, rushing up the stairs. She slammed the suitcase shut and nervously pressed down on it, trying to close it.

Nick furiously followed her upstairs. He opened the door to the balcony, grabbed the suitcase, and tossed it out the window. It landed on the patio below.

Sandra ran over to the stairs, but Nick caught up to her and dragged her back.

"I said you're staying," he yelled hoarsely. "I warn you not to leave since I'll find you and then I'll do something terrible," he threatened her.

His eyes flashed coldly at her like a pair of blades, which made Sandra tremble in fright. She realized she was helpless against his violent nature.

She couldn't free herself from him at the moment. She burst out in tears, and her pent-up emotions were unleashed. She lost control of herself and clenched her hand into a fist, slamming it into his face.

Nick recoiled. He stared at her for a moment in shock and surprise, before raising his arm and striking the face of the terrified woman, who lost her balance and rolled down the steps.

In the ambulance, Sandra's eyes were closed, and sweat was beading on her forehead. Her husband sat next to her, nervously drumming on his knee with his fingers. They didn't say anything or look at each other. At the hospital, after putting on the cast, the doctor told them that fortunately, she suffered no other injuries apart from her fractured leg.

Nick stormed off without a word. Sandra was left all alone with her dark thoughts. She was intimidated by this sudden accident, and thus she was unable to think about the approaching period. She sadly called her mother to say that she broke her leg, so she wouldn't be able to come.

A few days went by, but there was still no sign of Nick. He made no inquiries into his wife's condition.

CHAPTER 93

She laid on her hospital bed half asleep, thinking about the events that happened recently. *How could he act so indifferently after what happened?* She pondered with an aching heart. She felt fear, yet she was still determined to go to Gale as soon as the cast was off her leg. That was six long weeks away.

A young nurse appeared in the doorway and approached her bed with light steps.

"So how is our patient today?" the nurse asked, handing her a thermometer.

Sandra smiled at her. "Fine, apart from my wooden leg." This nurse wasn't like the other hospital employees, who wouldn't do a thing unless they got a tip.

The nurse returned for the thermometer fifteen minutes later.

"Great, it's perfectly normal," she noted with satisfaction, hurrying off to do her work.

The patient dozed off. She stirred from her dreams to find someone sitting next to her bed. The lights weren't on in the room, so she couldn't make out his face. The unknown man probably noticed that she'd awakened since he turned the lights on and sat back down.

"Is that you?" she asked in surprise. "But, but how …" She didn't finish the sentence since she remembered that he knew her address.

"Easily. Remember that hotel room in Rio, when you first disappeared from me? You left a letter behind. The envelope had your address from Marbella." He didn't mention that he knew her address regardless of the envelope.

He thinks I'm absent-minded, she thought. *He didn't mention that we spoke at the gate before when he was looking for Nick.*

"Your neighbour told me that an ambulance came for you." He rubbed his chin with his right hand. "Hmm. The last time we met was at the hospital in Rio. Remember? Now we meet at another hospital."

"Funny."

"It is," he muttered in reply. "You know, they reassigned me. Perhaps I mentioned it before. I'll be working here for a while. I had some time, so I thought I'd like to visit you."

"That's easy when you're a detective."

"I wouldn't say that," he noted as a cloud passed over his face. "How is your leg. Are you in pain?"

"Thanks for asking, but I'll survive," she replied politely. "What case are you working on? Or is that a secret?"

"Pretty much, but with some luck, I can soon fill you in on that, if you'll still be interested. Unless you run away again, that is." He squinted.

She has no idea that I have enough things to investigate as it is, he thought.

Sandra smiled since she felt safe with him around. She wanted to share her problems with him and tell him that she was afraid of Nick and ask him for advice. However, she fell silent instead.

"Glad to see you again," said Robert Grey.

"So am I," she replied sincerely. "Is it tough?"

"What?"

"The case you're working on."

"Yes, unfortunately. Things are coming along very slowly, even though we've been working on it for years."

"Well, now you know my address." She jotted her mobile number down on a piece of paper, which she handed to Grey. "If you want to see me again, call me," she added in a friendly tone.

He was surprised that the woman wanted to stay in touch. Perhaps she had a good reason to do so.

"What happened to you?" he asked. "I can see you broke your leg, but how did it happen?"

Sandra licked her lips in concern. "It was an accident. I fell the stairs," she explained, yet she suddenly clenched her hand into a fist as it rested on the covers.

Robert had a good eye. He noticed the motion at once, along with her confused look. He was practically convinced that things happened differently, yet he decided not to question her since he knew she wouldn't answer him anyway. He stood up.

"I have to go now. I brought you some reading material," he said, pointing at the magazines he had placed on her nightstand.

"Thank you."

"That's the least I can do for you at the moment. If you need me, promise to give me a call," he suggested.

She eyed him gratefully since it was good to know that she had someone to count on.

After he left, she pulled out her mobile phone.

"Hi, honey," she said after Antonio picked up. "How do you like your hospital work?"

"I'm still learning things. I don't have much time and I'm always busy, but that doesn't matter. How are you doing?"

"I've been better. I fell down the stairs and broke my leg. I'm still at the hospital. I'll probably have a lengthy recovery."

"How could this happen to you?" cried Antonio in surprise.

"I was careless, that's all." She didn't want to tell him the truth.

"Where is it broken?"

"My knee."

"That's not good at all. You'll have to take good care of your knee, even after they remove the cast. I'm sorry that I can't be with you. Do you have any help?"

"I don't know yet, but don't worry, it's no big deal. I'll take care of myself somehow," she said, suddenly thinking of Yvonne.

"Is Nick around?"

"He isn't," she replied, even though she had no idea about the truth.

"Call my grandparents over."

"No, I don't want to do that."

"I have to go now. I love you. I'll get in touch," he added as the line broke off.

She pondered at length before finally making up her mind and calling her mother.

"Mom, don't worry, once I recover – which will take some time, I will visit you. Say hi to Dad for me."

"You promised to move here."

"I'm sorry, but I'm afraid that won't work out, at least not for the time being."

The mother could tell that her daughter was in trouble. "Do you want us to come over?"

Sandra thought of Nick and fended the matter off at once.

"No, no," she said in fright. "I'll take care of everything."

"Still, call us if you need our help," her mother said anxiously. "I'm sorry. I wish you a speedy recovery, and get in touch with us as soon as you can."

CHAPTER 94

Sandra was back home. She leaned on a cane as she hobbled around the house, trying to take care of things. Fortunately, the gardener's wife stopped by every other day to help out. It was hard for Sandra to move around because of the cast and she couldn't come down from upstairs without help, so she slept in the room downstairs. She hadn't seen Nick since their fight, so it seemed he had disappeared again, completely abandoning her.

Two weeks later, the intercom buzzed. She leaned on her cane as she limped over to the door.

"Who is it?"

"Yvonne!"

When she heard her girlfriend's voice, Sandra cried out in joy. "What a surprise! You're here, just when I need you the most!"

"What happened to you?" Yvonne asked, noticing the cast on Sandra's leg.

"It was an accident. Come, sit down, it's more comfortable that way. I'm sure you're tired. It's so great to see you again. I can never manage to make it over to see you."

"Come now, I understand," said Yvonne. "You have your own life, which is why you have no time for me. Not to mention the distance. We live too far apart. If you would live in Paris, things would be a lot easier, but this way, it's a bit tricky. Is Nick around?"

"No, he isn't."

"The truth is, I like being with you, but only when he's not home."

"I know, honey, I know, even though we haven't talked about this yet."

"I'm sorry," Yvonne said, regretfully thinking of the huge mistake her girlfriend made by marrying this scoundrel. "Before I came to surprise you, I called your mother. She told me that you just got out of the hospital and that you'll surely be thrilled to see me. That's why I came unannounced. I tried calling you once, but the line was busy."

"Thank you. I'm really glad you're here since I was feeling lonely. I haven't seen Nick for three weeks."

"As far as I can tell, you don't mind?" Yvonne raised an eyebrow.

Sandra avoided the subject. Instead, she told her, "Go, help yourself. Have a drink."

"What about you?"

"Perhaps I could use a glass of red wine, but I think we have to open a bottle first."

Yvonne finally managed to uncork a bottle with some difficulty. She filled their glasses and sat back down.

"Cheers."

"You too."

"So, tell me, how can you cope with him?" Yvonne asked cautiously since Sandra had never complained to her about a thing.

"It's hard, but hopefully it won't last forever now."

"What do you mean by that?" Yvonne perked up.

"I want to leave him—if I can get rid of him, that is."

"What was that?"

"You heard me. He doesn't want to let me go," Sandra admitted with teary eyes as the trouble starts to settle on her face. "If I protest, he can be very mean. Still, I openly told him that I won't put up with this any longer."

"And how did he take it?"

"Badly. Here's the result," she said, pointing at her leg in a cast. "Despite that fact that he wasn't around for a long time before it happened."

Yvonne turned pale. "You mean he did it?"

"Yes. I fell down the stairs because of him, since he didn't want to hear another word of me leaving." She briefly told Yvonne what happened.

"Oh, that is tough. But listen here," Yvonne said, leaning close to Sandra. "If you want to leave him, then come straight to Paris. You can stay at my place. Remember how well we got along together? Paris is the best hiding place for you. Until you get a divorce, he won't find you there, and then there's nothing he can do about it."

Sandra sceptically shook her head. "That's where we met in the past. Nothing can change his plans if he makes up his mind." she said, nervously biting her lips. "I'm sure you remember our escape and how quickly he found us when he kidnapped Antonio," she added, halting abruptly.

Yvonne didn't understand what that had to do with Nick, but she didn't force the subject since she didn't want to talk about that terrible incident.

"Don't worry, I'll try to help you out somehow." She thought of her boyfriend, André, who could surely figure out something.

Sandra pondered as she drummed her fingers on her leg. Yvonne glanced at the cast.

"When will they take it off?" she asked to distract her girlfriend's perturbed thoughts.

"I think they'll take it off within two weeks," Sandra replied with a shrug. "I can't move until then, but that's okay. I'm more afraid of him showing at any time."

"Don't worry, I'll be here with you." Yvonne wanted to change the subject at all costs. "So, which room will be mine?"

"The one next to mine. Go and make yourself at home."

While Yvonne disappeared, Sandra limped over to the kitchen to fix something for dinner.

Later, as they ate, Yvonne mysteriously glanced at her friend.

"What is it?" Sandra asked.

"I met a man, and we've been living together for a few months now."

"Really? I'm happy for you. You could use some love … but then I can't accept your offer."

"Come on, you won't get in the way since my partner isn't around during the day."

"What does he do for a living?"

"You won't believe me."

"Come on, tell me," Sandra said, eyeing her curiously.

"He's a detective."

"What?"

"Yes. That's why I'm here. He had to come to Marbella at once. He's wrapping up some drug case with a local colleague. I don't know the details since I don't ask him about his professional life."

Sandra laughed. "That's funny."

"What's so funny?" Yvonne asked reproachfully.

"Now it's my turn to say you won't believe me."

"Why?"

"Because I have a new friend as well, who's also a detective. Although he's not new at all."

Yvonne stood up at once, and they both burst into laughter.

"How did you find him?" Yvonne asked.

Sandra happily told her about her trip to Rio, carefully omitting the reason for her visit.

"I hope he's good-looking," Yvonne said.

"He's not bad at all. But actually, we're just friends. Even that might be an exaggeration. We're just acquaintances. That's it."

"Well then, you can be safe. Nothing wrong can happen to you," Yvonne said, and they shared another light-hearted laugh.

CHAPTER 95

Yvonne was spending her second week with Sandra. The house was quiet. They were both readings until the shadows grew long in the garden.

"It's better if we go inside now. Come on," she said, taking Sandra by the arm. They chatted at length in the living room and listened to some music.

"I'll call the hospital tomorrow. I want to know when they'll take this damn cast off my leg."

"Poor thing," said Yvonne regretfully and stood up. "I'm hungry, so I'll fix a quick dinner," she said, heading over to the kitchen.

Sandra limped after her with her cane, and they had dinner in quiet. Suddenly, the door slammed open. Nick stopped in the doorway and glared at them in annoyance.

"What are you doing in my house?" he growled at the Frenchwoman, who shuddered, at his harsh tone.

"I invited her over," interrupted Sandra.

Nick raised his hand, pointing his middle finger at her. "I didn't ask you."

"Yes, she called me over. Someone has to help if you won't take care of her," interrupted Yvonne.

"That's none of your business," sneered Nick with a dark look on his face.

"Nick, stop it, I want her to stay, since she's my girlfriend and I need her," Sandra said, raising her voice.

He didn't react to her or look at her at all. He stubbornly levelled his gaze at Yvonne. "Be out of here by tomorrow morning."

"You can't send her away. Do you hear me?" Sandra cried.

"Be quiet. Shut up!" he shouted in rage.

"Okay, I'll leave," Yvonne interjected, afraid of how out-of-control Nick was becoming. "Just stop fighting."

"Wait!" cried Sandra anxiously. "If he's sending you away, then I'm going with you. I don't want to stay here with this..."

The man came to life. He leapt over to his wife, grabbed her by the arm, and suddenly yanked her out of her chair. She winced in pain. "Don't, please, watch out!"

Nick kicked her leg in the cast in response. "Your words mean nothing, understand? If you open your mouth one more time, I swear you will regret it," he hissed at her threateningly.

The fear petrified the women. Yvonne slowly backed away to the door, but the man stopped her.

"Listen up, you bitch, if I see you around here again, you'll be sorry, too, understand?"

Yvonne nodded in terror. She wanted to slip off to her room and call her boyfriend to ask for his help. Nick, however, changed his mind and simply walked out on the women, who watched him leave in shock.

Sandra gripped the table leg with trembling hands, trying her best to get up.

"Wait, let me help," said Yvonne, but it was hard to help Sandra up because of the cast. "What do you want to do now?" she asked anxiously.

"I already told you. We'll leave at once."

"Are you sure about that? Even if we managed to get away,

he might find us. It's better if I leave on my own. I'll talk to André, and I'm sure he'll come up with something."

"Don't worry. He won't find us. Please, help me pack my stuff into my suitcase," Sandra said nervously, supporting herself on her cane as she hobbled over to her bedroom. "The suitcase is damaged since that madman threw it out the window upstairs before I broke my leg."

"Where will you go?"

"A hotel, anywhere. Can you help me go upstairs?"

"Sure, come on."

She pushed the clothes aside in the wardrobe with trembling hands and leaned over, enter the secret code to the safe. She emptied its contents into a scarf and carefully closed it. She quickly checked her papers one more time before dumping everything in her bag.

In the meantime, Yvonne moved the clothes piled up on the bed into the damaged suitcase, but she just couldn't seem to lock it.

"Are you ready?" cried Yvonne from downstairs.

"Yes," came the response.

She hurried upstairs to help Sandra come down. "I couldn't close the suitcase," she said tensely.

"There's another suitcase in the storeroom under the stairs. I'll look for it, but first I have to come down from here. Or I can look for a belt which the two of us can use to hold it shut."

"Don't worry about that, I'll fix it. Watch out," Yvonne said, wrapping her arm around her tighter. "Hold on, or you might end up breaking your other leg."

Sandra nervously laughed. Her helplessness drove her crazy. Her girlfriend fumbled with the suitcases for a while before dragged it outside and stuffed everything into the car. They hurried back inside and Yvonne went to the bathroom before shouldering her bag.

Sandra eyed her gratefully. "Thank you."

"That's okay, honey, just hurry up and pick up whatever else you want to bring and let's get out of here as fast as we can."

Sandra focused hard, gathered a few more belongings, and stuffed them into the duffel bag on the sofa. She looked around the living room she was about to leave for good just one more time.

"Can we get going?"

"Yes." Sandra locked the door and sadly glanced at the garden for a moment.

As they reached the car, Yvonne tilted the front seat forward so Sandra would have more space in the back. "Come on," she urged her friend.

Sandra hopped down on the seat. She slipped inside the car as far as she managed so there would be more room for her leg. Yvonne's mobile rang quietly. She answered it.

"Yes, we're just leaving, and we'll soon be at the hotel. No, you don't have to come here. We'll get going right away." She turned off the phone and started up the motor. "I called André while you were upstairs," she explained. "I told him what happened and got him to write down the address in case I don't get back to him."

"Fine," Sandra said happily. She firmly pressed the button of the garage door, slowly retracting it.

Yvonne suddenly stopped the motor.

"What is it?" Sandra asked.

"Look," Yvonne said, pointing ahead of them.

They were out of luck. Nick's car suddenly stopped in front of them.

They were too late. Their escape route was blocked.

CHAPTER 96

Nick slowly opened the car door and took his time getting out before approaching them with an ashen look on his face.

Yvonne dialled André's number with trembling hands.

"André, please answer," she begged, but the other end of the line was busy.

She motionlessly stared into space, preparing for the worst to happen. However, much to their surprise, nothing happened at all.

The man calmly spoke to them through the window.

"OK, I thought things over, you can stay. Sandra needs you. Come on, get out," he said, opening the door and even helping his wife to get out.

As they clambered out of the car, the girls held on to each other and walked back inside the house. They didn't say a word as they exchanged troubled glances. Their eyes were filled with concern and a sliver of hope.

In the meantime, Nick parked both cars inside the garage and closed the automatic door. He moved the suitcases to his car. Finally, he searched the women's bags, which they had left in the car and was satisfied to see that they contained their passports. He brushed off all their suspicions by carrying the bags back inside and tossing them on the sofa.

"You left them in the car," he said listlessly before heading over to the kitchen. Sandra distrustfully opened her bag to check her belongings. She was reassured when she saw that everything was accounted for.

Nick walked over to the bar. He pulled out three glasses, filled two of them with whiskey, and handing them to the women. He even raised his glass to a toast.

"To a better mood," he said, before drinking his whiskey in a single gulp. He wiped his face before expectantly eyeing them with a sneaky look.

"Well, come on, drink to our peace," he urged them.

The women flashed glances at each other. They knew they'd better do what he said to keep the peace.

However, Nick brought the bottle over and poured them some more.

"Let's drink," he suggested in a changed, rough, authoritative tone. Sandra, however, wouldn't drink anymore. "What are you waiting for?" he growled hostilely at his wife.

"I had enough," protested Sandra.

He eyed her coldly. "Drink," he said, gripping her wrist and lifting the glass with his other hand.

"Please don't," she said, turning her head away in fright.

Nick suddenly grabbed her by her long red hair, yanking her head back. "Open your mouth," he ordered before forcing the drink down her throat, some of which spilt down her chin. He grinned when he was done and saw that Sandra had drunk enough.

Yvonne didn't see this at all. She'd turned away and was fumbling with her phone. Nick noticed her attempt. He took her phone from her without a word, tossed it to the ground, and impassively crushed the phone with an evil grin on his face.

"Your glass is still full. What are you waiting for?" he warned her coldly. For some reason, he had always hated this woman.

Yvonne didn't wait for him to get violent and quickly drank the contents of the glass. It slipped out of her hand, empty. She hesitantly sank to the sofa with a drunken smile on her lips. The room swayed around her. Nick seemed to double in front of her.

The man walked upstairs in satisfaction, calling his henchman.

"Prepare the yacht, I'll be there soon," he barked his brief order.

It was getting dark outside. Nick closed the door to the patio and pulled the curtains shut. He didn't turn the lights on just to be safe. His hunch was right since a car stopped in front of the house and someone soon rang the bell.

Nick let go of the girl as he was dragging her out to the car. The bell buzzed again. He motionlessly eyed the figure from behind the curtains as he walked along the fence. Nick quickly headed over to the bathroom from where he could keep an eye on the unwanted visitor.

The stranger stopped in front of the house for a while before disappearing. Nick listened with bated breath until he heard the sound of a car driving off.

He didn't hesitate. Things are heating up, he thought. I have to hurry up. He picked up the girl as her legs slipped out from under her from time to time.

"What do you want?"

"Nothing," he said, dumping her on the front seat. "I'm taking you to a nice place where things will be better," he said, dumping her bag in her lap.

"Uh-huh, that's great," muttered Yvonne haltingly.

Sandra felt completely numb as she dozed off with half-shut eyes, yet she clung to her bag as if it were her final lifesaver.

Nick left it in her arms. "Come," he said, carrying and almost lifting her with some difficulty as he took her out to the car, where he nervously tried dumping her on the back seat. In the meantime, he quickly cursed for not taking her to the hospital first so they could remove this clumsy cast.

He drove off to the Puerto Banus yacht port. An hour later, the yacht with a little group of people was crossing the open waters. The women motionlessly dozed in the cabin. Nick was up on the deck with two of his men.

"If they start stirring, give them some booze, but not too much. I left it there on the counter," he said to one of them. He omitted the part about previously mixing drugs into their drinks.

The men exchanged meaningful glances in the half-light. They'd been working for Nick for a long time, and they knew exactly what his cold stare meant. It was better to stay away from him when he was in a foul mood, especially if he was drugged up.

The prow of the yacht ploughed through the waves, and the wind picked up. Nick gazed out on the water with a steely look in his eyes while dark thoughts whirled through his mind. He had no plan since when he thought about it, he realized he was still devoted to his wife after all these years.

Yvonne opened her eyes and tried drunkenly to identify her surroundings. She sat up with some difficulty. In the dim, she faintly noticed Sandra's leg in the white cast. She groped at her body as she lay next to her in a stupor. She leaned over her and shook her.

"Wake up," she muttered with a bad feeling in her stomach as she heard the monotonous whirring of the engine. She realized that they must be on the sea.

"What … what is it?"

Yvonne let go of her as her head reeled and tried kneeling up to stare out the round windows.

The door quietly opened, and a dark figure stumbled into the cabin with a certain bottle of booze.

"Come here, honey," said the man, wrapping his arm around her waist from behind and pressing her head close to him, pushing the bottleneck into her mouth.

Yvonne was forced to swallow the booze, and her brain became dull and blunt.

The man set the bottle down and squeezed her tighter as his hand groped at her body. He quickly finished his act and replaced her skirt. He even wrapped a blanket around her. He took a swig of the bottle and leaned over the other woman. She was sleeping, so he didn't touch her. He turned around and cheerfully went back up on the deck.

Before mooring, Nick came down to the cabin. He collected the women's papers. A few photos fell out of Sandra's bag. One of them was a picture of a familiar red-haired girl. Since he was busy at the moment, he put it in the bag and went back upstairs, forgetting about the photo.

As usual, things went smoothly. Once they get there, things will be okay, he grinned to himself.

He slipped through Tangier without any difficulty. His plan worked out. *Women are always good alibis. No one has a clue what's behind all of this,* he thought confidently.

CHAPTER 97

Lucy was sitting at the airport in Malaga with a good vantage point of the arrival times of the planes. The electronic display next to the flight from Madrid lit up. She had a cup of coffee before patiently waiting next to the arrivals gate.

She finally spotted her uncle amongst the passengers, looking for her. She quickly waved her arm to him. He soon noticed her and approached with a broad smile on his face.

"Hey, I think we met somewhere before," joked Lucy as she leapt into his arms.

Pedro warmly reciprocated her welcome.

"How was your trip? Are you okay? Would you like a coffee or something else? Or maybe you're hungry?"

Pedro laughed. "You're just like a mother hen. We should better get going. Where's your car?"

"Here in the parking lot."

"You look great," he complimented her.

"You too, despite the grey hairs on your brow," she giggled teasingly.

"Time moves fast."

"That's right," she said with a pout, pulling the smaller suitcase along on the ground. "You sure put a lot in this one."

"I know. Trust me, it wasn't easy to clear out everything."

As they reached the car, Lucy opened the trunk and let Pedro squeeze the suitcases into the car. There was only room for the hand luggage on the back seat.

They took off. Lucy stopped at a traffic light and glanced at him.

"I'm sorry she passed away. You said you were doing fine in the early summer."

He turned grim since his wife's death was still a sensitive subject for him.

"True," he admitted. "That's because I didn't want to burden you with our problems. We never gave up on our hopes."

"Did she suffer?"

"Quite a lot. Unfortunately, cancer doesn't spare the body. But let's drop the subject. I don't feel like talking about it," he said dismissively. He turned away and gazed out the window as the sadness suddenly settled in between them.

Pedro tried recalling his wife's suffering expression, her thin lips and her final-stage condition. Yes, she suffered greatly, even though he'd hoped for her recovery. Finally, she gave up the fight and took a step back. She wisely realized that no living being had power over destiny.

He could still see her motionless face on the crunched-up pillow. Her final, hazy stare locked with his gaze, and her eyes glazed over. Life departed from her body. She was gone for good.

He swallowed his tears as they burst to the surface. He sighed heavily since he knew death was cruel. From one day to the next, it could take away the ones we love.

"Now I'm here all alone," he said, almost to himself.

Lucy respected her uncle's pain. "Yes, you're still here, but you must live on without her." She knew this feeling well, and she sadly thought of her baby who died so suddenly all those years ago. For a moment, she thought of Vicky.

Pedro glanced at her. "Thanks for the kind words."

"Talking is easy." She wondered how strange life was. *Here we are, living our lives one day, and then suddenly trouble hits you.* She anxiously wondered whether her mammography would come up positive or negative. Fortunately, hope lasts the longest. She suddenly stirred from her grim thoughts.

"What happened to Amy? Why did you leave her in Rio?"

"She left with some hippy. She doesn't even know her mother died."

Lucy glanced at him in surprise a moment. "Is that true?"

Pedro nodded.

"It's hard to believe that. She was such a decent girl." She clenched her mouth tightly and gripped the steering wheel for some reason she wasn't fully aware of.

The traffic picked up before they reached Marbella, and the cars came to a stop as they piled up in a row.

"We're stuck," she noted with annoyance, glancing back at Pedro, who had certainly changed. His old sense of humour might be gone for good, she thought, blinking profusely.

The man listlessly eyed the familiar hilly landscape of Andalusia.

"So, what's going on here at home?" he asked suddenly. "Are you still running around the place all on your own?"

"You could put it that way. You know, it's easier this way. No commitments and I can do whatever I want to."

"That's true," he agreed. She had been independent at a young age. He recalled the times she eloped from her house in the past.

"Patricia?"

"Mom is fine, and I think she can barely wait to see you."

He scratched his chin. "What's up with the house in El Palmar?"

Lucy eyed him quizzically. "What do you mean?"

"Nothing, I just remembered the place. When was the last time you went there?"

"I don't remember. A long time ago," she added, starting the car back up.

"I have enough time now, so I might head down there in the

next few days."

"It wouldn't hurt. I'm sure you remember that the keys are still in the oldhiding place," she reminded him.

"Okay, but first I have to buy a car since I can't get anywhere without one."

"Don't worry about that. I'll lend you mine until you buy one for yourself."

"Oh no, I'm sure you need it."

"I have two cars."

"I didn't know that. Well thanks, I'll take you up on that."

CHAPTER 98

Robert Grey was sitting in front of a huge table, caught up in his thoughts. After his investigation in Rio, he was continuing his unpredictable work in Marbella. He'd managed to wrap up quite a few cases, yet he still had a few which remained unresolved. The case they were currently working on seemingly couldn't be solved since the extensive criminal network was professionally fine-tuned. They were dealing with tough, experienced men. All members of the taskforce were aware of the danger at hand.

Grey liked a challenge. He was a natural-born tireless cop, yet the current case has proven to be a tough one; the suspect always slipped through his fingers without a trace. He still wasn't entirely certain whether Nick Winkler belonged to the Barcelona or Marseille gang. However, if his instincts were right, then perhaps Nick was the most important liaison.

He'd been working on this case with his colleague for ages, running back and forth between countries with no results forthcoming. Last week, his boss chewed him out over this, demanding quick facts and final results.

At dawn, he started up his car and soon reached Sandra's house. He walked over to the villa in concern. He just wanted to see her, since he couldn't get through to her over the phone. He thought about their flight to Rio. At the time, he still thought she was involved in the case, but he now knew beyond a shadow of a doubt that she was innocent.

He ran his fingers through his hair as he reached the gate and rang the bell, repeating the action a few seconds later. He heard the bell ring inside the house, but there was no sight of anyone. He pulled out his mobile and tried calling her, but his attempt was unsuccessful. *Where could she be?* He wondered as he walked down the narrow path running along the fence.

He stopped next to a low stone wall for a moment and looked around for a while before suddenly jumping over the wall and disappearing amongst the bushes. He silently circled the house before peeking into a window. The house seemed deserted, and he saw no sign of an alarm. He stopped in front of a window without grates in the back, since his sharp eyes noticed that it wasn't locked.

He looked around again. Dense hedges ran along the fence, blocking out everything. He quickly pushed down on the frame which popped open from the pressure. He slipped through the narrow opening at once, finding himself in the bathroom. He cautiously opened the door and peeked into the living room from the narrow corridor. When he was convinced that the coast was clear, he silently ran upstairs. He nimbly searched through the bedrooms without finding anything suspicious.

He quickly raced down the steps. Spotting a crushed mobile phone on the floor of the living room, he cautiously slipped it into a bag before pocketing it. There were two glasses and an empty bottle of whiskey on the low table. A third glass lay on the floor next to the sofa. He searched through the bins in the kitchen and found nothing of interest. *Things are far too clean,* he thought in annoyance.

Suddenly, the doorbell disturbed the silence in the house. He hurried back to the bathroom and squeezed through the window, which he pulled back into the frame. He quickly leapt over the fence before calmly approaching the gate.

"It looks like they're not home," he said to the woman waiting at the gate, who turned to him in surprise.

"Then it seems there was no sense in coming here," she muttered reluctantly.

"I just rang the bell myself. Do you know them well?" he asked her.

"Yes, but who are you if you don't mind me asking? We haven't met yet."

"I'm sorry," he said, holding his hand out to her and introducing himself.

"Carmen Stone," replied the woman, sizing him up.

"I wanted to talk to Nick Winkler," explained Grey.

"It seems he's in Barcelona again, or maybe he flew back to Marseille," explained the woman with ease.

"So, if I'm not mistaken, you're an old friend."

"Pretty much."

Grey eyed her with a piercing stare before slowly pulling out his badge and showing it to her. "I'm a detective," he added in a factual tone.

"Really? That's surprising." *So, Nick stooped this low,* she wondered, raising her eyebrows with a blink. "Poor Sandra..." she noted.

"Look, if you know anything, it would be a great help."

"I'm sorry, but I'm afraid I can't do anything for you."

Grey reached into his pocket and handed her his business card.

"Well, give it some thought. Something might occur to you later on." He turned around, about to leave. "Oh, by the way, did they travel somewhere, perhaps to their summer home?"

Carmen silently hesitated for a second before mentioning the house in El Palmar.

"Have you been there before?"

"Yes," she replied hesitantly, hoping she could stay out of

this murky matter. However, the sweet revenge she'd sought for so long seemed to be finally manifesting itself.

"Do you go there a lot?"

"Nick does."

"What does he do there?"

"I'm not sure, but the last time I went there with him, I felt uncertain."

"Tell me more," urged Grey, perking up.

"I have nothing much to say."

"Well, you could still give it a shot. What kind of a man chooses, to neglectfully hide behind his wife, while letting his children turn against their grandparents without love?"

He thinks in such a smart, mature way, acknowledged the mother convinced that this provocative woman would finally give him the lead he was looking for.

"I don't know anything," said the woman, backing down, anxiously adjusting her hair. "Still, it wouldn't hurt to look around Canos de Meca," she added hesitantly.

"Tell me something more specific."

"Unfortunately, I don't know the address. The truth is that I was there about two weeks ago with Nick. We stopped next to a gate with an archway. I stayed inside the car. I couldn't see anything from the tall wooden gate, and it was pretty dark outside. Nick disappeared behind the gate and didn't return for a long time. I was getting worried."

"And?"

"I remember that when he returned, he rubbed his shoulder as he nervously got in next to me."

"Was he injured?"

"I saw the mark of the blow later on," she noted, "when he got out of the tub." She awkwardly averting her gaze.

"Do you do anything for a living?"

"Not at the moment."

"Are you married?"

"Yes, but we're getting a divorce," she added quickly.

"So, Nick Winkler is your lover."

Carmen blushed. "What if he is? That's not a crime. We broke up."

"Indeed, it isn't. Still, I have to ask you to make yourself available tomorrow. Come with me to Canos de Meca. If we have some time, you can show me the house in El Palmar."

"Me? But why?"

"Come now, don't worry, I just want to find that house fast, which I can't do without you."

"Is that an order?"

The man smiled and slightly tilted his head to the side.

"Let's just say I'm taking you out on a trip." Without waiting for her to agree, he added, "I'll come to pick you up at nine." He pulled out his notepad.

"If you give me your address, that is."

Carmen was forced to give him her temporary address.

"Fine," she said, "see you at nine."

The man smiled in satisfaction. "Thank you for your help. Can I give you a lift home?" he offered politely.

"Unless your car is covered in graffiti. You know what I mean?" she replied in a happier tone.

Robert Grey smiled. "Come on then."

CHAPTER 99

It wasn't hard for them to figure out they were back in Marrakech, back at the bloody riad. They glanced at each other in terror, but they were somewhat reassured by the fact that they were in a comfortable room on the ground floor.

After they rested up, they were welcomed by the sight of a nicely set table on the patio the following day at noon. The servant silently tended to her work.

Once they finished their meal, Sandra sat down under the arcade to take in their surroundings. Two middle-aged women worked at the house. An older man was leaning back on a narrow stool, dozing off in the tiny room next to the entrance, killing some time on an uneventful day. Thus, she felt reassured as she returned to her room.

Nick had brought them here because he urgently needed an alibi. His wife was a great burden with the cast on her leg, yet this was still the best and quickest solution he could come up with. Within a few days, he had to take care of the last shipment before finishing everything and disappearing. He still had much to do before then. He knew that all it took was a tiny mistake to ruin everything. He had been planning on finishing the whole thing for some time now and disappearing somewhere in the south, especially since the gang leader wanted to move his operations to Marseille. He had a feeling this was because the cops were catching up to them.

He had amassed a huge fortune over the years, which was more than enough to live the rest of his life in style and prosperity. It often occurred to him that he wasn't 100 per cent sure about himself anymore since he had been boozing and taking drugs for some time now. Due to his unstable condition, he was afraid he would make a mistake, and then it would all come to an end. He'd soberly planned on relocating to Brazil after this last shipment. He had everything figured out. He would take Sandra with him and try to please her and shake off the excess pleasures and even go to rehab, if necessary.

He sat next to a cup of coffee on the balcony of the Hotel Atlas around noon. He had just spoken to the local contact, going over the precise handling of the shipment one last time. They had to work precisely without any mistakes. If they managed to pull this off, the gang would make millions on this. The thought of it made Nick sneer, and he finished off his coffee in satisfaction.

He caught a glimpse of a young woman swimming in the pool. She glanced at him from time to time before finally climbing out of the water and slowly walking past him. Nick could never miss out on an opportunity like this. He cleared his throat.

"Hello there," he called out to the beautiful walking past him with swaying hips.

The woman turned around and daringly smiled at him. "Are you talking to me, honey?"

He raised an eyebrow and quizzically looking around. "Is there anyone else here?" he replied, putting on a show. "Can I get you a drink?" he added quickly as he openly feasted his eyes on the alluring siren's suntanned, dripping-wet body.

The sense of adventure at hand crossed the woman's features for a moment.

"Sure, why not, I'm thirsty anyway" she replied nonchalantly, sitting down at Nick's table with ease.

"Vodka on the rocks?"

"Sure."

Nick elegantly raised his hand as he introduced himself.

"Pussy," said the woman in introduction with a seductive look, intentionally leaning forward, offering him a close view of her cleavage.

"Funny," he quipped with suppressed cheer, his eyes glued to the shapely lumps bulging under her bikini.

"Yeah," said the siren in reply.

The waiter brought them their drinks. Pussy finished hers in a single gulp before sadly staring at her empty glass.

Nick frowned. "You sure seem to be experienced," he noted with a grin.

"Yeah."

"I assume you're staying here at the hotel."

"Yeah."

"With your husband, right?"

"Yeah."

"You don't speak much, now do you?"

"Is that so bad?"

"No," he pouted. "If you want to, we could have another drink in your room," he noted, getting right to point, while furtively glancing at his watch. He still had some time, since it was barely past noon. He perked up at the possibility of this sudden fling.

"Not a bad idea," noted the racy woman encouragingly, quickly reaching for his glass. She dipped her index finger into the rest of his drink before sticking it into her mouth and meaningfully glancing at him.

"Mmm, delicious."

"Then finish it," he encouraged her.

Pussy swallowed the rest of the drink without any hesitation. Nick didn't waste time and quickly paid for the drinks before hurrying off to the elevators.

The fifty-something waiter eyed them longingly. He knew a lot about affairs like this and the men from Europe passing by, looking for some relaxation while they stayed in town "for business" and partied through the days and nights, sexually making the most of themselves before flying home to their families. *He was sure he wouldn't forget a night with a woman like this,* he thought in agitation. His boss shook him up from his daydreaming.

"Get going," the man growled at him.

The waiter shuddered before collecting the tray from the counter and skilfully darting between the tables.

In the meantime, the elevator took off. The young woman turned towards the mirror, flashing a lewd smile at the stranger she'd just picked up, who moved up close behind her, wrapping his arm around her waist, pulling her close to him, making his intentions clear. Pussy reached back and latched on to him.

They reached her room a moment later. Nick kicked the door open with the heel of his shoe and tried getting out of his clothes.

"Wait. Let's have a drink first," she purred to him, before picking up the phone and ordering a bottle of booze. They made sure not to waste any time while waiting.

Nick let go of the woman when there was a knock on the door. She took the bottle in the open doorway while handing the waiter the money and slamming the door in his face.

Pussy slipped the packet into his hand, which Nick opened at once.

"Perfect fit," he acknowledged with a grin.

The woman grabbed the bottle, took a long swig from it, and handed it to the man. Nick handed it back to her after a few gulps. Pussy took another swig. She tilted her head back, voluptuously waiting for his sexual assault. Nick leaned over her and concluded their quick number.

He made it back home around three. The sun was streaming down onto the patio. He cautiously peeked inside his wife's room; she was blissfully asleep on her bed. Her red hair was scattered across the pillow with her dreams bringing a happy smile to her suntanned features.

She still seemed innocently alluring, he thought as he eyed her at length. He would have loved to lie down next to her, yet he decided on closing the door instead after his previous encounter.

In his room, upstairs, he took care of some extended phone calls in a low voice. Once he concluded his business, he took a long shower in the bathroom before lying down naked on the bed. He was still angry at himself for loving that innocent, red-haired beast. He just couldn't get rid of her no matter how many women he surrounded himself with. Yet he didn't want to get rid of her, he realized. If he managed to pull off this last shipment, it will change our lives, he vowed for the umpteenth time.

CHAPTER 100

The slim sailboat returned to Spain without any difficulty. The lights on the shore were shining by the time they entered the house in El Palmar. Nick was still impeccably polite as if nothing happened at all. He gently helped his wife upstairs before carrying the suitcases up after her.

"Nick."

"Yes?"

"My leg is itchy under the cast. We should have it removed."

"I still have a lot to do, but we'll see what we can do once I'm done," he said before turning around and walking out on the women.

Yvonne eyed him suspiciously. She walked over to the window and peeked out after him. She saw Nick cross through the yard and head out the gate towards the shore. He soon disappeared in the twilight.

She headed down to the living room in search of something to eat. Much to her surprise, she found some fresh bread, ham, and a few cans of food on the kitchen table. She pulled out the drawers in search of utensils and came across a long knitting needle. She smiled and quickly fixed some sandwiches. She found two cans of beer and a big bottle of water, which she put on the tray with the needle. In the meantime, she thought how a few days ago, back in Marrakech, they were both terrified that things were starting all over again. Fortunately, this wasn't the case. She had to admit that Nick behaved impeccably. *Perhaps things would take a turn for the better,* she thought naively.

As they finished their dinner, she handed her friend the long needle.

"You can use this to scratch your leg," she suggested, and the house resounded with their laughter.

Yvonne stood up. "I think we could both use some rest, so it's better if we go to bed. It's getting late."

She helped Sandra out into the bathroom before walking her back to her room.

"Sleep tight," Yvonne said to her friend, closing the door on her way out.

Sandra lay in the dark with her eyes open. She couldn't sleep from her memories. A long, long time ago, in this house, perhaps in this very same bed, she had spent a few lovely nights with Pedro. Oh, how happy she was at the time. She covered her head with the pillow, doing her best to fall asleep with her old, lovely memories.

Yvonne woke late at night to the sound of some noise. She peeked out the window. The pale moonlight illuminated their surroundings. The gate was open. She saw two men doubled over, struggling with some heavy package. She pulled her head back in alarm. She listened for a long time, but only heard the sound of the waves murmuring in the distance. No one came inside the house, so she lay back down and her eyes soon grew heavy and closed shut.

The following day, Yvonne helped Sandra down to the ground floor. Nick was nowhere to be seen, so they enjoyed the undisturbed silence and calm surroundings.

"If you don't mind, I'd like to look around the neighbourhood," Yvonne said, but she wanted to call André and tell him where they were.

"Go ahead, honey, I'm just fine sitting here. See, I have something to read, too."

Yvonne headed off to the gate. The dusty road in front of the house, which led straight down to the shore, was deserted. The neighbouring buildings seemed deserted. After she had taken just a few steps, a black, worn-out jeep turned the corner and suddenly came to a halt beside her, stirring up a big cloud of dust.

Yvonne perked up in surprise.

Nick jumped out of the car and grabbed her arm. "Don't go anywhere, do you hear me?" he hissed while eyeing the intersection.

She glanced at the dark figure sitting in the car before turning to Nick reproachfully. "I have to buy something to eat. All we have is a bottle of water."

"Don't worry about that, I'll get you something later on. The store is far away from here," he replied, forcing himself to stay calm while gently ushering her through the gate. "Take Sandra upstairs at once," he ordered her in a harsh tone.

Yvonne felt it was better to obey him, so she helped her girl-friend up the stairs with some difficulty before peeking out onto the street through the half-opened window. She couldn't see the jeep at all.

CHAPTER 101

Nick kept his promise and finally returned in the late afternoon. He shouted out to them from the living room, announcing that he had brought them some water and something to eat. By the time Yvonne came down, he had already disappeared. She shrugged. They were better off without him around. She was hungry, so she unpacked the bag and fixed an early dinner.

Sandra was sitting in the old, worn-out armchair, trying her best to slip the long needle under the dirty cast.

"It's scratchy," she complained nervously. Spotting the tray full of food stopped her activity at once.

They eat without saying a word. Perhaps Nick has come to his senses and will take us back to Marbella, Yvonne thought hopefully.

"I was hungry," Sandra said. "You too?"

"Yeah," nodded Yvonne as she stood up, hearing some noise from downstairs.

"Hush," she said, lifting her finger to her mouth and quietly creeping out of the room. She slipped over to the hallway and peeked downstairs.

Two men stood in the entrance, staring at each other, ready for action.

"Think hard about what you're about to do," said one of the men in a low voice. They disappeared behind the house when they heard the sound of the footsteps.

Yvonne anxiously locked the door. She hung the key from the rack on the wall and hurried back upstairs at once.

"Did something happen?" Sandra asked.

"I'm not sure. I saw two nasty-looking strangers at the door, but only for a moment since they disappeared as soon as they heard me.

"Did you lock the door?"

"Yes."

"Good. Hopefully, things will be fine."

Unfortunately, they weren't.

Nick showed up an hour later to take the women to a nearby apartment while things went down. He had an ashen look on his face from his temper. He'd just had a nasty argument with his companions, who were upset that there were strangers at his house, even though he tried convincing them it was for his alibi. The truth was that he didn't trust the guys. This was no surprise since no one could be trusted in this shady business. He grudgingly agreed to take the women elsewhere while they took care of the shipment. *A few days later he would disappear from here anyway,* he thought.

Sandra eyed the perturbed man with a piercing gaze. "What are you up to, and who were those men?" she asked in a slightly harsh tone.

Nick was edgy as it was, so her remark enraged him at once. "That's none of your business. You better not get involved in this. Never, do you understand?"

"What are you talking about? Yvonne just saw two creeps at the door. She had no idea they were your pals. Yes, your dubious-looking friends. I don't know what you got into, but it stinks."

"Silence, you red bitch," he hissed, nastily tugging at her arm. "You better not say another word or me..." He left the sentence unfinished, as Sandra lost her balance and fell in front of the window.

Yvonne rushed to her aid. "Leave her alone. Isn't it enough that you broke her leg?"

Nick slapped her at once.

"Shut up," he snapped, and then halted, as Yvonne had fallen over and accidentally bumped her head. She lay on the floor, unconscious.

Sandra sat up with some difficulty. She stared at the motionless body in shock. "What did you do?" she screamed in terror.

"Keep it quiet. You saw for yourself that it was an accident," he growled at her, nervously leaning over the woman. He didn't have any time to waste with them, he thought. He picked his bag up from the living room along with a glass of booze and ran back up the stairs to the bathroom, where he prepared the drugs.

Sandra was still sitting on the floor, leaning up against the armchair, futilely trying to help Yvonne.

"Wait, let me do it," said Nick, appearing in the doorway. He walked over and nervously pulled his wife up into the armchair. He lifted the glass to her lips. "Drink up, you can use it."

Sandra was parched, so she downed the booze in a single gulp.

"What did you slip into my drink?" she asked.

"A sedative. It'll make you feel better."

"What's up with Yvonne?"

"Everything will be alright, she just blacked out. I'll take her over to the other room and lay her down on the bed."

First, however, he ran back downstairs. He rummaged through the drawers until he found some robust string. By the time, he went back up, Sandra was knocked out, leaning back against the chair. He quickly tied her leg in a cast to the bars in front of the window so he wouldn't have to worry about her anymore. He closed the window as best as he could before turning to the Frenchwoman. Was she dead? No, she couldn't be. He fended off the unpleasant thought.

He glanced at his watch. He had to hurry, so he grabbed Yvonne's arms and dragged her over to the other room. He dabbed a towel into some water and wiped the small amount of blood off her forehead. Finally, he lay her down on the bed and propped her head up with a pillow. He shook the girl a bit to wake her up, but she didn't move. He pressed his hand down on her temple. He sighed in relief once he felt her pulse.

He tossed the towel into the bathroom in a hurry. He yanked out two blankets from the closet, draping one of them over the motionless woman before changing his mind and placing two big pillows on her body. Finally, he pulled in the shutters and closed the door.

He carried the other blanket over to Sandra, who dozed in the armchair. After pausing for a moment, he closed the door on his way out. He ran downstairs with his bag and locked the front door. He carefully placed the key in its hiding place in the damp half-light. The silent house was plunged into darkness.

CHAPTER 102

Pedro stretched and got dressed early in the morning before running down to the shore with long strides. The waves barely moved across the surface of the water, and the sand stretched out in front of him into the distance. He started into a slow, comfortable, perhaps too cosy jogging tempo. At the edge of the water, he found a man busying himself with his fishing pole. He greeted the man.

The stranger kindly reciprocated. "It looks like a nice day," he added.
"Yes. Have a good catch," Pedro motioned to the man before he carried on running. He was glad he'd come home and that he could go running on the shore again.

A young man passed him with a dog. The Yorkshire terrier playfully jumped back and forth, lagging and sniffing or raising its paws. Its owner threw a tennis ball for it to catch, causing the dog to race off ahead.
Pedro turned back and ran to the house. He doubled over at the house, supporting his hands on his knees, panting heavily. *Man, you're in bad shape,* he thought to himself.

He brewed some coffee and had a hearty breakfast. His niece wasn't around, and his sister was still fast asleep. He suddenly came up with an idea and packed his most important belongings into a duffel bag. He jotted down a few lines to Patricia, telling her that he was heading down to El Palmar to look around his old house. Off he headed in the car Lucy had loaned him.

He got caught in traffic as he passed through Marbella. That was to be expected in the morning hours, he acknowledged patiently. However, the toll-based highway was practically deserted, and he quickly made it down to Gibraltar. He slowly drove down the winding road past Algeciras.

He glanced out at the ocean from time to time. The beautiful view was captivating as always. He slowed down near the wind turbines and unconsciously turned off the road and drove down a dirt path which twisted and turned through a cork woods. He was already pleased, hoping to find his old friends. He hadn't been here for close to twenty years. He never wrote them a line from Brazil, since he didn't have anything to write to them. *Perhaps they might not be living here anymore,* he thought sadly. The gate was locked and no one appeared when he rattled the bars, so he went on his way, feeling depressed.

As he passed by Tarifa, his eyes gazed out across the familiar landscape. Later on, he had seen the road lined on both sides by wind turbines. *Yes, the twenty-first century undeniably had made its presence felt here,* he thought to himself. *We're growing in numbers, so we need the energy.*

He stopped at a parking lot on the far side of Barbate and bought something to eat and drink, which he packed into the trunk before carrying on. He slowed down as he reached the shady pine forest. He'd always loved this stretch of the road; the contrast of the bright colours of the sandy soil and the clear blue sky accentuated the green foliage of the trees. The road sliced through the treetops before the slope and the impossibly bluish-green the sea spread out in front of him.

A group of hippies sat at the side of the road at the junction to Trafalgar. He thought of Amy. *God knows where she is now,* he thought sadly. 1, he cheered up when he finally reached El Palmar. He stopped the car for a few minutes and nostalgically eyed the long, sandy beach stirred by the wind blowing in from the west.

He parked the car as he reached the house. Much to his surprise, the gate wasn't locked, but he didn't worry about that at the moment. He sighed heavily and quietly spoke up.

"Well, you finally made it, pal. Welcome back!" he cried out loud.

He loved this old, ramshackle house, with its crumbling walls. I should get the place fixed up, he thought. The garden was neglected as well. The hedges running along the fence seemed more like thickets, and the palm tree he'd planted in the past had grown incredibly high. This made him a bit emotional.

He looked up at the house and noticed the window upstairs was slightly ajar. This was another surprise. He quickly went to fetch the key from the hiding place. Once he put his hand over the crevice, he smiled as he thought how Patricia never dared reach into the hole for the fear of something grabbing her hand. At such times, she always muttered, "I didn't lie, I didn't lie." That was a long time ago, he recalled, as he opened the door with a slight click. It seemed like only yesterday since he'd left that kind, red-haired girl here all alone.

The smell of the stuffy room hit him and brought him right back to the present moment. He opened the windows and brought everything in from the car. He opened the fridge, which was plugged in, but there was only a bottle of water inside, which seemed odd to him.

He walked out onto the patio and leapt into the air like a teenager, punching upwards. This was the first time he'd felt joy since his wife passed away. The pressure inside of him faded and disappeared. He opened a bottle of beer, finished it off, and rushed upstairs.

He opened the room opposite the stairs. The stench of blood hit him at once. He instinctively felt that something was amiss. He looked inside the bathroom where he found a towel on the floor. As he picked it up, he noticed it was still wet.

"Hmm," he muttered. I guess someone is or was here, after all, he wondered with a frown. As he put the towel back on the rack, he noticed it was bloody. He took a closer look and smelled it. Yes, he wasn't mistaken.

Again, he thought of the strange, heavy smell in the room. He quizzically went back inside and opened the shutters. Light flooded in. He looked inside the closet, which was practically empty, with only a suitcase inside. He didn't bother with the suitcase and instead thoughtfully slid the door back into place. He stood by idly for a while since he could still sense the smell in the room. He glanced at the heavy pillows on the bed and the twisted covers, which he suddenly pushed aside.

"Who is this?" he cried in shock, cursing himself for not noticing her sooner. He skilfully groped at the motionless woman's carotid artery. He couldn't find a pulse, yet the body was still warm. He placed his hands one over the other and attempted CPR before checking for a pulse again, which he could faintly make out.

He ran down to the living room and rummaged through his bag for his mobile. He glanced at the table and bookshelf in passing before noticing an old phone book, thickly covered with dust. He slammed his fist on it, recoiling from the cloud of dust. He quickly flipped through the book. He found the number he was looking for and quickly called an ambulance. He was so excited that he knocked off a book from the shelf, and it fell to the floor with a thud. He seemed to hear some noise from upstairs. He ran back to the unknown woman and checked her pulse again. He laid her on her side and noticed the slight injury on her head, the look of which he didn't like at all.

After a while, he heard a distant siren and rushed out to the corner. In a few minutes, the ambulance had whisked the woman away.

For a while, he was left thinking about the odd turn of events, yet he quickly grew hungry and walked over to the local restaurant. The last time he'd visited the place years or rather decades ago, he had been a regular customer. He sat down at a table outside. He focused on the menu under the parasol, and an unknown waiter took his order and soon returned with some cold beer. Pedro drank half of it off at once. He walked back to the house once he'd finished his meal.

CHAPTER 103

Most people rested lazily in the afternoon siesta when the sun beat down punishingly from above. *A good Spanish tradition,* he muttered to himself. After the fine meal, he quickly made himself comfortable on the covered patio.

He was half asleep when he heard a whimpering sound from upstairs. *That's right,* he recalled, when he arrived, he saw the window upstairs was slightly open, so that's probably where the noise came from, although he wasn't sure. Perhaps he was just dreaming. He got up and walked around the house to look up at the windows. Yes, one of them was still open. It suddenly occurred to him that he'd forgotten to check the other room because of the unknown woman he found upstairs.

Suddenly, someone rattled the gate out front. Pedro hurried over to the entrance.

"How can I help you?" he quickly asked the stranger.

"I'm Detective Robert Grey," said the man, showing Pedro his badge. "Can I come in?"

Pedro opened the gate in surprise and expectantly eyed the man, who slowly walked over to the house.

"How can I help you?" he asked, following the man inside.

"Do you live here?" asked the man, slowly turning back to face him.

"Yes, for a few days. I just arrived. Dr Gomez," he said in the introduction, holding his hand out to him.

"Pleased to meet you." While shaking Pedro's hand, the man followed up with another question. "When exactly?"

"About two hours ago," he said impassively. Although he wasn't offended, Pedro had no idea what the man wanted. He'd come down here after all these years for some relaxation, but he'd already found a strange woman lying unconscious in bed – who might be dead by now – and now a detective was questioning him.

"Where do you live?"

"In Marbella," Pedro replied grimly. "Could you tell me why you're asking me all these questions?"

Robert attentively eyed Gomez. "I have a good reason."

"Then tell me what that reason is," he snapped disapprovingly. "Look, I came here to rest. I have to decide whatsoever to get involved in anything."

"You already are."

"What do you mean by that?" Pedro asked in surprise.

"I'm sure you know the answer to that better than me."

"Come on, tell me, what is it I should know about?"

"That woman in the hospital might not make it. Do you understand now?"

"Ah," he sighed in relief. "Yes, when I arrived, I found her upstairs. I tried giving CPR and called an ambulance at once. I'm really glad she's alive. That means that hopefully, I saved her life. That's all. I must add that I don't know her. I've never seen her before in my life."

Grey listened to his account while sizing him up with a scrutinizing gaze.

"Where do you work?" he continued his questioning, taking out his notepad to jot down the details.

"Nowhere yet."

"What do you mean by that?" Grey perked up.

"Look, that's private. Get to the point and tell me what you want, then I'm going to have to ask you to leave me alone."

"I have my fair share of official duties to deal with as well," said Grey. "You have to answer my questions if you don't have anything to hide. But even if you do, you still have to answer my questions," he added firmly.

Pedro replied awkwardly in a more moderate tone, "I just returned a few days ago, from Rio de Janeiro. For good. I lived there for a long time and worked there as well. But I moved back now."

"Why?"

"My wife died and my daughter, or rather my stepdaughter, disappeared with a hippie. So, I was all alone. I am currently staying at my sister's house. I'm a doctor and as soon as I get back to Marbella, I'll look for a job at a local hospital or maybe open a private clinic. I'm not sure yet. That's it. That's all I have to say. Oh, and this is my house. This is the first time I came here after about nineteen years. I'm pretty sure there weren't many visitors who stopped by in the meantime – except this unknown woman who was taken away by the paramedics."

"Do you have any idea how she ended up here?"

"I don't. It's a mystery to me too."

Pedro heard again a whimpering sound coming from the open window upstairs. They both perked up when they heard the sound and rushed upstairs at once.

Pedro pressed down on the handle of the door and was surprised to find it locked. He rammed his shoulder against it, but the heavy wooden door wouldn't budge. He knocked on the door and listened with bated breath.

"Let me try," said Grey. He took a step back from the door and ran against it with full force. The door suddenly burst open, and the detective fell forward into the room.

Pedro was holding a hand out to help him up from the floor when he caught sight of a red-haired woman sitting in front of the armchair on the floor. Her leg, in a cast, was grotesquely tied to the metal grate of the window.

The men were left speechless in surprise. Robert Grey came to his senses first, although he was shocked by the sight as well since the unfortunate the woman was none other than his former acquaintance, Sandra Winkler.

The detective nervously rummaged through the bag at his side. Once he found his pocketknife, he quickly cut through the durable cord and cautiously lowered the woman's leg to the floor. He motioned for Pedro to help, and the two of them picked up the woman together and lay her down on the bed.

"She's alive," muttered the doctor, tenderly shaking the woman's shoulder while rushing over to the bathroom. He pulled out a clean handkerchief from his pocket and quickly moistened it before hurrying back and carefully wiping the woman's worn-out face. He searchingly looked around the room and spotted a woman's handbag lying on the floor. He leaned over and rummaged through the bag before he came across a small bottle of perfume, which he unscrewed and held under the woman's nose.

"Is it bad?"

"I hope not," muttered the doctor. "I'll bring some water," he said, racing downstairs. He was wondering what Antonio's stepmother was doing here while he opened the fridge in confusion. He grabbed the bottle of water along with a glass from the shelf and ran back upstairs with his bag, where he routinely examined the woman.

Sandra was still lying on the bed with her eyes shut. Pedro reached under the back of her head and gently lifted her head. "Drink, darling," he said quietly. "I'll call an ambulance at once, she needs one."

"I'll call them," said Grey, coming to his senses.

This was the second time an ambulance had been called to the same address. Pedro motioned for the detective to step outside.

"Yes?"

"I'll go with the woman because I want to take a look at the other woman as well. I'll put the suitcases in the trunk and take them after them. Are you coming?"

Grey glanced at his watch.

"Unfortunately, I can't. I have to stay in the neighbourhood. You could give me your number because I'd like to look around the house sometime in the evening if that's fine with you."

"I don't mind," he replied, readily giving the detective his number.

"If you have time, you can stay here now."

"Thanks, then I'd rather stay."

"Fine. Come on, I'll show you where to leave the keys when you're done."

After a short wait, the ambulance arrived. They carried down Sandra Winkler, since they couldn't turn around the bend in the stairwell.

As he followed the ambulance, Pedro quizzically thought about the shocking events and the odd coincidence of finding Antonio's stepmother at his house in such a condition.

CHAPTER 104

Robert Grey entered the house. He thoroughly searched all the rooms on the ground floor, pulling out the drawers and even checking the books, but he couldn't find anything of note.

In the back of the kitchen, there was a small Moroccan rug hanging from the wall. He noted its beauty and unintentionally ran his hand over its surface – and that's when he discovered a lump under the rug. He folded the rug to the side. Much to his surprise, there was a low door behind it which was locked. It occurred to him that he had seen a bunch of keys somewhere. *I'll give it a shot,* he thought. *But where were they? Oh, I know.* He opened the low cupboard under the sink and crouched down. Behind the detergents, he found an old cardboard box filled with rusting keys. He patiently tried each of them and laughed out loud when he tried the seventh key. "Seven will be my lucky number from on," he muttered to himself as the lock creaked open.

He crawled through the door and turned a light on. He found himself in a pantry filled with all sorts of piled-up bric-a-brac. As he rummaged about, a few empty cardboard boxes fell on top of him.

He dusted himself off with a few curses and then gazed at the background in surprise. The previously well-disguised room led out to a huge room that was filled with cardboard boxes taped shut. He tried lifting one of them, but it was too heavy. He carefully opened one of the boxes with a knife and found some precisely packed antiques in the box. He looked around the shelves and found masking tape, which he used to carefully close back the box. He turned the lights off and finally locked the door. He pocketed the key since he would need it later on. The other keys, he put back into the cupboard under the sink.

He pulled out his phone. "I'm here at the house. Bring your dog. Hurry up, because it's getting late." He hung up and dialled another number. "Call me at once if you see any cars approaching," he ordered, ending the brief call and continuing his search.

He went upstairs and entered the room where Pedro found the other women on the bed, but he already knew everything about that. He searchingly looked around the room. Something shimmered in the last rays of sun filtering in through the window between the nightstand and the bed. He reached in and pulled out a woman's handbag with a metallic top. He emptied its contents onto the bed. He found what he was looking for in a little packet. He read the name of Yvonne Siran, French citizen, from the certificate. He immediately called André Breton, who had been looking for his girlfriend in vain. The last time she spoke with him, she was at Sandra Winkler's home in Marbella. They were about to leave, and then they had mysteriously disappeared.

"I found them. They're both in the hospital in Cadiz," he informed Breton. "You can pick up your girlfriend's suitcase from Pedro Gomez. He might already be at the hospital by now. I have her handbag along with her papers." As they talked, Grey walked over to the other room where they'd found Sandra Winkler. "Oh, and good luck," he said in parting to Breton before focusing back on his work.

He noticed a smeared blotch on the floor. What happened here? he wondered as he examined it. Even the foot of the bed had some blood on it. As he headed towards the door, he noticed a drop of blood on the threshold. He carefully noted down everything in his little notebook before leaving the house with the Frenchwoman's handbag. He locked the door and slid the key back in its place, just as Pedro Gomez had asked.

He quickly looked around the yard but failed to notice anything with his sharp eyes. As he moved on, he spotted a formidably sized round cistern behind the house. He walked past the cistern and then backtracked. He opened the metal door on top of the cistern; it was rather dark for him to see what was inside of it. He leaned over, picked up a stone, and tossed it inside. He heard the quiet splash of the water. He noticed that there was a narrow ladder leading downwards under the narrow opening, but he didn't go down inside. *He'd wait for his partner and his dog to show up,* he thought, quietly closing the metal lid.

His narcotics partner still hadn't returned, so he walked over to his car. He put the bag of the poor Frenchwoman in the trunk. He issued some orders over the phone to covertly keep tabs on the house night and day. While waiting, he summarized the facts in his mind. They'd found two women upstairs, one of whom might be dead by now. He had the feeling something was fishy about the house.

A few days ago, he'd managed to more or less define the location of the suspicious house in Canos de Meca with the help of Carmen Stone. Since then, they'd been monitoring the whole street, although the high stone walls and the wooden gate would surely fend off prying eyes. The wire-fence running behind the street ran immediately beside the picturesque nature preserve. From that side, they could keep an eye on any possible movement, yet they could only approach it on foot. Although two plainclothes cops were already watching the neighbourhood, it was still possible that craftier types would notice this at once, and then he would have to start it all over again.

His man finally arrived, leading a beautiful German shepherd on a leash. The finely trained animal stopped next to its owner in a disciplined manner while the men quickly welcomed each other.

"Come on, let's hurry up," urged Grey, quickening his pace. He opened the door to the house and then the door to the storeroom. The dog pushed its way ahead before listlessly sitting on the threshold.

"He didn't find anything," warned his companion.

"Go upstairs."

Grey did a quick, precise job. As he finished scanning the ground floor, he put the rusty key back with the other keys before heading upstairs after them.

The dog excitedly sniffed around. It sniffed at the bloodstains and reared up to the edge of the sink in the bathroom and started yelping. The dog's handler leaned over, checked the top of the marble surface, and ran his palm over it. "There are some traces of drugs here," he said.

Grey listlessly closed the door. He'd hoped for more. "Let's go look around the garden and the garage as well."

They thoroughly checked all around, but couldn't find a thing. The detective stopped behind the house, discouraged.

"This is all we have left," he said, opening the door to the cistern. The dog suddenly leapt on top of the cistern and started scratching at the entrance and barking. His owner called its name and stroked it, but the dog anxiously lay flat on its stomach, whimpering and peeked into the opening, sniffing in the air.

The man moved on to the narrow metal ladder and disappeared into the deep. He carefully flashed his light on the walls above the water.

"Did you find anything?" asked Grey anxiously, leaning over the lip.

"I don't know yet."

The neighbourhood was quiet. A few minutes later, the detective called down inside the cistern again.

"What's going on, what's taking you so long?" he asked in a hushed tone. The man's head reappeared in the opening.

"My flashlight isn't bright enough, give me yours. I think

we're on to something," he whispered before disappearing into the hole again.

In the meantime, the detective stared down into the cistern, nervously biting his lip.

"Well, what is it?" he urged impatiently.

"Bingo. We've found the stuff. Seems like quite a cache," he said, climbing back up with a grin on his face.

"Did you take a sample?"

"There's no need for that. I trust my dog."

"OK, but I want to see it too," Grey said, taking the flashlight and climbing down the ladder.

He flashed his light along with the approximately three-meter-long round structure. Just above the water, he noticed a niche with a huge, bale-like package. He felt the tension rising inside of him. He stuck one of his arms through the rung of the ladder and gripped the light between his teeth, thus freeing up his other arm. He dug out a bag from his pocket along with his knife and used the latter to cautiously poke a hole with the sharpest steel edge of the blade into the side of the waterproof package. He pressed his finger into the package and tasted the white powder that stuck to his finger. They were dealing with drugs – very good quality drugs at that. He took a tiny sample into the bag, which he pocketed. Finally, he covered the hole with some tape. Once he was done, he climbed up the ladder and quickly closed the metal door of the cistern.

He leaned over. "Thanks for helping me out," he said, gratefully stroking the dog's head before rising back up. "Now let's get out of here," he added. As they reached the car, Grey spoke up again. "I'm staying here."

"I guess that means you're saying we should leave the stuff right where we found it, correct?"

"Exactly. I want to catch them with the drugs. But I'm going to need more men to do that – the very best I can get. You understand me, right?" he asked his companion with obvious excitement. "Get to it. I want them to park in front of the restaurant once they get here. Not here, but further down next to the intersection, and then

I want them to cautiously spread out. I want you to stay close by, along with the dog. Man, thanks for helping me out, along with your finely trained pooch," he praised the dog again, patting its head.

"All in a day's work," muttered his colleague with satisfaction.

The sun dipped below the edge of the horizon with the sound of the lapping waves in the distance as the only noise coming from the shore.

Grey got in his car and backed up amongst the weeds on an empty lot. He called up his boss to tell him about the case as well as to speed up the backup he needed. *They mustn't lose track of this top shipment,* he thought with growing alarm. He also called up André Breton, who was still at the hospital.

"How is your girlfriend?" he asked.

"Not too good. She's in a coma."

"Is there any hope for her?"

"Not much."

Robert regretted the events.

"Look, come down here once you're done. We found the drugs, so all we have to do now is wait for them to come to pick it up."

"That's great news. Congratulations, pal."

CHAPTER 105

They finally removed her cast. The doctor watched the woman closely.

"I'll let you go, but you have to promise me that you'll get some rest. You're going to have to use a cane for a while and be gentle with your leg."

"I understand, and thank you for everything."

"That's my job," the doctor replied, thinking how all his patients reacted the same way before the door closed behind them, but that's the way things should be. *Many of them got stuck there and could never get back to normal life – or leave for good,* he thought sadly.

"Can I ask you something?"

"Go ahead."

"My girlfriend might be here."

"What's her name?"

"Yvonne Siran, a French citizen."

The doctor spoke with the nurse before saying goodbye and hurrying off to work. After some waiting, the orderly arrived. He sat her down in a wheelchair as she thought of Antonio and smiled faintly. Perhaps he's doing the same thing right now, but that's okay since he'll become a doctor in a few years.

The man took her to the second floor and carted her inside room number 16. Yvonne was lying motionless on the bed next to the window.

"Is she, all right?" Sandra anxiously asked the nurse.

"Not exactly, she's in a coma," said the nurse laconically. Sandra gripped her girlfriend's hand with a pang of conscience, quietly sobbing at her side. She hated Nick. This was his fault.

"Please, open your eyes and tell me everything is okay. I need you to do this for me, or I'll feel guilty for the rest of my life," Yvonne, however, didn't respond. Even her face was motionless. Sandra sadly bowed her head and thought back to the recent events.

She was utterly confused by Nick's odd behaviour. She didn't understand why he took them to Marrakech for a few days before bringing them back to El Palmar. Why wouldn't he leave her alone and disappear from her life? He was getting increasingly unpredictable, whilst she longed for peace and a carefree life something she never experienced at his side. She made up her mind to return to Marbella at once and put an end to all of this. She wouldn't let him treat her like a puppet anymore. She faintly formulated a plan and decided to go far away as soon as she could – anywhere, as long as it was some unknown place. *Once Yvonne hopefully recovers and is discharged from the hospital, I will go with her so I can take care of her,* Sandra vowed as she eyed her friend silently.

Someone put a hand on her shoulder. She shuddered and turned around. "It's you!" she cried in surprise.

"Do you mind?" asked Pedro quietly.

Sandra blushed and awkwardly shook her head.

"I just wanted to know how the poor woman who was in my house was doing," he said with a grim look on his face. "Along with you," he added.

"She's my girlfriend. But what do you mean 'along with me'?" she asked ominously.

"I'm sorry, I should have known better," he said and explained everything in detail. "I spoke with the doctor," he said, glancing at the woman lying on the bed. "She's in a coma. But he let you go."

Suddenly, his mobile rang, so he had to leave the room.

"I have to ask you urgently to leave your house at once," he heard from the detective on the other end of the line.

"But you can't order me to do something like that."

Robert Grey took a deep breath and patiently explained why he was asking this. Of course, he didn't mention the drugs.

"Look," Grey explained, "I don't want you to get in danger. We have to keep the house under surveillance for an indeterminate period, probably one week at the most. Trust me, I have a good reason to order this. I don't want Sandra or you to suffer any harm. As you can see for yourself, the Frenchwoman is in a coma. Thus, I'd like to ask you again to return to Marbella today," he said firmly.

"One of my colleagues spoke with the doctor, who said that he would be releasing Sandra as well," Grey added. "If you don't mind, I'd like to ask you to take her with you."

Pedro hesitated for a moment. He glanced at the woman sitting with her back to him through the doorway for a moment.

"Fine, I'm still here at the hospital. Sandra Winkler is with me in the Frenchwoman's room. Naturally, I'll take her with me – if she agrees, that is. We'll be at the house an hour from now at the latest. I'll get my stuff, and we'll head back to Marbella. You'll find me there if you need to."

Grey was relieved. "Thank you for your cooperation. I'll get in touch." He ended the conversation.

Pedro visited the head nurse and asked for Sandra's discharge form before hurrying back to her.

"Come, we have to go now," he said, carting Sandra out into the hallway. "Do you have any personal belongings in your room?"

"No. My suitcase was at your house. As you can see, I have my bag with me."

"Great, then let's get going. I have your suitcase with me."

Sandra eyed him quizzically, yet still, let him cart her down the corridor. At the main entrance, she absent-mindedly stood up. If he hadn't been there to catch her, she would have surely fallen to the floor.

She realized that her legs weren't strong enough for her to stand on her own. *Where is my husband when I need him?* she wondered forlornly.

She felt awkward.

"Look, I don't want to get in the way. I'll call a taxi to take me back to Marbella."

"There's no need for that since I'm headed there as well," said Pedro.

"I hope you don't mind the company?"

She didn't want to offend him. "Thank you for your help," she whispered awkwardly.

"That's only natural." He opened the car door and helped her get in, feeling this woman stir up old memories in him yet again.

They both fell silent. Neither of them had any idea what the other was thinking about.

Well, we've crossed paths again, thought Sandra. She wanted to know how he had happened to show up here so suddenly again, since Rio de Janeiro was far away. Were his wife and daughter with him as well? She decided not to ask any questions, clenched her finely curved mouth shut instead.

Pedro spoke up as they reached the house.

"Stay here, I'll be right back," he said. "I'll just pick up a few things. But if you want to come in, I can help you out."

"Thank you, I think I'll stay in the car."

Pedro closed the windows of the house. He unplugged the fridge and opened its door. He placed the previously purchased food in a bag. Who knew when he'd come back again? His duffel bag sat untouched on a chair in the living room, just the way he left it. He picked it up and slung it across his shoulder. He looked around one more time before finally closing the door. He replaced the key in its hiding place.   The kilometres ran by, yet they didn't say a word to each other. Pedro occasionally glanced at the woman, who seemed dismissive and reclusive.

He opened his mouth twice to start up a conversation, but each time decided to stay silent. The tension was practically tangible between the two of them. He saw her tightly clenching her fists in her lap and fumbling her fingers.

"You're nervous because of me, right?" he said finally.

Sandra blushed in response.

"Why won't you say a thing?"

"I feel awkward to rely on your help and that I'm wasting your time." She had never wanted to rely on anyone in her life, yet her fate had forced her to do so on multiple occasions, she thought bitterly.

"That's not true. We're headed in the same direction," he assured her.

"Well, that's still how I feel. But I'm still thankful for your help."

"You already said that."

Their conversation faltered again. The tension still loomed between them.

"Something happened to him, right?" he asked after a while.

"Who?"

"Your husband."

"Oh, I don't think so," she said quickly. *Nothing ever happens to Nick,* she thought. "I'm worried about Yvonne's condition," she said to change the subject.

"How did her injury happen?"

She wondered what she could say to that. After all, Nick was still her husband.

"I don't know. I was sleeping." She didn't tell him that the doctor told her that she was drugged, even though she begged to differ.

"Did you speak with the detective?"

"No. But …"

"So?"

"But I did speak to Yvonne's boyfriend, André Breton, at the hospital. He's also a detective," she explained.

"That's a good thing."

A lengthy silence settled in between them. Pedro thought

about what kind of husband would leave his wife like this on her own. He recalled the summer when they spent their vacation in Marbella. Amy enthusiastically told him that Antonio's parents were nice, especially the father. *Ha! What a kind person,* he thought, thinking about the way he had spotted this poor miserable woman behind the door as it popped open, left on the floor with her leg twisted to the side for God knows how long.

"I don't want to pry, but at least tell me how you ended up at my house with your girlfriend?"

"The house belongs to you and not to Nick?"

Pedro suddenly slammed on the brakes and veered over to the side of the road, turning on the lights in the car. The fury gleamed in his eyes. If what he thought was true … "Nick what?" he demanded.

"What do you mean, what?" cried Sandra in fright. "Winkler!"

"That's not what I meant. I know he's Winkler, but what does he look like? Where did he come from?"

The look on the man's face made her swoon, so she buried her face in her hands and sobbed out loud. Pedro hesitantly caressed her head.

"Don't cry. Please, forgive me, I lost it there for a moment. But please, you have to tell me what your husband does for a living. I'd like to know."

"He's about the same age as you. He's from London," she added faintly. "He deals with antiques, but actually, I don't know," she explained before she started rummaging through her bag with trembling hands.

"Here's a picture of him," she said, holding it out to him.

Pedro recognized Nick at once. He got out of the car with a pale complexion and nervously ran up and down. He clenched his hand into a fist and hissed, "So you crossed my path again."

The wind started blowing fiercely, which quickly sobered him up. He got back in his car and carried on.

CHAPTER 106

Meanwhile, In Canos de Meca, Nick was finding himself in a tight spot with Rodrigo, who urged him to hand over the shipment at once.

"I'm not going yet, only at night. Everything is ready by now."

"Why are you freaking out? It's a quiet neighbourhood."

"We have to wait," Nick said stubbornly.

Rodrigo eyed him with a sneaky look on his face. "I have to be in Marseille by tomorrow."

"I know that," Nick retorted in a snappy tone. "Is the money here?"

"Sure, but I want the drugs first. A deal is a deal."

Nick gazed at the tip of his shoe to compose himself.

"Will do. Don't worry. You always get what you want, right?" He pulled his straw hat down low, turned around, and hurried out of the building. Rodrigo watched him walk away.

Nick got into his car, all riled up. He inserted the key in the ignition with a slightly trembling hand before taking off as slowly as possible. He didn't move his head, yet his eyes watched the street in front of him, which was quiet as always. He looked back behind him at the Trafalgar intersection, but no one was following him. He parked in front of the local restaurant, where he had lunch. He paid the bill and disappeared on foot behind the houses. He stopped at a deserted apartment and opened its front door before disappearing behind it. He peered out of the window into the darkness. *The coast was clear,* he agreed. He set his alarm clock for two o'clock before slumping down onto the bed. He thought of the following day, leaving his tense thoughts far behind.

He'll pick up the cash in the evening before sailing off to Morocco with Sandra. They'd spend a few days there before heading over to the Canary Islands if the weather held out. His plan was for them to fly off to Lisbon from there before taking a big detour and landing in Brazil. He wanted to start a new life with a pocket full of cash and his wife at his side, he thought sleepily. He felt the gentle billowing of the breeze in his sleep, which stirred the wind on the beach. A family was having a carefree weekend nearby, laughing and having fun.

He suddenly woke up and glanced at his watch. *I still have time,* he thought, lying back down on the bed. He thought of his dreams. As far as he could remember, he was always alone. He'd lost his mother at an early age and didn't know his father. He was raised by his grandfather for a long time in London. One day, he left everything behind and somehow ended up here and decided to stay.

Perhaps for the first time in his life, it occurred to Nick that he'd never really had a family – or rather, he never really bothered about them. His thoughts briefly strayed to Antonio and then his wife, who was still at the house on the beach with her girlfriend. He didn't have time to deal with them, but they'll just have to stay put for the next few hours. *Everything will change from tomorrow,* he vowed.

CHAPTER 107

The darkness blanketed the surroundings. The waves of the Atlantic Ocean rolled far inland on the sand.

Robert Grey's men inconspicuously monitored the house all day long, yet they saw no movement apart from Pedro and Sandra picking up their things. In the meantime, André called to tell them that they had enough men in El Palmar, so he would rather head over to Canos de Meca if Robert didn't mind.

The detective agreed to the idea. Since he had been waiting in the jeep for hours, his back was starting to hurt from all the time spent sitting, so he stretched – though without losing focus on the surroundings. For the time being, he had nothing to do but tensely wait.

He thought of Nick Winkler and hoped that he would finally catch the man today. Nick had to show up sooner or later. Grey was sure that a package worth its value in gold wouldn't stay at the bottom of a cistern for long. This was the only dusty road that led to the house, winding through the thickets. Grey and some of his men were carefully secluded as they kept an eye on the building. He was filled with hope that he could finally wrap up this long-drawn-out case tonight. If he managed to pull this off, he could finally go somewhere and enjoy a long, deserved rest. *But let's see how things play out first,* he sighed hopefully.

Later that night, Grey sleepily groped for his thermos. He unscrewed the cap and filled it with hot coffee. He slowly drank the coffee, relishing the hot, aromatic liquid. *It wasn't nearly as good as Brazilian coffee, but he would have to make do,* he thought. *Half a loaf is better than none,* he recalled the adage.

An hour later, he got out of the car to move his cramped legs. He walked down the plank and disappeared amongst the dunes, cautiously sitting down on a log. He could see to the house in the dim light of the streetlamp, yet the short cul-de-sac was entirely deserted.

He sat there at length, gazing up at the starry sky. The wind was picking up and clouds were racing over the heavens. During his extended wait, the moon crossed over to the other end of the heavens, peeking out from time to time from behind the increasingly dense clouds. He stood up as his legs grew numb and kicked out into the air before sitting back down on the log. As he glanced over at the shore, he suddenly noticed a barely perceptible dark blotch approaching. He had no time to run back to the car, so he leaned over and quickly hid under the log, tensely listening and watching. After a brief wait, he heard a man pass by and approach the street.

Grey saw the figure approach the house under surveillance. His mobile beeped faintly.

"Yeah, I saw him. He came in from the shore. It seems like the fish are taking the bait. Don't move yet, only when we take them. I'll give the signal," he whispered and quickly turned off the phone.

He was getting incredibly anxious, no doubt about it. He would have loved to creep after the man, but that's precisely what he couldn't afford to do. He couldn't take any risks, and he had enough men on the other side of the house. This was the only way they could take the package from the house by car. They had no other options. He could catch them with ease from here, he thought, ready for action.

CHAPTER 108

Nick entered the gate, quietly opened the door to the house, and tiptoed over to the bookshelf in the living room. He unbuckled the bag from his belt and hid it behind the books, cautiously groping in the dark. He kept only his driver's license on him. Once he was done, he would come back for Sandra and pick up his bag, he thought.

He quietly locked the door and put the key back in its hiding place before expectantly sitting down on the worn-out chair on the patio, propped up against the wall. He stretched his legs out and lay back in the chair. He'd walked along the shore from Trafalgar to approach the house. His plan worked out since he met no one at this late hour. Although he was slightly exhausted, he didn't mind. The whole thing was much safer this way. His old jeep was parked nearby on the footpath.

He had a good sense of intuition, so he'd carefully thought out and prepared the delivery of the shipments. He'd been covering his moves with women for some time now. In this clever manner, he managed to fend off even the slightest suspicions. He was now especially careful with the final shipment. There was a lot at stake – perhaps the highest stakes he's ever had to deal with. Once he handed over the drugs and grabbed the cash, he would disappear at once from the area as well as the whole country for good.

He waited anxiously for the men to show up. *They should be here by now,* he thought. As experienced as he was, it was hard for him to deal with his nerves at the moment. *Don't worry, everything's going to be alright,* he assured himself. He had to stay level-headed, so he hadn't been drinking or doing any drugs for two days now. However, this frayed his nerves.

He broke off his pondering and focused on scanning the darkness around him. The boys had to get here any minute now, he thought anxiously.

He heard some noise on the right side of the yard from behind the bushes. He could faintly make out the two dark figures who crawled onwards.

He quietly hissed at them.
"Over here, follow me," he whispered to them. He lay flat on his stomach at the corner of the house, and all three of them crept over to the cistern. A few minutes later, they reached the covered concrete ring. Nick slowly raised his arm, groped for the metal handle of the lid, and silently opened the door to the cistern. He looked up at the sky. The moon cast a silver glow on the clouds above them. The wind blew fiercely at them.
"Let's wait a bit," he whispered.
"I think we should hurry up. Let's bring the goods up as fast as we can and get out of here!" whispered the long-haired man impatiently as he crouched on the grass next to Nick.
"No, wait!" Nick ordered in a whisper, pressing his shoulder back down. Nick wasn't fond of his companions and didn't trust them. They weren't particularly sharp either, yet he had been forced to work with them for some time now.
"But why?"

"Look up at the sky. The clouds will soon block out the moon, and then we'll get down to business."

The other agreed reluctantly, forced to realize Nick was right. When the moon finally disappeared behind the clouds, they both suddenly disappeared down the cistern. Roberto expectantly stayed behind. As they reached the third rung, Nick spoke up. "You stay here," he whispered. "There isn't enough room for both of us."

He removed a tiny flashlight from his pocket and cautiously crept down the metal ladder. Once he reached the hiding place, he cheerfully muttered, "It's here, everything is OK."

The little flashlight he clenched in his teeth didn't emit much light, but it was enough for him to move the shipment worth millions. He slipped one of his arms through the ladder and grabbed the rope bound around the package, which was fastened to a hook. He managed to unhook it with some effort before holding up the end of the rope forced into the depression to his companion holding onto the ladder above him.

"Are you holding it firmly enough?" he asked with a whisper.

"Sure."

"Pass the end on to Roberto," he whispered, "but tell him not to stand up, and make sure you wrap the end around your arm. Let me know when you're done."

"I'm ready," whispered the other man almost instantly.

Nick pulled the package out of the niche and supported one of its corners on the ladder's rung.

"Can we pull on it?" asked the long-haired man anxiously.

"Not yet." He descended a bit further to support the heavy bale with his shoulder from below. "Now, pull, otherwise it might fall into the water," he said, concentrating with all his might on the delicate manoeuvre before they managed to pull the heavy package upwards with united force, inch by inch.

The long-haired man appeared in the hatch.

"Put your back into it, grip it tighter," he whispered to his companion lying on his stomach above him, who cursed in reply.

"Easy does it," warned Nick from below before the package finally slid out onto the wet grass with a rustle.

All three of them lay flat out on the ground for a few minutes and paused and listened, panting for a few moments, but they heard nothing in the night-time silence. The clouds still blocked out the moon, and so they tugged and pushed the package onwards together, which was no small feat. Finally, they lifted the precious cargo to the top of the fence. Roberto doubled over and jumped over the low fence at once. The long-haired man forced the package over the fence with half of it still on top.

"Hold it for a moment so it wouldn't fall over," whispered Nick before jumping over the fence and gripping the package from the other side.

"Jump," he urged their cursing companion, who quickly followed the others before lowering the precious package down into the neighbour's yard.

They breathed heavily as the sweat covered their pores since they were over the worst part. A few minutes later, they listened with bated breath, yet the neighbourhood was still quiet.

The neighbour's yard was covered with bushes, so it was fairly easy for them to disappear into the dark. They crawled along the ground as they dragged the package to the end of the yard where they repeated the previous manoeuvre. They lifted the bale over to the other side before carrying it along the footpath a hundred yards, panting until they reached the jeep awaiting them. The car's trunk was open, so they silently placed the goods inside.

"Don't close it yet," whispered Nick cautiously. He quickly opened the front door. He gripped the steering wheel with one hand and grabbed onto the front of the car with his other hand. At the same time, the men behind him started pushing the jeep. They sweated heavily as they worked hard on the topsy-turvy track.

Nick knew the terrain well. When he'd brought the jeep here, he'd taken a good look around and moved two large stones, thus allowing them to roll the jeep here the narrow footpath down to the paved road leading out of the village.

"Close the trunk and get in," he called out quietly to the men. He didn't turn the headlights on just yet out of precaution and thus they drove on very slowly. Once they reached the intersection, he turned right and finally turned on the dimmed headlights and started rolling at normal speed.

"You could push that pedal a little harder instead of dawdling along," cursed the complaining man from the back. "Let's get it over with."

"What's the problem, are you freaking out? We're already done with the hard part by now," laughed Nick, recovering from all the pressure he was under. The road was deserted in the late-night hours, yet he still didn't want to take any risks.

"Damn you," cursed the nasty-looking man.

"Settle down," hushed Roberto, who had remained silent until now.

"You can go running off anywhere you want to with your cash in half an hour."

"That better be true," muttered the other man ominously.

After the Trafalgar intersection, Nick rolled onto the unpaved road. He turned off the headlights again just to stay safe. Although he progressed slowly, he finally passed through an open gate and followed the lights which faintly glimmered for a moment from the back of the garage. Nick cautiously drove the car inside before he sighed heavily, stopped the car, and disappeared inside the building.

Someone silently closed the garage door. The complaining man called out "We got it" to the man waiting next to the car.

"Get out and bring the stuff inside," said the hulking man, motioning towards the car.

CHAPTER 109

A dim light glowed in the living room. The fat Rodrigo sprawled across the tubby armchair. He held a large cigar amongst his thick, pudgy fingers. When he saw the package, he took a hit from his thick Cuban cigar and puffed the smoke into the air with satisfaction. "Go check it," he said to his companion, who quickly got to work.

"Well?" asked the fat man.

"Excellent."

Nick made a face. "It's always excellent," he noted smugly.

Rodrigo ignored the sarcastic remark.

"Take the stuff away and store it," he issued the order.

"Where's the cash?" asked Nick, getting right to the point.

"What's the rush?" grinned the man with a sneaky look on his face.

"It's late. I'm tired."

Well, you'll have plenty of time to sleep now, thought the fat man, standing up with some difficulty. "OK, come on. You're right, let's get it over with," he motioned with his head and slowly strolled over to the other room. Nick followed him.

Rodrigo panted as he sat down on the chair behind the desk. "Have a seat!" he said, pointing at the armchair opposite the desk.

Nick reluctantly sat down.

Rodrigo poured some booze from the bottle on his desk into two glasses. He pushed the salt and the drink over to Nick.

"Have a drink with me to our fine catch," he said, leaning forward to clink glasses.

Nick slightly frowned and swallowed the drink at once before licking the salt off the back of his hand.

Rodrigo lifted his drink to his mouth as well – just as someone entered the room. Nick turned around. As he did, the fat man quickly spilt his drink on the floor and licked the back of his hand to cover up his move.

"Get the cash," he said to the man who entered the room before pouring some more into the glasses.

Nick drank some more and set the empty glass down on the edge of the desk. It fell to the floor. This was surprising since Nick swore he'd set the glass down properly.

The fat pig was explaining something to him, which sounded oddly incomprehensible. Nick slowly leaned back as his head reeled. Everything became blurry in front of him.

For a moment, he saw himself getting on a plane with the bag full of cash. The stewardess politely showed him to his seat. Sandra was sitting at the window, just like the good old days, smiling at him, but the scene disappeared into the darkness. He silently slipped down onto the ground. He didn't even notice Rodrigo mockingly spilling the glass full of drugged alcohol onto his face.

Nick couldn't sense a thing. He wasn't sure whether or not he was about to leave this cruel world which wouldn't let him fulfil his final dream.

"Put him in his car and take him away. Leave him somewhere on the hill," said the fat man, puffing into the air. He ran his foot over the carpet beneath his desk, which hid his cache filled with the multi-million-dollar shipment.

The complaining man reached the edge of the village, where he cautiously drove onto a stretch of land covered with groves and shrubs. He stopped the motor and listened for a while before dragging Nick over to the driver's seat. He turned the handbrake off and quickly slammed the door of the car. Finally, he gave the jeep a push from behind. It rolled down the incline, first slowly and then gradually picking up speed.

Now that he was done with his job, the long-haired man quickly left the scene. He peevishly thought how only two hours ago, Nick was still fumbling with the package at their side, and now he was rolling down the hillside towards the ocean in his car. For some reason, the man didn't like this at all.

He returned to the house after a twenty-minute walk. He looking for his third companion, who was nowhere to be seen. He made the mistake of walking into the bathroom, where a cord slipped around his neck from behind.

CHAPTER 110

The stars grew pale, yet he didn't see any movement at all. Robert Grey finished off the rest of his coffee and sleepily got out of his car. He stretched after waiting for so long. Something was fishy. Could it be that Nick slip through his fingers again? No, that couldn't be, since he and his men had been monitoring the house all night long. Since dawn was fast approaching, he pulled out his phone and called his colleague.

"Nothing happened, right?"

"Right."

"Come down to the gate," he ordered and hurried off to the house with long strides. He couldn't wait any longer; he had to check on the cistern again. He might get the drugs to a safe place while his men kept an eye on the cistern. He was uptight of his long night-time wait didn't yield any results.

They entered the yard as soon as they reached the gate. Once he got to the patio, he checked the key, which was still in place. *But then, who was that lonely figure he saw in the night?* He had a bad feeling about it and anxiously ran behind the house. Much to his surprise, the door to the cistern was open. He knew at once that he had a problem. He disappeared through the hatch at once. He turned his flashlight on and exclaimed in protest before crawling out with an angry look on his face.

"The package is gone," he noted anxiously. He lost the game. His companions exchanged puzzled looks.

"That's impossible," noted one of them, blushing.

Grey's mobile started ringing, so he walked a bit further away.

"What's the matter?" he asked peevishly.

"We sensed some movement, but everything is quiet at the moment. What's your plan?"

"The drugs are gone," he relayed the bad news in a depressed tone, "but wait until I get there. Suddenly he had an idea. Turning to the other two policemen, he said, "Stay here and call me if anything happens."

He ran to his car, jumped in, and impatiently pushed down on the accelerator – a bit faster than necessary – racing down the road as fast as he could to Canos de Meca. He cursed himself for waiting in the car all night long instead of going after the man he saw at night.

The sky was getting brighter, and the edge of the horizon was turning red. A bit further away from the house under surveillance, André Breton waited in a car with three of his men.

Grey slowed down and stopped next to them. He leaned out the window. "Follow me!" he cried anxiously and parked his jeep in front of the gate of the suspicious house to block any possible way of escape. The Frenchman parked his car right behind.

Grey used his mobile to alert his men who were hiding behind the house. "All units go!" he ordered briefly, and the commandoes silently jumped over the high fence. The raid happened in a matter of minutes as they systematically combed through the house.

They found a fat man fast asleep on a broad bed. He was snoring out loud with his mouth open. Grey motioned to his men in the pale light of the early morning hours to handcuff the man as they hurried over to the other room with the Frenchman.

The first gunshot went off, reverberating dully throughout the house. The detective cried out and fell to his knees. The commando behind him fired back, and someone fell to the floor in the dimly lit room. One of their men turned the lights on, whilst the Frenchman took solid aim at the other, figure who was trying to escape through the window.

"Drop your gun, hands in the air!" he cried in a rough tone. The man straightened out and slowly raised his arms into the air. Breton hurried over and handcuffed him at once before frisking him and finally motioned to one of the policemen to take him outside. He turned around to Grey, whose leg was bleeding. "Call an ambulance!" he cried out to the policeman.

The detective's injury wasn't serious, so he limped on as he followed his French colleague.

"Let's head over to the garage," he suggested. They found it deserted apart from two empty cars. "We have to thoroughly search the whole house," he panted excitedly. "We need a dog. The drugs have to be here somewhere."

They found two bodies in the cellar. One of them muttered something one moment and was dead in the next.

In the meantime, the ambulance arrived. The workers tended to Grey's leg, but he wasn't willing to go with them. Instead, they took the casualties and the two bodies belonging to the gang.

The police thoroughly searched all the rooms in the house. They found multiple traces of drugs, yet the package was nowhere to be found. There was one more room to check: the study. They found a bottle of tequila on the desk, not full. They spotted a glass on the floor. They could still make out the stain of the booze on the floor, which the dog sniffed at and started scratching.

"We have to take the bottle and get it analysed," said Grey, handing it to one of the policemen.

Suddenly, the dog started whimpering and sniffing under the desk, scratching at the carpet. The detective crouched down with some difficulty. He ran his broad palm over the carpet, which was covered by the huge, hulking desk.

When his hand seemed to run into some obstacle, he cried out excitedly, "Help me! Let's get this off of here."

The officers came over and pushed the heavy desk aside. Grey folded the carpet to the side at once. They pried open the small hatch and discovered a hidden entrance. Grey and Breton walked down a wooden staircase, which creaked under their heavy footfalls.

In the windowless room, they found the package covered by a worn-out piece of tent canvas. Grey examined the box from every side, and when he found the tiny piece of tape he'd left on the box after sampling its content, he cried out, "Mission accomplished!"

He winked at Breton in satisfaction. "We made a big catch today!" he cried. He forgot all about his injury and leapt up in joy. "Perhaps the greatest catch so far," he added, wincing as he cradled his wound and the men high-fived.

There was still one piece missing to wrap up the case since the prime suspect was nowhere to be found. Perhaps he was wrong, and Nick Winkler had nothing to do with all of this? Maybe the man was fast asleep at home. Grey issued his final orders before leaving the site.

"Comb through the neighbourhood and keep monitoring the house at the beach."

CHAPTER 111

He had dinner with the commandoes who took part in the mission. They were celebrating, and they had every reason to do so. Robert Grey knew how lucky he was when the first gunshot was fired since he could have easily ended up dead. He knew well that his profession always entailed this kind of danger. However, he forgot all about his injury for the moment and was glad he could finally wrap up the case.

"Come on, let's have another drink," he offered to Breton after the meeting.

"I'd love to," the Frenchman said with a grin on his face.

Grey gazed at him cheerfully. He dug out his keys from his pocket, opened the door to his hotel room, and turned the lights on. He glanced at his watch. It was a few minutes after midnight. He picked up two glasses from the shelf before pouring them some cognac from the bottle on the table.

"Cheers," he muttered, downing the scorching liquid in a single gulp before comfortably leaning back in the sofa.

"You know," Grey went on, "I still feel a bit hazy about Nick Winkler and his wife. I'm not sure whether or not they had anything to do with all of this. Not to mention Pedro Gomez's sudden arrival, which shook things up a bit. What do you think about this?" he asked while reaching out for the bottle.

"I thought the woman was suspicious for a while. But ..."

"What do you mean, but?" asked Grey, leaning in closer.

"Yvonne shared a secret about her," replied Breton. "She asked me not to tell anyone about it. But since she might never come to, I'll share the secret with you."

"I'm listening."

"Yvonne's father passed away recently."

"And?"

"He was a famous plastic surgeon, who performed several operations on Sandra's face many years ago before she met Nick Winkler."

"What?" cried Grey in surprise, excitedly finishing off his cognac.

"Take it easy. I think I know what her secret is," he noted, relating the story about Morocco.

"Shocking."

"Yes, it is. You know, I was surprised too when Yvonne told me all about it."

"It sure is an unusual tale," muttered Grey. He stretched his legs and stared at the wall at length. His mind felt numb from all the booze, so everything was muddled up inside of him.

Breton noticed his colleague's numb since he was starting to feel the same way himself. He stood up and said, "It's late, so I'll go get some rest. Goodnight, pal."

Grey heard the door quietly slam shut before his head tilted back drowsily. He fell asleep right on the spot on the narrow sofa.

The following morning, he awoke with a headache. He yawned and sleepily scratched his head. He filled the tub with warm water and enjoyed the pleasure of taking a bath. He thought of Sandra – the cold-eyed, mysterious woman he'd been attracted to since the first time they met.

He got dressed later on. He was brewing a pot of coffee when the phone rang.

"What?" he cried in shock. "Are you sure it's him?"

"Yes. We found his driver's license in his pocket."

An hour later, he examined the body before hurrying back to his office. He decided not to put off relating the bad news. He called Sandra at once.

She acknowledged the death of her husband in a thin voice.

Grey warned her that she would have to come down to identify the body. He thought of her leg and promised to send a car to pick her up and then take her back to Marbella.

After the identification, Sandra prepared to head out with clenched teeth. It was hard to believe that she wouldn't see him again. He was gone for good, she thought, as her heart ached. She leaned on her cane as she sadly, hobbled over to the parking lot.

Robert Grey politely helped her get into the car.

"I would like to pay you a visit after the funeral," he noted, waiting for her consent.

She nodded before turning away, and the car slowly headed off.

Grey could tell that she was only willing to meet the detective in him, even though he secretly hoped that perhaps one day he could get closer to this gorgeous woman. He knew for sure by now that he no longer stood a chance.

He started working on his next case a few days later. A 15-year-old girl had died from a drug overdose.

He glanced out the window. The rain was drizzling outside. The phone rang, and he peevishly turned around to pick it up.

"Yes, I'll head over right away," he replied in an apathetic tone.

CHAPTER 112

After the funeral, Grey asked for an appointment and visited Sandra Winkler, who was wearing an elegant black dress. The sadness showed on her pale, freckled face. Her long red hair was tightly combed back.

"Have a seat. Can I get you a drink?" she asked sullenly.

"I'll have one if you have one."

"Whiskey?"

Grey nodded. He comfortably leaned back in the armchair before motioning at her with his glass and taking a sip.

"I came to see you," he began, "because a few things still aren't entirely clear, which I would like to ask you about."

"What do you have in mind?" she asked, quizzically raising her eyebrow.

"The case is closed. We might not see each other again." He paused for a moment. "Please, tell me how you met Nick Winkler in the past."

"But why? This has no relevance whatsoever. He's dead and gone."

"I know. I just wanted to know to tie up a few loose ends," he replied patiently.

"Fine," she acknowledged the matter with a nod. "What would you like to know?"

"Why did you undergo plastic surgery in Paris?" he asked her suddenly.

She blushed in surprise. "How do you know that?"

He waved it off. "Let that be my little secret. So?"

"It's very hard for me to discuss this."

"Well, you can still give it a try," he urged her benevolently. "Trust me, you'll feel better once you get rid of your secrets. That's always the case," he encouraged her, eyeing her expectantly.

"Well actually," she began slowly, "this is my third face. Frankly, I'm a three-faced woman."

"What do you mean by that?"

"I lost my original face many years ago, in Marrakech."

"How did you end up there?"

"I was kidnapped, but that's a long story. It's practically my whole life."

"I'm listening. I have plenty of time," urged Grey, comfortably crossing his legs.

She started to relate the tale of her chaotic life. Her complexion seemed tense and confused.

"Are you okay?" he asked in concern.

Sandra hesitantly shook her head, yet still carried on.

"I lost a man who I loved dearly, whilst my face was irreparably damaged," she continued relating her odd story before suddenly bursting into tears.

Grey sat down next to her on the sofa, wrapping his arm around her shoulder and handing her a tissue. He waited for her to cry her tears of bitterness.

Sandra suddenly perked up.

"I was left in an Arabic world with a mangled face, like a dog without a home. I was nobody," she whispered.

The tears welled up in the detective's eyes. "I'm sorry," he said gently.

"But that's not all since I soon found out that I was pregnant." She uttered the words to the detective, increasingly perturbed as she related her unusual tale." It sounds just like a fairy tale, right? I hope you understand."

Robert reservedly nodded.

Sandra felt like she did want to rid herself of all her secrets. She wanted to rid herself of the shadows of her dark past, so she carried on.

"We lived in Nick's riad until we managed to escape one day, yet my son was kidnapped after we made the crossing. As promised, Yvonne took me to Paris, where I had plastic surgery at her father, Dr Siran's, clinic. You can see the results of that yourself."

"How did you meet Winkler again?" he asked.

"Later on, I was working at a hotel where we bumped into each other. From that point on, he wouldn't let me out of his sight, which I was thrilled with since I was convinced that I could only find my son through him – which finally happened after a long time."

"So, he's the father."

Sandra flashed a dark glance at him and slowly nodded. Grey noticed her uncertainty.

"You married a man you didn't love," he noted, practically to himself.

"Well actually, I grew fond of him."

"What was your husband's occupation?"

"That's a tough question. I don't know. I think he was trading in antiques."

"Did you notice anything suspicious during your marriage?"

"He travelled a lot, often heading off for months to Barcelona, Marseille, London, New York, the Far East, and God knows where else."

"I have one more question to ask."

"I'm listening."

"Why did you go to Rio de Janeiro?"

"Do you want to know?"

"I'd appreciate it."

She sighed heavily.

"It was a strange coincidence," she said as if talking to herself. "My son fell in love with the daughter of Pedro Gomez, which I had to stop."

"But why?"

She glanced at him with an utterly devastated look on her face.

"Because Antonio and the girl were half-siblings."

"What?" cried Robert in disbelief, jumping up from the sofa. "So, that's why you brushed me off!"

"Yes, because I wanted to deal with the problem on my own."

"That means that Gomez and you..." He left the sentence unfinished.

"Yes, we loved each other, before we were cruelly separated by fate.

I thought that Pedro died. But one day, my son introduced us to his daughter. That's what started the landslide."

Grey suddenly recalled his recent conversation with the doctor.

"Now, wait just a minute," he noted, eyeing her with growing confusion. "You just said that Nick..."

"Yes, that's what I said. The truth is, I don't know who the father of my son is."

"How come you don't know?"

She fell silent.

"Please, tell me."

"Because I slept with two men in one week. I loved one of them, whilst I didn't have a chance to say no to the other. That's all."

Grey could barely hide his shock. He suddenly finished his drink and stood up.

"Look, I can help you with the dilemma of your son."

"How?" she asked anxiously.

"Because I know that your son and Pedro Gomez's daughter aren't siblings, even half-siblings."

"I don't understand."

"But it's simple," said the man with a grin.

"No!"

"Yes."

"So, you mean that the girl..." she didn't dare summarize the facts.

He interrupted her. "I meant that Pedro Gomez isn't Amy's father. She was from the first marriage of his wife, who passed away recently."

"Oh!" she gasped. "It was all because of me … my dear son. I separated them for no reason," she stammered incoherently.

He grimly eyed her for a moment before sitting back down next to her and squeezing her hand. They sat in silence for minutes. The room was slowly cast into the half-light, so he turned the lamp on.

Sandra suddenly cried out, as if stirring from a dream. "But I can't tell this to Antonio!"

"Come now, you're being far too dramatic. I'm sure your son will understand. Just don't shut him out. The problem is that you have too many secrets, and problems are piling up inside of you which you can't cope with anymore. You know, the best solution would be to tell all of this to him. You would free yourself from a heavy burden. Trust me," he added regretfully, glancing at his watch. "I'm sorry, but I have to get going now. Thank you for your time. Please, promise me you'll reveal your past to those who are close to you."

Sandra, however, didn't say a word and left the matter unanswered.

CHAPTER 113

After the funeral, Antonio flew straight back to New York. He promised to return in mid-December, and perhaps they would be able to spend Christmas, the most beautiful holiday of the year, together in Gale. The truth is, he had grown fond of his grandparents. His grandfather was full of wisdom concerning the matters of life and people's problems. He was crazy for his grandmother's fruitcake, her teary-eyed laughter, and their intimate conversations. He felt happy with his mother in the sunny villa since he felt surrounded by their love.

Sandra was left alone now, which further increased her sadness. Nick was gone for good, and her son had a life of his own. Even though she'd gotten him back for a brief period, she might, sooner or later, end up losing him for good because of the rest of her secrets, since she couldn't bear telling him the truth that Amy wasn't his sister after all and that she didn't know for sure that Pedro was his father in the first place.

She locked herself up for a long time and didn't meet anyone. She was bored as she puttered around and read books and watched

TV in the villa, or huddled on the couch and mourned her complicated life. The weather grew colder. The sky was blanketed in heavy clouds. It was unusually cold and almost constantly raining.

One day, the phone rang, as it did on so many occasions. However, this time, she reached out and picked up the receiver without thinking.

"Hello," she said quietly.

"So, you're home. Well, I tried calling you a lot, and I thought something happened or perhaps you left. Can I see you?" asked Pedro, getting right to the point.

Sandra was surprised, yet her pulse quickened. "If you want to."

"Of course, I want to, I'd love to," said the man on the other end of the line, fending off his excitement. "Today, tomorrow, the day after tomorrow?" he asked in a happier tone.

"How about tomorrow at five?"

"I'll be waiting for you in front of the gate."

"Fine, tomorrow it is," she added, yet she doubted herself at once, wondering whether she had done the right thing by agreeing to see him since her husband had only passed away a few months ago.

She checked her email. She received some great offers from a well-known travel agency. She had been thinking about this matter for weeks. She kept thinking about travelling to some distant location and disappearing for good. But who was she running away from? She wondered again, as she did so often on this matter. Nick was gone, so she had no reason to worry about him. But then who was she afraid of? she agonized relentlessly. She was unable or unwilling to answer this question.

She took a bath and washed her hair. The mirror was misted over in the steam. She wiped at its surface with her hand as she dried her hair and gazed at her image in the mirror at length. *You're alone, utterly alone,* she thought anxiously. *Your youth has slowly disappeared. Oh, my ugly youth,* she thought. *Well, that won't make me sorry,* she noted absently, slipping into her robe.

She hopped down on the sofa in the living room. What would happen tomorrow? And what did she want from Pedro anyway? Not to mention Amy. Oh, the whole thing was so absurd. No, she couldn't go through with all of this. As soon as she got out of one tangle, she fell straight into the next one. She felt like banging her head on the wall for being so cowardly as to keep her secrets to herself in Rio.

Ever since Robert Grey visited her and told her that Pedro was merely Amy's stepfather and that his wife had died, she had been thinking a lot about him. She pulled her legs up and rested her head on her knees, moping around at length. I'll leave, she decided suddenly. She turned her laptop on and reserved a flight online. She stood up in relief and walked down to the kitchen for a bite to eat.

She was pleased with her decision. There was no sense in sitting at home, locked up like this, ruminating over her irreparable past. She had to overcome herself and deal with the incessant agonizing which captivated her again and again. She thought of Dr Siran, who had tried shaking her from her depression in Paris with these very same words.

She felt completely changed by her sudden decision. She was swept away by travel fever. She flipped through her calendar and marked the day of her departure. She had four days left, during which she had plenty of time to take care of everything. Packing wouldn't take much time. Whatever she needed she could pick up on the way.

She walked over to her chest of drawers and searched for her passport. Her hands hovered over the secret compartment. It occurred to her that she hadn't opened it for years. The lid was stuck, so she had to make an effort to open it. She found a sealed envelope in the drawer. "To Sandra," she read in Nick's handwriting. She opened it in surprise and read:

In case something happens to me, my bank is located at the following address. Set Antonio off in his life. Once he's graduated, set up a private clinic for him. The rest is up to you. Nick

The bank's address was in Switzerland, and the letter was dated two years earlier. She found a key to a safe in the envelope along with the letter.

She was left standing puzzled for a while before she put the letter and key back into the drawer and carefully closed the lid of the recess. They were the only ones who knew of this hiding place.

She turned the lights off and lay down on the bed. She couldn't fall asleep for a long time. She tossed and turned, thinking of Nick. What should she do about the money? she wondered tensely. Robert Grey had gone to Madrid or God knows where else. Should she inform the police?

No. The case was closed, she assured herself. For Antonio's sake, she couldn't do that. The letter had been lying there for two whole years. Nick must have made quite a profit from his extended business deals. Yes, she recalled the way he always encouraged her, saying she could "spend as much as she wanted." There was no evidence that he was a member of a drug ring. His accident happened elsewhere. His body was found far away in the wreck of the car. The cause of his death was a drug overdose. The fat man they caught in Canos de Meca had been behind bars for months. Nevertheless, she decided to try to get in touch with Grey.

Still, she tossed and turned, thinking of the next day's encounter with Pedro. Oh, this was going to be hard. However, the next moment she thought the opposite. *OK, I'll go down to the gate, but I'll get right to the point and tell him to never come to visit me again,* she decided as her thoughts piled up uncertainly.

The following day, she made all the arrangements for her trip. When she came home, she spoke with the gardener and paid him three months in advance. She had known him for a long time. He was a decent man, and she trusted him. Finally, she dug out Grey's card and dialled his number, but she couldn't get through to him.

Her meeting with Pedro was fast approaching, and thus she grew increasingly anxious. She readied herself and rummaged through her wardrobe at length. She picked a coat and skirt and tried it on, critically eyeing herself in the mirror. She turned to the side and decided she didn't like the cut of the skirt. She took it off and went through her clothes again. *You're still mourning,* she reminded herself, putting on a black dress and untying her long red hair. No, that's no good. Finally, she nervously tied her hair up with a clasp made of pearls. She applied a faint layer of makeup to her face. Her simple, natural looks were reminiscent of her younger years.

The phone rang.

"Sandra Winkler," she answered at once.

"Is that you?" asked the detective in surprise, having forgotten her phone number. "How are you?"

"Thank you, I'm fine," she said, telling him about the letter. "What should I do?"

"Nothing. Don't do anything. This is up to you. We caught the gang, and Nick Winkler's death was an accident. Since we found no additional traces, we concluded the case as a drug overdose. I'm afraid I have to go now. Take care of yourself, and good luck."

Sandra held the receiver in her hands for a while before putting it down, feeling clueless.

CHAPTER 114

It stopped raining. She glanced at her watch. I have to go down to the gate, she thought. She draped her cardigan over her shoulders in the unusually overcast weather and walked out the gate. Pedro came walking up to her with an umbrella in his hand. He hastened his steps as he noticed her.

"It's good to see you," he said nonchalantly as if they had only met yesterday. Sandra welcomed him with a faint smile on her lips.

The rain was about to pick up again, so they hurried over the nearby bar on the beach before sitting down to a table, feeling cold. Pedro looked at her curiously.

"How about an Irish coffee?" he asked.

"Thank you, that sounds lovely. It's unusually cold, isn't it?"

"Yes, but hopefully it will pick up in a few days. At least that's what they say on TV, which isn't exactly scripture," he added. They furtively eyed each other for a while, yet they both smiled when they locked gazes.

She warmed up from the hot beverage. She felt somehow relieved. She was simply enjoying his company. His charming looks had somewhat changed over the years. There were some crow's feet around his eyes, yet his striking face, eyes, and slim shape hadn't changed at all. Okay, maybe he'd put on a few pounds. No one could imagine how much she had been thinking of him over the years. She thought of Antonio. What kind of woman could tell the man at this moment that he had a son? Oh no, that would be impossible.

"What are you thinking about?" asked Pedro, jolting her back to the present moment.

"Nothing special," she replied awkwardly, faintly shrugging.

Pedro felt he must be careful if he wanted to see her again, which is exactly what he wanted. He'd thought of her a lot since finding her at the house in El Palmar. He would be deeply pleased if they could at least be friends. Yet he hesitantly sensed that she didn't want to get close to him. This was their first person-to-person encounter for months. He faintly smiled. He opened his mouth several times, yet he didn't have the courage to speak of his past and was afraid of her rejection. Instead, he decided to have a light chat to avoid any awkward subjects.

"The detective mentioned that your wife..." she started, trailing off.

"I'm sorry," she added, awkwardly averting her gaze.

Pedro nodded with a sullen expression on his face. "My condolences for your husband," he noted, perhaps a bit too coldly.

"Thank you." The widow and widower thought Sandra cynically.

Their conversation halted again, and the pent-up tension grew between them. Finally, they managed to carry on a conversation, avoiding any important subjects and discussing frivolous matters before he walked her home.

"Can I see you again?" he asked a bit forlornly. Sandra had anticipated the question. She nodded awkwardly and quickly disappeared behind the gate.

Her silence scared him off. *It's better if I forget all about her,* he decided. He grimly turned around and bowed his head as he strolled down the street, caught up in his thoughts and puzzled by his behaviour. Despite that, the following morning, he called her number but slammed the receiver down after a single ring. *It's too early, I have to wait,* he warned himself.

He waited for three long days and called her again on the fourth day. There was no answer. *I'll try later,* he thought. He called her the following day and the day after that. Finally, he mustered his courage and rang the doorbell in the middle of the week.

The gardener peeked out from behind the fence.

"Can I help you?"

"I'm looking for Ms Sandra."

"She isn't home. She went away."

"Do you know where?" Pedro asked in shock.

The gardener shook his head.

"Do you know when she's coming back?"

"She didn't tell me," muttered the man suspiciously.

"Do you come here every week?"

"Yes, every Thursday."

Pedro nodded. "I'll keep in touch." He walked away peevishly. He was convinced that she was trying to avoid him or that she didn't want to see him again.

Pedro felt lonely as he sadly walked down the street. He had no one apart from Patricia and Lucy. God knows where Amy went. He didn't even have any friends he could meet up with, he thought sullenly.

CHAPTER 115

After the holidays, as always, Antonio flew back to New York, whilst Sandra continued wandering through the world like a hounded beast. One day she grew fed up of living out of a suitcase and decided to fly over to New York.

Her son looked worn out and tired when he welcomed her. There were dark rings around his eyes, which was no wonder since he regularly worked at a hospital while studying. Sandra was alarmed at the sight, so she stayed with him until the end of the semester. Every day, she patiently waited for him to come home and tended to him, helping him in any way she could. After exams, they both sighed in relief as the second year of his studies came to an end.

"It seems like you could use a longer vacation and some rest. How about flying off to Italy and then from there, on to Kenya?"

"That sounds great. I would love going with you," replied Antonio, having freed himself from a great deal of pressure. "The truth is that I'm a bit exhausted. You know, it's not easy to provide for your future," he added in an ironic, old-man-like tone. "Oh, by the way, I got a letter from grandma. They're doing fine, feeling well, and looking forward to our return. They told me to say hi, and asked me to tell you to stop by their place at the end of your journey – of course, with me in tow."

"I planned the same thing, but on a longer tour."

They spent a month in Italy. Naturally, they first visited Rome, which was slightly exhausting, since they wanted to see all the sights. They were captivated by Michelangelo's Pieta, the Vatican, the Sistine Chapel with its frescoes on the ceiling, the Coliseum, and the rest of the sights. Of course, they had to sample Italian cuisine as well. They often had lunch at small eateries where they browsed the menu in pleasure, the half of which was incomprehensible for them, but they always had some help. The waiter kindly welcomed them with a huge smile on his face and brought them an inevitable bottle of red wine.

One evening, they stopped in the crowd at the Trevi Fountain.

"Impressive, isn't it?" Antonio said.

"Yes, it is," his mother agreed. "The most famous baroque fountain in the world. Suddenly she winced and turned around. Someone had punched her in the rump. She awkwardly eyed her son.

Antonio smiled. "I think they thought you're my girlfriend or maybe my sister," he noted with obvious pride. He rested his hand on his mother's shoulder and planted a kiss on her face. This made both of them laugh. Indeed, she was quite a sight. Her red hair fell to her shoulders, and freckles dotted her suntanned skin. Her eyes glowed, and she seemed entirely carefree. It seemed like she was an entirely different person altogether. They spent their last two weeks in Florence and the Island of Capri before returning to Rome.

They left the Italian capital and flew off to Nairobi. Sandra thought of Nick, with whom she already visited Kenya a long time ago. She glanced at her son, overjoyed to have him at her side. After a long flight, they finally stepped out onto the red soil of Africa.

During their rich, diverse range of activities, they enjoyed the huge distances and the beauty of unspoiled nature. The taste of adventure and the proximity to the wild animals was an unforgettable experience for both of them. They had a chance to get a glimpse into the lives of the natives, which had remained unchanged for centuries. The natives' colourful clothes, proud bearing, and simple huts stirred up their emotions. The huge disc of the sun towered over the flat-top acacia trees on the endless savannah, reaching the edge of the horizon. Flocks of birds passed through its rays in the sky. A herd of elephants passed by in the distance. Nearby, dust billowed in the sky, which the torrid winds blew in their direction. It was as if a ghost drifted over the arid savannah.

"I think this is the most beautiful, diverse, and exciting continent I've ever been to," cried Antonio in exhilaration. "Africa is a continent of superlatives."

At night, they camped down and silently stared up at the starry sky above, which stretched like a canopy over the savannah. The proximity to nature unintentionally reminded them of their distant ancestors, as if those ancestors were sitting next to them. *It's true,* thought Sandra. Even after thousands of years, the descendants carrying their ancestors' genes still felt an inexplicable feeling taking control of them as if they had lived in the same place themselves. It was like walking into paradise, from the present into the past.

Sandra thought of how these intense feelings couldn't be described and had to be experienced. She felt that the beauty of nature was entwined with the way the people and animals living here struggled for their everyday existence. She thought of how the tangible closeness of life and death belonged to this wonderful landscape.

"Mom, where are we?" cried Antonio enthusiastically, again and again.

"It feels like we turned back the wheel of time."

Sandra laughed. "That's right, my son."

They went on hikes and exciting safaris. These dusty trips also revealed things they shouldn't have seen. In Nairobi, the inhabitants of the hobbled homes of the shantytowns lived amongst indescribable conditions. The poverty was apparent in the villages as well.

"I have to admit that I'm deeply moved by Africa," said Antonio. "Ever since I came here, I keep wondering what must be like in the rest of the countries? I might just come back here to help them out." Sandra had similar feelings.

"We've seen quite a few films about Africa, but it's different being here and seeing their real, everyday existence," continued the young man.

Three days later, they arrived in Switzerland. Before dinner, Sandra pulled out Nick's letter and handed it to her son.

Antonio read the brief message. "What should we do?" he asked in surprise.

"That's why I brought you here. We'll head over to the bank tomorrow," she said firmly before starting her meal.

The following morning, they opened the safe in the bank. Sandra pulled out the drawer, which contained various documents, stocks, gemstones, and pearls. Sandra glanced at her son, feeling clueless.

"Come on, we have to talk to someone," she said. "I don't know much about such matters

The bank clerk discreetly informed them that they were dealing with a lot of money and stocks. The man suggested they keep everything just the way it was. He opened an unlimited bank account for both of them. After dealing with official matters, they had lunch on the last day of their trip.

"So, what would you like to do?" asked Sandra with feigned ease. "Don't forget, you have to finish your studies first," she raised her finger in warning. Antonio nodded before thoughtfully raising his eyebrows.

"Nothing. I won't do anything for the time being. Just as you told, or rather ordered, me to do," he added with a grin. "I'll finish my studies first, and then I'll work at the hospital for a few years. I need the practice."

Sandra looked at her son with satisfaction. She was undeniably pleased that her son wasn't swayed by their fortune and didn't have a greedy nature. She was thrilled that he wanted to support himself on his own. They flew back to Lisbon in the evening and were reunited with her parents two days later.

The end of the summer was fast approaching. Sandra continued her journey across the world. She still didn't want to return to Marbella. She didn't want to meet the man she'd lost before, who might still be waiting for her.

She flew off to Shanghai, as far away as possible. Yet her thoughts still trailed back to her home.

CHAPTER 116

Antonio returned to Marbella for a brief period, since his mother asked him to take care of a few things for her. He opened the windows and doors to air out the house.

The dog days were in full swing in mid-August. He paid the gardener and took care of the things his mother had entrusted to him before heading down to the beach. He suddenly thought of Pedro Gomez, his father, who had no idea that he had a son. Antonio had been interested in the subject for quite some time, but he still didn't want to discuss the matter with his mother. He was apprehensive about meeting Pedro. Perhaps he wouldn't even dare ask about Amy's whereabouts. His wandering mother had been away for ages as if she was running away from someone. It occurred to Antonio suddenly that perhaps it was precisely this confession she was fleeing from.

After a few hours on the beach, Antonio had a bite to eat at a tapas-bar. He strolled home in the late afternoon, pondering and sorting through his thoughts. He made up his mind, hopped on a bicycle, and aimlessly cycled through the streets along the beach before hesitantly turning down the next corner. Yes, this was the place, he remembered now. After Nick's funeral, Pedro had explained to Antonio where he was living. Nevertheless, as he reached the gate, his courage seemed to fade away. It's a good idea to visit him, but what could he say to him, where to start? He hesitated for a while in front of the house before finally pushing the doorbell.

"How can I help you?" asked the woman who appeared at the gate. He blushed and explained that he was looking for Pedro Gomez.

The woman furtively eyed him through the gate. Perhaps she hesitated for too long since the young man started explaining that he knew the man.

"OK, OK, I'll open it right away," she replied, slipping the key into the lock. "If you want to, you can bring your bicycle inside," she offered.

"Thank you," he said in reply and introduced himself. The woman smiled at him. "Come inside," she said in a friendly tone. "Go ahead, he's sitting over there," she said, pointing at the spacious patio next to the swimming pool and leaving him alone.

"Hello there," Antonio said awkwardly.

Pedro looked up and cried out when he saw him. "Oh, is it you? Wow, what a surprise!" He sat up and stretched his limbs. "I was resting for a bit, but it's great to see you. It's been quite a while. Have a seat," he offered, pointing at the armchair next to him. "I'll be right back. I'll just fetch something to drink."

Antonio sat down and rested his gentle, delicate hands on the armrest. He crossed his legs and made himself comfortable. The garden exuded a sense of peacefulness in the approaching twilight. The air was filled with the sweet scent of jasmine bushes. *It's a nice place,* he noted to himself. He watched a squirrel dash by.

Pedro returned at once. He held out a can of beer to Antonio whilst opening the other with a quiet hiss.

"Salud," he noted cheerfully before taking a few sips. He was overjoyed to see his visitor.

"So, what is it like in New York?" he asked attentively.

"Well, I have a lot of studying to do, plus I'm working at a hospital. I hardly have any time for other things."

"How much have you got left?"

"I'm about to start my third year."

"What are you majoring in?"

"Dermatology."

"Great. Get in touch once you've graduated. You know, I've been thinking about starting up a private clinic for some time now. So, what do you say?"

"Are you kidding?" the young man said, blushing.

"No, this is no joke at all."

"I'm sure Mom would be glad to hear about it."

The man laughed out loud.

Antonio looked at him awkwardly, shaken by the unexpected offer.

"If you're serious, I would gladly accept your offer," he said with a huge smile, flashing his impeccable teeth. He lifted his can of beer and drank from it. "Thank you for thinking of me," he added, wiping his face, "but I still have a lot of studying left to do."

"No problem. It's done then," declared Pedro. "You know, this whole plan of mine is still further down the road," he continued, as if talking to himself. "It all depends on when I can get together the capital to pull it off. I found the right building, but the renovation would take up a lot of money, which is stalling the matter. Not to mention the furnishings, medical equipment, machines, and the rest of the things, which aren't exactly cheap either. Still, despite all the problems, I hope to open the clinic in the coming year."

Antonio almost offered financial help, but he stopped himself just in time. He wanted to discuss the matter with his mother first.

"So, tell me about yourself. What is the reason for your sudden visit? I haven't seen you since your father's funeral."

"He wasn't my father," Antonio noted carelessly.

Pedro Gomez was baffled from what he heard.

"What do you mean by that?"

"My mother faintly referred to a secret from her past. That's why I'm here."

"I'm listening," said Pedro, turning serious. An odd sensation seemed to press down on his chest.

"Back in Rio, I broke up with Amy because of Mom's secret," he explained, forcing himself to utter the awkward sentence.

"But why?" Pedro asked in shock.

"Because Amy's my sister."

"How is that possible?" cried Pedro in surprise.

Antonio related a few events from his mother's dramatic life, including plastic surgery in Paris.

Pedro laughed out loud. Suddenly, it was all clear. How could he have been so blind? Even since he saw her in Rio, he had been thinking about those long-lost days. Yet he always shooed away these absurd thoughts, since Sandra didn't resemble Vicky. Now it seemed as though he wasn't daydreaming after all.

"Look, if that's true, then..." Pedro left the sentence unfinished. The two men glanced at each other before suddenly jumping up and hugging each other.

"I'm proud to have such a tough young man as my son," he noted as the tears welled up in his eyes. He realized that he was no longer alone.

Antonio swallowed hard, struggling to subdue his feelings. Why had he waited for so long? He thought of how absurd it was to cover up these secrets.

Pedro gripped his shoulder.

"Look, I have something to tell you, too. Amy isn't your sister."

"What?" Antonio recoiled, turning deathly pale.

"The explanation is simple," Pedro said. "Amy was from my poor wife's first marriage. Your mother had no way of knowing that," he added, thinking of the scene in Rio when she wasn't willing to have a toast with them.

Antonio glanced at him in relief. "Why didn't she come here with you?" he asked.

Pedro sadly bowed his head. "Because, son, she ran off with a hippie. She severed all ties with us. I have no idea where she is and what she's doing. She doesn't even know that her mother died."

"I'm sorry. Then it seems like..." he started, without finishing the sentence.

"Yes, I'm afraid so."

"I'm flying back to New York tomorrow," Antonio noted, changing the subject. He started to write down his contact information.

"Wait," said Pedro, fetching a business card. "I want you to have my number as well."

"Thank you. It would be great if you could come to visit me."

"I might just do that," Pedro noted emotionally, eyeing Antonio oddly before asking the question, they had both avoided until now. "Where did your mother go?"

"She's probably already in Shanghai," Antonio told him. "She's been travelling for a long time now. She wants to be alone. Still, we spent the summer together in Italy before flying off to Kenya and learning all about Africa. You know, that continent blew us both away. We have some great memories of the place."

Pedro fell silent, with unformed sentences swirling inside of him. He envisioned the kind-faced woman in front of him again, the woman he had been futilely seeking for so long.

"And can you tell me how long she'll be away?" he asked.

"I don't know, but it seems like she needed to do this. She simply wants to forget," Antonio explained, awkwardly glancing at his father. "She has been coping with depression for some time now, but nobody noticed it. Including me."

"I didn't know about that," Pedro said.

"Do you remember when we were at your place in Rio?" asked Antonio.

"Sure."

"The following day, she told me I mustn't marry Amy because she's my sister, and then she attempted suicide that same evening. If I had gone home a half-hour later, she would have wound up dead. Do you understand?"

Pedro blushed. "Did she say anything else?" he asked numbly.

"Not at the time, but later on, she told me about her whole life. But fortunately, that's all behind us by now," he added, falling silent.

He hesitantly eyed his father, since he wanted to ask the man what had happened between them, but he simply didn't dare bring up the delicate subject. *Perhaps some other time,* he thought.

It was getting late. Dark shadows crept along with the bushes in the garden. The lights turned on behind the windows of the neighbouring house.

"I have to go," Antonio said finally, "but I'll be back for Christmas. I'll keep in touch," he added, standing up awkwardly. "I hope things will work out," he added without any insinuations.

"Son, I'll do everything I can." They hugged each other one more time at the gate. "If you need any help, I mean financial help, I'll be there for you."

"Thank you, but I can take care of myself. As I mentioned, I'm working at a hospital while studying at the university. I have enough money," he noted, thinking of the Swiss bank account.

"Still, don't forget that I'm here for you," Pedro assured him. "Take care, and see you soon. Have a safe trip."

Pedro watched as the young man cycled off into the distance. It was hard for him to believe that he had a son, yet he was thrilled with all his heart.

CHAPTER 117

Patricia glared at her brother confusingly. "Who was that good-looking young man?"

"You won't believe me," he noted with a grin on his face.

"Come on, tell me," she urged him curiously.

"My son."

"What? That can't be right. Where did you keep him in hiding until now?" she demanded, deeply offended.

"I didn't hide him. I didn't know he existed until now, understand?"

His sister cried in relief. "Come on, speak up, tell me everything!"

"I'm sorry, honey, but I have nothing to say since I don't know the details."

Patricia loved her brother. She was deeply upset when he moved to Rio for such a long time. Later on, he sent her a letter telling her that he got married. Although he showed up two years ago with his family, it was only for a brief visit.

Patricia had been mostly alone, and the years relentlessly passed over her. She still occasionally performed at a few events, but her success faded away. Lucy unexpectedly burst into the house, as she always did.

"What's wrong with you two?" She looked at both of them curiously. "Did something happen?"

"What makes you think so?" asked Pedro mysteriously.

"I can tell from the look of your nose. Something is making you happy."

"You have a great sense of foresight. It's true that I just found out the great secret," he explained cheerfully.

"Then tell me, let me share in your joy."

Pedro laughed out loud. However, Patricia answered the question for him.

"Would you imagine, he has a son, a good-looking, charming young man. He's around twenty-some-odd year old if I'm not mistaken. Right?" she asked, glancing at her brother.

"Twenty-one," noted Pedro.

Lucy was always fast to catch on, so she spoke her mind. "It's Antonio, right, the one I referred to previously?"

"You're right, it is him. It's still hard for me to believe it, but I'm pleased to have him," replied Pedro gladly.

"You know, when he rang the doorbell, I stared at him for a while for some odd reason, since his face seemed familiar. Come to think of it, he has your features," Patricia mentioned.

Pedro fell silent as he thought of the red-haired woman. He decided he must find her. He wouldn't let her run away from him again.

Lucy felt uncomfortable at the news since she clearly remembered that wild night she spent with Antonio. Luckily, they both had too much to drink and nothing happened between them, otherwise, she wouldn't be able to bear to look Pedro in the eye. Yet she thought that Antonio was Nick's son, she reasoned to settle her conscience.

But now the situation has changed. They were relatives, tied by blood bonds, and a chill ran down her spine. *You nasty whore.* She scolded herself for sleeping with anyone she happened to lay her eyes on. She went out into the kitchen and secretly took a swig of the bottle of vodka. She popped a candy she found on the table in her mouth so her breath wouldn't be so bad.

I was incredibly lucky, otherwise, this sin would have marked even my callous heart. And if Pedro found out about this, he would surely disown me for good, she thought as she anxiously sat back down to listen to her mother.

"I'm really glad that our family has been expanded by another person," she muttered awkwardly before getting up and leaving.

She needed a drink, so she went to a bar. She recalled Nick's funeral when she could openly take a good look of Sandra. Even then the woman had reminded her of Vicky, but she'd discarded the suspicion since she simply couldn't believe in such an odd coincidence. She thought back to the time of their escape. The last time she saw Vicky was at the riad in Marrakech. She lay motionless on the tiles of the patio, her face covered in blood. So, it seems she didn't die after all. *No, that can't be, since Nick told me she was dead,* she pondered hesitantly. Eh, she'd discuss the matter with Pedro when things settled down. Only the red-haired woman knew the whole truth about everything.

Lucy pondered the events of the past for a while before she thought of David, a man she had met at Nick's funeral. They'd gotten close to each other since. It was the beginning of a new chapter in her life. She thought differently about things now, which often surprised her. She'd grown fond of David and wanted to spend time with him. They got along just fine. The reason she'd come to see her mother was to share the news, but she decided to put it off for a while because of the newly revealed secret.

Pedro retreated to his room, where he kept on daydreaming. He had a son, and a red-haired woman he thought was dead had mysteriously resurfaced in this life. The thought deeply disturbed him, and it kept him up throughout the night. He searched his memories to recall her, yet her looks had faded from his mind over the long years. All he could focus on was Sandra's gentle complexion.

He was no longer alone, he thought as the magical sentence occurred to him again. He had a great song, and somewhere out there was a kind woman he would love to find. After a while, though, the resurfacing of this old secret wore at his nerves. He was afraid the whole thing was just a dream. *Why didn't she tell him in Rio that they had a son?*

Suddenly, he was filled with doubts. If she had any feelings for me, she wouldn't have run away, yet she disappeared a long time ago. He was uptight, and he kept tossing and turning in bed. In his dreams, he tried to hug his sweetheart as she grew increasingly distant from him.

CHAPTER 118

Sandra returned to Marbella in early December. The La Concha Mountain was shrouded in clouds. The western wind stirred, chasing dark clouds over the endless waves. The gusts buffeted the tops of the palm trees. The leaves of the orange trees in the square in front of the mayor's office were bunched up in the cold, with the oranges defiantly swaying to and from in the stormy winds. The sky grew darker, and the rain slowly began drizzling. She buttoned up her coat and wrapped her shawl around her neck. She hurried along a narrow street in the old district of the town, which seemed deserted. She dug out her umbrella from her bag and turned to face the fierce winds as she struggled to open it. The umbrella twisted inside out and broke. She dropped it in the nearest waste bin in annoyance and ran off to her car, freezing in the cold air.

She soon walked through the broad glass doors of the La Cañada shopping mall. She stopped at one of the bars and asked for a cup of coffee while eyeing the barista, who was working with her back to Sandra. When the coffee came sputtering out of the machine, the girl placed her cup under the spout and set it down in front of her customer with a faint smile on her face. Other people were waiting for her attention at the counter, so she turned to deal with them. Sandra ripped open a packet, poured sugar into her cup and slowly stirred the fragrant liquid which was a far cry from the Portuguese bica.

Someone touched her shoulder.

"Hola," said Lucy in welcome. "Well, we've finally met," she noted cheerfully. "I haven't heard a thing about you since Nick's funeral," she lied as she sat down on the tall bar stool next to the astonished woman.

"You look great!" she added whilst closely scrutinizing the woman's face and recalling the hardship they'd shared in the past. *Yes, Sandra and Vicky could easily be the same.*

Sandra stood her glance for a while before suddenly speaking up.

"What is it? What do you want from me?" she asked in a rather hostile tone.

"Nothing," Lucy pouted. "I'm just glad that we've met, that's all."

Sandra's tension filtered away and she unintentionally recalled the old times. She remembered the young girl she picked up in her car all those years ago. The thought made her ease up and smile. They locked glances as the past slipped through an invisible hourglass within a single second.

Lucy suddenly gripped her hand. "Look, I took a good look at you at the funeral, and I already had the feeling that it was you." She got right to the point. "I'm glad you're alive and that you didn't die back in the riad. I've been thinking a lot about those times since I was the cause of your misfortune. It was all my fault. Please, forgive me."

"Don't blame yourself," said Sandra through her shock at being recognized. "It wasn't your fault at all."

Lucy's eyes glowed from her reply. "Yes, it is. If I wouldn't have stopped, those two henchmen wouldn't have caught up to me," she sniffled. "And then those horrible things wouldn't have happened to you and the people around you. Please, can you find it in your heart to forgive me?"

"Oh, come on, forget about it. That's all done and dusted. I think our fates are written in a big book somewhere. I never thought for a moment that we could choose our future."

Lucy eyed her in relief.

"You might be right. We haven't seen each other for a long time, and I thought you died. But please keep in mind that I never forgot you over the years. I'm sorry about Nick. I knew him well since I was his wife for a brief period."

"What?"

"You didn't know about it?" Lucy cried in surprise.

"I didn't know it was you.

"Ah! Don't mind, it makes no difference now," she said and laughed out loud.

"Why are you laughing?"

"Do you remember the time I asked you for a ride and that Jaguar was trailing us with two men inside, Nick and Pedro? Did you think our, fates would be so closely entwined, perhaps for good? That we would meet again, after all these years?"

Sandra shook her head. "No, not really. I think that's what they call an odd coincidence."

"Yes. Please, if you're feeling lonely and need someone, just let me know. I'm here for you, understand?" she added in a practically demanding tone. "We've known each other for ages, and we've crossed paths several times, right?" she asked, falling silent as she suddenly recalled the time she was forced to overhear Nick and Antonio's bickering. She finished her coffee to hide her confusion.

Sandra was moved by what she just heard. She thought back and remembered how Lucy wasn't the type to easily open up to someone.

"Will you accept my friendship?" Lucy asked, looking Sandra deep in the eye, her face still reminiscent of her former features.

Sandra held her hand. "Absolutely. I already accepted it all those years ago," she added, leaning over and caressing the younger woman's face. "So how is life treating you?" she asked, kindly changing the subject.

"What do you mean?"

"I was just asking. I don't mean to pry."

Lucy ran her fingers through her thick hair.

"I guess you know David, right? Since he was there at the funeral..."

"Yes, in passing," Sandra laughed mysteriously.

"Well, we've been seeing each other for a while, and we get along just fine."

Sandra turned serious as she looked at Lucy. "I've known him for a long time, and I consider him my friend. Don't forget, he's an open-hearted and exceptionally decent man. He's been disappointed twice. I hope you won't be the third time this happens to him?"

"No, definitely not. I think I've become more mature, even if it's a bit too late for that."

"Great."

"I love him and want to stay with him," she added hesitantly, "if that's what he wants." She ran her hand over her smooth forehead. "What about you?"

"Hmm, nothing has happened to me, and nothing will happen," she replied with a sad look on her face.

Lucy giggled as she furrowed her eyebrows.

"Did you say something?" asked Sandra.

"No, not a thing," noted Lucy, giggling before she finally spoke her mind. "I think something's going to happen to you soon," she grimaced mysteriously. She suddenly glanced at her watch. "I've got to go now. I have a date with David."

CHAPTER 119

Lucy gladly glared at the ring glimmering on her finger. David had proposed to her, and she'd said yes – perhaps a bit too quickly. She had been living on her own for a long time. She hadn't exactly been an angel. She'd enjoyed her life and gone from one fling to the next before growing jaded and living up too much of her youth. Perhaps she didn't love anyone... maybe except for Nick. She secretly admitted that she had always been a selfish, calculating person, but she felt that she'd changed since she met David.

"You seem out of sorts," he said to stir his suspiciously silent fiancée. Lucy lifted her glass. "Salud. I think we're going to get along just fine."

He toasted with her in satisfaction. The waiter smiled as he brought them their dinner and wished the loveable couple bon appétit.

"Do you like it?" asked David.

"Yes," said Lucy as she skewered another piece with her fork. "Taste this."

"Hmm, that's not bad, but mine is better," he said as he saved the most delicious bite for Lucy.

"Aha," she teased him as she focused on the taste and smacked her lips with a serious look in her eyes. "It is delicious. I'll ask for it the next time we come here."

"I'll remind you of that," grinned David, but his smile wasn't due to their tasty dinner. He was simply enjoying her candid behaviour. She can't keep any secrets or lie, he thought. Yes, this is a lot better than stumbling through the dark. He thought of Carmen for a moment, who'd fooled him for years.

If two people want to be together with the least, they can do is be honest with each other, he thought. *Sincerity is an indispensable form of love, not to mention that it restores our inner self and internal balance. Although, indeed, no one is perfect, yet many things – if not everything – can be pardoned.*

She watched him for a while.

"What?"

"Would you believe it, I bumped into Sandra today," Lucy mentioned.

"And?" asked David, eyeing her attentively.

"My assumption was right."

"What assumption?" he asked quizzically.

"Sandra is none other than Vicky, a woman I thought was dead," she explained, briefly telling him about their shared past.

Well, well, it seems all secrets are revealed in time. So, she finally admitted it. He was pleased by this unforeseen development since he'd charged her and perhaps even harassed her with the same information in the past. The freckled lady with gentle features would never admit the truth to him.

"Oh, and there's another secret," continued Lucy, slightly leaning forward to him.

"Go ahead," said David, holding back his laughter.

"Would you believe that Pedro, my uncle, is the father of Sandra's son, Antonio?"

David turned grim. "As far as I know, Nick was the boy's father, and the mother passed away a long time ago," he explained in surprise.

Lucy laughed and related the old story to him. "You know, if Nick was still around and caught wind of this, Sandra would be in trouble."

David tactfully fell silent. It's a small world. Many years ago, he was with Vicky for a short time, although that might be an exaggeration...

"How old is he?" he asked, cutting off his train of thoughts.

"Who?"

"Antonio."

"I don't know exactly. He's in his twenties and attending university."

David suddenly understood Vicky's unspoken rejection and the reason for her sudden disappearance, yet he dropped the subject and focused on a more important matter.

He glanced at his future wife. "So, when should we schedule the wedding?" he asked, looking deep into her eyes.

Lucy happily giggled at him. They started brainstorming and quickly got caught up in the planning of their future joyful event.

CHAPTER 120

When Sandra finally came home, she carefully put down packages full of Christmas gifts on the sofa and called Antonio.

"So, when are you coming?"

"Four days from now. I'll come on the usual route, through New York, Lisbon, Faro, as agreed."

"Fine, see you at the airport in Faro. I can hardly wait to see you."

"Me too."

She felt a lot better now that she'd finally taken care of the last, most beautiful holiday of the year.

She walked into the bathroom, turned on the water, and took a long, warm bath. She closed her eyes and lost herself in her thought. His image appeared in front of her again, yet she was still uncertain. She was apprehensive of him, herself, her surroundings and perhaps even her family since she simply couldn't bear to discuss her secrets openly with him. She might be mistaken, and Antonio might be Nick's son after all. She always felt worried as she thought about things like this.

No, she didn't dare tell him the truth about what happened at the riad all those years ago. She knew it was easy to do a paternity test nowadays, but for some reason, she shied away from this. If Nick was Antonio's father, she didn't want to know. She dried herself and donned a bathrobe before impatiently combing her tousled red hair. She wanted to brush her teeth, but her electric toothbrush wouldn't start. She reached into the drawer and searched for some batteries in annoyance, yet could only open the device's battery case after a lengthy struggle. The device finally whirred to life. After brushing her teeth, she reached out for her jar of cream and applied some on her face.

Tomorrow, she decided, she would write Pedro a short letter. That would be the best and most comfortable solution. She turned the lights off and headed to the bedroom. The lamp cast a dim light next to the bed. Their former marriage bed reminded her of Nick. She felt cold as she slipped under the sheets and there was no one next to her she could cuddle up to.

She breathed calmly as she slipped into a deep sleep, departing to an unknown location. Could it be that she lived a life with two homes? Perhaps that was true for all of us, and the dreams we experience in a far off realm take place.

The following morning, she wrote the letter and excitedly mailed it off. *I finally did it,* she thought with a sigh, yet her heart still felt heavy. She started panicking and felt increasingly anxious. In the afternoon, she quickly gathered up her belongings, stuffed them into her suitcase, and dragged it over to the garage before putting it into the trunk with some effort. She practically ran back inside. She picked up the Christmas gifts and carefully placed them on the back seat. She smiled in relief at the thought of spending the approaching holidays with her family. In the evening, she fixed herself a bite to eat, which she polished off with little interest. After taking a bath, she set her alarm clock. *I want to have an early start,* she thought as she sat down to watch TV.

In the meantime, Pedro was standing outside the house. He saw the lights come on in the living room. He stopped in front of the gate and rested his hand on the buzzer but didn't dare to press it.

He could finally recall the faint birthmark under her shoulder. He would have to check for that. If it was there, then she was Vicky, the girl he'd presumed dead a long time ago. He anxiously wondered how could he check for it – he couldn't just ask her to get undressed and show him her birthmark. Eh, damn it, he'd had enough of this. All he had to do was patiently wait for the right moment to come. But how long he would have to wait? These unresolved matters made him increasingly anxious. He simply had to talk to her. He had been planning this for a long time, and he kept looking for her.

He was caught up in his thoughts and failed to notice that he was already walking across the sandy dunes of the beach. It seemed like he would be ready to open his new clinic in the first half of the next year. He had taken care of almost everything, except one thing: Sandra, the redhaired woman, who seemed unapproachable.

He quickly turned around and headed back to the house with a determined stride. What would he ask from her? he wondered, since he already knew what counted. Antonio had personally shared the secret with him, he thought, faltering for a moment. He hesitated before finally pressing the doorbell and eyeing the entrance with bated breath. When he heard her approaching steps, he nervously bit the edge of his mouth. He simply couldn't think of anything to say.

"Who is it?" asked a familiar voice from behind the locked gate.

"It's Pedro. I want to talk to you. It's urgent," he added with an aching throat.

She swooned; it seemed her premonition had become real. He couldn't have read the letter yet since she'd only mailed it in the morning.

The key quietly rattled in the lock and the door opened. The full moon illuminated their anxious faces.

"I know it's late, but..." began Pedro.

"That's okay," interrupted Sandra quickly. She tried hiding her tension by hurrying ahead with quick steps. As she reached the house, she offered him a seat with a frightened look in her eyes.

He didn't sit down.

"A drink?"

"No."

His face was pale as he faced her with a perturbed look in his eyes before moving up to her and gripping her shoulder. Sandra averted her gaze with a blush, yet she felt his gaze boring into her, which urgently forced her to look him in the eye. They understood each other without saying a word. Pedro tenderly embraced her, and the old, unspoken love for each other vibrated in the air between them. Suddenly, the joy of their reunion swept all their problems away. When Pedro left in the early morning hours, Sandra remembered the letter. If he finds out the truth, he won't want to see me again, she thought with a twinge in her heart.

The sky was turning red on the eastern horizon, yet she still felt his burning embrace and kisses on her body, which made her tremble. She buried her face in her pillow with concern. She simply couldn't afford to lose him again after all these years, she winced in despair. She was stirred from her gloomy thoughts by the sound of her alarm clock. She composed herself and got up. An hour later, she was racing down the highway towards Algarve.

CHAPTER 121

He got up late. His sister giggled as she asked him, "Were you out frolicking late last night?" She handed him a cup of coffee without waiting for his answer.

Pedro grinned without saying a word.

"So, you were," repeated Patricia, her attention shifted to him. *He's in a good mood, he seems entirely different,* she thought.

"Do you think I'm that type of guy?" he asked mysteriously. He picked up a slice of toast from the bread basket and put some spread on his plate.

Lucy burst into the room with a beaming smile on her face.

"*Hola,*" she welcomed both of them and sat down at the table opposite Pedro.

"Help yourself," said her mother encouragingly.

Lucy poured herself a cup, filled it with coffee and two lumps of sugar, and slowly stirred while glancing back and forth between her mother and Pedro, who was now flipping through the morning paper. She set her hand on the table, so they would notice the ring.

"You came early," her mother noted.

My God, how time is flying, thought her mother about the good old days. For some reason, she remembered a summer afternoon with Nick running towards the beach with her daughter before splashing in the water with shrill laughter. Yes, that was the beginning of something. That young man was a lot younger than her, yet she still went through with that absurd relationship. She already knew at the time that it was futile, yet the sense of adventure swept everything else away. Years later, she felt a bitter sense of jealousy when she found out that Nick had married her daughter, and the hatred found its way into her heart.

"What happened, there's something you want to tell us, right?" she asked, glancing at her daughter again.

Lucy fell suspiciously silent. She played with her napkin with the hand carrying the ring, and since no one noticed the glittering piece of jewellery, she spoke up: "I'm getting married soon."

"And who is the lucky man, if you don't mind me asking?" her mother asked in surprise. Pedro peeked out from behind his paper without saying a word.

"David Stone."

"Do we know him?" Patricia asked her brother, who shrugged in response.

"We would like to have dinner on Saturday so you could get acquainted with each other," Lucy added quickly to fend off any further explanations.

"Well, isn't that a modern introduction. I hope I won't offend you by asking how long you've known this gentleman, what's-his-name? I trust he is a gentleman."

"Well, it might be hard to believe, but he is," insisted Lucy in a serious tone.

The mother sensed her unusual emphasis, which somehow had a comforting effect on her.

"How long have you known him?" she asked in a level-headed tone.

"About a year. But Mom, don't worry, this time it's different," she said, thinking of Nick. "Look," she added, raising her hand in the air. "Isn't it pretty?"

The mother glanced at the ring. She could tell at once that it wasn't a cheap trinket. "Yes, it's nice," she said, finally smiling at her daughter.

"I'm sure you're going to like him too," she noted, glancing at Pedro, who folded up his paper and eyed the ring. "It's nice," he said, standing up. "So, it's the day after tomorrow at when?" he asked briefly.

"We'll pick you up at eight."

"Fine," he noted with a smile. "Congratulations," he added, walking out on the women.

He went up to his room and stared out the window at length. The rain was pouring outside, casting the day into the gloom. He engrossed himself in some reading for a while before suddenly closing the book, unable to follow the story. He couldn't stop thinking about Sandra. He went over to the phone and dialled her number, but there was no answer. He restlessly began pacing up and down the room before hopping down on the sofa. *Get yourself together,* he warned himself, yet he ended up calling her again ten minutes later.

He impatiently put on his coat in the late afternoon and headed over to her house. As he reached the house, he pressed the doorbell. He slipped his hand back into his pocket and waited for a while, yet the house was silent behind the garden.

Where did she disappear to now? he wondered despondently. *Could It, be that she ran away again?* No, that couldn't be, since she'd embraced him so warmly last night. Nevertheless, he walked back home with a heavy heart after futilely waiting at length.

"Aha!" he cried out. Perhaps she'd gone out shopping. He looked around in alarm, wondering if anyone had heard him, but the street was deserted. It suddenly occurred to him that he'd forgotten to check for her birthmark, which he didn't mind at all. As he got home, he noticed his sister had left. He sat down and waited for a while, yet there was no sign of Sandra. He poured himself a drink, which he relished. He felt cold after his lengthy stroll in the chilly weather.

The fire was barely flickering in the fireplace. He removed the grate and tossed another log on the flames. He leaned back in his armchair and thoughtfully stared at the fire. Even if she's lost, I'll still have to find her," he repeated to himself.

He spotted the white envelope on the table, addressed to him. He opened it at once.

"What?" he cried in shock, reading the lines over and over. He angrily crumpled up the paper and tossed it into the flames. He felt so anxious that he didn't know what to do with himself. He dialed her number, yet the phone just kept on ringing over and over. *Why hadn't she said anything last night? So that was why she'd disappeared so suddenly. She'd run away from the awkward subject like a coward.*

He gazed at his empty glass and picked up the bottle. He thought of Antonio, his high forehead, intelligent gaze, and athletic shape. He barely knew the young man, yet he'd still grown fond of him somehow. He couldn't lose his son already, yet this was no laughing matter. He poured himself another glass and his head felt heavy, which of course, didn't resolve this outrageous situation.

CHAPTER 122

Sandra was preparing for the holidays with her loved ones in another house. She was glad to be with them and sat enjoying the warmth of her home in front of the fireplace.

The fire was burning low and the cinders had crumbled into dust, so she tossed another log onto the heap. Her parents and Antonio were already fast asleep, yet she was still snuggled up in the armchair with her arms pulled up close. She stared at the flames as the wood turned into glowing embers, thinking of Pedro. *He must have received the letter by now,* she thought with a heavy heart.

The following day, she was helping out in the kitchen. She leaned over the sink while washing some fruit under the running water and looked out the window.

Her mother was happily busying herself around the kitchen.

"Watch what you're doing, your shirt is soaking wet," she warned, folding her daughter's sleeves up without waiting for a reply.

"Thank you," Sandra said, lovingly glancing at her.

Her mother noticed the golden bracelet at once — the one they'd bought for Vicky's twentieth birthday all those years ago.

"Are you still wearing it?" she asked emotionally.

"What?" Sandra noted with a start.

"That," her mother said, pointing at the bracelet. "I haven't seen you wearing it before."

"I lost it, but since I found it, I hardly ever take it off," she said, leaning over to her mother and planting a kiss on her cheek. "Since it's from you. That makes it more precious to me than the Koh-I-Noor diamond," she said with a mischievous smile. She slowly started humming the song her mother used to sing to her a long time ago when she was a little girl. She even nodded her head to the tune while dicing the vegetables on the cutting board.

The tears welled up in the woman's eyes as she recognized the familiar tune.

"Watch what you're doing, don't cut your finger," the mother warned again.

She thought of how attentive Sandra was. Her daughter never let her labour on her own in the kitchen. She'd raised a good child, as opposed to the woman living in the neighbouring villa, who complained that when her son comes to visit her for the holidays with his family, he never helped her out. They told her that they came for a vacation, not to work. Well yes, without any love, they just used her both financially and morally. She was lucky that her child wasn't like that, she thought as she furtively glanced at her daughter.

"Something smells good," said the father as he entered the kitchen, curiously peeking into the pot.

"You could open the bottle of wine. The lunch is almost done," said the wife, happily smiling at her husband.

"Antonio!" cried Sandra.

"Yes?"

"Wash your hands and set the table."

"My hands are clean."

"But still, wash them," Sandra insisted. She stirred the stew again before taking out the tablecloth from the drawer and handing it to her son.

She kept looking out the window during lunch, often glancing out at the raging sea. It was raining outside. The dark clouds were running low, blanketing the sky. She wanted to go for a walk on her own, but she didn't dare set out in such stormy weather.

The villa was quiet in the late afternoon hours, and her parents lay down for a nap. Sandra was sitting in the living room with Antonio, flipping through magazines and newspapers.

"After our vacation, when you asked me to take care of a few things in Marbella," began Antonio slowly, "I visited Pedro, who told me that he will soon open a private clinic. Can you believe that he told me, I could work at his place once I finish university?"

Sandra's heart fluttered in her chest. "And?"

"I accepted the offer at once. What do you say? It would be a great opportunity."

Sandra smiled. "That's up to you," she said anxiously.

"He also mentioned that he has to get some money together to realize his dream. I almost offered him my help, but I wanted to discuss this with you first."

"I would wait with that if I were you." She thought of the letter and the fact that Pedro surely knew the truth by now.

"Fine, I'll wait if you think that's what I should do." He stood up and looked out the window.

"You know, I finally told him to his face that he was my father," he mentioned the delicate subject, turning back from the window.

"What? What did you tell him?" she stammered as she stood up.

"Yes, I told him the truth, since you would never do so," he said, his words bouncing off towards her like ping pong balls across the table. "This is my business too."

"It is, but you could have spoken with me first."

"Why, since nothing happened after all these years? You always put off delicate matters like this. I have the feeling that you've been keeping secrets all your life. You've retired into yourself. You don't trust a soul. I'm not the type to stay silent. If something is bothering me or if I'm facing something unpleasant, I want to clarify it as soon as possible to free myself of the nagging thoughts. You, on the other hand, you always keep your problems locked up inside of you, and I'm sure you keep worrying about these things."

"I don't want to listen to this anymore," said Sandra, putting her hands over her ears. She stood up and turned to the window before suddenly running off to her room. She fell on the bed and bitterly cried over what her son had just told her, and also over the letter she had written to Pedro. Antonio was right – she always kept secrets. Yet it occurred to her again, that she didn't even know for sure what the truth was.

The twilight was settling over the house when Antonio quietly slipped into her room. He sat down on her bed and caressed his mother's head.

"Please don't be mad at me for being so tough on you and telling you what happened and what my feelings are. Believe me, I didn't do it to hurt you. The truth is, I want to help you. And I've been wanting to help for a long time, understand? But I don't know-how. Ever since Nick died, you've been travelling from one place to the next. I don't want you to keep on wandering from one country to the next just so you wouldn't have a home. I would like you to find your way back to yourself, for you to finally open up to everyone. I think that if we open up and let the other person know what we're really like, we will probably be accepted and understood."

Sandra sat up. She lifted her arms and pulled her only son close to her, running her fingers through his thick black hair.

"I know, son, I know you're right. I've been forming the sentences inside Me, to tell the truth, but something always scared me. I was frightened, and I still am frightened of myself and everyone else, life, surprises, and unforeseen developments, but the scariest of all are the coincidences which always interrupt my life again and again."

Antonio looked her firmly in the eyes. "Don't be afraid, do you hear me? I'm here for you. Grandma and Grandpa are here as well." He faltered for a moment, thinking of Pedro, his father. "We're all here for you, whatever happens. Do you understand?"

She hesitantly nodded.

"I don't like it when you back off and run away from everyone," he continued in a softer tone. "When I look at you, I feel concerned."

"What are you afraid of?" she sniffled.

"Don't you think I noticed how men stared at you in Rome?"

"One of them even pinched my butt, do you remember?" she giggled through her tears.

Antonio laughed as well. "I remember." He was glad that his mother was smiling again and that perhaps she could set aside her fears for a while.

"Look, have the courage to face yourself. We all know that life is short, don't waste it," he said with a mischievous smile in his eyes. "You know, a few years ago, I read on the Net that a woman is living in Georgia who's 130 years old, completely healthy and, listen to this, she drinks vodka every day." They shared a laugh over this. "Would you like some?"

Sandra shook her head. "Thank you for consoling me," she said to her son, "for giving me faith."

"I love you," said Antonio in conclusion. "Get some rest until dinner," he suggested, walking out of the room.

CHAPTER 123

The meeting was a success. Patricia instinctively liked David at once.

"Lucy can count her blessings," she said to her brother in satisfaction when they got home late at night.

"I like him too. He seems like a decent, normal man."

"That's true. If you don't mind, I'm going to bed now, since I'm a bit exhausted," said his sister in parting.

Pedro remained seated in the armchair for a long time. Well, at least Lucy is happy, he thought morosely. He felt lonely since the redhaired woman had disappeared from his life again. She'd vanished like a fairy that appears in your dreams. She charmed him and then left him all alone. He thought of Antonio as well. Of course, it was strange for him to suddenly have a young man as his son, yet when he read her letter, his joy flittered away and his dreams were dashed. An odd twist of fate, he thought bitterly.

The following day, after taking care of a few phone calls, he headed down to the kitchen before lunch.

"Can I help you?" he asked his sister helpfully. She noticed her brother had grown sad and quiet recently.

"Oh yes. Could you open a bottle of white wine? Lunch is almost ready," she said in a hurry, carefully turning the fish over in the pan.

"Smells promising," he noted hungrily as he removed the cork with a quiet pop. The phone rang, and Pedro answered it. "Hello?"

"Happy holidays!" said Antonio warmly.

"Same to you, son! I wish you all the best."

"Dad," said Antonio absently, surprising himself. Pedro's heart was filled with warmth.

"Yes," he said quietly.

"Mom is here with me. You're the only one who's missing. Five hundred kilometres? Not so bad. If you would like to spend the holidays with us, I would love to see you here in Gale at my grandparents' villa."

Pedro almost dropped the receiver in surprise.

"Are you still there?" asked Antonio in a louder tone.

"Yes, I'm here, but what will your mother have to say about this? I don't think she would be glad to see me."

"Don't worry about her, I'll take care of everything, just come and visit us. Leave as soon as you can," he said, giving the address. "If you have any problems on the way, just call me. You know my cell phone number, right?"

"Yes."

"Great. So, what do you say?"

Pedro hesitated for a moment before making up his mind.

"Fine, I accept your invitation, and I'm grateful that you thought of me," he said firmly.

"Of course, I thought of you! You're my father, so you have to be with us during the holidays. I'm looking for your call. See you soon!"

He was left pondering in the room. He'd agreed to come, which meant he accepted what Sandra wrote to him, but he had no other choice. He suddenly realized that he didn't want to lose the red-haired woman, whether her name was Vicky or Sandra. If Antonio wasn't his son, he'd still love him like he was. This thought relieved him, and he returned to the kitchen full of hope.

"Did something happen?" asked Patricia, noticing the joy on Pedro's face at once.

"Yes, I'm heading off to Portugal tomorrow. Antonio invited me over to Gale to spend the holidays with him."

Patricia nodded. "You must go if he invited you," she said with a sigh. "I hope you'll find your happiness." Even if I couldn't, she thought as she served the fried fish on the plates.

CHAPTER 124

Pedro took off. He stopped to buy some gifts at the La Cañada shopping mall, aimlessly wandering from one shop to the next before buying a chess set for Antonio, a bottle of Metaxa and a box of truffles for the grandparents, and finally some Dior perfume for Sandra. He left San Pedro behind, heading on to Gibraltar, Seville, and Huelva before reaching the Portuguese border. An ethereal bridge spanned the River Guadiana in front of him, linking the countries. Suddenly, a car veered off the road and headed straight towards him. He seemed to watch it all in slow motion before things blacked out. He opened his eyes and felt a piercing headache. He spotted a sixty-odd-year man lying on the bed next to him, engrossed in reading a newspaper.

Pedro sat up with some difficulty. He didn't feel any pain, yet he could tell that he was injured. He tried recalling the accident, but he had no idea what happened to him.

"You better lie back down," suggested the stranger. "The nurse said you were really lucky. You could have easily ended up dead," the man added benevolently. "Sometimes our life hangs by a thread. I think we're all programmed, liked computers. Anything can happen to us, but we won't die unless it's time for us to go. However, we aren't programmed for our brains to comprehend the fact that we're just visitors here on Earth. But for how long, a few years or decades? We always naively keep up our hopes, even though the clock of our time keeps ticking on. Some people's clocks are faster than others."

Pedro politely nodded. "You might be right," he replied in a rather hazy state. He tried standing up, and the nurse entering the room cried out at him at once.

"You better lie back down. You have to rest. Here are your belongings – at least, what was left of them. Your car is a wreck," she added briefly. She put his bag down on the bed and got the patient to lie back down.

"What happened to me?" he asked hesitantly.

"The head physician will do his rounds soon, so ask him," she replied dismissively.

When she left, his neighbour spoke up: "That nurse is always nasty, so, it's better if you don't ask her anything."

He groped at his body under the covers. His legs were fine, but he felt some pain along his spine.

During his rounds, the head physician stopped in front of Pedro's bed. "Sit up," he ordered strictly.

Pedro sat up with some difficulty.

The doctor prodded his back and even tapped at it gently.

"Does it hurt?" the doctor asked attentively.

"No."

"Since Christmas is here, you can go home tomorrow," the doctor said, walking out of the room.

"Good for you," said the other patient, glumly eyeing the ceiling. "I'm not as lucky as you. I have to stay put."

"What's the matter?" asked Pedro, turning to face the man.

"I'm not sure. Although I'm not in pain, I am somewhat paralyzed. I can't stand up since the accident."

Pedro didn't want to get involved in the man's troubles since he had his fair share as it was. He fished his mobile out from his bag and called up Antonio.

"It's Pedro," he said and hesitated for a moment. "Your father," he added quietly.

"Where are you? I've been waiting for you to call."

"Son, I can't come. I had an accident on the road."

"Are you at the hospital?" Antonio asked anxiously.

"Yes, but fortunately, it's nothing major. They'll let me go home soon."

"Are you sure about that? Because if you're not, I'll get in the car at once."

Pedro smiled. "Thank you, there's no need for that. Don't worry," he added emotionally.

"I'm sorry my plan didn't work out."

"Me too," Pedro muttered sadly. "Merry Christmas and Happy New Year to you, your mother, and your grandparents."

"The same to you. Look, if you need anything, just give me a call," Antonio said before hanging up.

Pedro dialled another number. He didn't want to get Patricia all worked up for no reason, so he called up Lucy instead and told her what happened.

"When will you get out?"

"Tomorrow morning."

"Great, then I'll come to pick you up with David. Get some rest until then. Don't worry about anything, OK?"

"Thank you for your help."

"Of course. See you tomorrow."

He lay in bed motionless for a long time. He cynically thought of how something always came up in his life.

The following morning, he underwent a few routine check-ups before they finally discharged him from the hospital.

Lucy came to pick him up, as promised, with David.

He greeted his sister that evening. She was surprised, yet pleased, to see him.

"So, the meeting didn't work out, huh?"

"No, but I think we'll get along just fine this way, right?"

She eyed him gratefully. "I assume you're all hungry," she asked with care.

"You could say that," replied Lucy at once.

"Then wash your hands, and I'll warm up the food."

Pedro smiled. He was overjoyed to be at home and that nothing bad had happened to him. He was really lucky since things could have ended up a lot worse, even tragically. In the bathroom, he looked in the mirror and squinted, faintly smiling at his image.

"You're a lucky man, pal," he repeated quietly.

"Come on, dinner is getting cold," he heard Patricia's beckoning voice.

"One minute," he replied with ease.

After dinner, Pedro told them about the accident and his brief stay at the hospital. His sister turned pale as she listened to him.

"You were really lucky," she noted with alarm in her eyes. "You always hear about accidents in the news. Indeed, everyone drives too fast in this country, and they never keep a proper distance from the car in front of them. I ran into some trouble myself a few years ago. I was slowing down when a car ran into me from behind. Can you believe it, the guy who ran into me was the one who was shaking his fist at me?" she explained, gesturing. "But I reciprocated the compliment and gave him the middle finger through the window." Having concluded her tale, she lifted her glass and savoured the rest of her drink.

They forgot all about the accident and shared a few laughs.

CHAPTER 125

The holidays went by quickly. Sandra watched the raging sea from the top of a cliff. The wind buffeted her, and she turned up the collar of her coat against the cold. The waves hammered the rocks below, spraying water high into the air. The fierce winds slightly pushed her back and forth. The rain started drizzling, and she quickly headed back to the villa. The wind raged and fought against her every step.

Antonio was standing at the window. He saw his mother was being battered by the wind, so he quickly put on his coat and hurried over to her, taking her by the arm. "You shouldn't come out in such terrible weather."

Sandra remained silent.

As they entered the villa, her mother appeared with a tray in hand, bringing them both a cup of fragrant, honeyed tea.

"Darling, drink this as hot as you can. It will do you good."

Sandra gratefully nodded and smiled.

It's a shame Dad couldn't come, thought Antonio. He'd subconsciously felt or at least hoped that the two of them would get closer to each other, yet this bond was still very weak and shaky. He indeed knew very little of their muddled lives. Still, he never dared ask his mother about this subject, since that was their business. He secretly hoped they would find their way back to each other.

As he pondered this matter, he thought of Amy. He tried recalling her face. She was surely surrounded by a heap of children by now. Hippie families worked hard at that, he thought, making a wry face. *What about me?* he wondered, clueless. He'd had a few flings and even a few relationships, yet none of the girls could get his heart racing. He hoped he would meet the right one eventually.

"You're freezing, aren't you?" he asked his mother with concern.

"Yeah, a bit, but this tea will sort me out."

Antonio headed over to his room for no particular reason and ended up staying there. Later on, he grew hungry and returned. His family was engrossed in a discussion in front of the fireplace.

"When's dinner?" he interrupted their conversation.

"It's still early, so you can wait a bit longer," chided his mother. His grandmother laughed. "Come now, I'm getting hungry too," she noted, glancing knowingly at her grandson before getting up and nimbly walking over to the kitchen. Sandra followed her at once. She never let her mother work alone.

In the meantime, Antonio set the table and brought himself a glass of milk. His grandfather brought a bottle over and leisurely poured it out into the glasses before comfortably sitting down next to his grandson. They smiled as they tapped on the table like a piano to urge the women in the kitchen to hurry up.

"We're ready, so where's the dinner?" cried the grandfather.

"I'm coming," said the grandmother, bringing them bread and salad.

"Is that all?" pouted the man, humorously winking at his grandson.

"What is it?" asked his wife with annoyance.

"Friday," replied the grandfather.

"The thirteenth?" retorted the grandmother with a grimace.

"No, just the third," added the grandson, bursting into laughter as he eyed the calendar.

The grandfather fell silent and smiled to himself. In the meantime, Sandra brought a few delicacies over. After their meal, they chatted at length and laughed at ease in a great mood.

Antonio went back to study after the holidays. Sandra returned to Marbella as well, where it was raining ceaselessly. She never left the house due to the foul weather.

Much to her surprise, she got a letter from André Breton a week later, telling her that Yvonne's condition was improving and she could already go home. "Visit us if you can," he wrote.

She cried tears of joy. She reserved a seat on a flight to Paris at once and called up André to tell him she was coming.

CHAPTER 126

She was finally back in Paris after a lengthy absence. The girlfriends cuddled up with teary eyes and wished each other Happy New Year. They quietly clinked their champagne glasses. André discreetly left them alone, taking the empty bottle with him.

"I'm glad that you recovered from your lengthy illness," noted Sandra emotionally. "I asked your mother from time to time about your condition, but..."

"Yes, I know. When they released me from the hospital, my, mother didn't want anyone else to take care of me. As you can see, I'm much better now."

"Thank God."

"Thank you for coming," Yvonne noted before mysteriously whispering, "I have some news."

"What is it?" Sandra asked curiously.

"There's going to be a wedding next month."

"Who's getting married?"

Yvonne pointed towards the kitchen and then back at herself before biting her lip and waiting for Sandra's reaction.

"That's amazing! Congratulations!" cried Sandra, clapping her hands.

"Thank you," laughed Yvonne out loud.

"What's that noise?" cried André, rushing into the room. The women grabbed hold of him from both sides and planted kisses on his cheek.

"Allow me to sincerely congratulate you on the occasion of your upcoming wedding," said Sandra. Suddenly, the women exchanged glances and shared a laugh as they held onto each other, tears rolling down faces since André now had lipstick marks on both his cheeks.

"What is it?" asked the man quizzically.

"Friday," giggled Sandra, digging her camera out of her bag and taking a few shots of André.

Yvonne embraced her fiancé and the camera rattled off a few more shots.

"Okay, now let me go or I'll burn the dinner," he said, but they just wouldn't let go of him.

"We'll take care of that. You can go to the bathroom," they insisted, pushing him through the door as the girls eavesdropped, holding back their urge to laugh.

"Damn it!" they heard André cry in annoyance.

The girlfriends ran to the kitchen, and their laughter echoed throughout the house. Yvonne quickly opened the second bottle of champagne, and the cork flew up high into the air before Sandra nimbly caught it. Yvonne giggled as she filled the glasses before picking up two of them. "Here's yours, now follow me," she urged as they ran back to the bathroom. When the door opened, she handed a glass to her man, thus settling the matter.

André was away working all day long, so the girls had plenty of time to do whatever they wanted.

"You have a beautiful flat."

"Yes, I love it."

"Let me take a look at your work."

"The truth is that I haven't visited the studio for quite some time now," she explained as she revealed her hidden boudoir to Sandra.

The sun coursed through the huge windows in slanted rays.

"Oh, this is lovely," gushed Sandra.

The middle of the room was dominated by a comfortable leather armchair. Yvonne's easel was propped up behind an old Chinese folding wall. Next to the wall stood an old cupboard with numerous drawers, most likely from the sixteenth century, which contained her paints and accessories. A range of paintings of various sizes was propped up against the wall and on the floor. A half-fastened brocade curtain dangled in front of the floor-to-ceiling windows. An antique armchair, slightly faded from the sun, sprawled in front of the easel, nonchalantly covered by a beautiful tapestry.

Sandra appreciatively eyed her girlfriend's paintings.

"They're really pretty, congratulations. You have to keep on painting. Don't give up."

"Yes, I'll carry on. But first, if I have the time, I'll buy a new easel," she noted, mainly to herself. "Come on," she invited her over and approached the desk, where she puttered around for a while. "All I have to do now is mail out the invitations," she said. "Here you go, here's yours."

Sandra read the invitation and planted a kiss on her friend's face.

"Thank you for thinking of me."

"Don't be silly," she said, furrowing her eyebrows. "You're my only true girlfriend, so you have to be there at our wedding. But that's not all since I'd like you to stay here until the wedding." She swayed her head from side to side with some ulterior motive. "I could use your help along with my Mom's help."

"Aha, so you want to use me." Sandra eyed her lovingly. "If you want me to, I'd be glad to stay. But first, I have to share an old secret with you," she explained with a grim look on her face, "which I never dared tell you because of Nick. If I tell you my secret, you might get angry at me and won't want me to stay," she added with an alarmed look in her eyes.

"Whatever you say, you're staying here," said Yvonne in a firm voice. "I'm listening."

Sandra began her confession. She related the story of her relationship with Nick before and after their wedding and explained to her how long she had to wait for him to finally come home with Antonio.

"You poor thing," Yvonne said, pulling her close. "I understand. Everyone keeps secrets, and you probably have more than most of us, but that doesn't count. All that counts, is that you got your son back," she said, planting a kiss on her face. "Let's just forget about the whole thing, okay?" Sandra gratefully nodded.

The time flew by with the preparations and shopping. One day, Sandra was out for a long time. She visited all the antique stores until she finally found a beautiful easel. But she didn't know where to hide it from Yvonne. The owner of the store offered to send the wedding gift to her on the designated day. Sandra gratefully thanked him for the offer.

As she walked back down the street, she wondered what to buy for André that would make him happy. As she entered the Galeries Lafayette, she finally found what she was looking for. She bought a pipe and a leather notepad with a pen. She wanted to get him a long cashmere hat, but she didn't know his size.

Finally, the big day was upon them. The doorbell rang in the morning amidst all the hustle and bustle.

"I'll get it," said Sandra, suddenly jumping out of her chair and glancing at her watch. Her hunch was right since indeed, it was a delivery-man with the easel she'd purchased previously.

André peeked outside into the foyer.

"Stop snooping around and help me out instead. Please, take this over to the studio," she whispered. "I want to give it to her now." Sandra disappeared into her room and quickly fetched the gift she'd bought for André. She walked into the living room with a flushed complexion and spoke up. "I would like to present you with my wedding gift," she noted emotionally and presented the package to André.

He opened it at once, cried out in laughter, and quickly stuck the end of the pipe in his fiancée's mouth. "That's for you!"

Yvonne giggled and recoiled. "It's beautiful, but it suits you better," she laughed, sticking it back between André's teeth before wrapping the scarf around his neck.

"You still need a hat, but I didn't dare buy it since I didn't know your size. This way, you look more like a modern version of Sherlock Holmes," she noted, conspiratorially glancing at her girlfriend and holding her hand out to her. "Come with me!" she invited and led Yvonne over to the studio. She opened the door and gently pushed her friend ahead. "My present for you," she said, pointing at the wrapped-up package.

André was close behind them.

"Wait, I didn't even thank you," he said warmly. "I appreciate the gift." He kissed Sandra on the cheek before stepping up and removing the wrapping on Yvonne's gift.

The easel stood in front of Yvonne, who emotionally noted, "I love it, it's just what I was looking for." She blinked with teary eyes, and the women embraced.

Before the ceremony, Sandra critically eyed her girlfriend, who was oddly silent and timid. Yvonne left everything up to Sandra, who made a few final adjustments to the bride's hair and beautiful long gown before finally raising her hands with a smile.

"It's perfect, she can go now, right?" she asked Yvonne's mother, who was almost as nervous as her daughter.

André had already left so he wouldn't see the bride. The ceremony took place just the way they planned it, and it was marvellous. At the end of the wedding, the bouquet flew towards Sandra, who caught it in surprise. Yvonne spun around and knowingly squinted at her.

CHAPTER 127

As Sandra returned to Marbella, a sense of loneliness suddenly settled over her. She rested lazily in bed, surfing the Web, reading, and watching TV all day long. She rarely went down to the kitchen and usually ate something cold or some fruit when she got hungry. She felt depressed in this house, which lacked cheerfulness, laughter, and happiness. She even considered selling the place.

Meanwhile, she lost a lot of weight, and the freckles on her skin grew darker. She could barely sleep at night. She kept thinking over and over about her unsuccessful life. Her loved ones were far away, and she was all alone. She didn't go anywhere and met no one. She wasn't looking forward to the upcoming spring, which kept rearing its head through her shuttered windows.

Her hair was tied up in a ruffled, tousled manner, and she felt no inclination whatsoever to deal with it. Her face seemed worn out without makeup, and her sneaky depression surfaced again. She was exhausted by life and grew increasingly sadder – whether due to the lengthy spell of bad weather or her memories, she wasn't sure. Whenever the phone rang, she covered her ears and walked over to the other room. Occasionally the doorbell rang, yet she still didn't budge.

The weeks went by and spring has arrived. Thrushes and other little birds were chirping and flittering from branch to branch as they built their nests. The sunshine improved her mood. She opened her windows, donned a worn-out old straw hat, and went outside to putter around in the garden. She eagerly ripped out weeds and cut back bushes. She punctured her glove, so she removed it, and her hands were soon coated in dirt. The garden shears soon raised blisters on her hands. *What happened to my carefully groomed, polished nails?* she wondered for a while. For the first time in months, she smiled.

The hours went by, and the sun was dipping down across the sky. She wiped at her perspiring forehead with her right hand and stretched. She was exhausted from work and her waist ached. She tried massaging with her hand, yet her body and soul still felt much lighter.

She spotted the outlines of a man on the other side of the fence. He had been eyeing her for some time now. Her heart beat frantically.

"Pedro, it's you?"

"Yes."

"So, you've been spying on me," she noted with fake indignity whilst joy flittered in her heart. She rubbed the dirt off her hand and awkwardly shuffled her feet.

"Can I come in?" asked the man hopefully.

"Sure, if you want to, but let me go fetch the keys." I must look terrible, she thought. Whatever, she added with a shrug. He will never forgive me for my letter and my long silence anyways. It's better if he sees me like this, she consoled herself as she opened the gate. She raised her dirty hands in the air, stepping back. "As you can see, I'm pretty dirty."

Pedro suppressed a smile. For a moment, he thought about leaning closer and kissing her on the face, but he restrained himself. He was practically convinced that she would recoil from him.

Instead, he turned around and closed the gate before following the ragged-looking, jeans-wearing woman who kicked her old outdoor shoes off in the doorway.

"If you don't mind, I'll straighten myself out. Please, help yourself and have a drink."

"A beer is fine for me," he replied tensely.

"You'll find some in the fridge. Help yourself."

"Wait," said Pedro.

She turned around.

"I'd like to take you out to dinner. I'm sure you're hungry after all that work, right?"

Sandra searchingly eyed him for a moment. "Is that really what you want?"

"Indeed, it is."

"Fine," she said with a smile. "In that case, you're going to have to wait a bit longer."

He was thrilled. "That's fine, just take your time. I'll be fine with my beer."

She hurried up the stairs and walked over to the bathroom. She took her clothes off and had a shower.

In the meantime, Pedro finished the beer. *Don't rush and be careful, Otherwise, you can ruin this promising encounter,* he warned himself as he looked around the living room. He glanced at the books on the shelves. He picked up a framed photo of Sandra, Antonio, and Nick laughing back at him. He put it back down with some annoyance before turning the TV on and watching the news.

She appeared in the living room.

"I'm finally ready. I sure made you wait a lot, right?"

He didn't say a word and averted his gaze. He wanted to take her in his arms, but an inner voice warned him not to.

"I'm thirsty," she said. "Will you have a beer with me?"

"I already had one, if you don't mind."

"That's OK if you're willing to have another one," she noted with a mischievous smile. "You know, drinking alone is bad for you," she noted, walking over the kitchen.

Pedro followed her. He opened two cans of beer and poured them into glasses. The foam spilt out of one of them. Pedro made a face.

"That was too fast," he noted apologetically with a smile.

Sandra suppressed her smile as she thought back to the first time they met. He'd spilt the beer down the side of the glass when pouring her drink that time too.

CHAPTER 128

They silently walked to the chiringuito down on the beach, side by side. After ordering their meals, they ate with a hearty appetite. When the waiter took their plates away, the tension settled back down between the two of them. Pedro suddenly reached across the table and took her hand. He had a serious look in his eyes.

"I've been waiting for this moment for a long time," he said. "The truth is that it was hard for me to cope with the series of failed attempts to seek you out."

He poured out the rest of the wine from the bottle, yet didn't touch the glass.

"I want to marry you. Will you be my wife?" he asked, cutting right to the heart of this delicate issue. Ever since they were reunited by fate, he had been undeniably attracted to her. The fact that her past was a muddled mess no longer counted. If this lovely woman was Vicky, and he believed she was, he had no reason to hesitate. Even if it wasn't her, he still wanted to spend the rest of his life with this woman. Nothing mattered anymore apart from finally, being reunited with the red-haired woman he had desired for so long.

Sandra anxiously closed her eyes for a moment.

"You … you didn't reply to the letter I wrote to you."

"Look," he started slowly, "I would be thrilled if Antonio is my son, but even if he isn't, it wouldn't change my feelings at all," he noted, levelling his dark, glowing eyes at the woman he loved.

She blushed and bowed her head in embarrassment. "If you want to, you can take a test to..."

"No, that's not important to me. But I'll do it for your sake or Antonio's sake."

"Antonio doesn't know about this since I would never dare tell him the truth."

"It's up to you," said Pedro, letting go of her hand, yet still intently gazing at her "So, tell me. Will you marry me?" he repeated with pent-up excitement.

Sandra looked up and they locked glances.

"Yes, I'll be your wife, if that's what you want."

Pedro leaned over and planted a kiss on her cheek. "I love you. You've just made me very happy. We'll get the ring tomorrow," he said happily, without knowing that his dream would come true this very day.

He motioned for the waiter to bring a good bottle of champagne. They clinked glasses.

"To our marriage, and to finding out way back to each other," whispered Pedro happily.

A month later, they held a double wedding, with Lucy and David getting married on the same day.

Sandra's parents emotionally eyed the couple with Antonio. The grandmother suddenly squeezed his hand.

"See son, that's what true love looks like, and I wish you the same thing from the bottom of my heart."

The young man eyed her with teary eyes.

"I know, Grandma, I know. I want the same thing."

After the ceremony, Yvonne whispered in Sandra's ear, "I intentionally threw the bouquet towards you in Paris. See, it still works this way," she laughed mischievously.

The gondola slowly slipped down the dark-water canal. The man kissed his wife's naked back where the tiny dark birthmark seemed to laugh up at him before carefully replacing the cardigan over her shoulder. He could still vividly recall the first time they'd met and how they loved each other. They were about to forget all about each other when they were brought back together by an odd coincidence.

Sandra glanced at her beloved husband sitting next to her, wrapping his arm around her shoulder. She could still hardly believe that she belonged to him now. The gondolier smiled. He loved couples like this. He pulled himself out straight and slowly paddled on before suddenly he started singing out, his voice carried down the canal. A tousled-haired woman cried down at him from up above, yet the Italian waved her off with ease and kept on singing without a reply.

CHAPTER 129

The summer sun was scorching over Andalusia. Pedro was racing down the road towards El Palmar with his little family. As they reached the house, they headed straight down to the beach. Antonio decided to stay on the shady patio. He was engrossed in a thick medical volume, reading about tropical diseases. The parasol provided the happy couple with some shade, otherwise, it would have been hard for them to tolerate the heat. The golden-yellow the sandy beach was crowded with vacationers.

"Come on, let's go swimming together," said Pedro, holding his hand out to her.

The clear waters of the Atlantic Ocean glimmered beckoningly with a greenish-blue glow. They relished drifting in the cold water and jumping on top of the waves that kept rolling in. The water wasn't deep, but the waves still slammed ashore fiercely. Sandra was careless and disappeared under the water for a moment, but Pedro grabbed her with his strong arms and hugged her with care.

"Watch out, here comes the next one!" he cried, and the wave swept them away. Sandra happily giggled in joy.

Later on, they lay down on their mats on the beach, enjoying the beauty of the summer and the joy of being together.

Pedro sat up, and he ran his hand over her back.

"Don't forget," he told her with concern, "whenever you're in the water, you have to pay attention to the waves washing ashore. The ocean is beautiful yet dangerous, and it will relentlessly pull you under."

"I know, but I'm always so clumsy. My dad warned me of the same thing when I was little." Suddenly, she recalled the crossing during which she blacked out on this stretch of water and almost ended up dead. The memory made her a bit sad.

Pedro leaned over to her and wrapped his arm around her while running his mouth over her shoulders.

"Are you okay?" he asked attentively.

"Yes," she gasped faintly, closing her eyes and listening to the murmuring of the ocean.

A few moments later she started smiling, however, as she recalled the blissful period all those years ago when she spent a few unforgettable days here with her Latin lover. She propped herself up on her elbows, resting her head on her chin while beguiling Pedro, who squinted and glanced off into the distance. She was overjoyed that they'd managed to find the way back to each other after all these years. She suddenly bent her head on her arms as her tears gushed forth. They weren't due to sadness but were rather tears of joy. She was unspeakably happy to be with Pedro. She could never imagine other women interfering with their lives with him at her side – as opposed to Nick, who hungrily devoured all the woman around him with his stares, doing everything he could to have another fling. Her previous marriage was humiliating and had caused much suffering. She slightly shook her head and suddenly cuddled up to her husband in order to chase away the bad memories for good.

Her thoughts strayed off. It all began when Lucy asked for a ride and the Jaguar started trailing her. From that point, her fate had been entwined with Lucy's, Pedro's, and Nick's – and she could even include David in all of this since they always seemed to cross paths. None of them knew at the time that they were tied together by invisible bonds. Those ties were further complicated by the arrival of Antonio, and odd coincidences seemed to surface again and again.

She sighed heavily. They were together now, and all their secrets had been revealed. Her husband would soon open his clinic, and Antonio would join him after graduation. Deep down inside, she felt that her son wasn't completely happy since girls were always missing from his life. He was only interested in his work. Even now, he was sitting on the patio with a thick medical book, studying.

Pedro was also thinking things over. He was overjoyed that he was reunited with Sandra. He ran his fingers through his wife's hair again. She bowed her head and lay flat out on the mat with her head bowed.

"Come on, I have an idea," he said mysteriously.

Sandra perked up curiously. "What is it?"

"You'll figure it out on the way."

He jumped up and held his hand out, helping his wife up from the sand.

"Come on, tell me!" She tapped his back gently.

He knew the curiosity was driving her crazy, yet he still turned away quietly and trotted off to the house, with Sandra nimbly following in his footsteps.

Antonio was still reading out on the patio. He perked up when they arrived.

"Come on, we're going somewhere," motioned Pedro to his son.

"I don't want to come," Antonio replied glumly.

"Come on," Pedro urged him. "Get yourself together. You could use the little trip," he said cheerfully, heading over to the bathroom.

Antonio spoke up when Pedro disappeared.

"Look, Mom, I found a bag amongst all the books."

"What's in it?"

"Dad's, or rather Nick's papers."

Sandra took the bag from him without a word, yet she didn't open it.

She ran upstairs and stuffed it inside a drawer. She didn't want Nick to get involved in their life anymore.

She quickly had a shower before putting on a light floral dress. She tied her hair up. Her suntanned face was fresh and youthful.

When Pedro saw her, he went over to her and planted a kiss on her forehead.

"What was that for?"

"Nothing, it was just a spontaneous thing," he beamed at her. "Come on, you two," he urged, hurrying to the car.

Antonio locked the house and nimbly climbed in the back seat.

CHAPTER 130

He drove slowly and comfortably. As they left Tarifa, Sandra asked him again where they were headed, yet he only laughed mysteriously in reply. As they headed down the winding road lined with windmills, he suddenly veered off the road to the left. Sandra laughed out loud. As she recognized the road, she suddenly realized what Pedro had in mind.

"If I'm not mistaken, you want to surprise our friends we haven't seen for ages, right?"

"That's right. So, you still remember them?"

"Of course, I do. You know, I came this way myself not so long ago, but I was out of luck. The gate was locked, and no one showed up."

"Let's hope we'll find them at home this time."

The cork wood still cast its shadows over the rough dirt road. Sandra recalled the two beautiful foals which stopped in front of her car before running off into the bush in alarm. She turned around. "Isn't it a lovely place?" she asked her son, briefly telling him where they were headed.

Pedro added, "This is where we met."

Antonio muttered something in reply, grinning at his romantic parents.

When they reached the house, they noticed that the gate was slightly ajar. Strangers were seated at the long table on the patio, set for dinner. The cheerful company was laughing out loud, but when they noticed the new arrivals, they fell silent. Pedro fell uncertain and awkwardly explained himself. "We're looking for our friends. Their names are Sarah and Juan."

A young, blond girl stood up at the end of the table at once.

"Then you've come to the right place," she said with a smile and approached them. She couldn't take her eyes off the good-looking young man.

"Angela," she introduced herself openly.

Sandra smiled at her. "You've grown a lot since the last time I saw you."

The girl glared at her in confusion.

"My parents are over in the kitchen, busying themselves with the dinner. Come," she said, beckoning with her hands.

"There's no need for that, we know the place," interrupted Sandra anxiously, almost rushing inside the house, Pedro in tow.

Antonio hesitantly stopped in front of the door, whilst the girl stopped next to him.

"Where did you come from?" she asked curiously.

"Marbella," he replied readily, attentively eyeing the girl.

"What a detailed response," noted the girl with a mischievous reply.

"I don't know what's going on," he apologized squeamishly.

"Me neither. Come on, let's go follow them. We might hear something interesting," she urged as she squinted at him.

Pedro and Sandra were standing in the door to the kitchen, holding hands and emotionally eyeing the two people in the room.

Sarah was just turning over the fried meat on the stove. Her slim figure had barely changed. Juan was standing with his back to them, fumbling with the cork of a wine bottle. The curls of his black hair drooped down to his shoulders.

Sarah suddenly looked up at the strangers and emitted a quiet shriek. She was so surprised that she dropped the knife, which fell to the floor with a loud clang.

"What's the matter?" cried Juan at his wife, who turned pale as she covered her mouth with her hands, staring at the doorway.

He turned around. He was so dumbfounded that he was unable to say a word for a moment before coming to his senses and setting the bottle down on the counter.

"Hey!" he cried out loudly. "We have some unexpected guests," he noted as the friends embraced and patted each other on the back.

"Well, pal, you sure haven't changed much, even though I've lost count of the years," said Juan with a broad smile on his face before hesitantly eyeing Sandra. Her eyes seemed familiar, yet her face was that of a stranger.

"Sandra, or rather Vicky, is my wife," noted Pedro emotionally.

"Oh. But she died," whispered Sarah.

"No, that's not true, I didn't die. It's me, Vicky, but now I call me Sandra."

Sarah was so startled that she forgot to welcome the guests. Sandra shuffled over to her with misty eyes and they embraced in tears.

The other guests left after dinner, while the old friends kept on chatting.

The youngsters were left to their own devices, sitting out on the patio, yet they weren't bored at all. The young man was getting increasingly interested as he lost himself in Angela's blue eyes. Their heads almost touched as they kept on chatting.

Antonio asked for her phone number. "I hope we can meet up again, while we're here," he said in an elated tone. He suddenly felt light, strong, and charming.

In the meantime, the girlfriends retreated to one of the bedrooms, where Sandra related her shocking story with a grim look on her face.

"You know, we met once a long, long time ago," she reminded her girlfriend.

"I don't think so."

"But we did, in Marrakech."

"That was a long time ago."

"Indeed. You were strolling through Djemaa el-Fna square and you asked for directions from me."

"I still don't remember it."

"That's no wonder, since I was wearing a black djellaba and covered my face with a shawl. I'm sure you thought I was an Arab."

"Why didn't you say something? Why didn't you say it was you?"

"I simply couldn't say a word because of my face."

"Your story sounds like a bad dream," said Sarah. "No one would believe it. We better forget all about it. Come on, let's go back to the others."

"Where are the kids?" asked Sandra.

"They went for a walk," noted Juan, exchanging glances with Pedro.

"Things sometimes repeat themselves or simply start anew," whispered Sarah and the girlfriends shared a laugh as they recalled an old story.

Sandra glanced at Pedro. She nostalgically recalled the first time they met, when they strolled off into the corkwood, without knowing the life of vicissitudes they would be facing together.

Perhaps Pedro was thinking the same thing since they suddenly locked glances, mirroring the joy of their reunion.

Three years later, Antonio married Angela and flew off to Sudan. The young doctor began his work as a trainee at a hospital in Khartoum, whilst his wife worked near the hospital as an office assistant. They were both filled with ambition and tried their best to help the people living there, fighting against various diseases, famine, and countless other challenges as Africa captivated their hearts for good.

About the Author

Maria Bárkányi was an informatics adviser and programmer in Budapest. Then, she followerd her husband to Africa, who has worked in Nigeria as an FAO adviser in Kaduna. Maria never worked again. After ten years, they settled down in Portugal's Algarve. Finally, as a retired couple, they lived in Marbella, Spain.

They travelled a lot in Africa and the rest of the world. They often spent more time in a Land Rover or aeroplanes than at home. She has seen many things and met many kinds of people and tribes. Her memory inspired her to write down the most exciting moments of her life and give pleasure to the readers.

She published three books. Two are about Africa, the third one is a novel.